"Strap in and start running your pre-checks. And remember, Tacco," he held up a warning finger to Lisa, "that you've only got the ventral launcher to work with."

"Yes, Sir."

Lisa pushed off the Missiles Station handhold and slipped past the captain to the Tactical Station. Travis was right behind her.

"What do you want me to do first, Ma'am?" he asked Lisa.

"Double-check the autocannon," she said. "Fore first and then aft. The weapons crew is shorthanded, and we've been having serious trust issues with the status board feed. Chief Wrenner is working on the laser plasma feed—stay on the intercom with him until he's finished, then run a remote diagnostic on the laser. I'll do the missiles and launcher."

"Yes, Ma'am," Travis said. A quick look at the tactical—"Three hours yet to begin raising impellers?"

"Engineering's still spinning up the reactor," Lisa told him. He looked at her, and she shrugged. "Regs," she said with a wry smile.

"Yes, Ma'am," he said. Yet another eminently sensible peacetime regulation that had now come back to bite them. From both safety and reactor efficiency perspectives it made sense to require ships to use shore power when moored to a space station.

In peacetime.

He looked at a side display, a hollow feeling settling into his stomach as he examined the icons of the ships theoretically prepared to sortie in Aegis Force's support. *Damocles*, *Erinye*, and *Perseus*, and none of them able to move for at least another three hours. By then, the intruders would be barely twenty minutes from their turnover point for a zero-zero intercept with Manticore.

And if the invaders got past Aegis and its theoretical supports, there'd be nothing between them and the capital planet.

BAEN BOOKS by DAVID WEBER

MANTICORE ASCENDANT: *A Call to Duty* with Timothy Zahn • *A Call to Arms* with Timothy Zahn & Thomas Pope • *A Call to Vengeance* with Timothy Zahn & Thomas Pope

THE STAR KINGDOM: *A Beautiful Friendship* • *Fire Season* with Jane Lindskold • *Treecat Wars* with Jane Lindskold

HONOR HARRINGTON: *On Basilisk Station* • *The Honor of the Queen* • *The Short Victorious War* • *Field of Dishonor* • *Flag in Exile* • *Honor Among Enemies* • *In Enemy Hands* • *Echoes of Honor* • *Ashes of Victory* • *War of Honor* • *At All Costs* • *Mission of Honor* • *Crown of Slaves* with Eric Flint • *Torch of Freedom* with Eric Flint • *The Shadow of Saganami* • *Storm from the Shadows* • *A Rising Thunder* • *Shadow of Freedom* • *Cauldron of Ghosts* with Eric Flint • *Shadow of Victory* • *Uncompromising Honor*

HONORVERSE, EDITED BY DAVID WEBER: *More than Honor* • *Worlds of Honor* • *Changer of Worlds* • *The Service of the Sword* • *In Fire Forged* • *Beginnings*

MULTIVERSE SERIES: *Hell's Gate* with Linda Evans • *Hell Hath No Fury* with Linda Evans • *The Road to Hell* with Joelle Presby

BAEN BOOKS by TIMOTHY ZAHN

Blackcollar (contains *The Blackcollar* and *Blackcollar: The Backlash Mission*) • *Blackcollar: The Judas Solution*

The Cobra Trilogy (contains: *Cobra*, *Cobra Strike*, and *Cobra Bargain*) • *The Cobra War Trilogy* (contains: *Cobra Alliance*, *Cobra Guardian*, and *Cobra Gamble*)

COBRA REBELLION: *Cobra Slave* • *Cobra Outlaw* • *Cobra Traitor*

To purchase any of these titles in e-book form, please go to www.baen.com.

A CALL TO VENGEANCE

★ BOOK III OF ★
Manticore Ascendant

DAVID WEBER &
TIMOTHY ZAHN
with THOMAS POPE

A Novel of the Honorverse

A CALL TO VENGEANCE:
BOOK III OF MANTICORE ASCENDANT

This is a work of fiction. All the characters and events portrayed in this book are fictional, and any resemblance to real people or incidents is purely coincidental.

Copyright © 2018 by Words of Weber, Inc., Timothy Zahn, and Thomas Pope

All rights reserved, including the right to reproduce this book or portions thereof in any form.

A Baen Books Original

Baen Publishing Enterprises
P.O. Box 1403
Riverdale, NY 10471
www.baen.com

ISBN: 978-1-4814-8373-5

Cover art by Dave Seeley
Maps and interior artwork by Thomas Pope

First mass market paperback printing, January 2019

Library of Congress Catalog Number: 2017053918

Distributed by Simon & Schuster
1230 Avenue of the Americas
New York, NY 10020

Pages by Joy Freeman (www.pagesbyjoy.com)
Printed in the United States of America

A CALL TO
VENGEANCE

BOOK ONE

1543 PD

CHAPTER ONE

THE SPANISH INQUISITION HADN'T BEEN THE first political and religious witch-hunt in Old Earth's violent history. Nor had it been the last, or even been the bloodiest. But for some reason, the memory of its long and persistent reign of terror had lingered in common human memory up to the Diaspora and throughout the long centuries since.

Lieutenant Travis Uriah Long, late of the cruiser HMS *Casey*, didn't know why that was. Perhaps it was the faintly exotic name that continued to catch the human ear and imagination. Perhaps it was the cautionary proverb of a long-forgotten pre-Diaspora philosopher, who had warned that nobody expects the Spanish Inquisition. But whatever the reason, he was familiar with the history of that particular malevolence, and had always wondered how the victims felt as they faced their stone-eyed accusers.

It was, he suspected, probably a lot like he was feeling right now.

"... I do so solemnly affirm," the clerk prompted.

3

"I do so solemnly affirm," Travis repeated.

The clerk gave a brisk nod and raised his voice. "Long life to the King."

"Long life to the King," Travis repeated. This time he was joined by the rest of the men and women seated across from him in the hearing room.

All of whom, he had no doubt, grimly recognized the irony of the sentiment.

Long life to the King...

At the center of the long, curved table, Prime Minister Davis Harper, Duke Burgundy, cleared his throat. "We are assembled today," he intoned, "to examine the events of 33rd Twelfth, and the events and decisions leading up to the loss of His Majesty's corvette *Hercules*—" he paused, just noticeably "—and the resulting death of Crown Prince Richard Winton. Do you understand, Lieutenant Long?"

"Yes, Your Grace," Travis said. *Nobody expects the Spanish Inquisition.*

Only in this case, it was not only expected but virtually guaranteed.

Never mind that four other ships of the Royal Manticoran Navy had been destroyed, with the loss of their entire crews. Never mind that half a dozen others had suffered damage, with some of their crew members also dead or injured. Certainly the Battle of Manticore had brought with it more than enough death and trauma to go around.

But those deaths were relatively anonymous except to the families and friends who had lost their loved ones. Richard's name and face, in contrast, were known to everyone in the Star Kingdom of Manticore. He was the symbol of the Navy's desperate defense, and as such had become the center of the swirling questions of How and Who and Why.

The Star Kingdom was solidly focused on Richard. That went double for the members of Parliament. It went triple for the Committee of Naval Affairs.

And Travis had no doubt that half the members of the latter group were determined to find Travis's commander, Commodore Rudolph Heissman, personally responsible for the Crown Prince's death.

Which was both ridiculous and a complete waste of time. The Navy's Board of Inquiry had already cleared Heissman of any wrongdoing. The rest of the long, official hearings had ended a week ago. What was going on in here today was nothing but political posturing.

Travis hated political posturing.

Burgundy was running through the standard welcome routine, thanking Travis for his service to the Crown and emphasizing the importance of the testimony he was about to give. Listening with half an ear, Travis let his gaze drift over the line of men and women arrayed against him, his eyes and brain automatically running threat assessments.

The Chancellor of the Exchequer, Anderson L'Estrange, Earl Breakwater, was clearly out for blood. Not specifically because it was Commodore Heissman on the hot seat—Travis doubted the Chancellor even knew Heissman—but because anything that besmirched the Navy's reputation could only put his own Manticoran Patrol and Rescue Service in a better light. MPARS's contribution to the battle had been minimal, mainly because only two of its ships had been in position to help. Still, those two ships had acquitted themselves well.

But Breakwater was never satisfied with the simple gathering of laurels. He much preferred gathering his laurels with one hand and wilting those of his political opponents with the other.

The embodiment of that opposition, Minister of Defense James Mantegna, Earl Dapplelake, would of course be pulling the opposite direction, for similar but reverse reasons. The Navy had suffered huge losses in the battle, and Dapplelake had no intention of letting any more of the Star Kingdom's limited shipyard and manpower resources be siphoned off to MPARS than was absolutely necessary.

The two men's political, economic, and philosophic rivalry had been going on for a long time—the entire fourteen T-years that Travis had been in the Navy, at least, and probably longer. Most of the Committee members had also been in various positions of power for much of that time, and they'd long since sorted out which team they preferred to kick for. Secretary of Bioscience Lisa Tufele, Baroness Coldwater, and Shipyard Supervisor John Garner, Baron Low Delhi, typically lined up behind Dapplelake: Low Delhi because his family and Dapplelake's were friends, Coldwater because boosts to Navy funding often meant more money for *her* budget, as well. First Lord of Law Deborah Scannabecchi, Duchess New Bern, and Director of Belt Mining Carolynne Jhomper tended to vote with Breakwater: New Bern because she was a big believer in legal balance and thought the Navy threw its weight around too much, Jhomper because the more patrol ships MPARS put into her area of responsibility, the better. Secretary of Industry Julian Mulholland, Baron Harwich, and

Foreign Secretary Susan Tarleton didn't favor either side: Harwich because all ship-building projects made him happy, Tarleton because Foreign Secretary was largely an honorary position and no one ever paid much attention to her anyway.

As for Prime Minister Burgundy himself, who had assumed chair of the Committee, he would be trying hard to stay neutral. But as a close ally and personal friend of King Edward, Travis had no doubt that his judgment would be at least somewhat skewed.

Which direction that bias might run, though, was a question all its own. In public, the King had studiously avoided saying anything beyond the simple acknowledgment of his son's death, with no judgment or recriminations. What he said in private was something Travis doubted more than a handful of people knew.

"Let's start with the basics, Lieutenant," Burgundy said. "Where were you when it first became apparent that the distress call you were responding to was, in fact, an invasion?"

"That recognition was more an ongoing process than the result of a single bit of data or insight, Your Grace," Travis said. "But to answer your question: I was on *Casey*'s bridge during the entire time in question."

"I see," Burgundy said, and Travis thought he could see a flicker of approval in the Prime Minister's eyes. It was all too easy to second-guess decisions and actions after the fact, but matters were seldom obvious to those in the middle of a given situation. Travis's reshaping of the question should help to underscore that reality for the rest of the Committee. "When it *did* become evident—or at least likely—that an invasion was underway, what was Commodore Heissman's response?"

"We're particularly interested in his deployment of his four Janus Force ships," Breakwater put in. "Why was *Gorgon* put into aft-relay position instead of the Crown Prince's ship, *Hercules*?"

For a moment Travis was sorely tempted to play out a little rope in the hope that Breakwater would manage to hang himself somewhere down the line. But he resisted the urge. Breakwater was a master manipulator and politician, and if Travis tried to play any games the Chancellor would have him for breakfast. The truth, as straightforward and open as possible, was his best bet. "*Hercules* was a corvette, My Lord," he said. "*Gorgon* was a destroyer. As such, *Gorgon* had aft weaponry—specifically, autocannon—which *Hercules* didn't. Since *Gorgon* was already farthest from the enemy when it was time to flip and decelerate, and was therefore most likely to survive the opening salvo, Commodore Heissman elected to leave her there as our best chance of getting full sensor data back to Aegis Force."

"Really," Breakwater said with clearly feigned surprise. "I'd have thought that *Casey* herself, with aft autocannon *and* an aft laser, would be the best suited for such survival. So why didn't Commodore Heissman put his own ship in that position?" He glanced both ways down the table, as if inviting agreement. "After, perhaps, bringing the Crown Prince aboard?"

Dapplelake stirred. "That kind of personnel transfer requires the entire force to cease deceleration while a shuttle makes the run. They had little enough time to prepare as it was. The loss of that hour would have—"

"Would have what?" Breakwater interrupted. "Commodore Heissman lost three quarters of his force as it is. Three hundred and fifty good men and women. Including the Crown Prince."

Travis squared his shoulders. Enough was enough. "If I may, My Lord?" he spoke up as Dapplelake opened his mouth to launch another verbal salvo.

Breakwater turned to him, and for a second Travis thought the Chancellor was going to lay into him for daring to interrupt a private conversation. Then he seemed to remember where he was, and the reason they were all there, and the surprised outrage smoothed away from his face. "Of course, Lieutenant," he said. "You were about to say...?"

"I was about to expand on the reasoning behind Commodore Heissman's decision, My Lord," Travis said. "First of all, as Earl Dapplelake has said, it would have cost us an hour to transport Prince Richard to *Casey*, with our wedge down much of that time. Our mission at that point was to stay between the invaders and Manticore as long as possible. As it was, we unavoidably sped through missile range very quickly. Shortening that time would have meant even less time for us to inflict damage on the enemy."

"Exactly," Dapplelake muttered, and out of the corner of his eye Travis thought he could again see a glint of approval from the Prime Minister.

"More important, though, were the tactical realities of the situation," Travis continued. "*Casey* had counter-missiles in addition to her autocannon. *Gorgon*, *Hercules*, and *Gemini* each had only autocannon. Putting *Casey* at the rear of the formation would have meant our counter-missiles couldn't help in the defense of the other ships."

He held his breath, fully expecting Breakwater or

one of the others to call bogus. In theory, he was correct: *Casey*'s counter-missile spread could indeed help protect the other ships. But as a practical matter, that kind of screening formation was seldom used unless a battlecruiser or other high-value ship was in play. With *Casey* the biggest and most powerful ship of her small task force, her counter-missiles were mostly useful for her own defense.

But no one spoke up. Those who weren't familiar with such military minutiae—which was probably the majority of them—were apparently willing to accept Travis's logic at face value. Dapplelake, who *did* know how it worked, would certainly not do anything to undercut Travis's testimony that way.

"So what you're saying," Breakwater said after a moment, "is that Commodore Heissman's entire focus was on the upcoming battle. And that the life of the Crown Prince was never even a factor in his strategy."

"The lives of *all* his officers and crew were a factor, My Lord," Travis said. "But more important even than that was the Star Kingdom and her citizens. Offering our lives in their protection was the oath we all took when we accepted the RMN uniform." He focused on Burgundy. "*All* of us. Including the Crown Prince."

He hadn't expected a round of applause for his little speech. But he wasn't prepared for Breakwater's thinly veiled sarcasm, either. "Yes, I'm sure Prince Richard would invoke such sentiments, too, were he here," the Chancellor said. "Which, of course, he's not. It seems to me that Commodore Heissman was also rather caught off-guard by the appearance of the—what were they called? Oh, yes: you tagged them early on as Bogey Two. The two enemy destroyers that the MPARS corvettes *Aries* and *Taurus* took care of for you."

Travis clenched his teeth. That was *not* how it had gone down. Not exactly, anyway. "Those ships came in coasting with their wedges down, My Lord," he said stiffly. "Effective sensor range under those conditions is extremely short."

"Yet Commodore Heissman knew they were out there," Breakwater said. "Shouldn't he have been more alert?"

"We already had our hands full with the ships of the main attack force."

"You can't focus your attention on two directions at once?"

"It's not a matter of focus, but of firepower," Travis said. "We knew where the main force was, and turning toward a potential flanking force would simply have left us open to the main force's attack." He hesitated. "To be perfectly honest, My Lord, Commodore Heissman probably didn't expect any of us to survive the engagement. His goal at that point was to do as much damage to the enemy, and get as much data back to Aegis, as possible."

Breakwater gave a snort. "So RMN officers now go into battle expecting to get their entire crews killed?"

"Sometimes Navy personnel have to do just that," Travis said, feeling anger rising inside him. "Especially when our ships are undermanned, underequipped, and—by some—underappreciated."

There was a small stir around the table. Travis winced, realizing too late that he'd probably gone too far. "My apologies, My Lords and Ladies; Your Graces," he said. "I didn't mean to sound unappreciative."

"Yet you did," Breakwater pointed out stiffly. "Perhaps we should allow you a few moments to collect yourself before we continue." He turned to Burgundy and inclined his head. "With your permission, of course, Your Grace."

"I think we could postpone the rest of Lieutenant Long's testimony until tomorrow morning," Burgundy said, peering at his tablet. "We're approaching the noon recess anyway." He looked at Travis. "Tomorrow at oh-nine-hundred, Lieutenant. You're dismissed."

"Yes, Your Grace," Travis said. Silently berating himself for once again sticking his foot in it, he picked up his tablet and pushed back his chair.

"Oh, I'm sorry—one last question," Breakwater spoke up suddenly. "The technique you used to destroy that enemy battlecruiser. Very clever, that. Whose idea was it, exactly?"

Travis felt his stomach tense. Breakwater knew perfectly well whose idea that had been. "It was mine, My Lord."

"Not Commodore Heissman's?" Breakwater asked. "Or Commander Belokas', or Tactical Officer Woodburn's? Yours?"

"Yes, My Lord."

"I see." Breakwater inclined his head. "Thank you, Lieutenant. You may go now."

"Yes, My Lord."

Ninety seconds later, Travis was walking down the wide corridor toward the exit nearest the visitor parking lot. Wondering what the hell that last bit had been all about.

Wondering perhaps a little too strenuously. Vaguely, he became aware that someone was calling his name—

"So are you ignoring the whole world? Or is it just me?"

Travis twitched with surprise, guilt, and embarrassment. "No, of course not," he said hastily. "I mean—"

"Apology accepted, Travis," Lieutenant Commander Lisa Donnelly said, the warm impishness of her smile erasing any lingering suggestion that she was actually mad at him. "I'm surprised you have any brainpower left at all after that." She nodded back behind them. "Let me guess: Chancellor Breakwater was playing his usual games?"

"Yes—Ma'am," Travis belatedly remembered to add. Lisa had been his best and closest friend for four years now, probably the only person he'd ever truly been able to relax with. As near as he could tell, she was just as comfortable in his presence as he was in hers.

But she also outranked him, and here in public the correct forms of military etiquette had to be strictly adhered to. "And I'm pretty sure he won."

"Only *pretty* sure?"

"Yes. Mostly because I have no idea what the game was."

"Ah." Lisa glanced around and gestured to a set of empty chairs grouped around a small table in a conversation alcove at one side of their corridor. "Let's sit down and you can tell me all about it. If you've got time."

"Yes, Ma'am, absolutely," Travis said, already feeling the tension melting away. He hadn't had a chance to see Lisa for several weeks before the battle, and the thought of spending even just an hour with her was definitely something to look forward to. "They don't want me again until tomorrow."

"Good." She glanced conspiratorially to both sides as they headed toward the alcove. "And you know, if we keep our voices down, you won't even have to call me *Ma'am*."

Travis felt his face warming. Lisa didn't call him on his strict adherence to rules very often, but when she did she was painfully efficient at making her point. "Yes, Ma—I mean, yes."

"So *tomorrow*, you say," Lisa said thoughtfully. "Sounds like Breakwater got what he was looking for. Okay, let's see if we can figure this out. Was there any point where he seemed happier than he was the rest of the time?"

"Well, he threw in a last-second question as I was being dismissed," Travis said as they both sat down. "And he went out of his way earlier to remind everyone how his two MPARS ships took out one of Tamerlane's destroyers."

"He's not going to let anyone forget that," Lisa agreed. "Especially since Cazenestro had ordered the MPARS ships to stand down. If Hardasty and Kostava hadn't ignored him and moved in anyway, things would have gone a lot worse." Her eyes shifted over Travis's shoulder. "Speaking of which." She lifted a hand and raised her voice. "Townsend? Over here!"

Travis felt a sudden jolt of tension as he twisted around in his chair to look. Sure enough, the big Sphinxian lumbering toward them was Petty Officer Charles Townsend. *Chomps* Townsend, to his friends.

A long time ago, Travis had been one of those friends. Not anymore.

But Chomps was smart enough not to show animosity toward a senior officer in public. He smiled at Lisa as he came up, gave the exact same smile to Travis, then came to a smart halt and executed an equally smart salute. "Commander Donnelly; Lieutenant Long," he greeted them. "What heinous crime have you committed, may I ask, to have been hauled into this den of political machination and chaos?"

"And what would *you* know about Parliament?" Lisa asked dryly.

"Oh, I've sailed these waters myself of late, Ma'am," Chomps said. "Two days ago, in fact. Possibly later today, too, if they really want to put themselves through a repeat performance." He glanced at the wall chrono. "Though probably not until after lunch."

"At least you get to go in on a full stomach," Lisa said. "I'm guessing we're all here for the same reason."

"Which is?"

"Lieutenant Long and I were just trying to figure that out," Lisa said. "Care to join us?"

"Thank you, Ma'am," Chomps said. "If I may suggest: as I say, it's lunchtime. Would the two of you care to join me for a small repast? My treat, of course."

"Hmm," Lisa said, her face wrinkled with feigned uncertainty. "I don't know. Enlisted *and* MPARS. What do you think, Travis? Can we legally accept such an invitation?"

"If it helps," Chomps offered, "we could consider it my apology for calling you by your first name in front of your fellow officers."

Travis sat up a little straighter. "What?" he asked carefully.

"It's okay," Lisa soothed him, her eyes twinkling with amusement. "It was on Casca, and the Cascans don't care so much about proper etiquette."

"I was also trying to save my skin, Sir," Chomps added to Travis. "Which for a while looked like they also didn't care much about."

"But as you see, we made it through," Lisa said, standing up. "Very well, Townsend, we accept. To the cafeteria?"

"Or to a little place just around the corner, Ma'am." Chomps raised his eyebrows at Travis. "It's Italian, Sir. I seem to remember that you like Italian."

"Yes," Travis confirmed warily, searching the man's face for some hint of the resentment or hatred he was surely still feeling for Travis and the damage to his career that had been a result of Travis's damning report about Chomps's computer hacking.

But if there were any such emotions there, Travis could see no evidence of them. Chomps seemed genuinely cheerful and relaxed, friendly to both him and Lisa, and not at all ashamed of the MPARS uniform he was wearing.

But then, Travis had never been good at reading people. For all he knew, Chomps could be planning right now exactly how and where he was going to slip the knife between Travis's ribs.

"Travis?"

He looked at Lisa. She was eyeing him, a questioning expression on her face. As if the lunch thing was his decision and not hers.

Squaring his shoulders, Travis looked back at Chomps. If the other was planning some revenge, they might as well get it over with. "Sounds good," he said. "Please; lead the way."

CHAPTER TWO

CAPTAIN TRINA CLEGG TAPPED THE RELEASE, and the hatch into *Vanguard*'s bridge slid open in front of her. She grabbed a handhold, noting as always the misaligned pair of plates on the inside of the pocket that had yet to be fixed. A lot of these older ships had been slowly warped and twisted over the years from missile launches, high accelerations, and simple age.

Also as always, she turned her eyes resolutely away as she pulled herself through the hatchway. *Vanguard* still needed a lot of work to bring her to full fighting strength. Nonvital internal plate assemblies were way down on the priority list.

The ensign at the tracking station glanced up, stiffened.

"Captain on the bridge!" she called.

At the front of the compartment, Commander Bertinelli swiveled around. His lips compressed, just noticeably, before he smoothed them out.

"Welcome, Captain," he greeted her gravely.

The words were correct, and delivered in the correct

tone. But Clegg wasn't fooled. As far as Bertinelli was concerned, Clegg was an interloper, a Johnny-come-lately who had no business being on this ship.

And who *certainly* had no business being flag captain of the newly restructured Aegis Force.

On one level, Clegg could sympathize. Bertinelli wanted to command a battlecruiser. Wanted it so badly he probably had fever dreams about it. A few years ago he'd been offered the cruiser *Gryphon*, but he'd turned it down, preferring to stay on as *Vanguard's* XO. His theory, as far as Clegg could tell, had been that he'd somehow thought staying where he was would put him first in line once the position of *Vanguard's* captain was finally vacated.

If so, he'd been sorely disappointed. Six months ago, a slightly doddering Captain Davison had announced his retirement. Bertinelli had probably gone out the next day and ordered the champagne to celebrate his imminent promotion to *Vanguard's* captain, and he was probably the only person who'd been surprised when it wasn't offered.

Personally, Clegg was surprised his career had survived turning down the cruiser command at all. In fact, she suspected that only connections in high places had prevented his relief and reassignment to the kind of slop duties normally given someone who declined to sit the first time they pulled out the captain's chair for him.

Not surprisingly, at least for anyone who knew him, Bertinelli didn't see it that way. Instead, he blamed Clegg.

"Nothing to report, Captain," Bertinelli continued, unfastening his straps. Again, his words and tone were correct, but Clegg couldn't shake the feeling that he believed the universe's highly unmilitary state of serenity was also somehow her fault. "Very quiet out there."

"Quiet is good, XO," Clegg told him, giving each of the displays a quick but careful look as she floated past them. "I think our recent exercise demonstrates that, don't you? Speaking of which, what's happening with *Bellerophon*'s sidewall snafu?"

"Last I heard, they were still working on it, Ma'am."

"Which was when?"

She looked at Bertinelli in time to see another quick twitch of his lip.

"About three hours ago, Ma'am."

Three hours. Clegg managed to not roll her eyes, but she pitched her voice quite a bit crisper as she turned to the com section.

"Com, signal *Bellerophon*. I want an update on their sidewall situation."

"Yes, Ma'am." Quickly—maybe a little too quickly— the petty officer turned to his board.

Bertinelli's face had gone stony.

"You have a comment, XO?" Clegg asked.

The commander took a deep breath.

"No, Ma'am," he said stiffly. "Except that I already instructed *Bellerophon* to report if there was any change. I doubt they've forgotten."

Clegg regarded him thoughtfully, wondering just how stupid he really was. Aegis Force had returned from its most recent underway exercise to its overwatch position in Manticore orbit ten hours ago. There were many arguments in favor of simply staying in orbit and carrying out simulated exercises, but Clegg agreed with Admiral Kyle Eigen that the only way to be confident of a warship's systems was to actually use them, not just *pretend* to use them. That was particularly true when the ships in question were as long in the tooth and short of spares as the Royal Manticoran Navy. That consideration had been given an extremely sharp and painful point just three weeks earlier, when too much of the RMN had been reduced to wreckage.

And when *Bellerophon's* captain was forced to report that his Number Two sidewall generator was down for maintenance, Commander Bertinelli had missed the minor fact that Captain Stillman should have reported that *before* the exercise, not in the middle of it.

Nor was that the only system failure the exercise had turned up. The ancient art still known as *gundecking reports*, the practice of somehow failing to note any embarrassing items which might reflect poorly upon ship or officer, was alive and well.

In the shrinking, underfunded, peacetime RMN, that had been merely contemptible. Three weeks ago, it had also become criminal dereliction of duty.

But not everyone seemed to have gotten that particular memo, which was why Clegg had requested end-of-the-watch updates from *Bellerophon*—and every other ship in the squadron—on the status of any major equipment casualties, including state of repair, estimated time of completion, and *actual* time of completion. Since the watch had changed over an hour ago, Captain Stillman's report should have been waiting in her message queue when she entered the bridge. And an XO who could find his rear end with both hands and approach radar should already have asked Stillman—respectfully, of course—where it was. And should then have referred the matter to the squadron's flag captain. Who could be just a bit *less* respectful when she asked for it.

"There's *probably* been no change," she acknowledged. "But it never hurts to make sure of that."

In your long and illustrious naval career? Bertinelli didn't actually voice the comment, but the sentiment was plastered all over his face.

"Understood, Ma'am," he said, again managing to keep his tone sufficiently north of insubordinate. "May I point out—?"

"Bridge, CIC," Lieutenant McKenzie's terse voice came from the bridge speaker, interrupting Bertinelli. "Commander, we've got a hyper footprint at zero-eight-nine by zero-zero-two, relative to the planet. Range is ten-point-six-two LM—call it one-niner-zero million kilometers."

"Acknowledged, Lieutenant," Clegg replied. "Commander Bertinelli, I have the ship," she added formally, grabbing the handhold on the back of the Missiles station and turning her casual drift into a human missile vector. Bertinelli had just enough time to get himself clear of the command station before she hit the back of it, did a stop-and-corkscrew maneuver that she'd developed back when she was a lieutenant, and shoved herself into place. "Astro, plot me an intercept course. Engineering, bring impellers to immediate readiness, but do not bring up the wedge. Com, alert *Bellerophon* and *Gryphon* of the situation. Order them to Readiness Two, but inform both of them that they are not—repeat, *not*—to bring up their wedges or transponders."

"Aye, aye, Captain."

Taking a deep breath, Clegg flipped up the protective cover. She touched the Alert key, blasting the earsplitting klaxon onto the ship's intercom system. She gave it three seconds, then turned it down to a background buzz.

"General Quarters, General Quarters," she announced. "Set Condition Two throughout the ship. Repeat: set Condition Two throughout the ship. Admiral Eigen, please report to the bridge."

She keyed her mic back to the dedicated Combat Information Center channel.

"Talk to me, Lieutenant."

"Yes, Ma'am," McKenzie's voice replied. "We don't have a firm count, but it's definitely five-plus. I can't say how many more there are until they get closer or spread out enough for us to see past the leading wedges to the trailers."

"But your minimum number is solid?"

"Yes, Ma'am," McKenzie said firmly. "Tracking is confident of at least five impeller signatures."

Clegg's earbug pinged. "Bridge, Eigen," the admiral's voice came. "What do we have, Captain?"

"Unknown ships have entered Manticoran space, Sir. They're approximately thirty thousand kilometers outside the hyper-limit and about two degrees above the ecliptic. That's all we've got right now."

"Have you alerted System Command?"

"No, Sir, not yet."

"Well, they probably already have as much information as we do, but go ahead and give them a heads-up anyway. You've informed *Gryphon* and *Bellerophon*?"

"Yes, Sir, and moved them to Readiness Two."

"Good. Plot us a running intercept and have CIC start squeezing the ether for everything they can get. I'll be there in five."

"Yes, Sir."

The admiral keyed off, and Clegg looked over at Bertinelli, hovering stiffly in the cramped space between her and the helm.

"You were about to say something, XO?"

His eyes flicked to the display above her head as it changed from engineering status data to full-on tactical.

"No, Captain," he said. "Nothing at all."

Clegg nodded and shifted her attention to the maneuvering plot, a hollow sensation in the pit of her stomach. She'd been aboard *Vanguard* three weeks ago, supervising the battlecruiser's recent work, when Admiral Tamerlane blew into the system, demolished Janus Force, and came within an ace of doing the same to Admiral Carlton Locatelli's big, fancy Aegis Force. *Vanguard's* meticulous reconstruction work had instantly shifted to an insane scramble to get the wedge up so that Clegg could take the unarmed, undermanned, paper tiger of a ship out to face the attackers. Pure bluff; but combined with the unexpectedly brilliant defense thrown together on the fly by the Navy and MPARS, it had done the trick.

At the time, Clegg had been enormously frustrated that she and her ship hadn't been able to actually do anything to help. Now it looked like the universe was offering her another chance.

Because there was no reason for this many ships to come into the Manticore System all at once. No reason at all.

Unless they were Round Two of the invasion.

"System Command has transmitted Code Zulu to all commands and units, Ma'am," Com announced.

"Very good," Clegg acknowledged.

"All departments reporting Condition Two," Tactical reported.

"Acknowledged," Clegg said, and felt a cold smile at the corners of her lips. *Vanguard* was still undermanned, and still very much underarmed.

But she was no longer just a paper tiger. She could fight.

And she damn well would.

☆   ☆   ☆

"...and so he got away," Lisa finished her story. "With our nodes down, there was nothing we could do about it."

"Mm," Travis said, taking a bite of his ravioli.

A fairly tasteless bite, actually. Not the ravioli's fault, but his. There was just too much uncomfortable camaraderie going on around the rest of the table for him to concentrate on his lunch.

The clever maneuver Lisa and Chomps had cooked up during the Battle of Manticore was bad enough. It gave them a connection and a personal history together that Travis would never be a part of.

But this Casca thing was even worse. Lisa had given him a summary of the murders and the following events years ago, right after she and *Damocles* returned. But until now he hadn't realized just how closely she and Chomps had worked together to bring it to its conclusion.

And it bothered him. He was embarrassed to admit it even in the secret depths of his own mind, but it bothered him.

He was glad Lisa was alive, of course. He was equally glad that her cleverness had kept Chomps from getting killed, too, both on Casca and in the recent battle.

But why did they have to be so happy and cheerful and *friendly* about it?

It was a childish reaction. He knew that. But that knowledge just made it worse.

He'd worked so hard to try to make himself someone who was unique in Lisa's life. Yet here she was, laughing over mutual private jokes with someone else.

"Travis?"

With an effort, he blinked away his silent brooding. Lisa and Chomps were both staring at him, puzzled expressions on their faces.

The *same* puzzled expression, probably.

"What?" he demanded.

"You're a million light years away," Lisa said. "Everything okay?"

"Of course," he said. "Ma'am."

Lisa's frown deepened a couple of degrees. Chomps's actually lessened, by the same amount. Was he amused at Travis's sudden awkwardness? Probably.

"Because if we're boring you—" Lisa began, then broke off abruptly, raising her wrist and keying her uni-link. "Donnelly," she said, her frown deepening.

Travis watched her face closely. The stiffness, the slightly narrowed eyes . . .

"Understood, Sir," she said, her voice taut and formal. "I'm on my way." She keyed off and pushed back her chair. "I have to go, Travis."

"What is it?" Travis asked as he and Chomps also stood.

"Hyper footprint," Chomps said, lowering his own arm to his side. Travis blinked with mild surprise; with his full attention on Lisa, he hadn't even noticed that Chomps had also received a screening. "Aegis Force picked it up, right on the hyper-limit. I expect *Excellent*'s got them by now, too."

"We're being recalled to our ships," Lisa said, already heading toward the restaurant door. "Cazenestro wants everything that can move out of orbit thirty minutes ago."

Travis cursed under his breath. *Casey* was in space dock with her starboard sidewall generators disassembled and a third of her nodes undergoing maintenance. Whatever was about to happen, he and his ship were out of it.

"Oh, wait—the check," Chomps said, stopping abruptly. "I need to—"

"I've got it," Travis cut them off. "Go."

"Thanks, Sir," Chomps said, already halfway to the door, Lisa right behind him. "I'll pay you back."

If you live through whatever's about to happen. Travis winced, even more ashamed of his uncharitable thoughts a few minutes ago. He'd seen the reports on the Navy's combat status, and it wasn't good. Nearly every ship that had been in the battle had taken damage, either from enemy weapons or self-inflicted by aging or improperly maintained systems that had been strained beyond anyone's shortsighted expectations.

The waiter was already on his way with his tablet. Travis pulled out his fob, squeezing his thumb against the reader as he tapped the tablet to transfer the funds. He and the waiter exchanged nods, and Travis hurried for the door—

And nearly collided with Lisa as she came charging back in.

"Come on," she said, beckoning sharply. "Townsend's getting his aircar."

"*Me?*" Travis shuffled to a confused halt. "I haven't been—"

"Haven't been called up," Lisa said, grabbing his arm and pulling him toward the door. "I know. But I just remembered that our ATO was reassigned to *Vanguard* and we don't have a replacement yet. Maybe you can take his place."

Three seconds later, they were outside.

"But I'd need orders," Travis protested as she steered him toward an aircar just settling to the street in front of them. "I can't go aboard without orders."

"She can screen on the way, Sir," Chomps called through the open side window. "If it doesn't work, you can at least enjoy the ride."

"Okay," Travis said.

This was happening way too fast and *way* too far outside normal procedures. But too many people had died in the battle three weeks ago. If this was going to be a replay of that invasion, the Navy would need every man and woman it had. Including Travis Uriah Long.

A week ago, Travis had been reminded of his stated willingness to die for the Star Kingdom and warned that he might well get the chance to do so.

This might just be that chance.

☆   ☆   ☆

The translation nausea faded away, and Jeremiah Llyn keyed on the repeater displays in *Pacemaker*'s private command center. If everyone had made the translation according to his orders...

They had. Mostly. The six ships of the Royal Starforce of the Free Duchy of Barca—an absurdly pretentious title for such a tiny navy, but Barca was like that—were a little out of position, but not too badly, given the vagaries of hyper astrogation. At least the two troop carriers were positioned behind the cruisers and corsair as Llyn had ordered, and all of them were a few thousand kilometers in front of Llyn's compact courier ship.

And behind *Pacemaker*, lurking far to the rear, were the two modest-sized freighters.

They were puny things, as freighters went: just under five hundred thousand tons each. They weren't nearly as efficient as the usual one- to two-million-ton ships, and they were often a source of amusement for the crews of bigger freighters when they arrived at a port. Many people considered them a sort of "starter" ship for people whose ambitions were way larger than their credit ratings.

Still, smaller ships could make a decent living if they focused on exotic—and pricy—luxury goods. Those who considered them a joke usually had a quiet laugh and then forgot them and turned their attention to more important matters.

Which was the main reason Llyn liked the ships so much. Warships in port were never ignored. Small freighters—even small freighters secretly packing the firepower of a top-of-the-line destroyer or cruiser—were.

"Signals from *Shrike* and *Banshee*," Captain Lionel Katura's voice came from *Pacemaker*'s intercom. "They report half a dozen civilian transponders within range, but nothing military."

"Thank you, Captain," Llyn said as the transponders' positions popped up on his repeater display. *Pacemaker*'s own sensors hadn't yet picked them up, but that was no surprise—the freighters' sensor suites were as sophisticated as their weapons, smart-skins, and ECM equipment.

There were members of the Axelrod Corporation board, he'd once heard, who had objected strenuously to spending the huge stacks of money required to design and build ships like *Shrike* and *Banshee*. Personally, Llyn couldn't think of a better use of money than the corporation's Black Ops division.

Diplomacy, bribery, cajolery, leverage, manipulation, and sheer purchasing power had their place in business negotiations. But sometimes, it just came down to force. And when it did, the wise negotiator made sure he had plenty of it in reserve.

Besides, there were even times when a freighter out here in the back-of-beyond had a *legitimate* need for defensive armament. Which made a nice cover if any pointed questions about armed ships happened to float to the surface of the Axelrod pond.

Not that there should be all that much force needed today. Three weeks ago, the Volsung Mercenaries had hit the system with more than enough ships, missiles, and proficiency to make quick work of the obsolescent Royal Manticoran Navy. A few of the Manties' smaller ships might have escaped destruction, and there were probably one or two still cowering over at Gryphon and Manticore-B, but they weren't likely to make trouble. As long as Landing City and the Star Kingdom's precious king were under the Volsungs' guns, Llyn should have no trouble delivering Barca's formal demand for the surrender of Manticore to the Free Duchy.

After that, he would withdraw and let Major General Sigismund Haus and his Axelrod advisory team take over. Once the Barcan occupation troops had been landed and Haus was settled into the Royal Palace,

Llyn and the two Black Ops ships would take a leisurely tour of the system and make sure there was no significant danger. Then Llyn would head back to Barca, assemble the permanent occupation force and civilian administrative corps, and escort them back here. The Star Kingdom of Manticore would cease to exist, and Manticore would become a permanent part of the freshly-expanded Free Duchy.

Haven might raise a stink, of course. The Solarian League would probably at least notice, though Llyn didn't expect anything more than a few raised eyebrows from that quarter. But the disapproval would blow over quickly enough. This kind of conquest wasn't exactly commonplace, especially this far from the conquering system. But it was hardly unique, either. Eventually Manticore's neighbors would adjust to the new reality, and life would go on.

Somewhere in there, the Free Duchy would quietly make an official deal with Axelrod for certain exclusive rights and trade privileges, an arrangement that no one was likely to notice. Then, when Barca "discovered" the Manticoran wormhole junction, Axelrod would be in perfect position to "manage" and "administer" the junction for them.

And Axelrod, which was already hugely rich and successful, would become a great deal more so.

He leaned back in his chair, watching the repeater plot as his squadron began accelerating in-system.

CHAPTER THREE

"WE'VE MANAGED TO REFINE THE ORIGINAL data now that they're moving in-system," First Lord of the Admiralty Admiral (ret) Thomas P. Cazenestro said as King Edward settled himself into his chair in the underground War Room. "No identification yet, but they've been in n-space for about eleven and a half minutes. They're definitely headed for Manticore and there are definitely nine of them, but they're only up to about five hundred and forty KPS and they're still over a hundred and ninety million klicks out. Everything we've got is scrambling to get underway, but for the moment, Admiral Locatelli has approved Rear Admiral Eigen's decision to hold Aegis Force in orbit until he's reinforced with whatever *can* get underway."

"Locatelli's still on his inspection tour of Thorson, I assume?" Edward asked.

Cazenestro nodded. "And he's not happy about being stuck there," he said. "But there's no way to get him out to join Eigen, and at least *Excellent* gives him good communications facilities."

"Yes," Edward said. And with everything spread to hell and gone around the system, that might be critical.

"Whoever these people are," Cazenestro continued, "they're holding their acceleration down to about eighty gravities, so we've got some time. Assuming they want a zero-zero intercept with the planet and maintain that accel, it'll take them over four hours just to reach turnover."

Edward nodded, feeling an unpleasant tingle as his hands gripped the chair's armrests. He'd held those same armrests barely three weeks ago as he watched the Manticoran forces fight their desperate battle for the Star Kingdom's survival.

As he'd watched his only son die.

He'd managed to mostly shove his feelings into the back corners of his mind since then. There'd been so much death and destruction that it almost seemed that *everyone* on Manticore had lost at least one friend or family member. They hadn't, of course; the Navy was too small, too understrength, for that depth of personal loss to touch all of his subjects. But in a sense, *all* of Manticore's dead belonged to all of her people, and Edward, as King, needed to keep his grief at the national level and not allow his private sorrow to take precedence.

His advisers had assured him that the people would understand if he took some time away for private mourning. But while Edward appreciated that, he also appreciated his duty.

A king's life is not his own. Edward's father Michael had reminded him of that four years ago, on the day he'd abdicated in Edward's favor.

Michael could mourn his grandson. Edward's daughter Sophie could mourn her brother, Queen Consort

Cynthia could mourn her son, and Edward's half-sister Elizabeth could likewise mourn her nephew. But Edward couldn't mourn his son. Not as deeply as he wanted to. Not yet.

And now, maybe not ever.

☆   ☆   ☆

"The irony is that Clegg wasn't supposed to be on *Vanguard* in the first place," Lisa said as Chomps blazed their aircar through Landing traffic.

Well above the speed limit, of course, and with complete disregard for normal traffic flow regulations. Travis winced with each veering pass; but for once, of course, there was good reason for it.

"She wasn't?" he asked, to take his mind off Chomps's driving.

"No, she was actually in line to be Locatelli's flag captain aboard *Invincible*," Lisa said. Maybe she was trying to keep her mind off Chomps's driving, too. "Only she didn't get it."

"Why not? What happened?"

"Secour happened," Lisa said. "After Metzger's performance there, Locatelli pulled strings to push her up the list and give her the gold star for *Invincible*."

"I imagine Clegg was annoyed."

"I believe the word is *pissed*, Sir," Chomps called over his shoulder.

"Officers don't get pissed, Townsend," Lisa admonished him. "Women don't sweat, either—we glow."

"I stand corrected, Ma'am."

"Actually, I don't know that she *was* annoyed," Lisa continued. "From what I've heard, she was more frustrated that she was supervising *Vanguard*'s refit during the battle and didn't get to join the fight."

"She may be about to get a chance," Travis said grimly.

"My point exactly," Lisa agreed. "Hence, the irony. Hold on." She raised her uni-link. "Donnelly." She listened a few seconds—"Acknowledged, Sir," she said. "He's right here—I'll bring him on my shuttle... Yes, Sir."

She keyed off.

"You're in," she said. "Your orders will be waiting at the shuttle."

Travis nodded. *I wanted this*, he reminded himself. *I didn't want to just sit on the ground and watch.* So instead of watching from the sidelines he was going to head back into battle.

But then, that was what he'd signed up for when he put on the uniform.

"Thank you, Ma'am."

"Don't thank me yet," Lisa warned. "With only one functional launch tube, we'll be going into whatever's about to happen with one hand tied behind our backs." She reached over and squeezed his hand. "But whatever we've got, I'm sure you'll come up with some clever way to use it."

Travis swallowed.

"Yes, Ma'am. I'll do my best."

☆   ☆   ☆

Llyn's tactical repeater remained singularly barren of useful information and he frowned thoughtfully.

There were a lot of civilian transponders in detection range—well, a lot for a star system this far out in the back of beyond, anyway. But not a single military ID.

Which wasn't necessarily worrisome. Admiral Cutler Gensonne, who should be the current master of this system, couldn't be certain who any newcomers might be. He knew the *schedule*, but schedules were prone to slippage over interstellar distances, and it probably made sense for him to be wary, at least until the newcomers' identities could be confirmed. Llyn understood that.

In fact, if he was surprised by anything, it was the fact that Gensonne was taking sensible precautions. That wasn't something he normally associated with the Volsungs' commanding officer.

☆   ☆   ☆

"Still no ID, Sir," Commander Bertinelli's voice rumbled over the speaker from CIC. "May I remind the Admiral that Bogey One has now been accelerating in-system for over fifteen minutes? That's more than sufficient time to bring his transponders online."

Seated at her station, Captain Clegg winced. As usual, Bertinelli's tone was correct enough, but she was pretty sure Admiral Eigen could hear the impatience under the words.

That was a problem, and not one that seemed likely to go away any time soon. Eigen needed to be publicly oblivious to tensions within his flagship's internal chain of command, Clegg knew, but he'd made it subtly clear to her that he wished she handled people a little better.

He probably had a point. Clegg had never had a high tolerance for fools, and seldom bothered to go out of her way to hide that fact.

Though after just three weeks commanding Aegis Force, it was likely that Eigen had independently come to the conclusion that Bertinelli did indeed fit that category. The man clearly believed *Vanguard*'s bridge was his rightful domain, and just as clearly resented having been banished to the Combat Information Center.

Clegg couldn't decide whether that was because Bertinelli opposed change simply on general principles or because it deprived him of his opportunity to shine directly under his new squadron CO's eye. Neither one spoke very well for him, though.

"Thank you, Commander," Admiral Eigen said calmly. "I *was* aware of the time."

"Yes, Sir."

Clegg winced again. Set up, smack down, and Bertinelli probably hadn't even noticed.

Still, she couldn't help wondering if she might have short-circuited some of this if she'd explained her thinking to her senior officers when she overhauled the arrangement of their battle stations. The unexpected test of the recent attack had demonstrated that the RMN's practice of concentrating all the senior officers on the bridge was potentially a disaster waiting to happen. The carnage of actual combat had demonstrated the need to separate a ship's senior officers as widely as possible to ensure that someone survived to exercise command if the bridge was hit.

Eigen had expressed his own approval of her analysis and solution, and had assured her that the rest of the Navy would eventually come to the same conclusion. So far, it hadn't. Even more unfortunately, neither had Bertinelli.

The man was overdue for a little career counseling. But now was neither the time nor the place for that.

"Force readiness, Captain?" Eigen asked.

"The Squadron is closed up at battle stations, Sir,"

Clegg reported formally, turning to face him. "Impellers are at full readiness."

"Good." Eigen smiled bleakly. "I'm sure our visitors will be suitably surprised when we bring up our wedges and turn on our transponders."

For a moment Clegg wondered if his last four words were an implied criticism of her decision to keep Aegis Force's transponders locked down when they went to Readiness Two instead of bringing them up, as the Book mandated. She opened her mouth to explain—

"Surprise is always a wonderful thing to have," the admiral added. "What's the flagship's status?"

So he *did* understand. Good. "As ready as we can be, Sir," she said. "We only have eleven missiles, and Laser One has some intermittent faults that the techs are still chasing down. On the plus side, the energy torpedo launchers seem to be functioning perfectly."

"Should we ever find ourselves close enough to use them."

"Yes, Sir. There's that," Clegg conceded.

"Still, it *does* happen, doesn't it?" Eigen continued, with another, less bleak smile.

"Yes, Sir. It does," Clegg said, and smiled back.

During her slow rise up the ladder, she'd had more than one discussion with her fellow junior officers about the relative value of missiles, lasers, and energy torpedoes. Most of those fellows had endorsed the received wisdom of "best practice" navies like the Solarian League that the missile was *the* decisive weapon. Not even a capital ship, like *Vanguard*, was likely to survive a single direct missile hit, and even a close near miss could result in a mission-kill. Of course, missiles could at least theoretically be intercepted or evaded, but it still took only a single hit, which could be achieved well before the opponents entered energy range.

Peacetime exercises had only confirmed that view on the part of most of her peers. But Clegg had always taken those exercises with a kilo-sized grain of salt. Missiles were far too expensive to waste in live-fire exercises, and she'd suspected that both accuracy and terminal effect—and the inefficacy of defensive fire—were overstated in the simulations' assumptions. That was why she'd always argued that those exercises badly understated the importance of close-range, direct-fire weapons.

Three weeks ago, missiles had, indeed, wreaked carnage in the opening phase of the engagement. But it had been HMS *Casey*'s energy torpedoes which had utterly demolished the first battlecruiser ever destroyed in combat by the Royal Manticoran Navy. Lasers, too, had played a critical role in the final slugfest before the enemy's withdrawal from the system.

The decisive impact of the despised short ranged weapons she'd championed for years only made her frustration at missing the battle even more acute.

☆   ☆   ☆

His Majesty's Space Station *Orpheus* was a madhouse.

Travis felt his head trying to swivel in continuous 360° motion as he and Lisa swam briskly across the micro-gravity section of the platform towards *Damocles*'s boarding tube, and not just because he couldn't look away from the chaos. He was afraid that if he *did* look away, the consequences might be fatal.

For three weeks, everyone had worried that the
Star Kingdom's attackers might return. For that same
three weeks, everyone had hoped desperately that
they wouldn't, because the severely mauled Royal
Manticoran Navy was in no state to resist a follow-
on assault. Two battlecruisers, a heavy cruiser, and
Casey were all down for major repairs, and half the
ships that weren't currently in yard hands should have
been. They were in line behind more important units,
but that didn't make them remotely combat-capable.

And of those that *were* theoretically combat-capable,
too many, in Travis's opinion, were scattered around
the Manticore Binary System. Every combat-ready unit
assigned to the capital planet's defense—which was a
grand total of three of them—were in Aegis Force.
Whether or not any of the other ships in Manticore
orbit—many of them at least lightly damaged—might
be available to support them was an open question.
He wasn't positive about *Damocles*'s condition, but in
theory, she, the heavy cruiser *Perseus*, the destroyer
Erinye, and the corvettes *Aries* and *Taurus*, constituted
the entire System Reserve Force.

The first three on that list had suffered at least
moderate damage in the battle. The two corvettes
had escaped unscathed, but they'd exhausted their
supply of missiles, and the RMN had never really
had enough of those to go around in the first place.
MPARS's attempt to get the Navy to hand over some
of its precious remaining birds, unfortunately, had
fallen on deaf ears.

Now, someone had apparently realized missiles
would be more useful aboard ships that could move,
even wretched little corvettes, than they would sitting

in stowage or in the magazines of lordly cruisers and destroyers that were dead in the water.

Unfortunately, transferring an impeller drive missile was a nontrivial task at the best of times.

Travis winced as one of the station's bright yellow cold-thruster tractors drove across the crowded docking bay gallery at at least twice the maximum speed regulations allowed and well outside the normal cleared lane. The pilot never slowed down, but merely leaned on the horn button while pedestrians scattered out of his path like fish surprised by a plunging shark. The two trailers behind the tractor carried power shunts for someone's sidewall generators, and Travis wondered which ship they were headed for.

He hoped it wasn't *Damocles*.

The demented tractor pilot wasn't the only lunatic on the loose. Everywhere Travis looked, parties of yard dogs ignored every conceivable safety reg as they worked frantically to get the warships ready to fly. Crews were frantically ripping away repair scaffolding, and even the nearest of the moored ships floated at least eight hundred meters from *Orpheus* at the end of individual boarding tubes and service umbilicals. The yellow hardsuits of the ordnance personnel threading through the whirlpool of frenetic movement were designed to be clearly visible, and Travis's jaw tightened as one of them took a glancing hit from a discarded scaffold structural member and went tumbling away from the missile its owner had been moving. That was probably a broken bone, or worse.

Travis knew he followed regulations and SOP more than most, and usually disapproved of those who didn't. But even though the mad chaos underscored exactly

why those regs had been written, he found himself
for once mentally urging on the violators.

They reached *Damocles*'s thousand-meter boarding tube and swam madly up it. It seemed a lot
more than a kilometer long and there was plenty of
traffic, but a hole opened magically before them as
Lisa bawled for the right of way. They reached the
shipboard end at last, and she waved a salute at the
ensign standing post as boat bay officer of the deck
without even slowing down.

☆   ☆   ☆

"Status on *Aries* and *Taurus*?" Admiral Eigen asked
quietly, never looking away from the main plot. Bogey
One had made its translation into n-space half an
hour ago, during which time it had traveled almost
two million kilometers towards Manticore. Its velocity
was now 1,412 KPS, continuing to build at the same
leisurely eighty gravities' acceleration.

"*Aries* has three birds aboard and two loading now,
Sir," Bertinelli replied from CIC. "*Taurus* has two
stowed and two loading."

"Casualties in the transfer crews?"

"Unknown, Admiral." Bertinelli's tone sounded
faintly surprised.

Eigen clenched his teeth. Of course the question
would never have occurred to him. "Then I suggest
you find out," he bit out.

"Yes, Sir," Bertinelli replied.

Eigen inhaled deeply. He shouldn't have lost his
temper that way. Not as he prepared to lead his force
into combat. His officers and crews needed to know
he was fully and coolly in control.

"*Orpheus* reports three injuries so far, Admiral,"

Bertinelli's voice came, sounding subdued. "One of them is considered serious."

☆   ☆   ☆

Damocles's bridge was a hive of quietly tense voices and flickering displays as Lisa and Travis slipped in through the hatchway.

"Tactical Officer reporting for duty, Sir," Lisa called as she maneuvered her way through the tight maze of stations, displays, and other people towards the CO's station.

The man and woman floating together at the station turned around. Travis recognized the man as Captain Hari Marcello; the woman wasn't familiar, but from her insignia she was obviously the XO, Commander Susan Shiflett.

"Welcome back, Commander," Marcello greeted Lisa. His eyes flicked to Travis. "You must be Lieutenant Long. Welcome aboard."

"Thank you, Sir," Travis said, giving his best salute. "I was given orders to come aboard—"

"Yes, I know," Marcello cut him off. "I was the one who approved them. I presume you remember how destroyers are laid out?"

"Yes, Sir," Travis said, his mind flashing back to his assignments aboard *Guardian* and *Phoenix*.

"Good." Marcello nodded behind him toward the double TO/ATO station at the forward end of the bridge. "Strap in and start running your pre-checks. And remember, Tacco," he held up a warning finger to Lisa, "that you've only got the ventral launcher to work with."

"Yes, Sir."

Lisa pushed off the Missiles Station handhold and

slipped past the captain to the Tactical Station. Travis was right behind her.

He had indeed served aboard two other destroyers. But back on *Guardian*, he'd been a mere gravitics tech third class, while on *Phoenix* he'd been a forward weapons officer. Neither post had given him much time on the bridge, and certainly hadn't allowed him any time at the ATO's station.

Fortunately, the control layout was very similar to the setup aboard *Casey*, where he *had* spent considerable time. He strapped himself in and gave everything a quick look, making quick mental notes about the handful of mostly minor differences.

"What do you want me to do first, Ma'am?" he asked Lisa.

"Double-check the autocannon," she said. "Fore first and then aft. The weapons crew is shorthanded, and we've been having serious trust issues with the status board feed. Chief Wrenner is working on the laser plasma feed—stay on the intercom with him until he's finished, then run a remote diagnostic on the laser. I'll do the missiles and launcher."

"Yes, Ma'am," Travis said. A quick look at the tactical—"Three hours yet to begin raising impellers?"

"Engineering's still spinning up the reactor," Lisa told him. He looked at her, and she shrugged. "Regs," she said with a wry smile.

"Yes, Ma'am," he said. Yet another eminently sensible peacetime regulation that had now come back to bite them. From both safety and reactor efficiency perspectives it made sense to require ships to use shore power when moored to a space station.

In peacetime.

He looked at a side display, a hollow feeling settling into his stomach as he examined the icons of the ships theoretically prepared to sortie in Aegis Force's support. *Damocles*, *Erinye*, and *Perseus*, and none of them able to move for at least another three hours. By then, the intruders would be barely twenty minutes from their turnover point for a zero-zero intercept with Manticore.

And if the invaders got past Aegis and its theoretical supports, there'd be nothing between them and the capital planet.

CHAPTER FOUR

"—ABOUT THE SIZE OF IT, YOUR Majesty," Cazenestro said, looking up from the display recessed into the tabletop before him. "We've got better data on them, but I still wouldn't call it *good*. And our ships..."

"Yes," Edward murmured, gazing at the screen. He'd seen plenty of tactical displays when he was Captain His Royal Highness six years ago, but none of them had painted a bleaker picture. There were a lot of numbers involved: positions, accelerations, times until wedges could be raised, times to arrival at Manticore.

But the bottom line was that too many of the Navy's ships were off at Sphinx and Gryphon, and none of them could get here ahead of the intruders. "Well, this is what we have to work with. Let's focus on what this better data tells us."

"Yes, Your Majesty," Cazenestro said. "I'll just mention in passing that Admiral Locatelli's observations from *Excellent* track very closely with the ones we're getting from Eigen and Aegis Force."

"I assume *Excellent*'s launchers are also ready?"

Edward asked, turning to the com screen where Admiral Locatelli sat in the Thorson command room.

"As ready as they can be," Locatelli said, his image on the com screen tight-lipped. He'd been pushing for years to upgrade the missile launchers on Manticore's single lunar base, Edward knew, but as always there was never enough money to go around.

Still, the missiles that *were* there offered at least a theoretical last-ditch defensive shield.

"We've IDed four warships with a high degree of confidence," Cazenestro continued. "*Vanguard*'s CIC calls it at seventy-five percent; Commodore Osgood's people on *Excellent* call it eighty-five. We still haven't been able to get anything I'd call a good look at them, but we've picked up active radar emissions from at least two sources that look an awful lot like HighLink Sevens or Eights. Coupled with the formation they're maintaining, it looks like at least four warships—probably nothing bigger than a cruiser, judging from the wedges—screening four or five ships pulling civilian-grade accelerations."

Edward pursed his lips. The Solarian-made High-Link radar systems were ubiquitous among naval vessels, including the RMN's own, but their cost and maintenance issues meant they were seldom found on merchant vessels. "Four or five transports, you think?"

"Hard to see what else they could be, Your Majesty," Cazenestro said grimly. "I'm not sure why they've turned up three weeks *after* the attack, but it has all the hallmarks of an occupation force coming in to tidy up."

"Maybe." Edward planted his forearms on the tabletop. "But as you say, why wait three weeks? Why not come in with the attack force and wait outside the limit until the shooting had stopped? Or at least take up station a few light-hours out and wait for a courier to come get them?"

"We don't have an explanation," Locatelli said. "My best guess is that they simply screwed up their intended coordination. We don't know where the attack originated, and we don't know what their own logistic and timing constraints may have been. Maybe there was a delay loading the ground troops, or maybe one of the transports had an engineering issue and they were delayed repairing it." He gestured somewhere off-screen. "But the fact that they've been in-system for over half an hour and still haven't said a word suggests they aren't exactly here to make friends. I think we have to operate under the worst-case assumption that this is exactly what it looks like."

"Agreed," Edward said. "The question is how we want to respond. I'm inclined to go with the argument that this is a chance to get some of the intel we desperately need. Drawing them deeper in-system may give us an opportunity to take some prisoners and, if we're *very* lucky, perhaps even capture a computer system more or less intact."

"But if we let them *too* far in-system, it makes a battle significantly more likely," Cazenestro warned. "At their current profile they'll reach turnover in three and a half hours. At that point, it's fight or surrender."

"Or blow straight through the system and hope we can't hit them," Locatelli added. "It seems to me they're putting in way too much time and effort just to surrender or run. I agree that we need to learn more about them, Your Majesty, but at this point I think keeping them away from Manticore is the more important goal."

"As do I," Cazenestro said.

"Very well," Edward said. As King, he could still override them, But much as he wanted to know who the hell this was who was threatening his people, keeping those same people safe had to be his first priority. "I just wish we had a better idea what we're facing. If the biggest thing they have is a cruiser, then a battlecruiser with a cruiser and destroyer in support ought to be more than they'd care to tangle with. But if this is Tamerlane's backup, it's probably got a heavy tech advantage, and that could even things out considerably."

"We'll see what we can do about getting you that information, Your Majesty," Locatelli promised.

Edward nodded silently. He just hoped they could get it while they could still use it.

☆　　☆　　☆

"Excuse me, Mr. Llyn."

Jeremiah Llyn looked up as the *Pacemaker*'s captain appeared on the intercom display. "Yes, Captain?"

"Signal from *Hamilcar*, Sir," Katura said. "General Haus is asking—again—if he should go ahead and initiate contact."

"Getting a little anxious, is he?" Llyn suggested.

"I'm sure he wouldn't put it that way, Sir."

"No, I'm sure he wouldn't," Llyn said, frowning at the chrono. The Axelrod/Barcan force had been headed in-system for almost forty minutes, and still nothing from Gensonne.

Llyn could think of some reasons the Volsung commander would take his sweet time about checking in.

Not *good* ones, perhaps, but Gensonne always enjoyed proving his own cleverness.

Still, Llyn had always held to the rule to never ascribe to malice that which could be explained by incompetence. Especially when the individual in question had such an abundant store of incompetence to draw upon.

General Haus had been something of a pain throughout the voyage to Manticore. Still, on this one he had a point. His four ships represented a significant chunk of the Royal Starforce of the Free Duchy of Barca, with an equally significant percentage of Barca's troops aboard those transports. Under the circumstances, it wasn't unreasonable for him to be nervous about the ongoing silence.

"Very well," he said to Katura. "Put me through."

"Yes, Sir."

Katura's image disappeared, replaced a moment later by the distinguished, square-jawed, silver-haired Haus.

"General," Llyn greeted him courteously. "How can I help you?"

"I've been going over Admiral Gensonne's timetable, Mr. Ichabod," Haus said. As always, he leaned just a bit on the name, his not-so-subtle way of saying that he didn't believe for a minute that was the operation organizer's real name. "It seems to me that he should already have hailed us. Since he hasn't, I suggest we go ahead and com the planet directly."

"I think we should probably wait on that, Sir," Llyn said "Admiral Gensonne's firepower was more than sufficient to deal with the Manticoran Navy, but it's possible that he took some damage, or that he's still dealing with Manticoran fugitives dodging around the system. If he's had to go farther in-system for some reason, he might not yet have detected our wedges."

"In that case, shouldn't he have left one of his lighter units orbiting the planet?"

"I'm sure you'd have done exactly that," Llyn agreed. "So would I. But again, the Manticorans may have decided to be pesky."

"Perhaps," Haus said with an impatient wave of his hand. "The Admiral had best notice us sometime in the next two or three hours, though. Otherwise, you and I will be having another conversation."

"I'm sure there's nothing to worry about, Sir," Llyn soothed him. "Nothing at all."

☆　☆　☆

"Ready to proceed, My Lady," Captain Ermolai Beckett said.

"Thank you, Ermolai," Admiral White Haven replied, never taking her eyes from the icons in HMS *Nike*'s main display. So far, their information on Bogey One's composition was one hell of a lot vaguer than she could have wished, but she was confident additional information was en route. Twenty-eight light-minutes was a long way for a message transmission to come.

And even longer for a pair of warships to cross.

"My Lady," Beckett said quietly, "I really think—"

"I know what you think, Captain," White Haven interrupted. "But micro jumps are too risky. You know how easy it is to be off by as much as four or five million kilometers even on a longer jump. On a micro jump, that margin of error goes up catastrophically."

"I realize that, My Lady. But—"

"The last thing Locatelli and Eigen need is for us to wind up somewhere the hell and gone away from where they expect us. And the last thing *we* need is to find these people—whoever they are—far enough inside us that they can finish Eigen off in detail before we can join forces with him."

Beckett was silent for a long moment. White Haven turned her eyes from the display and met his gaze coldly. For a moment they held that pose, and then Beckett looked away.

"With all due respect, My Lady, I intend to log my formal disagreement with your decision."

"Do whatever you think right," White Haven said, letting her tone frost over. "In the meantime, you will get the squadron underway."

"Yes, My Lady," Beckett replied. He looked at *Nike*'s helmsman and astrogator, both of whom had been studiously deaf during the conversation. "Proceed as directed," he ordered.

"Aye, aye, Captain."

A moment later *Nike* was on the move, accelerating away from Sphinx at 1.57 KPS^2—twice Bogey One's reported acceleration, but of course she had a lot farther to go. The plain, ugly fact was that there was no way in hell they could reach Manticore in time to make any difference at all to the upcoming battle.

We never should have been stationed here to begin with, the admiral thought bitterly. The fact that she'd said so at the time was of little consolation now that she and the rest of the Star Kingdom were looking the consequences of that disastrous decision squarely in the eye.

Her mind ran the relentless calculations yet again. *Nike* was ten hours from Manticore orbit; Bogey One would enter planetary orbit in only three hours and forty minutes.

She might be there in time to pick up any remaining pieces. But nothing more.

☆　　☆　　☆

"I understand, Sir," Eigen said, studying Locatelli's expression on the com display. As always, there was no way to tell which side of the prisoners-and-intel versus keep-them-at-arm's-length argument he'd come down on. Locatelli definitely knew how to play the political game.

"I'm sure you do, Kyle," Admiral Locatelli replied. "And let me underscore that no one disagrees that we still need all the intel you can squeeze out of this."

"We just have to do it from farther away."

"Exactly," Locatelli said. "How soon can you break orbit?"

"*Vanguard, Gryphon,* and *Bellerophon* are ready to go now, Sir. *Aries* and *Taurus* are still loading missiles, though, and the rest of the Reserve is still over an hour from bringing its impellers online. I want those corvettes as close to fully rearmed as I can before we head out, and I want the Reserve close enough to be another factor in their thinking."

Locatelli frowned. Probably considering the implications of where *Vanguard* was headed, Eigen guessed, and the negligible contribution a corvette was likely to make in any confrontation.

At least on paper. Because Eigen also knew that Locatelli couldn't help but remember how, three weeks ago, the corvette HMS *Phoenix* had made a contribution to that battle that was far beyond anyone's expectations.

Though at a cost. A terrible cost.

Locatelli stirred, and Eigen could see him pushing back the memories. "Bit of a judgment call about the corvettes," he observed out loud, his voice remarkably toneless.

"I know, Sir," Eigen said. "But if the object is to make a show of force and convince these people to go elsewhere, the more platforms I have with me the better. And if I'm going to be taking them into harm's way, I'd really like them to actually be able to shoot at the bad guys if they have to."

"Can't argue with that," Locatelli said, his expression grim. Again, pushing back memories. "When do you want to leave orbit?"

"As late as I can and still be sure they see me coming well before turnover," Eigen said. "The longer I can wait, the better prepared our people are going to be. And the better picture I'll have of the Reserve's actual readiness, for that matter. I understand that we want a cushion, though. Call it another fifty minutes for the corvettes to load birds, and another thirty or forty, maybe forty-five, if I wait for the Reserve."

"That'll put them less than an hour from turnover," Locatelli pointed out.

"I know, Sir." Eigen looked across his bridge to meet Clegg's gaze for a moment. "That would be my best-case timing. If Admiral White Haven and *Nike* were in Sphinx orbit when the alert message got there, they'll still be at least five and a half hours from Manticore orbit even on a least-time profile at that point. Unless our visitors *really* take their time, that means all they'll likely be able to do is pick up whatever pieces are left."

"True," Locatelli said grimly. "On the other hand, if you can stall them off that long, White Haven *might* still have a chance to get in on the fight."

"Not if Bogey One's paying attention. Regardless, it

would be nice to know going in whether I'll have the Reserve to work with. And, to be honest, it's probably even more important to know if I *don't* have the Reserve to work with."

"A point," Locatelli conceded. "I'll give you until the corvettes' launchers are all loaded or there are no more birds *to* load, but that's it. If we wait too long to show our faces, our visitors may figure out that we're less than totally confident in the state of our shipboard systems. And, as you say, we want them to have as much time as possible to think things over short of their turnover point."

"Yes, Sir," Eigen said. "In that case, though, I intend to make my initial acceleration only a hundred and twenty gravities. That will get us underway as soon as the missile loadout allows, which will tell Bogey One we're on our way. But our acceleration will be low enough that the Reserve can overtake us before we reach combat range, even if Bogey One keeps on coming. Also, seeing a second echelon coming up behind *Victory*, *Gryphon*, *Bellerophon* and the corvettes may give them additional pause to think."

"Seems reasonable," Locatelli said. "And of course, how you handle your squadron's up to you. I'll endorse your decision, and I don't expect anyone planet-side to overrule you." He looked at something off-screen, and Eigen saw his lip twitch. "And just when we needed it most, some more bad news. It seems Admiral White Haven has decided that returning with all due speed means running straight through n-space. *And* to the planet itself."

Eigen exchanged startled looks with Clegg. "She's *what*?" he demanded.

"Running to Manticore," Locatelli confirmed bitterly. "Straight through n-space."

Eigen stifled a curse. He'd known for years that Karina Alexander was an idiot who'd essentially achieved her rank via money and political clout. But he hadn't realized until now just how much of an idiot she truly was. "Any chance of countermanding her orders?" he asked, running a quick calculation. If White Haven headed to the hyper limit and did a microjump, she could come in behind Bogey One. Still way out of position to affect whatever was happening here, but that would at least throw in an extra intimidation factor.

"I can countermand all I want," Locatelli said. "But it wouldn't help. By the time the orders could get to her, and she could decelerate and reverse course, she'd be even more behind the curve. No point, really."

Eigen nodded heavily as he ran his eye over the numbers. Locatelli was right. "So she's effectively taken *Nike* completely out of the tactical equation."

"Pretty much," Locatelli said. "And with Flannery and *Victory* at Gryphon..."

Eigen nodded again. And sitting in the Manticore-B system, Admiral Thomas Flannery and Red Force were completely unaware that anything was happening. "So this really *is* all we've got to work with."

"Looks like it," Locatelli said. "You still want to hold to your timetable?"

Eigen looked at Clegg. The flag captain's face was grim, but she nodded her agreement. "Yes, sir," he told Locatelli.

"Right." Locatelli pursed his lips. "I'd be just as happy if no one else got killed today, Admiral. If anyone has to, though, do your damnedest to make sure it's *their* people, not ours."

"I'll do that, Sir. Eigen, clear."

The display blanked, and Eigen looked at Clegg.

"Pass the word to the rest of the Squadron, Trina, and then check in with Captain Timberlake. Tell him I need a running update on *Erinye's* estimated completion time."

☆   ☆   ☆

"I think we've got the laser plasma feed issue resolved, Ma'am," Travis said, looking up at Lisa. "Chief Wrenner gives it an eighty percent probability it'll hold."

Lisa punched a key, dropping a summary of Travis's work onto her display. He watched tensely as her eyes went back and forth in quick study.

"Looks good," she said. "No worse than the skyhooks everyone else is running on right now. And we've still got the secondary for at least partial backup."

"Sort of," Travis agreed, looking back at the readout of Wrenner's jury-rigs. He wasn't any happier with it than Lisa was, but it was the best anyone was likely to get right now.

"Going to be a lot of *sort-of* going around, I'm afraid," Lisa told him. "Beats the stuffing out of *God-I-hope-this-works,* though. Okay, go ahead and run a full diagnostic."

"Yes, Ma'am."

Travis called up the laser readouts on his multifunction display, glancing at the master status board while they loaded. Seventy minutes before Aegis brought its impellers fully online and broke orbit, and *Damocles* and the rest of the Reserve were still seventy-five minutes from *initial* impeller activation.

Forty minutes behind *Aegis*, which was better than he'd initially dared hope. Not great, but at least they'd be close enough behind Admiral Eigen that he could slow or even reverse his accel long enough for them to join forces before anyone reached weapons range.

Assuming nothing else went wrong, of course, and he winced as he read the casualty board. Only one dead, thank God, but they had over thirty injured.

So far.

His earbug pinged as the laser readouts appeared. Putting his concerns about the status board out of his mind, he got back to work.

☆   ☆   ☆

"Captain Timberlake reports *Erinye* is almost ready to go, Sir," Clegg reported, running her eyes down the status reports. "Just chasing down that sidewall glitch."

"Acknowledged," Eigen said. He lowered his voice. "Don't let it get to you," he added quietly.

Clegg frowned at him. "Sir?"

"White Haven's bonehead maneuver," he said. "You're still seething over it."

For a second Clegg wondered if protocol demanded she deny it. Bad-mouthing a superior officer, especially to another superior officer, was generally frowned on.

The hell with protocol. "Yes, Sir, I am," she said. "I've never been impressed by the Admiral, but I would have expected better of Captain Beckett."

"Oh, I have no doubt Beckett tried to dissuade her," Eigen said. "But she's the admiral, he's her captain, and those decisions are hers."

"Yes, Sir." And if there was any justice in the galaxy, Clegg thought bitterly, it would be the last decision White Haven ever made as a flag officer in command.

She glared at the master display, as much for something to distract her from her fury as anything else. But she couldn't stop thinking about it. White Haven and her squadron were at least close enough they *could* have responded in some kind of useful time frame. And if Sphinx had been Thomas Flannery's station, that's exactly what would have happened.

But Flannery was at Gryphon, thirteen light-hours away. Even if it had been possible to transmit a message that far, everything would be over long before he even knew anything was happening.

Her eyes narrowed. Unless...

She keyed her mic.

"CIC, this is the Captain," she said. "Tell me more about—" she craned her neck at the plot "—contact Sierra-Three."

"Sierra-Three...Ma'am?" Commander Bertinelli repeated in a tone of obvious surprise.

"Do you need me to repeat the order, Commander?" Clegg demanded icily.

"No, Ma'am." There was a moment of silence. "Sierra-Three is listed as RMS *Hyderabad*, Ma'am," he responded rather stiffly. "Eight hundred thousand tons, registered to Samuel Tilliotson, under charter as a Navy transport."

"*Thank* you." Clegg turned to Eigen. "Sir, I've just had a thought."

☆   ☆   ☆

Captain Estelle O'Higgins, CO of RMS *Hyderabad* watched her plot, a numb feeling in the pit of her stomach. *Not again*, she thought. *God*, please *not again!*

There was a flicker as the plot updated the projected vector of the glaring icon that indicated the intruders' position. Eight ships, maybe more, heading toward Manticore.

Once again, the Star Kingdom was being invaded.

"Signal from MPARS, Ma'am," Lieutenant Slocum spoke up. He was trying to hide his own dread, O'Higgins could tell, and not doing a very good job of it. "Basically the same Code Zulu that System Command sent an hour ago."

O'Higgins nodded. At the moment, *Hyderabad* was less than three minutes from the Manticore-A hyper-limit en route to Manticore-B on the freighter route between the companion stars. Usually, traffic between the Manticore System's two stellar components was handled by the far cheaper sublight freighters, running a sublight trip of three days instead of the half hour it would take in hyper. Given how few hyper-capable freighters Manticore owned, most of the time it was considered wasteful to use one of them merely to shave a week or so off the round-trip voyage.

But that had changed three weeks ago. In the wake of the attack on Manticore, and with quick transport time now of vital concern, *Hyderabad* had been commandeered to transport priority Navy spares, personnel, and missiles to the squadron detailed to protect the planet Gryphon in the event of another attack.

The squadron, O'Higgins reflected, which was in exactly the wrong place to defend the planet *Manticore*.

To defend Manticore . . . and O'Higgins's son Brian.

Because while *Hyderabad* was well out of any danger out here at the hyper limit, Brian and his ship, HMS *Taurus*, were squarely in the middle of it.

And there was nothing O'Higgins could to do help him. Nothing.

"Ma'am?" Lieutenant Slocum's voice broke into her reflections. "I've just receipted a message from System Command."

"An update on their Code Zulu?" O'Higgins asked, frowning. There was something odd in her com officer's tone.

"No, Ma'am. It's a burst transmission from Admiral Locatelli. And it's specifically addressed to you."

☆   ☆   ☆

"Jasmine! *Get out of there, Jazz!* The bird's—"

Lieutenant Brian O'Higgins, HMS *Taurus'* tactical officer, felt his jaw tighten as the warning shout came over his link to the missile-loading crews. The pop-up ID on his screen strobed, identifying the source as the master chief supervising the loading of the after quad launcher, and his eyes darted to the screen dedicated to the master chief's crew.

Oh, Jesus, O'Higgins thought sickly, watching the twenty-meter missile twist as one of the tethers snapped. He'd hated dropping so many safety procedures, though under the circumstances he'd never even considered protesting. So far *Taurus* had been lucky: only two injuries, and neither of them serious.

But now—

The missile pivoted slowly, but the reloading crews knew how much every second counted. They were cutting margins even closer than they'd been told to, and O'Higgins closed his eyes as the three hundred-ton missile impacted on *Taurus'* hull and one of the green icons on his display turned suddenly crimson. Like all too many of her fellows, Petty Officer Jasmine Falcone had been sent out in a standard vac suit instead of the hard suit The

Book specified, although it probably wouldn't have mattered if she hadn't been.

"Get it off her!" the master chief barked, even though he must know as well as O'Higgins that it was far too late. "Get her out of there!"

Another crimson code flared suddenly on O'Higgins's panel, and he swore viciously.

"Captain, we've lost the ventral mount's Number Three Cell," he announced. "The bird they were loading twisted on its way into the tube. Looks like at least half of the actuator hard points are down."

"Time to repair?" Commander Carpenter demanded.

"Probably at least thirty-five or forty minutes. If it's a full replacement situation, make that two or three hours."

An estimate which also tacitly assumed that *Orpheus* had the parts on hand. Which it probably didn't.

A second later, a sobering thought slapped him across the face.

Why the hell was he getting so upset over losing a tube when somebody had just been killed trying to load it?

"Status of the missile?" the captain asked.

"Unknown."

"Well, find out. If it's still up, there may be time to transition it to *Aries*."

☆   ☆   ☆

"Acknowledged," Admiral Flannery said, studying the face on his day cabin com screen. He'd never met Estelle O'Higgins before, but he couldn't imagine she looked this strained and tense on a normal day.

Or this sick, for that matter. Even without the sound of someone still retching behind her it would have been obvious that *Hyderabad*'s skipper hadn't wasted any time decelerating before making her transition back to n-space. "Good job, Captain. I'm glad you were in position to play courier."

"*I'm* glad you weren't in planetary orbit," O'Higgins said. "Admiral Locatelli said you might be."

Flannery cocked an eyebrow. Locatelli's exact words, he suspected, had been *should be*. "The stars have been kind," he said, deflecting the whole question. "You can stand down, Captain, and give your crew some recovery time."

He shifted his eyes to the second face on his display. "You got all that?" he asked.

"Yes, Sir," Adelaide Meyers, his flag captain, replied. "Astrogation estimates approximately one hundred minutes before we can enter hyper."

Flannery nodded. There weren't any standing orders to cover a situation like this one—*although there damned well ought to be*, he thought grimly—but Meyers was the sort to use her own initiative. "Execute," he ordered. "Time to the Manticore-A hyper-limit?"

"Astrogation makes it two and a half hours—one hundred forty-three minutes, to be precise—from now," Meyers replied. "Planetary orbital insertion in another six hours plus."

Flannery scowled. Eight and a half hours until they could do anything.

And it would have been a lot longer if he'd been sitting neatly in Gryphon orbit as his official orders had intended, and as Locatelli had probably assumed.

Ironically, when Flannery had asked First Lord Cazenestro for the authority to interpret those orders a bit liberally, he'd been more concerned about boredom than anything else. Aside from the Manticoran citizens on Gryphon, there was exactly zero in the system to protect, and sitting around all day drinking tea was a good way for a crew to go stale. Fortunately, Cazenestro shared his reasoning, which was why Flannery had felt comfortable asking permission to spend some of their time out here running drills.

And run them he had. He'd put his ships and their crews through the most demanding series of drills and tactical problems he could think of. If Tamerlane ever came back, Flannery was determined that Red Force, at least, would be up to whatever challenge he could throw at them.

He'd also been careful to keep his ships between Gryphon and the hyper-limit at all times, of course. Whether or not Manticore-B was the best place for Red Force to be, the fact remained that the protection of the people on Gryphon was Flannery's primary responsibility. But it wasn't coincidence that he'd picked his locations so as to keep him significantly closer to the hyper limit than a Gryphon orbit could offer.

And now, because of that paranoia-tinted foresight, Red Force was just under two light-minutes inside the limit, rather than the nine minutes inside where they might have been. Three and a half hours closer to the limit—and to Manticore-A—than they would have been.

He felt his eyes narrow as he studied the data packet *Hyderabad* had brought. Assuming the numbers were correct, *Victory* would make her alpha translation back into n-space just about the time Bogey One reached its turnover point.

And when that happened . . .

"Red Force is on its way, Admiral," Captain Meyers reported. "Forming up on us."

"Good," Flannery said. "Make sure the other captains get the data packet. I want everyone at their absolute top game."

"They will be, Sir," Meyers assured him. "You've made sure of that." She gave him a tight smile. "I guess there's something to be said for maneuvers, after all."

"Indeed there is," Flannery agreed. "Let's hope Chancellor Breakwater makes note of that at the next budget conference."

☆   ☆   ☆

Among the elite of Axelrod's operatives, there were some who advocated the occasional use of what was referred to as Rule Thirteen: dealing with someone who'd really, really pissed off the operative by shooting him between the eyes in front of his subordinates.

Llyn would never do such a thing. It was crude, it was messy, and worst of all it left witnesses. Still, if Cutter Gensonne was playing childish games with him, he might actually consider it.

The ominous part was that this had stopped feeling like a game, childish or otherwise.

The problem was that he had two conflicting sets of non-data. The first was Gensonne's persistent and infuriating absence from the scene. Llyn's force had been in-system for two hours and forty minutes, and there was *still* no sign of the Volsungs. If, in fact, Gensonne was somewhere else, deeper inside the hyper-limit, it was entirely plausible for him to be unaware of their arrival. But he knew the schedule, and Llyn's part of it had allowed sufficient slippage for Barcan inefficiency for them to arrive almost exactly on time.

It was still possible that Gensonne was sitting right there in orbit and simply keeping a low profile. If the Volsungs had taken heavier losses and damage than anticipated, it could be that they hadn't yet picked up on Llyn's arrival.

There was, unfortunately, another possibility. It was conceivable, however unlikely, that Gensonne had managed to lose. The odds were so overwhelmingly against that outcome that it was hard for Llyn to even take it seriously.

Even if he did, even if Gensonne had managed to lose against the ragtag Manticoran Navy, why hadn't the Star Kingdom challenged or so much as even messaged the ships that were headed towards its capital? Their passage across the hyper-limit without identifying themselves constituted a major breach of interstellar law, which reasonably should have sparked irate demands for identification. Especially in the wake of Gensonne's attack, whether it had been successful or not.

That was the second set of non-data. Either Gensonne was being coy, or the Manticorans were.

Still, even if the Volsungs had somehow been driven off, they'd surely inflicted major losses on the RMN in the process. Given their numerical advantage, it was impossible for Llyn to believe that they hadn't inflicted at least as much damage as they'd taken. That still didn't explain the absence of any communication from the Manticorans...unless they'd accepted that all of Llyn's units were what they appeared to be.

That could be it. They could be looking at their sensor data and thinking all they were facing was three or four cruisers and four freighters. Unless Gensonne had mauled them beyond any resistance at all, maybe they thought they could afford to let Llyn keep coming until his force was too far inside the limit before they showed themselves.

Which could be the last mistake they ever made. They didn't know about *Shrike* or *Banshee*, or the fact that they were actually looking at the equivalent of *six* cruisers, not just four, or the fact that the two warships they didn't know about were newer, more modern, and a lot more dangerous than any cruiser in the RMN, especially at missile ranges.

If there were any remnants of the Manticoran Navy to sweep up, Llyn had a damned good broom.

☆   ☆   ☆

"Anything more on that launch cell, Tactical?" Captain Vincent Carpenter demanded.

"No, Sir," Brian O'Higgins said, shaking his head. "Still waiting for a response from *Orpheus* on the hardware."

"Then tell them to forget it," Carpenter growled. "We're leaving in ten minutes."

"Sir," O'Higgins said respectfully, "we still got station personnel completing umbilical connections on two of our birds."

"I know." Carpenter said, looking at his displays. "Tell them they might want to expedite. Otherwise, they may be going on an unexpected journey."

☆   ☆   ☆

"The Squadron will proceed as ordered, Captain," Admiral Kyle Eigen said formally.

"Aye, aye, Sir," Clegg responded, equally formally, and nodded to *Vanguard's* helmsman. "Take us out, Chief. Com, the rest of the Squadron is to conform to our movements." She pursed her lips. "If anyone's still working on the corvettes' missiles, they might want to get a move on."

"And after you've done that, Lieutenant," Eigen added, "stand by to contact our visitors."

☆ ☆ ☆

"There they go," Lisa said quietly, and Travis looked up from the diagnostic he was currently running as the tactical display changed.

Aegis Force's data codes changed abruptly as the open-ended triangle that indicated an active impeller wedge sprang up about its ships. Travis felt his stomach tighten as they began to move, accompanied by the two corvettes who'd been attached to them at the last moment. Their icons looked proud and confident, but he knew too much about their systems' reliability issues.

And he remembered what had happened to so many of those icons' fellows only three weeks before.

He gazed at them another moment, then looked at Lisa, nodded once, and returned his attention to his panel's flowing datacodes.

"Impeller initiation in seven minutes, Captain," *Damocles*'s chief engineer reported over the intercom.

CHAPTER FIVE

"MR. LLYN, YOU'D BETTER LOOK AT this."

Katura's voice sounded much tighter than normal, and Llyn looked up from the book chip he'd been reading. The book was rather boring, but he'd learned that that kind of casual activity was a good way to demonstrate professional calm, especially in the face of general uncertainty and growing tension. He took one look at the captain's expression, then dropped his eyes to the navigation display.

He felt his own facial muscles tighten. Five icons, each burning the crimson of an unidentified unit, had left Manticore orbit.

And unlike the handful of obviously civilian impeller signatures *Pacemaker* and his special ops ships had detected, these were headed directly towards the intruders instead of away from them.

"What do we know about them?" he asked, keeping his voice calm and unhurried.

"Not much, yet," Katura replied. "At least one of them is probably a battlecruiser, judging from apparent wedge strengths. Hard to say about the others, but a couple of them look a lot smaller than that. Acceleration's one-twenty gravities, so they're obviously military, but that seems on the low side for a battlecruiser. That's all we've got so far. Be another seven or eight minutes before we get anything light-speed."

Llyn frowned. Katura was right about how low that was for a warship. But the real question wasn't their acceleration profile, but who they were.

It could still be Gensonne. In fact, given the ongoing silence from any Manticoran authorities, it probably *was* Gensonne, although exactly what he was playing at now was unknown.

Well, Katura was also right about the limitations of light-speed transmissions. Even assuming those icons had activated their transponders at the same moment their impellers came up, it would be another—he checked the time—six and a half minutes before those IDs reached *Pacemaker*.

He sat back to wait.

☆   ☆   ☆

"The Squadron reports all units underway, Sir," Clegg announced, exactly as SOP required.

And thoroughly unnecessarily, Eigen reflected, since his display had already shown him that. "I assume the yard dogs all got clear in time?"

"Yes, sir." His dour captain gave a small snort. "They were moving rather more enthusiastically than usual there at the end."

"I'm sure they were." Eigen checked the chrono. "All right, they've had time to see our IDs. Com: go ahead and transmit."

"Yes, Sir." Clearly bracing himself, Lieutenant Messner pressed the *send* key.

☆   ☆   ☆

"We're getting transponders, Sir," Katura said.

Llyn watched the icons change. They remained the same bright crimson, but data codes began popping into existence beside them. "According to their IDs, they're Manticoran warships," Katura continued. His voice was under control, but there was a hint of concern beneath it. "HMS *Vanguard, Gryphon,* and *Bellerophon*—a battlecruiser and a pair of cruisers. The other two are showing as corvettes, HMS *Aries* and HMS *Taurus.*"

Llyn's eyes narrowed. For the last several minutes, despite everything, he'd allowed himself to go on hoping it was Gensonne. The IDs pretty well ended that one.

Or maybe not. It was just barely possible Gensonne had relabeled his ships in order to fool any unexpected visitors before they realized there'd been a change of management.

That would be a bit cleverer than he would have anticipated out of the Volsung admiral, but it would also have been one way to entice any of those visitors into a range at which they had no choice but to surrender. It probably wouldn't matter one way or the other if someone *had* figured out that Manticore had just changed hands, but it would certainly be more convenient to keep that information under wraps until the troops had landed and made sure the change stood up.

Unfortunately, not only would that have required more brains and imagination than Gensonne had thus far demonstrated, but it didn't match what Llyn was seeing on his display. Not unless the Volsungs had been hammered one hell of a lot harder than they should have been. Besides, if those smaller units really were corvettes, not destroyers showing false transponder codes, they couldn't be Gensonne's, because he hadn't taken anything that small to Manticore in the first place.

Could the idiot have lost after all? Even as the uncertainty had swirled higher and higher around Llyn, he'd never really let himself believe that could have happened. Even with the unexpectedly de-mothballed ships his last pre-battle intel pass had spotted, the RMN's state of rust and inexperience had still left Gensonne with a solid seventy/thirty edge. How could the Manticorans have somehow won with that big a disadvantage?

Or, to put it another way, how could Gensonne have screwed up and *lost* with that big an *advantage*?

"Sir, should we activate our own transponders?" Katura asked.

Llyn chewed his lip. The Manticorans were transmitting their IDs, but they'd made no attempt to communicate further. Under the circumstances, he was disinclined to give them anything at all.

"Negative," he said. "Let's get a little closer first."

"Yes, Sir."

☆   ☆   ☆

"Impeller initiation sequence begun, Sir," *Damocles*'s engineer announced. "Everything looks optimum now."

"Thank you, Commander Papadakis," Captain Marcello acknowledged.

"Get ready to spin up the sidewall generators for test, Travis," Lisa instructed.

"Aye, aye, Ma'am," Travis replied and began entering commands. Because a sidewall had to interface with a ship's wedge, it couldn't really be tested until there was power to the beta nodes. In fact, Engineering would have to be a good ten minutes—five, at the very least—into impeller light-off before the generators could come up.

At least everything else looked good. Or, as Lisa would say, at least it all looked better than *God-I-hope-this-works*.

☆   ☆   ☆

"Mr. Llyn, we have a transmission."

From Katura's tone, it was clear who the transmission in question was from. Or, more importantly, who it *wasn't* from. "Put it up," Llyn ordered.

"Yes, Sir."

An instant passed, and then a compact, square shouldered man with dark hair and disconcertingly sharp gray eyes appeared on the master display. Whoever he was, he wore the uniform of a Manticoran admiral and he didn't look especially pleased at the moment.

"Unidentified force, this is Admiral Kyle Eigen, Royal Manticoran Navy, commanding His Majesty's battlecruiser *Vanguard*." Eigen's voice was strong and excruciatingly confident. "You are in violation of Manticoran space. You are instructed to identify yourselves and reverse acceleration immediately. If you do not, you will be considered hostile, and we will react accordingly."

He stared coldly into his pickup for another two seconds, then gave a brisk nod. "Eigen, clear."

Llyn stared at the display as Eigen's challenge began to repeat, cold fury seeping through him like ice water.

He'd been right. Gensonne had screwed up. The damn stupid, *arrogant*, S.O.B. had completely and totally screwed up.

And now Llyn's plan—in fact, his entire reason for being here—was equally screwed.

Eigen had barely gone into his second repeat of his message when the frightened yips began.

"Signal from *Hamilcar*, Sir," Katura reported, his voice tight. "General Haus has copied over *Vanguard*'s message and is demanding to know what you plan to do about the situation."

"Thank you, Captain," Llyn said, contempt mixing with his anger. Copied over the message, as if Llyn might somehow have missed hearing the Manticorans' announcement? Making fearful demands, as if Llyn didn't already have a plan prepared for every eventuality?

The truly irritating part of that was that he didn't.

He'd planned for Gensonne to have won. He'd also planned for Gensonne to have lost, but in the process turned the Manticoran defense into splinters.

What he *hadn't* planned for was for Gensonne to have left even a single damn battlecruiser alive and kicking.

Stupid. Criminally stupid, even. Llyn had been lulled by the fact that everything else in the operation had gone pretty much exactly according to plan, and now the unexpected had turned around to bite him.

It was a mistake he wouldn't make again.

"Time to missile range?" he asked.

"Seventy-nine minutes, assuming we both maintain constant acceleration," Katura replied. Obviously, he'd been working the numbers while Llyn had been cursing Gensonne.

"And if we reverse acceleration?"

"If we reverse accel and they maintain one-two-zero gravities, we enter missile range in just over one hundred minutes, Sir. Closing velocity at that point will be thirteen-point-five thousand KPS."

"If we reverse and they stop accelerating?"

"We still enter missile range in an hour and a half. Closing velocity would be down to two-point-two thousand KPS. But we'd still be twenty minutes from a zero velocity relative to Manticore. If we reverse acceleration this instant, we'd still need six hours and twenty minutes to recross the hyper-limit."

Llyn scowled. Not only was his plan screwed, so was he. Unless the Manticorans reversed acceleration, they were going to reach missile range whatever he did. If these people were feeling belligerent, Llyn couldn't avoid action even if he wanted to.

He pursed his lips, his frozen brain starting to function again. Maybe he wasn't as screwed as it looked. There was only one battlecruiser in that force, and it was accelerating at only three quarters of its book accel. That suggested damage, possibly serious damage. *Hamilcar*, *Hasdrubal*, and *Mago* might be less than cutting-edge by the Solarian Navy's standards, but they were far more modern and capable than almost anything Manticore had boasted even before Gensonne took out the rest of their fleet. *Mylae* wasn't as heavily armed, but she was just as modern. And that didn't even count *Shrike* and *Banshee*.

Unless *Vanguard* didn't have a ding on it, Llyn's force should be able to take it without even the need to sweat. A pair of corvettes wouldn't change that very much, either.

And if the RMN had anything more to throw at them, they'd surely have trotted it out by now.

"Signal to the Barcans," he told Katura as he reached for his makeup kit. "Have them activate their transponders but hold their present profile. And only activate their IDs," he added. "They're to keep every other com silent. Make sure they understand that."

"Yes, Sir. And *Shrike* and *Banshee*?"

"Activate their Barcan cover transponder codes. And tell Captain Vaagen and Captain Rhamas to begin prepping their weapons."

"Yes, Sir."

One of Llyn's most rigid private rules was that his actual face should never be seen by anyone outside of his own colleagues and trusted Axelrod employees. For coms, CGI overlays were the usual technique for that kind of masquerade: faster and more convenient than wigs, facial hair, and facial plastic strips. Most high-level operatives, Axelrod's among them, went that route.

But Llyn was more of a perfectionist. More importantly, he knew CGI overlays could be penetrated and identified as such if someone was willing to put in the necessary time and effort. If that someone had a great deal of ingenuity on top of it, the whole thing could even occasionally be dissolved, leaving the original face there in all its naked glory.

That kind of analysis *might* be able to show that a physically altered face wasn't the real one. But it could never be electronically unraveled the way a CGI could.

Good-bye, Jeremiah Llyn, he thought to himself as he started the transformation. *Hello, Count Ernst Bloch.*

☆   ☆   ☆

Travis sat back with a sigh of relief as *Damocles*'s sidewall generators spun up without faltering. He would never have called the destroyer's systems reliability anything close to good, but at least all of the critical ones were up. And, really, they weren't any less reliable than the RMN had been unhappily accustomed to dealing with for his entire career. In another thirty minutes, they'd be able to—

"Captain," Chief Ulvestad spoke up suddenly from Communications. The CPO's voice was crisp, but it was the sort of crisp, calm professionalism that training painted over something very different. "We've just copied a message from *Perseus* to *Vanguard* and *Orpheus*. Captain Conroy reports his entire port sidewall refused to initiate."

"Acknowledged," Marcello said calmly. "Ask Captain Conroy for an estimate on time to repair the fault."

"Aye, aye, Sir. I—" Ulvestad broke off. "Sir, *Perseus* now says her forward generator's going to require complete replacement. Her engineer estimates a minimum—repeat, a minimum—of five hours to get the aft generator back online."

An invisible fist punched Travis in the gut. Without a sidewall, *Perseus* would be at a deadly disadvantage if Conroy took her into combat.

But without the cruiser, with only *Damocles* and *Erinye*, Reserve Force would barely be worthy of the name.

His eye darted back to the time display, counting down inexorably to impeller activation, his brain feeling like a ground car skittering on ice.

☆   ☆   ☆

"Admiral Eigen, this is Count Ernst Bloch of the Free Duchy of Barca."

The voice boomed from the speaker, and Clegg gave the display a quick look. The man certainly looked the part, she decided. The image was a bit dithery—they must be right on the limit of Bloch's laser range, which might explain why he hadn't commed them sooner. But fuzziness or not, Bloch looked every inch the aristocrat: silvery hair with a single black streak through it, face lined with age and wisdom and an obvious love of the outdoors, a voice that commanded instant obedience, and piercing eyes that could see right into a person's soul.

He reminded Clegg a lot of her own father. He reminded her even more of the man her father had pressed very hard for her to marry.

Thank God there'd been the Navy.

"I wish to speak to your superiors," Bloch continued, his stern voice going a little sterner. "Specifically, I want to know the Star Kingdom of Manticore's connection with a group of pirates that have been plaguing our region."

"What the hell?" Eigen murmured under his breath. Then he cleared his throat.

"I'm sorry, Count, but I have no idea what you're talking about. I'm relaying your message to our System Commander, Admiral Locatelli, but I assure you we have nothing to do with pirates of any sort. On the contrary, we've spent the past decade doing our damnedest to find and destroy any and all such marauders. Eigen, clear."

He gestured and the message began its long journey back.

"Redesignate Bogey One as Barca Force," he ordered. "Make that Barca Alpha—there may be more of them on the way. Copy everything to System Command, and request that someone find me whatever the hell we've got on the Free Duchy of Barca."

"Yes, Sir," Communications replied.

"And in the meantime, Captain," Eigen continued, turning to Clegg, "it would seem that something new's been added. I think—"

"Excuse me, Admiral," Com said. "We've just received a priority signal from *Perseus*."

☆   ☆   ☆

Message turnaround time between *Vanguard* and Barca Alpha was down to fourteen minutes and falling. Between *Vanguard* and Manticore, it remained less than two seconds. Within two minutes, ONI had pulled up everything in the archives on Barca and its people. Three minutes after that, Clegg had read all of it.

There wasn't much, and all of it was at least fifteen years old.

The system was about two hundred sixty-eight light-years southeast of Manticore, nearly four hundred from Sol. It had been settled a couple of hundred T-years ago, and at last report was listed as reasonably stable, if not blazingly prosperous.

Why they should think Manticore was involved with pirates Clegg couldn't guess. But the fact that they'd sent a group of ships on a four-and-a-half-month journey implied they must have *some* good reason.

She looked forward to hearing it.

Assuming they were who they said they were, of course. The fact that they hadn't so much as announced their IDs before they were challenged was a clear violation of interstellar law which could certainly be construed as hostile. On the other hand, it could also simply indicate caution on their part, especially if they thought the Star Kingdom was in cahoots with a batch of pirates.

She just hoped it didn't indicate that they were the type to shoot first and crosscheck their data later. Along with Count Bloch's courier ship, the IDs the Barcans were now transmitting listed the force as four cruisers and four freighters. Given the state of *Vanguard*'s defenses, four cruisers could pose a serious threat, even with *Gryphon*, *Bellerophon*, and both corvettes in support.

Or rather, she reminded herself tightly, *without* the support of *Perseus*.

That fact clearly wasn't lost on System Command. Eight minutes after receiving Eigen's message, admiral Locatelli sent a response to be relayed to Count Bloch, repeating Eigen's assurances that the Star Kingdom wasn't involved in piracy. The transmission included a large attachment that purported to contain the complete record of Manticore's decade of pirate-hunting, which Eigen was ordered to likewise transmit to the Barcan force.

Vanguard sent it on its way immediately.

Six minutes later, Bloch's response to Eigen's last transmission came in.

"You'll forgive me, Admiral, if I can't simply take your word for that," the count said. "Eight months ago, our system was attacked by a powerful pirate force, and data we found in the wreckage referenced the Star Kingdom of Manticore. I'm not saying you or your government are necessarily in collusion with these marauders, but the fact remains that the trail leads here. We mean to find out why."

"I understand your anger and determination, Count Bloch," Eigen replied. "However, I assure you in turn that there's no place in this system where any such force could be hiding. Perhaps more to the point, we were ourselves attacked recently by an unknown force. If your pirates had information relevant to Manticore, perhaps it wasn't as their haven, but as their next target. At any rate, I've just sent you the data outlining our campaign against pirates over the past few years and suggest you at least examine those records before you draw any conclusions."

Once again, the delay began. The Barcans continued to drive towards Manticore, Clegg noted uneasily, ignoring *Vanguard* and her escorts. Bloch must be very sure of himself.

And likely with even better cause than he knew.

☆   ☆   ☆

"Captain Conroy, with all due respect, without a sidewall, *Perseus* isn't combat-capable," Captain Marcello said firmly. "If *anything* gets past your point defense—"

"I take your point, Captain," Conroy replied from Marcello's com display. "But if it comes to it, *Vanguard*—and the rest of you—are going to need our counter missiles. And let's face it: the initial exchange is going to be head-on, where sidewalls aren't going to matter one hell of a lot."

"Captain—Pierre," Marcello said, "if these people are who they say they are, it's not going to come to a fight . . . probably. And if it does—and if the range closes the way it did last time—the risk to your ship is, no offense, out of all proportion to her potential contribution to the engagement."

"Your view is noted." Conroy's voice was noticeably cooler than it had been. "The matter is not open for debate, however. Even if, as you say, these people *are* who they say they are, they may or may not be feeling reasonable. If they don't, Admiral Eigen is right about presenting them with the most forceful argument we can for *deciding* to feel that way. I think it's probable a cruiser and two destroyers would be a lot more forceful than two destroyers by themselves."

Marcello obviously wanted to continue the argument, Travis thought. Unfortunately, although he and Marcello were clearly good friends, *Damocles*'s CO was junior to Conroy. And equally unfortunately, the cruiser's captain had made several excellent points. Especially the psychological one.

Travis had scanned the same data Clegg had received, looking specifically for any information about Barca's military capability. There wasn't much, but there was the notation that, unlike the Star Kingdom, Barca built its own warships. That didn't necessarily prove anything, but given that the capability to do so had been developed only about twenty years ago, it probably meant the Barcans' ships were significantly later designs than anything Manticore had.

And that meant those four cruisers were probably a lot more dangerous, ton-for-ton, than those of the RMN, even if system reliabilities were equal.

Which almost certainly they weren't.

Bottom line was that Conroy was right. If Count

Bloch was feeling belligerent, Eigen needed every single scrap of argument in favor of *non*-belligerence.

☆   ☆   ☆

"Interesting," Bloch said from the com display. "I see you've been busy. Give me a few minutes to look this over, and we'll talk."

"Of course," Eigen replied. "I'll await your response."

He keyed off.

"Which isn't to say we're going to be just sitting on our hands," he added to *Vanguard*'s bridge crew. "CIC? Four of these people are identifying themselves as cruisers. Do we have any additional indications that that's accurate?"

"Sir, we're doing our best," Bertinelli's voice came back "but the range is still too far for us to tell you much more. All we've got to go on are their wedges, and at this point, our best guess from their signatures is that they are what they say they are. I can't guarantee that, of course."

The XO managed to sound whiny and faintly defensive, Clegg noticed, even though what he'd said was self-evidently true. On the other hand, it didn't exactly answer the question Eigen had asked.

And there were things other than emission signatures from which a competent tactical officer might draw inferences.

The operative word there being *competent*.

"Sir," Clegg said, gesturing at the master display. "I agree with Commander Bertinelli's comments on Barca Alpha's impellers, but I have to wonder why they would have brought *four* freighters with them. I suppose it's possible all four of them really are transports to carry a big enough ground force to let them actually occupy us, if they decided the Star Kingdom *was* involved with these pirates. But take a look at Barca Eight and Niner."

"What about them?" Eigen asked after a moment.

"It looks to me like Bloch is spreading them *wider*, rather than pulling them in tight behind his cruisers," Clegg said. "That's not something I'd expect someone to do with freighters when missiles might start flying. Especially not with freighters packed with troops and combat equipment."

"Indeed," Eigen said, rubbing his chin thoughtfully. "But that's the sort of thing a squadron commander might do to clear his units' sensors."

"That's one of the things I was thinking, Sir. It's also the sort of thing a CO might do to spread his missile platforms. Those things are showing commercial IDs, and they *may* be built on freighter hulls, but even though they appear to be much smaller than the other two they're probably still at least a half-million tons, six or seven times the size of one of those cruisers. Commercial transponder codes don't guarantee they aren't Q-ships or something even uglier, and God only knows what kind of firepower could be built into a hull that size. Which means—"

"Which means the odds could be even tighter than they look," Eigen finished her thought grimly. "Yes. Wonderful."

☆   ☆   ☆

"Instruct the Barcans to stop accelerating," Llyn said.

"Stop accelerating, not *reverse* acceleration, Sir?" Katura asked in the tone of someone making very certain he hadn't misunderstood.

Or, perhaps, suggesting some reservations with the order he'd just heard.

"That's correct," Llyn said, adding a bit of frost to his voice.

"Yes, Sir."

Llyn nodded his satisfaction.

Though he suspected he was probably the only person—aside from Vaagen and Rhamas, at any rate—who felt remotely satisfied by his actions. They were only fourteen minutes from the turnover point for a zero-zero intercept with Manticore at their current acceleration. Reducing their acceleration to zero stretched that to twenty-eight, which bought him at least a little more time.

On the other hand, if this Admiral Eigen decided to force the issue, they were already too deep inside the limit and going too fast to prevent the Manticoran warships from entering missile range. And if what he was coming to suspect about the state of the RMN was accurate, this was not a confrontation he wanted.

Sitting back in his chair, he gently ran a finger along his artificially wrinkled cheek and tried to think.

☆   ☆   ☆

"They're still coming," Lisa murmured.

Travis looked up from the panel in front of him. Barca Alpha was indeed holding course towards Manticore, despite having cut its acceleration.

"You suppose they're a feint?" he murmured back.

"They're sure acting like one," she agreed. "Only—" She waved a hand. "I don't see any follow-up forces making tracks towards us."

"Maybe it's behind them. That could be one reason they've cut accel. If what they wanted was to see what we had, they may be slowing their closure rate for something to catch up with them from astern."

"Aegis hasn't spotted anything. Yet, at least."

"I know." Travis hissed between his teeth. "You know, we really need something out there. A permanent patrol, or some kind of sensor buoy system close to the hyper-limit. Piggyback it off the NAVSAT array, maybe."

"Maybe," Lisa said. "But we can't do everything at once. Personally, I still vote for getting the battle-cruisers and cruisers out of mothballs and up to full fighting strength before we work on setting up a sensor net. If these people *are* up to something, and we had another battlecruiser or two to back Aegis..."

"I suppose. Ma'am," Travis added, remembering the proper honorific this time. Talking to her this way, it was easy to forget they were sitting on a bridge crowded with other Navy personnel. "In fact—"

He broke off, his breath catching in his throat. *Getting the battlecruisers up to fighting strength...*

"Travis?" Lisa asked.

Travis was vaguely aware that she was asking something, but his attention was on his board, fingers flying as he keyed for the status of *Damocles*'s impellers. The plasma flow... the alpha nodes... the beta nodes...

"Lieutenant Long?" The question was quite a bit sharper—and more formal—than Lisa's had been. Startled, Travis swiveled around to find Captain Marcello and Lisa looking expectantly at him.

As was the rest of the bridge.

"You have something, ATO?" Marcello prompted.

His question broke the spell. Travis shot another look at Lisa, realizing she must have said something to the captain while he was engrossed in his numbers.

"Yes, Sir," he said, looking back it Marcello. "What-ever Count Bloch is planning, *Perseus* really is—or should be—out of the fighting. But as I understand it, we really want to end this *without* any fighting."

His tone turned the final sentence into a question, and Marcello nodded.

"I believe you can take that as a given, Lieutenant."

"In that case, Sir, I think we could make ourselves look like a battlecruiser."

Someone in the aft section made a sound like the start of a snicker. Marcello's expression didn't change.

"Explain," he said.

"It's something I came across while I was on *Casey*, Sir. I was cataloguing a bunch of redundant files, clearing out the archives, and I found an old copy of a book by Vladislav Tremain. He was a Solly admiral a century or so ago—his book was in the files when the Navy took delivery of the *Triumphs*—and most of it talked about the evolution of tactics. And there was this really, really old trick he mentioned, a deception measure. He only mentioned it in passing, but I started poking around to see what it would take to make it work, and I think we could do it."

"Continue," Marcello said, his tone not giving anything away.

Travis braced himself. "Basically, if we run the impellers past the usual safe levels, and keep our acceleration down once we're moving, a gravitics array far enough out will see us as a much larger ship accelerating at its safe maximum. I think we could get a destroyer's signature all the way up to a battlecruiser's—for a while, at least, and at several light-minutes' range."

"Sounds risky," Commander Shiflett warned. "Besides, if it's so old, wouldn't everyone know about it?"

"Maybe not," Marcello said, his eyes narrowed. "It certainly isn't anything *I've* ever heard of. And even if Bloch knows about it, he might figure we're smart enough to realize *he'd* be smart enough to recognize a bluff when he saw it. Commander Papadakis? Thoughts?"

"I don't know, Sir," a severe voice replied. "Frankly, I've never even heard of something like that."

"No, Sir, it's not in the usual manuals," Travis said. "I only found it in Tremain's book."

"Yes, you said that." Papadakis didn't sound especially enthusiastic. "I'll remind the Captain that the alpha nodes are still being temperamental. If we do what our ATO is suggesting, we might burn them out and be completely helpless. Even if they behave themselves, we'd take months off their lifetimes and we're talking only a couple of hours before we'd have to scale down again. And let me emphasize that, as far as I know, no one's ever run nodes at anything like this level—with real impellers—aside from warship builders' trials, for at *least* fifty years. For that matter, *we* haven't done it since acceptance trials on *Nike* almost a century ago, and even then it was only for fifteen or twenty minutes."

"So you're recommending against it?"

"A moment, Sir. I'm running some numbers now."

"Run them fast," Marcello said, looking at Travis.

Travis waited, his pulse pounding unpleasantly, studiously not looking at Lisa. She was the one who'd brought Marcello's attention to this, after all, which meant her neck was on the block, too, if it went sideways.

"Okay, Sir." Papadakis's voice came back. "The numbers look...let's call them *fragile*."

"So you're recommending against?"

"That depends on what you want, Sir," Papadakis said. "If you want to make Barca Alpha think twice about tangling with us, I'd call it a fair risk. It gets a lot more questionable if they decide to keep on coming. Best-case scenario, it works and they break off. Best bad-case scenario, they keep coming and we end up a drifting missile platform when the meatgrinder gets within range. Worst-case scenario, we blow a node and vaporize one of the impeller rings. At least one. If we get a blowback into the plasma conduits—"

His voice gave the strong impression of a shrug and Travis winced mentally at the image his last few words had conjured up.

"Understood." Marcello shifted his attention to the com station. "Chief Ulvestad, record for transmission to Admiral Locatelli."

"Aye, aye, Sir," Ulvestad replied.

Marcello looked back to Travis, and his lips twitched in a small smile.

"In for a penny, in for a dollar. Right, Lieutenant?"

"Yes, Sir," Travis said, keeping his face firmly under control.

Because the suggestion was about to be put before Admiral Carlton Locatelli. And Travis and the admiral had not exactly had the most cordial relationship over the years. His only hope was that when Marcello presented the idea, Locatelli would assume it belonged to the captain and Travis's name would never come up. He opened his mouth to suggest that—

Closed it again. He'd already stepped far enough out on this branch. He didn't dare lecture the captain on the hidden politics of the case.

All he could do was hope. Because deep inside

him, he had a strong sense that rejecting the plan would be bad. For the Star Kingdom, as well as for Admiral Eigen's squadron.

"Hot mic, Sir," Ulvestad said.

Please don't mention my name, he thought earnestly toward the captain. *Please*.

"Captain Marcello, Admiral," the captain said into his pickup. "Sir, our ATO, Lieutenant Long, has come up with an idea I think has merit."

☆   ☆   ☆

"I admit it's risky, Your Majesty," Locatelli said from the display. "And it's unlikely they can keep it up for more than a couple of hours."

"Yes," Edward agreed, studying the big tactical display. "But a couple of hours should be enough to persuade Count Bloch to go home. Once he changes vector, Reserve Force can ramp down and pretend they're going back on standby."

"Exactly," Locatelli said, a slight edge to his voice. Clearly, the man wasn't happy.

Edward could hardly blame him. Tactical command was the System Commander's domain. Officially, the King and First Lord of the Admiralty were merely observers.

But Edward and Cazenestro had both been Navy command officers: Edward a captain, the First Lord an admiral. They knew something about strategy and tactics. And while the First Lord might be willing to follow protocol and sit quietly, awaiting Locatelli's staff's reports, Edward wasn't. He was the King, it was his realm and his people who were once again under fire, and by God above he was going to at least sit in on these crucial discussions.

"Marcello's a good captain with a good record," Locatelli added. "He wouldn't suggest this if he didn't think he could pull it off." He pursed his lips. "Besides that, the suggestion itself came from Lieutenant Travis Long, and he has a history of coming up with outside-the-lines ideas that pay off."

"Sounds like it's worth doing. Go ahead and give the order, Admiral," Edward said.

Locatelli's lips twitched in a small smile.

"Thank you, Your Majesty. I already have."

☆   ☆   ☆

"Last umbilical on Cell Two, PO Townsend," Spacer Second Class Huvoski announced, and Chomps nodded with satisfaction, despite the hollowness in his stomach.

The Battle of Manticore had left *Aries* and *Taurus* completely dry of missiles, and despite a lingering sense of loyalty to the Navy, Chomps shared the general MPARS opinion that leaving them that way had been particularly stupid of the Navy. Unfortunately, he was only a petty officer, which gave his opinions very little official weight.

At least they had five birds on board now, though the *Orpheus*-based ordnance crews were still finishing the plumbing connections on three of them. Well, two, now, thank God. Now if only—

His uni-link quivered against his wrist as a message came through.

Huvoski was hovering behind him in the cramped compartment while he monitored the Number Two quad launcher's progress. Surreptitiously, Chomps keyed the uni-link, wondering what this was about. Normally, official communications were delivered via the ship's intercom or computer systems. The only way to get anything to him via uni-link was to work through the back door of *Aries'* com system, and the only reason for anyone to do that was to keep the message dead secret.

And there was exactly one person Chomps could think of who could and would do something like that.

He was right about that.

Check vid message from Barca Alpha ASAP. GDF-3329-TDR. C.

"Good, Jacob," he said aloud. "Initiating diagnostics now. While I do that, get up to Missile One. See if there's anything you can do to speed them up without joggling their elbows."

"Right, Chief." Huvoski unstrapped and headed out the access way towards *Aries'* dorsal quad launcher at a fast float. Chomps waited until he was out of view, then swiveled the status display around so it wouldn't be visible from the open hatch, linked the larger display to his uni-link, and keyed the attached file.

It was the com feed from the Barcans, all right, with some silver-haired aristocrat type blathering on about pirates and vengeance and whatnot. Chomps watched the conversation play out—fortunately, the light-speed induced pauses had been edited out—wondering why anyone would want his input. This sort of thing was usually reserved for admirals, diplomats, or the Lords.

And then, Count Bloch smiled.

Chomps punched the freeze command and managed to hit it with the smile still in place. Staring at the image, he fumbled with his uni-link, hoping that whatever back door had been activated worked both ways.

It did.

"Did you see it?" she asked.

"Yes," Chomps confirmed. "It's him."

"No mistake?"

"I don't think so," he said. "Hair and face are different, but he can't disguise that smile."

"I imagine he could, only it never occurred to him to try." She hissed thoughtfully. "I just wish there was something we could do with this."

"Aside from breaking him down to his component atoms?"

"Not going to happen. You know what kind of shape the Navy's in, His Majesty knows what kind of shape the Navy's in, and even the *Navy* knows what kind of shape the Navy's in. Unless we *have* to fight them, no one down here has any interest in doing so."

"As one of the people up here, that one has my vote, too," Chomps agreed reluctantly. "I don't suppose we're going to get either of the other squadrons to reinforce us?"

"Probably not." He couldn't see the headshake at the other end of the link, but he knew it was there. "If Bloch doesn't decide to roll the dice and keep right on coming, the most likely thing for him to do is head back to wherever he came from. We're unlikely to get enough firepower in place soon enough to keep him from breaking back across the limit."

Chomps nodded, glowering at the frozen smile. He *owed* the man behind that smile, and the thought of its owner getting away clean a second time really, *really* pissed him off. If only—

He stopped, an odd thought starting to form in the back of his mind.

"Okay," he said slowly. "We can't kill him or get

our hands on him. But maybe we can at least snap his leash a little."

"I'm listening."

Chomps pulled up the tactical display. Not there. He thought for a moment, then shifted to an astro display.

Bingo.

"What do you think our friend would do if he thought we had a system-wide sensor net he didn't know about?"

"He probably wouldn't like it," she said. "Unfortunately, we *don't* have one."

"No," Chomps replied, grinning evilly. "But we *do* have the hyper-limit NAVSAT constellation."

"Yes, and everyone knows we do. For that matter, he can *see* it on his astrogation displays."

"No," Chomps said again. "What he sees is the *new* constellation."

"The—"

The other voice stopped, and he could almost see the sudden calculation in its owner's eyes. Each of the Star Kingdom's planets had its own Lagrange point constellation of astrogation satellites—still known by the archaic acronym, mostly because they were also used for navigation on the planets they orbited. Each stellar component of the binary system had its own hyper-limit constellation, as well: twenty-four individual satellites equidistantly spaced around the entire limit.

At the moment, however, Manticore-A actually had *thirty-six* hyper-limit NAVSATs. One of Earl Breakwater' infrastructure projects was the replacement of the original elderly constellation, but half of the old constellation had been retained as backups if the new system developed any glitches and to temporarily substitute for any of the newer satellites which went down for routine maintenance.

All twenty-four of the new constellation's beacons were clearly visible on Bloch's astrogation displays.

But . . .

"Interesting," she said after a moment, sounding intrigued. "We might make him blink. Even better, we might make him leery of coming back. Not only could we convince him we'd spot him farther out, but it would be a nice piece of disinformation. If he thinks he missed something that significant in his intel on us, who knows what *else* he could have missed?"

"Agreed, and agreed," Chomps said. "I'm not sure how we would pull that off, though."

"Leave that to me," she assured him. "Meantime, better get back to your day job. He's killed his acceleration, but he hasn't started *de*celerating yet. He might still decide to take a run at us."

☆   ☆   ☆

"Sir, they're reversing acceleration," Katura announced. "Not only that, they've increased accel by forty gravities."

"Reversing?" Llyn repeated with a carefully concealed flare of hope. If Admiral Eigen had decided to break off after all, that probably meant the odds were even more in Llyn's favor than he'd thought. And if that the case—

"More wedges coming up, Sir," Katura said suddenly, a moment later. "Manticore orbit. Computer's plotting positions and strength."

"I see them," Llyn confirmed, watching as *Pacemaker*'s computers analyzed the distant wedge data and spat its results onto the display.

And as the numbers came up, he felt his breath

catch in his throat. Three orbiting ships had spun up their wedges.

All of them read as battlecruisers.

He hissed out a vicious curse. So at least four of Manticore's five battlecruisers had survived the battle. Eighty percent of them. Gensonne had been even more incompetent than he'd realized.

Unless one of the warships was a visitor? None of the new units' light-speed transponder codes had yet reached *Pacemaker*. Maybe one of them—maybe even two of them—were visitors from elsewhere.

And the only possible candidate for such generosity was Haven.

The problem was that three weeks was far too short a time for the Republic to have heard about the battle and sent help. If one of the ships was Havenite, it had to have already been here when the battle began.

Maybe that was why Gensonne had lost in the first place?

"Sir, General Haus is signaling," Katura said into his musings. "He urgently recommends that we withdraw with all haste."

"I'm not surprised," Llyn growled.

And of course he was right. At this immediate moment, who owned which ships in the Manticore System was irrelevant. What *was* relevant was that Llyn's force had just gone from probably superior to outclassed as hell.

The trick was going to be figuring out how to make a graceful and plausible withdrawal without looking like they were cutting and running. The Manticorans were surely already at least moderately suspicious of his unexpected arrival. A panicky reaction could only hone that suspicion, and if it rose to even fifty percent certainty, Locatelli would probably send everything they had against him.

And if the Manticoran did that, Llyn's ships couldn't possibly kill their velocity and begin building an escape vector before the Manticorans brought them into decisive range. Which meant—

The display updated again as the new battlecruisers' transponder codes finally caught up with the appearance of their wedges. HMS *Invincible*, HMS *Nike*, and HMS *Swiftsure*.

Llyn cursed under his breath. A bunch of hayseeds in a two-for-a-credit excuse for a star nation, and out in the middle of nowhere to boot. There was no way someone like that should have been able to give a professional merc group this kind of drubbing.

That was what really frosted him, he realized. In fact, it bothered him more than the fact that he was very probably going to die in the next hour or two. It was infuriating to have been so effortlessly played for a fool by a star nation full of provincials who hadn't even known he was coming.

Or maybe they *had* known he and the Barcans were on their way. If they'd not only beat Gensonne but captured him, he'd spill his guts in a skinny minute if it might save his own neck.

But it didn't matter what they'd known. What mattered was that they'd played him perfectly. They'd delayed any response while he steadily built his velocity in-system and got farther and farther from any handy escape back across the limit. Then they'd shown him only Eigen's force to demonstrate how badly they'd been weakened against Gensonne.

And now he knew why their acceleration had been so low. They'd had no intention of building enough velocity to make it impossible for the battlecruisers hiding in orbit to rendezvous with Eigen before actually opening fire. But now that Eigen had him sucked too far into the trap to escape, the admiral was openly decelerating to kill his own velocity in order to hasten that rendezvous.

After which, the combined force would go back to the full hundred and sixty gravities the newcomers were showing and run down Llyn's ships—even the Barcan cruisers—well short of the limit.

At least they wouldn't be throwing any modern weaponry at him. But that was cold and thin consolation. Ancient missiles, especially in the numbers a quartet of battlecruisers could throw, would be more than enough to do the job.

Llyn had faced dicey solutions in his time, but there'd always been a way out. This time . . .

"Sir!" Katura said sharply.

"What?" Llyn snapped.

"Sir, *Banshee*'s detected a hyper footprint just outside the limit. Captain Vaagen's tracking three new impeller wedges." *Pacemaker*'s captain cursed quietly. "At least one of them appears to be another battlecruiser."

Another battlecruiser? Pure molten fury poured through Llyn's veins. So all *five* RMN battlecruisers had survived? Had Gensonne even bothered to show up at this battle?

And the sudden appearance of yet another Manticoran squadron astern of him was almost more disturbing than the fact that they'd taken so little damage from the Volsungs. He knew—he *knew*—they couldn't have prearranged this perfect a mousetrap. No one could have. Yet there the fresh threat was, its icons burning brightly as *Pacemaker*'s plot updated itself. However these bastards had managed to pull it off, Llyn's defeat was total, and there was nothing he could do about it.

And then, still seven minutes from the turnover point where he would have no choice but to continue all the way to Manticore orbit, Locatelli handed him the solution on a silver platter.

"Count Bloch, this is Admiral Locatelli," the system commander's voice said from the com. "It would appear we've both been guilty of a certain degree of misunderstanding. As I'm sure our documentation will demonstrate, we have no connection with the pirates who've been operating in Barca's vicinity. On the other hand, and while we don't wish to offend even our more distant neighbors, we've had some unfortunate experiences of late here in the Star Kingdom and we aren't really interested in hosting a foreign task force right now. I must therefore respectfully request that your battle force leave Manticoran space.

"I realize that until you've examined our evidence, you have no reason to simply take our word for our innocence. I think we can both agree that until and unless both sides can be convinced of the other's bona fides, it might be wiser to avoid any potential incidents which could arise out of continued misunderstanding. Accordingly, I've instructed Admiral Eigen to begin decelerating to remain outside his engagement envelope of your command. I've also transmitted orders to Admiral Flannery, commanding the squadron astern of you, to plot a course to Manticore which will keep him outside missile range of your force as you withdraw." The Manticoran admiral's expression hardened. "I have, however, been instructed by my Sovereign that if you choose *not* to withdraw, His Majesty's decision not to regard you as hostile units will have to be reconsidered."

Llyn treated himself to a deep, unobtrusive breath of relief.

So they hadn't beaten any information out of Gensonne after all. They were actually prepared to believe Barca truly had come calling on a pirate-hunting expedition.

"On the other hand, we have no objection to you and a one-ship escort continuing on to Manticore," Locatelli continued. "It would give us a chance to compare notes on our respective battles. With proper analysis, we might be able to determine whether they were the same force, two parts of the same group, or totally independent."

Right, Llyn thought with black humor. *When hell freezes over, defrosts, and freezes over again.*

He inclined his head, fighting to conceal his relief. It was harder than usual this time.

"All units reverse acceleration," he ordered Katura. He noted the matching relief on his captain's face, then punched the transmit key on his com panel again.

"I'm sure you'll understand that the Grand Duke would consider it a breach of my duty to offer myself as a potential hostage to a star nation we have yet to clear of collaboration with pirates," he said. "Perhaps after we've analyzed the data you've provided we'll be able to allay the Grand Duke's suspicions and can resume this conversation at a later date." A sudden thought occurred to him. "If you could also provide your data from the battle you mentioned," he added, "it would surely speed up that process. Regardless, since we're currently unwelcome, we will of course take our leave."

Another six minutes passed, interminable minutes during which Admiral Eigen continued to decelerate towards Manticore and the three battlecruisers still approaching from planetary orbit. *Pacemaker* and her consorts continued forward as well, covering another four and a third million kilometers. But their velocity dropped by almost 300 KPS in the same interval, their momentum taking them to a point ninety-eight and a half million kilometers from Manticore orbit. Assuming the Manticorans didn't change their minds about engaging the intruders, in another four hours they would come to a zero-zero point still fourteen million kilometers out from the planet and could be back across the limit in less than six.

Assuming, again, that the Manticorans didn't change their minds.

It was almost a shock when Locatelli's voice suddenly boomed again from the com.

"I'm sure the data would be useful to you," the admiral said. "However, since we ourselves have only barely finished our first-pass analysis, I'm sure you understand in turn that we can't yet release it to anyone outside the Star Kingdom. Regardless, have a safe voyage home, and we look forward to comparing notes more completely at some future date."

"I'll look forward to it," Llyn promised. "For His Highness, the Grand Duke of Barca, I bid you farewell."

He keyed off the com.

"Any other instructions, Sir?" Katura asked.

"I think not, Captain," Llyn said. "It's over now."

CHAPTER SIX

"STATUS CHANGE, CAPTAIN," TRAVIS ANNOUNCED beside Lisa, his voice clearly audible through the disciplined calm of *Damocles*'s bridge. "Barca Alpha's reversed acceleration."

"CIC?" Marcello called toward the intercom.

"Vector change confirmed, Captain," CIC replied. "Barca Alpha reversed on a reciprocal heading at eighty gravities two minutes ago at...mark."

Lisa breathed a silent sigh. She'd had every expectation that Travis's trick would work. But life and war were the province of uncertainty, and it was always a relief when theory and reality lined up.

"Bridge, Engineering," Papadakis's voice came. "Shall we ease back on the impellers, Sir?"

"Let's hold them where they are a little longer," Marcello said.

"Sir, if Barca Alpha's leaving, we really shouldn't strain the nodes any more than we have to," Papadakis persisted. "Every minute we hold them at this level takes at least *ten* minutes off their designed lifetime."

"I agree—*if* they're really leaving," Marcello said. "I'd like to be sure of that before I reduce the load. I might point out that System Command also hasn't authorized us to stand down yet. Shouldn't be more than another couple of hours," he added reassuringly.

"Aye, aye, Sir," Papadakis replied after a moment. If he was outraged, nervous, or concerned about the captain's decision, Lisa couldn't hear it in his voice.

"But I think we can at least secure from battle stations," Marcello added. "XO, set Condition Two throughout the ship."

"Aye, aye, Sir," Shiflett said, and Lisa heard her own quiet relief in the other woman's voice. *Damocles*'s officers and crew were as brave and dedicated as anyone in the Navy, but going into combat in a half-crippled ship wasn't anyone's idea of a fun time.

☆   ☆   ☆

Pacemaker and the other ships had finally killed their velocity towards Manticore and begun accelerating towards the safety of the hyper-limit almost six and a half hours ago. At the moment, the range between *Pacemaker* and Manticore had climbed back up to over thirty-one million kilometers, her velocity towards the limit was over seven thousand KPS, and the squadron which had arrived behind them—the transponder code of HMS *Victory* burning brightly in its midst—had indeed shaped a course to keep it outside missile range.

So far, so good.

Llyn had continued to keep a close watch on the Manticoran ships, however, wondering if Locatelli might decide at the last minute to insist the unannounced visitors come down for tea and crumpets, or whatever Kings did on little back-world planets like this.

But *Vanguard* and its escorts had continued decelerating until their own velocity relative to the planet had fallen to zero, and the other three battlecruisers had reduced their own acceleration to make rendezvous with Eigen at that point. Then they'd simply sat there, reducing their wedge strength to standby levels, waiting while *Victory* maneuvered to join them and keeping a watchful eye on Llyn's ships. The rats had been chased off, and the terriers were apparently content with that.

Llyn hoped the terriers were pleased with their small victory. It was very probably the only one they would ever have.

They were three hours and nearly a hundred forty-five million kilometers from the limit, and Llyn had just started to relax, when the whole thing again went sideways.

Bizarrely sideways.

"What kind of transmissions are we talking about?" he demanded.

"Standard com laser," Captain Vaagen's tense voice came from the speaker. "Semi-burst, centered on Manticore; we're only catching the edge of it because we're still so far from the source. It appears to be encrypted, with a system we've never seen before. We don't have it on file, anyway."

"Of *course* we don't have it on file," Llyn said with strained patience. "This is Manticore, not the League. Can you decrypt it?"

"We're trying. So far, the computer hasn't even found a base pattern."

"Frankly, I don't know what they could be transmitting, Mr. Llyn," Captain Rhamas put in. "Whatever's sending, it's not running any active sensors—we'd have picked those up on the way in. At this distance, I don't know what it can be reading."

"Well, it's reading *something*," Llyn countered, glaring at the icon which had appeared on the main plot. Rhamas was right, of course. In theory, something that far away and using only passive sensors shouldn't have a hope of seeing much besides his ships' impeller wedges.

But if that was all it had, why was it suddenly transmitting encrypted data toward Manticore?

Better safe than sorry, assuming it wasn't already too late.

"Prepare to pitch wedge," he ordered. "All ships. Pitch just enough to—"

"Pitch *wedge?*" Rhamas put in incredulously. "Sir, that'll add—"

"Just enough to block that satellite's line of sight down the throats of our wedges," Llyn cut them off. "Yes, it'll add some time to our exit. So what? The Manticorans aren't even trying to follow us. In fact, this thing's probably the reason *Victory's* been so damned obliging about swinging wide of us. It didn't *need* to maneuver to look down our throats; it could count on this thing to do it instead." He scowled at the display. "Whatever they're learning—or think they're learning—I want it to stop."

"Yes, Sir," Katura said briskly. "Computing pitch... transmitting order to Barcan ships."

"Execute as soon as you have acknowledgments."

"Yes sir. Executing...now."

Llyn watched the icons on the display shift positions. *Pacemaker's* projected vector tilted upward by just under forty degrees. It wasn't all that much, but whatever the damn satellite had been looking at, it wasn't looking anymore.

"And the new course will add...looks like just under two hours and forty-five minutes," Katura added.

"Good enough," Llyn said. He glowered at the icon marking the spot from which the transmission had come. "And make a good sweep of the area in front of us. If there are more of those damn satellites in our way, I want to know about it."

☆   ☆   ☆

"Sir?" Chief Ulvestad called tentatively from the com station. "We're getting something strange from NAVSAT HL-22B. Or, rather, from something right beside HL-22B."

"Strange how?" Marcello asked. "And what do you mean 'something right beside'?"

"Well, it's not from the satellite itself, Sir," Ulvestad replied. "It's still transmitting its standard beacon."

"Confirmed, Sir," Lisa said, checking the tactical display. "And the Chief's right—this is definitely coming from something else. And whatever it is, it's within no more than a couple of thousand kilometers of HL-22B."

"Could it be one of the old NAVSATs?" Commander Shiflett suggested. "That's the only thing I can think of that might be floating around out there. For that matter, it's the only thing that would be allowed within ten thousand klicks of any platform in the constellation."

"So what exactly is this transmission, Chief?"

"I don't know, Sir. It's...well, it's gibberish."

"And we're sure it's from something inside the constellation? Not from Barca Alpha?"

"Definitely not, Sir," Lisa said firmly, waving one hand at the master tactical display. "It's a good two degrees off their current heading and coming from a lot farther out."

"Could they have commandeered one of the satellites somehow?"

"Why would they do that?" Lisa asked, frowning as Travis pulled up the feed at her elbow. Both of them studied it, then looked at one another with matching frowns. Ulvestad was right; the computer was having no luck deciphering the data flow.

"Maybe it's a message to someone on Manticore," Travis suggested darkly. "Something they don't want to be associated directly with."

"Get this to System Command right away," Marcello decided. "Someone in crypto should be able to figure out what it is."

☆   ☆   ☆

"Interesting," Admiral Locatelli said from the main screen.

Edward looked up from the update that had just appeared on his own display.

"Are they coming back?" he asked.

"No, Your Majesty, they're still leaving," Cazenestro said. "They've just made an odd vector change, about forty degrees above the ecliptic."

Edward frowned at the big tactical display, feeling himself changing mental hats. For a moment, he was a Navy officer again, sifting through drummed-in memories of simulations, immersed in the details of impellers, weapons, and maneuvers, trying to read every nuance of the enemy's every twitch and grunt . . .

"If they're avoiding something, I'm damned if I

can see what it is," Locatelli said. "There's nothing out there except the NAVSATs."

"No, there isn't," Edward agreed. "Well, keep an eye on them, Admiral. And please signal my thanks and commendation to everyone involved. They caught us well and truly on the wrong foot, but our people did a magnificent job. Be sure they know I realize that. I'll be telling them myself sometime very soon."

"Yes, Your Majesty. Of course." Locatelli bowed his head, the tension in his face momentarily eclipsed by pleasure at his sovereign's praise. He was still in that posture when Edward cut the com link.

Edward inhaled a deep breath, exhaled it and turned to Cazenestro. "What do you think?"

"I think," the First Lord said with a malicious smile, "that Count Bloch has officially outsmarted himself."

"So it would seem," Edward agreed.

Because up to now all they'd had were suspicions that something in Bloch's formation felt odd, along with his violation of the hyper-limit without identifying himself, neither of which had exactly constituted hard evidence that he wasn't what and who he'd said he was.

But that was before Edward and Cazenestro had received the private com call advising them of the inspiration someone had had. Frankly, Edward hadn't really expected Bloch to bite, but he had. Now, with his blatant move to hide from the supposed sensor satellite, he'd effectively confirmed that he *had* something to hide. Something he hadn't wanted the Star Kingdom to know.

Something which would have exposed the fact that his ships weren't truly who and what he'd claimed.

Of course, there was still no hint as to exactly what

he was concealing, at least not in regards to his task force. That would have been extremely nice to know. Still, in time of war, every bit of information could end up being useful.

In time of war. Edward felt his throat tighten, and suddenly the mental hats shifted back. He was no longer just an RMN officer, but King Edward, responsible for the safety and well-being of the entire Star Kingdom.

And from that point of view...

"We probably should have let them get closer," he said, half to himself. "At least close enough for some decent readings."

Cazenestro looked at him in surprise.

"With all due respect, Your Majesty, I think Admiral Locatelli did exactly the right thing," he said. "We're not in any condition to fight anyone right now. Much better to make them come back when we're stronger."

"I know," Edward said with a sigh. "But now we've got confirmation that these bastards were up to no good, and it strains credulity to the breaking point to assume that two totally separate outlaw groups would just happen to attack the Star Kingdom in less than a month. We'll definitely need to up our game."

"*And* rethink our deployments," Cazenestro murmured.

Edward turned his head, glaring at the main display. In a way, the ship deployment that had just brought the Star Kingdom to the edge of destruction wasn't his fault.

In another way, it totally was.

Cazenestro and Locatelli had both argued—strenuously—against splitting up the Navy that way.

Edward had agreed with them, for whatever that was worth. Sphinx's entire population was no more than five hundred thousand, compared to the over three million of Edward's subjects living on Manticore.

A case *could* be made for assigning ships to the Manticore-*B* sub-system. While there were only around a quarter million people on the planet of Gryphon, the majority of them descendants of the TRMN's original, immigrant personnel, the system included an extensive system of asteroid mining and a robust Navy R&D setup. Even so, the system came in a distant second to the overwhelming need to protect the capital. Manticore was, hands down, both the most valuable and the only logical target in the kingdom.

Edward, the Admiralty, and Carlton Locatelli had all wanted to deploy their available forces accordingly. But however lightly populated Sphinx and Gryphon might be, the two planets were still home to over a third of the current peerage's holdings.

The men and women who controlled those holdings naturally wanted them protected. And unfortunately, given the Constitution's tilt in favor of the aristocracy, they possessed an entirely disproportionate level of political clout.

Their demand that the Navy provide direct protection would have been a pain in the neck under any circumstances. What had pushed things past that point was the fact that Chancellor Breakwater had supported the insistent peers.

In Sphinx's case, he'd leaned on the planet's steadily growing orbital infrastructure, arguing it was too valuable to abandon to an invader. For Gryphon, he'd had to get a bit more creative. Given their origins,

Gryphons tended to be highly loyal to the Crown, which meant the Chancellor was scarcely one of their favorite people. By loudly demanding that they deserved protection, he hoped to soften some of that animosity.

Personally, Edward suspected that his *real* motive in both cases was to collect favors and curry support as he shored up his power base in the House of Lords. That, of course, could never be publicly admitted, which made Gryphon's defense a particularly telling card for him to play. They were innocent civilians who deserved the Navy's protection, which gave Breakwater perfect cover for his favor-buying. But he also knew that both the Navy and the Crown were naturally inclined to protect those they saw as being uniquely their own. That fondness, he knew, would help undercut the fervency with which the Admiralty and the Crown opposed his arguments.

Breakwater and the affected Lords had pushed the Navy into splitting up its forces. That part wasn't Edward's fault.

But he was the king, and he should have cut off the debate with the kind of command decision that kings were supposed to make in such situations. The fact that he hadn't was entirely his damn fault.

"We will absolutely rethink our deployments," he promised Cazenestro.

"Thank you, Your Highness," Cazenestro said.

"And yes, we'll be stronger once we've had time to catch our breath," Edward said. "The problem is, so will they. And I'd really like to have better info on them than we do right now."

"I agree," Cazenestro said. "But I'm convinced we really and truly dodged the bullet here. If we'd backed them into a corner where they *had* to fight, instead of leaving them a convenient way out, they'd have found out in a hurry that there was only one battlecruiser in front of them. And *we* might have found out there were a hell of a lot more than four cruisers in front of *us*."

"I know," Edward said more quietly. "And we'd definitely have lost a lot more men and women if we'd done that. But I still wish..." He trailed off.

Cazenestro was right, of course. Certainly from the tactical perspective. If they'd forced a fight and those two "freighters" *had* turned out to be Q-ships, it would have been disastrous. *Vanguard* and her two truly combat-capable consorts might quickly have been destroyed, leaving no effective defense between the invaders and the Star Kingdom's capital. Flannery and Red Force would have been much too far astern of the intruders to prevent that from happening.

As a military man, Edward knew that. But as a king, he also knew that sometimes pawns had to be sacrificed in return for critical information, and that the pawns in question were men and women, flesh and blood.

King Edward Winton hated knowing that. But it was his *job* to know it.

And so even while he accepted Cazenestro's analysis, a part of him—the part responsible for discovering who and what had attacked his Star Kingdom, his subjects, his *people*—bitterly regretted how little concrete data they'd actually gained.

He would have sacrificed *Vanguard* and her entire company in cold blood if that had given him the information he so desperately needed. He would have loathed himself for doing it, but he would have done it.

But not today. Cazenestro was right. Not while the Star Kingdom still reeled from the devastation of the Battle of Manticore. Later, perhaps, but not today.

"I assume that once Count Bloch's made translation we'll get back to making repairs?" he asked, deliberately changing the subject.

"Yes, Your Majesty," Cazenestro said, his expression going a little more grim as he gestured to the repeater display from *Orpheus'* commanding officer's control room. "We're still sorting out how many *people* we lost," the First Lord continued heavily. "So far it appears we have only two dead—"

Edward suppressed a grimace. *Only* two dead.

"—but there are at least five more critically injured, and God only knows how many minor injuries are scattered around. And that doesn't even consider how much damage we did to the ships themselves—and to *Orpheus'* facilities, for that matter—scrambling to get the Reserve underway the way we did."

He shook his head. "We've come out of this a lot better than we might have, Your Majesty, but I'll be very surprised if we haven't added at least another couple of months to our repair time on *Damocles* and *Perseus*. Especially *Damocles*, if Marcello's engineer's estimates about her nodes are accurate. *Erinye* doesn't seem to have been as banged up as the other two, but that's a case of damning with faint praise."

"I know," Edward said bleakly, gazing at the tabulation of injuries on the repeater. It would seem he'd managed to sacrifice a few pawns today, after all.

He stood abruptly.

"I'll be in my office," he said. "Call me immediately if anything changes."

He strode off before Cazenestro could respond, his mind flitting to Locatelli's HQ on Thorson. He wondered what the system commander was thinking now, watching Bloch and his ships sweep steadily closer to the hyper-limit. Now that he could step back from the immediate threat.

The admiral was probably mourning his nephew, Edward thought. And it was right that he should. As this second attempted invasion passed without the pitched combat which had cost so many lives it was only proper that he should reflect upon those who died stopping the first one.

It was right that he should weep for his nephew. Just as it was right that Edward would someday mourn his son.

But not today. Later perhaps. But not today.

☆   ☆   ☆

With no further drama, and no further communication with Manticore, *Pacemaker* and its task force reached the hyper limit.

Two minutes later, they were safely in the Alpha band.

"Course, sir?" Katura asked.

"We head back to the rendezvous," Llyn told him. "We'll deliver our report, pull our people off the Barcan ships, and send everyone home."

"The Barcans won't be happy about that," Katura warned.

"Happiness hasn't been an option since we first entered this damn system," Llyn countered tartly.

"I only meant that—"

"I know what you meant," Llyn growled. "Don't worry, we'll make sure the Grand Duke gets his second payment."

"Yes, sir," Katura said. "Do you want *Shrike* or *Banshee* to accompany them? I understand Captain Vaagen in particular has become a pretty good diplomat where the Grand Duke is concerned. He might be able to smooth over any bad feelings at this setback."

Llyn scowled at the displays. Yes, it was a setback. But only a temporary one. The Axelrod Corporation wanted Manticore and the wormhole junction the fools down there didn't even realize they were sitting on. And what Axelrod wanted, Axelrod got.

But the Grand Duke might not see it that way. And if he got twitchy enough—and decided to look deeper into this mysterious benefactor who was offering him the Star Kingdom of Manticore—

"No," he told Katura. "We'll send a coded message to the liaison at the rendezvous point to release the payment and follow the Barcans back home. He can take whatever heat the Grand Duke feels like unloading on him."

"A bonus might be in order," Katura suggested.

Llyn snorted. A bonus, for doing nothing but flailing around and crying and getting underfoot? Yes, that was exactly how far too many people these days thought the universe should operate. "The Grand Duke can get a bonus when he earns it," he growled. "Sorry; *if* he earns it."

"Yes, Sir," Katura said, a little doubtfully. "Have you thought about Gensonne?"

"I've thought many things about him lately," Llyn said sourly. "Any one in particular you had in mind?"

"I was just thinking that if he was hit this hard, he's going to need help."

"If he survived long enough to make it back to

Telmach, he'll be fine," Llyn assured him. "His *ship* will need help—possibly a lot of it—but the man himself will be fine."

"Yes, sir," Katura said again. "I should point out that we could still split off *Shrike* or *Banshee* to deliver a report to the rendezvous."

Llyn grimaced. A report? On what? That Gensonne—and, by extension Llyn himself—had failed?

Not a chance. There was still a way to salvage the situation. Llyn just had to figure out what it was.

"No, I want both ships with me," he said. "After we say goodbye—and good riddance—to General Haus at the rendezvous, we'll head to Telmach."

"Understood." There was a short pause. "Are you expecting trouble, sir? At either place?"

"I don't necessarily expect it, Captain," Llyn said. "But I fully plan to be ready for it."

CHAPTER SEVEN

BEHIND THE CLOSED EYELIDS, THE YOUNG man's eyes were moving restlessly. Probably dreaming, Elizabeth Winton-De Quieroz decided as she carefully adjusted the blanket across his collarbone.

Almost certainly having a nightmare.

She lifted her eyes from his troubled face to the bandage wrapped around the top of his skull. He was one of *Damocles*'s injured, one of the ones caught in the blast when the ship's dorsal missile launcher exploded, sending deadly shrapnel bouncing down three passageways. Spacer Third Class Belgrand had caught what the doctors guessed was part of a monitor console in his chest and head.

At that, he'd been lucky. Five of his fellow spacers had also been injured, two of them worse than him. Three others had been killed outright.

Killed outright. Like everyone aboard *Phoenix* and *Sphinx*, *Gemini* and *Gorgon* and *Hercules*.

Including her nephew Richard.

Belgrand's face blurred as tears formed in Elizabeth's

eyes. A memory flowed in behind the tears: four years ago, just after the death of her beloved husband Carmichael, sitting with Richard at the palace after her father Michael's abdication. Richard had been only eighteen at the time, but he'd surprised her with the depth of his compassion, understanding, and wisdom. She could remember that even in the throes of her grief she'd made note of his maturity, and had envisioned the greatness he would someday bring to the throne.

Now, that day would never come.

She blinked back the tears. Mourning was fine in its place, but Richard was beyond her help. The other men and women in the ward weren't, and it was time she focused her full attention where it would do some good.

With a final look at Belgrand, she slipped quietly out of his room and walked down the corridor past the other quiet rooms and the soft conversation of doctors and nurses. Her visits to the physically wounded were mostly symbolic—the King's sister, dispensing comfort and blankets and all that. Her real work was with the mentally and emotionally wounded, the ones who those few hours of hell had left with invisible but equally debilitating scars.

She still had twenty minutes before her first appointment, plenty of time to look over her notes and prepare her mind. Just down the hall from the consultation room was a small lounge that was usually unoccupied at this hour, and she headed toward it, nodding silent greetings to the handful of medical staff she passed along the way.

Her first clue that the lounge *wasn't* empty was when she rounded the corner and spotted the two men loitering casually just outside the doorway. Large men. Watchful men. Armed men.

She came within an ace of simply turning around and walking away. Her brother had been on her case for the past two months—quietly and subtly, but on her case just the same—and she wasn't in any mood to hear one of his inspirational speeches on how she needed to get on with her life. Besides, she had important work to do.

But she continued walking, resignation mixing with her annoyance. Realistically, if the King wanted to talk to her, there was very little she could do about it.

It was only as she came close enough to recognize the men's faces that she realized that those weren't Edward's guards. In fact...

She picked up her pace a little. Of all the people in the Palace she actually wanted to talk to—

Crown Princess Sophie was sitting on one of the couches, her legs curled up beneath her, her elbow propped on the back of the couch, her head resting on her hand, her eyes turned toward the window and the glittering sunlit water of Jason Bay in the distance. Even with her face turned away, there was enough ache and depression in her body language alone to make Elizabeth wince.

"Hello, Sophie," she greeted her niece. "What brings you here this morning?"

"Hello, Aunt Elizabeth," Sophie said, not turning around. "I don't know. I just needed to get out of the Palace for a while."

"Ah," Elizabeth said, sitting down in the couch beside her. The girl still hadn't turned around. "Too many memories?"

"Too many broken people," Sophie said. "Mom and Dad... they're trying not to show it. But you can see it. You can see it in everything they say and do."

"And everything they *don't* say?"

Sophie's shoulders hunched briefly. "That's the worst. You know? What they don't say. It's like . . . they're hurting, but they can't show it. Not even to me. Not even to each other."

"He's the King," Elizabeth reminded her. "He probably thinks he has to put up a good front."

"I know," Sophie said. "That's what scares me."

"Why?"

Sophie exhaled, a long, tired sound. "Because some day that'll be me," she said, almost too quietly for Elizabeth to hear. "And I don't think I can do it." She turned around.

It was all Elizabeth could do to keep her own face under control. She'd expected puffy eyes, tear-stained cheeks, and all the rest of the aftereffects of a good, long, bitter cry.

What she saw instead was a face that was hard and cold and had had every bit of emotion burned out of it. "Sophie?" she asked carefully.

"You see?" Sophie's throat worked, the sole indication that there was anything going on behind the rigid exterior. "I try—I really do. But this is what I get. It's this or—" She broke off. "How does he *do* it, Aunt Elizabeth? How does he pretend that everything's all right. How does he smile?"

"I don't know," Elizabeth confessed. "But you don't have to. You're not him, Sophie. You don't ever have to be him."

"No, I just have to be the Crown Princess." Sophie closed her eyes, and for a brief moment some of the emotion buried inside leaked out. "I don't want this, Aunt Elizabeth. I never wanted it."

"I know, honey," Elizabeth soothed. She slid a little closer to the young woman and put her arm around her shoulders. "It's okay. It'll be okay."

For a minute they just sat that way in silence, holding each other as they reflected silently on their grief. Finally, Sophie stirred. "Thank you," she murmured.

"You're welcome," Elizabeth said. "It's what family's for."

"At least, what's left of us." Sophie took a deep breath.

And as Elizabeth watched, the fear and depression faded from her niece's face, to be replaced by her father's strength and dignity and force of will. "Okay," the young woman said.

"You ready to be Crown Princess again?" Elizabeth asked.

"I suppose," Sophie said. "You really *are* good at this, Aunt Elizabeth. You should be in politics."

"Not a chance," Elizabeth said firmly. "I'll take holding the hands of the wounded to refereeing Dapplelake and Breakwater any day."

"I don't blame you." Sophie wrinkled her nose. "I just hope they're not still going at it by the time I reach the Throne."

"Not a chance," Elizabeth said. "Your father's got at least thirty years of kingship in him, probably more like forty or even fifty. No, you'll have a whole set of brand-new problems and brand-new annoying people to deal with."

"Thanks a whole lot," Sophie said with a small smile. The smile faded. "I don't know, though. Politics can drive you crazy; but are you sure this job won't do that, too?"

"Meaning?" Elizabeth asked, hearing an edge of challenge in her voice.

"I just—fine. Does the phrase *pressing the bruise* mean anything to you?"

Elizabeth felt a lump form in her throat.

"I miss him, Sophie," she said quietly. "Miss him terribly. But my work here isn't just a backdoor way to feel sorry for myself. A lot of the people I counsel feel guilty that they survived while their friends didn't. I know how that feels—that peak bear could just as well have attacked me instead of Carmichael. I can talk to them on their own level, because I've been there."

"I know," Sophie said. "I see Navy people walking around Landing and I sometimes can't help wondering why they lived and Richard didn't. I just...I don't want you burying yourself here when there are bigger things you could be doing."

"Right now, this is as big as I want to get."

"Okay," Sophie said. "I just...I worry about you sometimes."

"As I worry about you," Elizabeth said. "That's also what family's for." She patted the girl's knee. "I know it may not feel like it right now, Sophie, but you're going to be a good queen someday. I can feel it."

"I hope so." Sophie made a face. "Though...I don't know. *Queen Sophie* sounds so...childish, I guess."

"You want to swap names?" Elizabeth asked dryly. "I've always liked yours better than mine."

"Really?"

"Really," Elizabeth assured her. "*Sophie* means *wisdom. Elizabeth* means my father was trying to get in good with his mother."

"It does not," Sophie scoffed. "It means *pledged*

to God. Besides, *two* Queen Elizabeths? Everyone will think the Royal House of Winton ran out of baby names."

"It could be worse," Elizabeth said. "I know brothers who both married women named Sherrie. Forever afterward, everyone had to call them *Matt's Sherrie* and *Mark's Sherrie* to keep them straight in conversation. At least you'd have *The Second* after your name."

"I'll take it under advisement," Sophie said. "You know what that means, right?"

"In our family? Absolutely," Elizabeth assured her. "Your father used that one for years when I was growing up. Usually when I wanted him to do something for me that he didn't want to do."

"I'll bet you were a pesky little sister."

"You have no idea." Elizabeth took a deep breath, let it out in a huffing sigh. "We do what we have to, Sophie. And that isn't always what we want to do."

"Like putting yourself between Dapplelake and Breakwater?"

Elizabeth forced a smile. "I'll take it under advisement. Until then, you take care of yourself, okay? And take care of your parents, too. You're the only one who can."

"I know." Sophie forced a smile of her own. "I'll do my best."

"You're a Winton," Elizabeth reminded her. "I think you'll find that your best is a lot better than you ever thought it could be."

"I hope you're right." Sophie stood up. "Good-bye, Aunt Elizabeth."

"Good-bye, Sophie."

She watched as Sophie collected her bodyguards

and headed back toward the lifts that would take them back outside.

Feeling guilty.

Yes, the Wintons were strong. And historically, at least, they'd always risen to the challenges of their places of authority.

But that authority came with costs. Some of those costs Sophie could already see facing her from her distant future. Some she would be shielded from until she could grow into them, or until she ascended to the Throne.

Some were things that had probably never even occurred to her.

Elizabeth shook her head. Sometimes those were the worst, if only because they reared their heads at the most awkward and unexpected moments.

Maybe she should have warned the girl about that. But that was Edward's job. Elizabeth had enough trouble handling the realities of life for her own three step-children without taking on that task for someone else's daughter. Even if that daughter was her niece.

Besides, that was the future. This was the present, and she had work of her own to do. *Sufficient unto the day is the evil thereof.*

Pulling out her tablet, she keyed for her first client's profile and started to read.

☆   ☆   ☆

"You're not listening," Chancellor Breakwater growled into his uni-link. "I don't care who *approved* it—Cazenestro, Dapplelake, or even King Edward himself. What I want to know is who in bloody hell issued the order in the first place?"

Seated at Breakwater's secretary's desk in the outer

office, Gavin Vellacott, Baron Winterfall, focused on the set of regulations he'd been tasked with slogging through and tried to ignore the controlled meltdown going on beyond the open door to Breakwater's main office.

A meltdown he couldn't fully understand. Breakwater's primary focus, as always in these situations, was to spin MPARS to its best advantage. Unfortunately— from the Chancellor's point of view—a non-MPARS person had come up with idea of inflating the two corvettes' wedges to simulate heavy cruisers, just as a puffer frog swelled itself to twice its size to scare off predators.

From Winterfall's point of view, it didn't matter where the idea had come from or who had given which order. None of it diminished in the slightest the crews' success in bringing their impellers to such an overstressed level *and* in maintaining the extra load for four hours without collapsing the wedge or losing any of the nodes. Winterfall didn't know a lot about the technical end of such things, but he knew enough to recognize that was an impressive achievement.

But Breakwater had never been the sort to settle for partial credit. For him, glory shared was glory lost.

"Well, *find out*." With a snarl, Breakwater keyed off the uni-link. He stormed through the doorway, stopping short as he spotted Winterfall. "What are *you* doing here?"

Winterfall blinked in surprise. "You asked me here, My Lord," he said. "You wanted a report on Harwich's meeting with Countess Acton—"

"I meant, what are you doing at Angela's desk?"

"I was running a regulation search for a constituent,"

Winterfall said. It was true, just not the *entire* truth. "I saw you were busy, and since I assume Angela has already left for the day, I thought I might as well put the idle minutes to use." He nodded toward Breakwater's uni-link. "If I may, My Lord, it's already on record that Admiral Locatelli gave the order for *Aries* and *Taurus* to inflate their wedges."

"Are you trying to deflect me, Gavin?" Breakwater rumbled, his eyes narrowing. "Because *I'm* the one who taught you how to shift a conversation where you wanted it to go."

"I'm not trying anything, My Lord," Winterfall protested, fighting against the reflexive defensiveness. Sparking defensiveness in an opponent was another technique Breakwater had taught him. "I'm just a bit confused. Is someone saying now that Locatelli *didn't* give the order?"

For a long moment Breakwater continued to stare at him. Then, his lip twitched. "That's not the order I'm concerned about," he said. "I'm trying to find out who told MPARS Sphinx Command to retask one of our navigational satellites to spew nonsense radio signals out into the void."

"I thought it was a programming glitch."

"Sphinx Command assures me that the broadcast profile changes couldn't have happened by accident," Breakwater said. "No, *someone* had to have ordered it."

Winterfall nodded slowly. An interesting question, given that all major orders or policy decisions that concerned MPARS should at least be reported to Breakwater.

It was especially interesting given that the pool of possible suspects was almost vanishingly small. The only ones Winterfall could think of were Defense Minister Dapplelake, First Lord of the Admiralty Cazenestro; and System Commander Locatelli. He opened his mouth to point that out—

"Yes, there are only three possibilities," Breakwater growled. "And it wasn't any of them. Or if it was, the perpetrator certainly isn't admitting to it."

Perpetrator. Odd choice of words. "Well, some tech has to have done the actual reprogramming," Winterfall pointed out. "We should be able to find him or her and backtrack up the chain."

"One would think so, wouldn't one?" Breakwater said acidly. "Only so far *that* approach isn't working, either. Whoever that tech was also seems disinclined to claim his share of the glory."

"Glory?" Winterfall echoed, frowning. "There's glory involved?"

"Of course not," Breakwater bit out. "But someone obviously did it on purpose, and I assume that person had a reason for it. Only I can't get anyone to tell me what the hell it was."

"Interesting," Winterfall murmured. In the three weeks since the Battle of Manticore he and Breakwater had run into several other instances of information silence. Usually it was just a matter of data that was backlogged or had been routed to the wrong person. But at least once it had appeared to be information that the Admiralty simply didn't want to share with its lesser MPARS cousin. "Do you want me to talk to my sources?"

"You mean your brother?" Breakwater snorted. "Don't hold your breath. As far as I can tell, he's become a pariah among the upper echelons. You saw how they brushed aside any recognition of his contributions during the battle. I don't know why Locatelli doesn't like him, but the tension there is quite visible. No, I doubt the Admiralty even listens to him anymore. They certainly aren't *talking* to him."

"You're probably right," Winterfall said, keeping his voice neutral.

Because he'd done some investigation of his own, and had come to a rather different conclusion. The Navy might not speak *to* Lieutenant Travis Uriah Long, but they certainly talked *about* him.

Not the whole Navy, certainly, and never on the record. But those who'd been his superiors over the past few years were quietly but solidly complimentary regarding his service.

In some places it went even farther. Despite the fact that Travis hadn't received any important commendations for his actions against Tamerlane, *Casey*'s commander had made it clear—*and* on the record—that the credit for the cruiser's survival during her part of the battle rested largely with Travis.

Competent military officers didn't ignore talent when they saw it. Senior officers like Locatelli didn't engage in feuds with officers that much their junior. In the end, Winterfall had been forced to the only remaining conclusion.

Travis's accomplishments were being downplayed because the Admiralty didn't want any glory to reflect off him onto Winterfall. And, by extension, onto Breakwater.

It was petty, in Winterfall's opinion. More so even than Breakwater's Travis/Locatelli feud theory.

It was also infuriatingly counterproductive. The Navy and MPARS were on the same side, after all, with both forces dedicated to the defense of the Star Kingdom. They just had different views on how best to do that.

But it got worse. Even as the Navy proclaimed victory and Locatelli basked in the warmth of public acclaim, the Admiralty was finding itself faced with a terrible and inescapable fact.

Namely, that Breakwater was right.

The record spoke for itself. All three of the invading ships that had been destroyed—two of them full-fledged battlecruisers—had been taken out by a light cruiser, a destroyer, and an MPARS corvette. David and Goliath matchups, all of them; and in each case the smaller ship had won out. Locatelli's battlecruisers, for all their size and glory and prestige, had accomplished precisely nothing.

The Star Kingdom didn't need a few big warships, like *Dapplelake* and *Cazenestro* wanted. What it needed was a larger number of smaller ships, ready to swarm and overwhelm any war party that dared to breach the hyper limit.

Which was exactly what Breakwater had been suggesting for the past fourteen T-years.

And the Admiralty knew it. Reason enough for them to try to freeze Breakwater out of important information. Motive enough to try to hold back the inevitable tide of history that was turning in MPARS's favor.

But how reprogramming a random NAVSAT figured into the grand conspiracy Winterfall couldn't imagine.

"I'll look into it anyway," he told Breakwater. "About Harwich's meeting...?"

"Later," Breakwater said, turning back toward his office door. Already a million kilometers away, Winterfall could see. "You said you were doing a regulation search. Did you figure it out?"

"Yes, My Lord."

"Then screen your constituent," Breakwater said. "From your *own* office. Be back here in one hour."

"Yes, My Lord."

Winterfall didn't actually have to go all the way back to his office for this one. But Breakwater had ordered him there, and lately the Chancellor seemed extra touchy about having his instructions followed to the letter. And so, to his office he went.

And from the privacy of his desk, he screened his mother.

She didn't answer until the seventh ring. About average for her, in Winterfall's recent experience. Probably dealing with her dogs, as usual, but not in the midst of some crisis that kept her from answering at all. The connection opened—"Hello, Gavin," Melisande Vellacott Long's voice came from Winterfall's uni-link. "I didn't expect you to screen at dinner time."

"Hello to you, too, Mother," Winterfall said. "Your dinner, or the dogs'?"

"The dogs', of course," she said, as if wondering why he even had to ask. "I never eat this early. Did you find that regulation I asked you for?"

"I did," he confirmed. "You were remembering it correctly."

"So I *can* run an *in vitro* breeding service here as well as my regular one? Wonderful. Where was it buried?"

"It wasn't exactly *buried*," Winterfall said. "It was part of a Landing land-use overview. And it didn't specifically mention dogs, pets, or *in vitro*, which is why your search couldn't find it."

"Well, good," Melisande said. "Now I can finally get that little bureaucrat off my back. Send me the link, will you?"

"Already done," Winterfall said. "By the way, I keep meaning to ask. Have you talked to Travis lately?"

"No. Why would I have?"

"I just thought you might," Winterfall said, floundering a little. The casualness of her dismissal—"There was something of a scare this afternoon. I thought you might have seen the news and checked to see if Travis was all right."

"I don't watch the news this late in the day," Melisande said primly. "If there was a problem with Travis I'm sure you would have screened."

Winterfall frowned. "Mother . . . when exactly *was* the last time you and Travis talked?"

"I don't know," she said in the same disinterested tone. "I have to go—Miggles is having trouble with his flews again."

"Wait," Winterfall said. "Three weeks ago—after the battle—didn't you even screen him then?"

"He didn't screen me," Melisande said. "Why should I screen him?"

"Because he could have *died*?"

"If he had, you'd have screened," Melisande said again. "And I really do have to go. Thank you for the link. We'll talk later." Without waiting for a reply, she keyed off.

Winterfall stared at his uni-link. *If he had, you'd have screened?* What in the *hell* kind of comment was *that*?

The comment of a woman who didn't really care about her younger son.

Slowly, Winterfall lowered his arm to his desk, an eerie feeling trickling through him. Years ago, during one of their infrequent get-togethers, Travis had tried to tell his older half-brother about the growing rift between him and their mother. At the time Winterfall had been too busy to give it much thought, and what little thought he *did* give it was quickly dismissed as the over-exaggerations of a frustrated teenager.

Clearly, the situation had gotten worse.

Maybe even pathologically worse. Briefly, he wondered if he should talk to her about getting some kind of therapy, or at least see if she would visit a counselor. Being aloof toward Travis was one thing; not caring whether he lived or died was an order of magnitude worse.

Winterfall winced. Not that he could claim any high ground. Time and again over the years he'd passed up a chance to meet with or even screen his brother. Three weeks ago, with the realization that the Star Kingdom was being invaded and that Travis was facing imminent death, he'd seen the terrible folly of his neglect, and had vowed not to let such opportunities ever slip away again.

Now, three weeks later, he had yet to carve out time to even have lunch together.

He swore under his breath. Well, that was going to change. That was going to change right now. He lifted the uni-link again—

It pinged before he could key it.

He clenched his teeth. Breakwater. "Yes, My Lord?"

"Did you see the King's latest announcement?" the Chancellor demanded.

"No, My Lord," Winterfall said, frowning as he keyed his computer. Palace announcements . . . there it was. "You mean the outdoor memorial service and requiem for the fallen next month?"

"Keep reading," Breakwater said stiffly. "The part about the Monarch's Thanks earlier that afternoon."

Winterfall skimmed the announcement. The senior officers from each of the ships that had taken part in the battle would embark from the Palace aboard the Royal Yacht *Samantha* and be taken to the Wintons' private retreat on Triton Island for a luncheon, returning to Landing in time for the memorial service. "Seems like a nice gesture," he said, wondering what Breakwater was seeing that he wasn't.

"Look closer," Breakwater growled. "The senior *Naval* officers are being invited. There's no mention of *Aries* and *Taurus*."

Winterfall gave the notice another look. The Chancellor was right: the two MPARS ships weren't specifically mentioned.

On the other hand, they weren't specifically excluded, either. Breakwater was probably reading more into the announcement than was actually there.

"I'm sure that's just an oversight, My Lord," Winterfall told him, choosing the most diplomatic approach to the problem. "If you'd like, I can call the Palace and have that clarified."

"You do that," Breakwater said. "And you make it clear that MPARS played a huge role in the battle and we will *not* be left out of the public consciousness. Whether Dapplelake likes it or not."

"Yes, My Lord."

"And when you're finished, come back here," the Chancellor continued. "I want to hear what Harwich and Acton had to say to each other."

CHAPTER EIGHT

WITH THE FLURRY OF ACTIVITY THAT had surrounded the brief Barcan incursion, plus all the reports and datawork afterward, it was three more days before the Committee hearings resumed. During that time Travis nurtured a private hope that they might have forgotten all about him, and that the glaring spotlight would move on.

No such luck. On the second day of the resumed hearings, he was ordered to report for testimony.

To find that Breakwater had managed to up the ante even higher. Not only had Travis been called, but Commodore Heissman had also been summoned to share the hot seat alongside him.

They sat there for over half an hour, answering questions, making statements, and occasionally spotting and respectfully disagreeing with some of the Chancellor's unstated and more slanted assumptions about the battle and the people who had waged it. For Travis, it seemed to last longer than the battle itself.

And when the session was over, and they'd been

dismissed, they finally learned what the Chancellor's true purpose had been in all of this.

"It seems clear, My Lords," Breakwater intoned as Travis and Heissman collected their tablets and other gear and headed for the door, "that the Naval Academy has proven itself woefully inadequate in carrying out its chartered duties. I think it's clear that, with a few exceptions, the officers commanding the Star Kingdom's ships relied almost exclusively on luck to see them through."

Travis paused, half turning back. They'd relied on *luck*?

"Let it go, Lieutenant," Heissman murmured from beside him.

"We need better than that," Breakwater continued. "It is therefore my intention to petition the government for a new training facility, one that will be used exclusively for MPARS personnel."

Travis's thoughts flashed back to his time at Casey-Rosewood and the Academy, and to the more recent horror stories he'd heard about how adding a trickle of MPARS personnel to the student body was already straining the Navy's resources to the limit. If Breakwater now raided those resources for a completely new facility—

"Because the last thing we can afford is the stale, by-the-book strategies and tactics we so recently witnessed," Breakwater concluded.

Travis had been fully prepared to keep his mouth shut, as Heissman had told him, and walk out of the room. But that one he couldn't let pass.

"Excuse me, My Lord," he spoke up. "That's not fair."

Every eye at the table turned to him. "Not fair?" Breakwater repeated, feigned puzzlement on his face.

"Not *fair*? Tell me, Lieutenant, from your vast military knowledge and experience: how is that *unfair*?"

Travis clenched his teeth. Once again, he'd opened his mouth without thinking it through. He really needed to stop doing that.

But it was too late to back out now. "With all due respect, My Lord, the tactics of response are defined by the tactics of attack. Tamerlane chose the vectors and timing; the commanders of each Manticoran group assessed and responded with skill and efficiency."

"The Navy lost five ships," Breakwater pointed out. "Tamerlane lost three. Is this your idea of efficiency?"

"Two of those three ships were battlecruisers," Travis countered. "I believe that gives us the win."

"Let me make my point clearer," Breakwater said calmly. "The *Navy* lost five ships. *MPARS* didn't lose any. Furthermore, it was an MPARS corvette that took out one of the enemy ships."

"With the aid of a Navy destroyer," Travis said. "And in all cases the victories were due to the skill and ingenuity of the officers and crew."

"Indeed," Breakwater agreed. "But again, the ingenuity of *junior* officers and *junior* crewmembers." He lifted a hand and started ticking off fingers. "Petty Officer Charles Townsend. Senior Chief Fire Control Tech Lorelei Osterman—all right; a senior, but a senior enlisted. Ensign Fenton Locatelli. And—if I may be so bold—Lieutenant Travis Uriah Long."

He favored Travis with a thin smile. "But thank you, Lieutenant, for making my case for me." The smile vanished. "And now, you and Commodore Heissman are dismissed."

☆ ☆ ☆

Heissman was silent during the long walk down the corridor to the building exit. He didn't speak again, in fact, until they were in their aircar and heading back to their shuttle. Even then he confined his conversation to the current state of *Casey*'s repairs and the details of upcoming work.

For his part, Travis didn't dare mention his stupidity in walking straight into Breakwater's trap. But such reminders were hardly necessary. Sooner or later, he knew, Heissman would have to bring up the fiasco, possibly as part of a formal discipline, possibly as a private, off-the-record dressing down. It was certainly no more than Travis deserved.

But it never happened. Heissman never mentioned the incident again.

Which wasn't to say that he was happy with how things had gone. Travis was pretty sure he wasn't. It also wasn't to say that he hadn't entered something scathing into Travis's record. Travis was almost positive he had.

There would be consequences for handing Breakwater more ammunition in his private war against the Navy. It was just a question of what those consequences would be, and when they would begin raining down.

☆   ☆   ☆

"Unfortunately, Your Majesty," Dapplelake said heavily, "for once, the man is right."

"Really," King Edward said, long experience first in the Navy and then in Manticoran politics allowing him to keep his voice unemotional and unreadable. "This is almost a first for you."

"I know," Dapplelake said sourly. "But if I'm going to call him when he's wrong, I have to be fair when he's right. And Casey-Rosewood and the Academy simply cannot accommodate the kind of personnel MPARS is going to need in the near future. We're barely holding our own now."

"If we don't give Breakwater his own training center, we'll have to cut back on Navy personnel," Locatelli added from the seat beside him. "And this would be the absolute worst time to do that."

"Agreed," Edward said, peering down at his tablet and the figures the Defense Minister had just sent across.

The numbers were impressive. Edward had assumed that the sheer number of deaths resulting from the battle would have a dampening effect on enlistment. It had been just the opposite. Manticore was mourning, yes; but Manticore was also mad as hell. The Navy recruiters were overwhelmed, and the data shufflers were having to scramble to process all the applicants showing up at the centers.

It was immensely gratifying to see his subjects coming defiantly together against their unknown enemy. But the surge of emotion that was driving this wouldn't last. As the memories of that terrible day faded, people would start returning to their lives and their hopes and their pre-battle goals. This was the time to grab as many people as possible, and everyone at the table knew it.

So, surely, did Breakwater. MPARS enlistments weren't nearly at the Navy's level, but they were definitely on the rise. Now, while the warm and willing bodies were still excited at the prospect of defending the Star Kingdom, was no time to put obstacles and cooling-off time in front of them.

"If he gets his own academy, you'll need to supply

him with some of the instructors," Edward reminded Dapplelake. "Possibly all of them. Can you afford to pull that many people?"

"No, but it's not quite as bad as it looks," Dapplelake said, tapping his tablet. Edward's own tablet flickered, and a new set of names appeared. "Our thought is to give him the smallest number of instructors we can get away with, and then fill in whatever else is needed with Navy officers whose ships are still undergoing repairs. Most of those officers and chiefs would be somewhat underemployed anyway, so we could probably spare them. That way Breakwater gets what he wants—and what the Star Kingdom needs, I suppose—without seriously damaging the Navy's own manpower buildup."

"It does seem the best of less-than-ideal options," Edward agreed, running his eyes down the list. He recognized a fair number of the names, and he mostly remembered them as competent. Some of them would squawk, of course, particularly some of the officers from the Peerage who had gone into the Navy for the prestige and what they'd thought would be easy jobs. One, in particular, he would bet money would use the term *slumming* in regards to a transfer to an MPARS training facility.

But at this point Edward didn't care about inconvenience or bruised egos. If Manticore needed a new training facility, it would get one.

And then, as he scrolled down the list, a message box suddenly appeared in the lower corner.

Princess on rooftop with glider. Advise.

Edward glared at the tablet. *Again?*

Why did his daughter always do this kind of thing when Cindy wasn't home to pin her ears back? She knew better than that—or if she didn't, it wasn't because she hadn't been told often enough.

An instant later his brief flush of anger morphed into a quiet stab of guilt. With some teens, this would be a cry for help or attention. With Sophie, it was simply a matter that she wanted to do something fun and resented the new restrictions on her life.

As a father, Edward could understand that. Hell, *he* resented his new restrictions.

As for the timing, as a former Navy officer, he also knew exactly why she pulled these stunts when her mother wasn't at home. It was called *tactics*.

Still, this had to stop. Edward had talked about it until he was blue in the face. Clearly, he hadn't gotten through. Maybe it was time for someone else to give it a try.

Call her Aunt Elizabeth to deal with it, he typed back.

"Your Majesty?" Dapplelake asked.

"My apologies," Edward said, looking up again. "You were saying?"

"I was just listing the facilities we could spare from Casey-Rosewood," Dapplelake said, tapping another list to Edward's tablet. "We're thinking that we might be able to move some of the advanced tech classes to the Academy. It'll take some schedule juggling, but I think we can pull it off." He made a face. "Of course, the cadets probably won't appreciate having to share space with enlisted. But at this point, I really don't care."

"Nor should anyone," Edward agreed. "Very well. Finalize your proposal, and we'll let the Cabinet and Naval Affairs Committee see it."

He tapped his tablet to bring up a new folder. "Next topic. At last report, we'd gathered a sizeable collection of debris from the destroyed battlecruisers. I want to hear the latest analysis results. We need to know who they were, and where they came from.

"And most importantly, what in the Star Kingdom is worth going to war over."

☆   ☆   ☆

It had been a stressful day already, and Elizabeth had just settled down to a relaxing cup of tea when the message and order came down from the king.

The Tower, as it was simply called, had been one of King Michael's pet projects a decade ago. Designed to resemble a classic castle tower, Elizabeth had always thought it looked a bit out of place compared to the rest of the palace. But Michael had been king, so they'd humored him.

What nobody had realized was that he was quietly building a home where he could retire after his unexpected abdication three years ago. A place that would be private and outside the palace proper but still on the grounds.

The fact that it was the tallest building on the grounds also made it the perfect launching spot for short hang gliding flights to other parts of the grounds.

Most of Elizabeth's walk and elevator ride was spent wondering whether she should resent her brother's high-handed move in ordering her to deal with her niece. Her reluctant conclusion, though, was that he *was* the King, and if anyone had a right to be imperious, it was him.

She found a very unhappy Sophie glowering in the middle of the rooftop, a counter-grav belt secured around her waist and shoulders, a partially assembled hang-glider at her feet, and a pair of equally unhappy guards at her sides. "Let me guess," Elizabeth said as she walked toward the trio. "These fine gentlemen refuse to let you jump off the roof?"

"I've been hang gliding since I was ten T-years old," Sophie said in a feminine version of the same lofty outrage Elizabeth could remember from the teen's father when they were growing up. "That's half my life and at least two hundred flights. I don't think that in the past month I've forgotten how this works."

Elizabeth sighed. The girl knew perfectly well what the difference was. She was just pushing the boundaries, looking for a way out of the velvet cage that had closed inexorably around her. "You're the heir to the Throne, Sophie," she said gently. "You can't participate in unnecessarily dangerous pastimes anymore."

"My grandfather does it," Sophie reminded her.

"Your grandfather abdicated three T-years ago. He's a private citizen and can do whatever he wants."

"He was racing jetboats when he was still king," Sophie countered, her tone starting to take on a belligerent edge.

"I know," Elizabeth said, an unpleasant shiver running through her. She would *never* understand the whole faster-higher-crazier fascination that afflicted her brother, father, and grandfather. For a long time she'd assumed it was a glitch in the Winton Y-chromosome; and then Sophie had popped up with it, too, which effectively scotched that theory. Nurture, not nature, presumably, and she could only thank God that she'd been immune to the influence. "What it boils down to is that a King can do what he wants, but a Crown Princess can't. It may not be fair, but it's how the universe works. I wish it was otherwise."

Sophie gave a deep sigh. "No, you don't," she

muttered. "If you had your way, you'd ground every jetboat, hang-glider, and hunti—" She broke off.

"And hunting skimmer?" Elizabeth finished gently for her.

"I'm sorry, Aunt Elizabeth," Sophie said. The anger and frustration had vanished, replaced by guilt and shame. "I'm sorry. I didn't mean to..." She trailed off.

"It's all right," Elizabeth said, forcing away the sudden knot in her stomach. "I don't need you to remind me that Carmichael's gone. My whole world reminds me of it every day of my life."

Sophie closed her eyes, a pair of tears trickling out. "What's the matter with our family, Aunt Elizabeth?" the girl said miserably. "My brother—your husband—so many of us. You look at our family tree—so *many* of us."

"There's nothing wrong with the Wintons, sweetie," Elizabeth assured her. "Most of those deaths were from the plague, and they had plenty of company among the general populace. It's just the swing of the pendulum. Sometimes it's someone else's turn; sometimes it's ours."

"I suppose." Sophie looked down at the hang-glider, blinking the tears out of her eyes. "Either way, no hang-gliding."

"Not today," Elizabeth said. "But don't give up hope. Your father's only fifty-seven T-years old, and as far as I know he's in perfect health. He and your mother are more than capable of having another child."

Sophie's face took on a slightly scandalized look. "That's *not* where I was expecting this conversation to go."

"Well, buck up, kiddo—that's what makes the world go round. But here's the thing. If they have another child, all you have to do is wait a few years, abdicate in his or her favor, and be hang-gliding that same afternoon."

"I could really do that?" Sophie asked, frowning.

"Your grandfather did it," Elizabeth reminded her. "You'd just be doing it a lot sooner."

"I suppose," Sophie said, frowning harder. "I don't know. Seems a little like cheating."

"Oh, it's a *lot* like cheating," Elizabeth confirmed. "But if you really don't want the job, that's your way out."

The frown cleared away, and Sophie smiled puckishly.

"And if I don't want my name and the family's honor in the sewer, I stick with it anyway? Is that where you're going with all this?"

Elizabeth shrugged.

"I'm not going anywhere, Sophie. Really. I'm just helping you figure out what's already in your heart and soul."

"Yeah." Sophie took a deep breath, let it out in a sigh. "Thanks, Aunt Elizabeth. If my parents do have another girl, I hope they name her after you."

"I thought *you* were going to take my name," Elizabeth reminded her. "How many Elizabeths do you want running around, anyway?"

"Personally, I don't think you can ever have too many."

"Well, thank you," Elizabeth said. "I still think your father would have a conniption if you tried it."

"Enough reason right there to do it. Maybe it would encourage him and Mom to get busy making a new heir." Sophie sighed again. "Fine. If a Crown Princess can't hang-glide, what *can* she do?"

"Well, I was just about to have a cup of tea."

Sophie rolled her eyes. "Terrific. Whatever. Let's go have tea."

"You'll love it," Elizabeth promised, taking the girl's hand and guiding her around the forlorn-looking hang-glider. "While we're at it, I can instruct you in all the finer nuances of tea party etiquette."

"Right. Don't push it."

☆   ☆   ☆

Travis looked up from his orders, his heart sinking. "I don't understand, Sir."

"The orders seem pretty self-explanatory, Lieutenant," Heissman said, his face an unreadable mask. "Three months from now you're slated to be transferred to Admiralty Building to serve as Beginning Tactics instructor for the new MPARS officers' section."

Travis looked back down at his orders. So that was it. After everything that had happened—after the Secour pirate attack and Tamerlane's invasion—after watching friends and shipmates die horrible deaths—he was to be summarily taken off *Casey*. And not just put on instruction duty, but to be teaching MPARS weenies.

All because he hadn't had the sense to keep his mouth shut when Chancellor Breakwater started dumping on those same friends and shipmates.

"Is there—?" He broke off. Of course there was no chance for appeal. *BuPers giveth, and BuPers taketh away*, the aphorism went; but BuPers never let junior officers argue their decisions. "Yes, Sir," he said instead, wondering if he should say something about how he would miss serving aboard *Damocles*. Probably not.

"Until then, of course, you'll still be one of my officers," Heissman reminded him, "and you'll be expected to carry out your duties with all due diligence and enthusiasm."

"Of course, Sir," Travis said.

"Good," Heissman said. "Then there's just one more thing, Lieutenant." He handed Travis a hard copy.

Frowning, Travis took it and started reading.

And felt his eyes widening.

From Admiral (ret) Thomas P. Cazenestro, First Lord of the Admiralty, Royal Manticoran Navy, to Lieutenant Travis Uriah Long, Royal Manticoran Navy. Sir: you are hereby invited to proceed to the Royal Palace on the Sixteenth Day, Fourteenth Month, Year Seventy-Four After Landing at eleven o'clock to attend the Monarch's Thanks.

Travis looked up again, his eyes still wide. Heissman still had that unreadable expression, but there was now a hint of a smile tugging at his lips. "Cat got your tongue, Travis?" the captain asked mildly.

With an effort, Travis found his voice. "Sir—I'm sorry, but I was under the impression that it was only the senior officers from each ship who were invited."

"They were," Heissman confirmed. "But as you see, our invitations included one for you." He raised his eyebrows. "Apparently, there are some people who want to meet you."

Travis opened his mouth. Closed it again. As had happened so often in the past, he had no idea what to say to that.

"Oh," he said instead.

"Just make sure you're at the Palace on time." Heissman lifted a finger. "And if you happen to run into Chancellor Breakwater, do us all a favor. Make an excuse, and walk away. Better yet, just walk away."

"Yes, Sir," Travis said with a sigh. "I will."

CHAPTER NINE

0600 Sunday
Embarkation for the Monarch's Thanks five hours away.

SERGEANT ROBERT HERZOG WAS SWEATING BULLETS. *Big* bullets.

Because the whole damn thing was ridiculous. Utterly.

It wasn't bad enough that the King, Crown Princess, former King, Prime Minister, and half the Cabinet were going on this little jaunt. Oh, no. Just the entire leadership of the Manticoran government, aboard a single ocean-going ship, within range of a well-placed missile or long-distance mortar attack from the shore. It was the same assassination choke point the King ended up in every time he and his family headed out to Triton Island, or even just for a cruise around Jason Bay.

And every single time Herzog and the rest of the King's Own security force walked on eggs until their monarch was safely back in the Palace.

But this time was worse. Far worse. For this trip, the King had effectively doubled the ante.

Because he'd also invited the Navy's top officers aboard. The self-same officers who'd risen to the challenge of Tamerlane's superior force, beaten him back, then chased him out of the system.

Which meant that theoretical well-placed missile or mortar round would not only take out the Star Kingdom's top political leaders, but its best military ones, as well.

Didn't the King realize that?

Probably not. Herzog suspected that Edward had his father Michael's easy-going and slightly naïve attitude toward assassination, which boiled down to the assumption that he was so beloved by the Manticoran people that no one would ever want to harm him. And if by some miracle someone *did* want to, the men and women of the King's Own would protect him.

Under normal circumstances, Herzog would have mostly agreed with both parts of that assessment. Certainly the King's Own were the absolute finest the Star Kingdom had to offer.

But these circumstances weren't normal. The Star Kingdom had just beaten back an invasion ... and Herzog's reading of military history indicated that invasions were often preceded by the infiltration of enemy agents. Agents whose job it would be to support the external attack with an internal one.

That was ominous enough. Even worse, the fact that they still didn't know where Tamerlane had come from meant there was no way to guess what sort of agents and weapons might be unleashed against them.

The King might not appreciate the risks, former

Navy officer though he might be. He was used to being surrounded by other dedicated officers, protected by multiple centimeters of armored hull and a flinkin' big impenetrable impeller wedge. He might not really understand how vulnerable he was down here at the bottom of a gravity well.

But if the King didn't get it, Major Blackburn certainly did. He'd had his people swarming like crazed bees ever since the announcement had been made public. Everything within reasonable attack range of the Palace and the yacht had been checked and double-checked.

Which was all well and good. But in the end, it came down to the last few hours. Those last hours when someone could smuggle a sufficiently powerful weapon into range and wait out the remaining minutes until he could change history.

That wasn't going to happen today. Not on Sergeant Herzog's watch.

The wind was brisk and cool, and getting brisker as the sun warmed the air. But Herzog didn't mind. He liked rooftops, the higher the better. Slowly, he turned on his latest three-sixty, peering at each of the nearby rooftops through the spotting scope slaved to the computer controlling his tripod-mounted M5A1 hypersonic sniper rifle. There were other spotters scattered around Landing's highest buildings, but this was the one with the best view of the Palace and yacht. An attacker with even half a brain would set up somewhere around here.

Herzog would be ready for him. The M5A1's computer did a continual read on air pressure, humidity, windage, distance, and every other factor that might affect how and where a bullet flew through the air. At the first sign of trouble—or even the first hint of a sniper nest in the making—Herzog could put a targeting laser built into his scope on that trouble and squeeze the trigger, and the rifle would put a round within two centimeters at a distance of three kilometers.

He paused. Down on the *Samantha*'s dock, among the people moving briskly about on their various errands...

He tapped his mic. "Nitro; Herzog," he said quietly. "I make a stranger ten meters on your ten."

"Blue shirt?" the reply came back instantly. "It's okay—he's got an ID pin."

"Yes, I can see that," Herzog said tartly. "He's still a stranger."

"Hang on, let me check."

The earpiece went quiet. Herzog peered at the unidentified man another second, then went back to his scan. Planting a screaming security anomaly in the most visible place possible was a classic diversionary tactic, and he was determined not to fall for it.

He hadn't found anything more suspicious before Nitro came back on. "Herzog; Nitro. It's okay—he's from one of the caterers."

"Caterers?" Herzog repeated, frowning. The Palace had a full kitchen staff of its own.

"Specifically, Sphinxian caterers," Nitro confirmed. "A few of the people coming on the cruise are Sphinxians, and the King wanted to get some authentic food for them. Don't worry—our people supervised the cooking and ran the usual tests, and sent everything over under full seal."

"And the seals are intact?" Herzog persisted, focusing his scope back on the man far below. He sure didn't *look* like a caterer, though now that Herzog thought about it he probably hadn't seen an awful lot of caterers in his lifetime.

"Checked 'em myself," Nitro assured him. "Relax, will you? You hawks just do your job up there and let us gophers do ours down here, okay?"

Herzog nodded, feeling marginally better. *Eagles* and *groundhogs* would have meant Nitro was under duress or otherwise had some suspicions that he didn't want to broadcast. But any other animal names meant things were all right.

At least, they were down there. Up here...well, the jury was still out.

Lifting his scope focus from the dock, Herzog settled it briefly on the distant patch of green midway to the watery horizon. Landing City was important, certainly. That was where the *Samantha* would depart from and return to.

But even more critical was Triton Island itself. That was where everyone would be spending three or four hours today.

Granted, an island was a big target. But it was also a *stationary* one. And even an unskilled idiot could hit a target that wasn't moving, provided he had a big enough weapon.

There were some in the security team, Herzog reflected, who considered him paranoid at best and something of a nutcase at worst. But he didn't mind the name-calling. He might be a pain in the butt to work with—a lot of team members said *that*, too—but at least no one had to worry about him overlooking or casually dismissing a potential threat.

Herzog had his end of the danger zone locked down. He just hoped the other end was equally solid.

0700 Sunday

Embarkation for the Monarch's Thanks four hours away.
Arrival at Triton Island six hours away.

GROWING UP IN THE HILLS OUTSIDE of Landing,
Major B.A. Felton had always loved the woods. Here
on Triton Island, he was starting to hate them.

It hadn't always been that way. Felton was old
enough, and had been in the King's Own long enough,
that he had fond memories of Crown Prince Richard
and Princess Sophie hiking in these woods. Often the
hikes degenerated into a game of hide and seek, usually with Richard attempting to lose his little sister.
Most of the time it had been a game, but occasionally
Richard had been exasperated enough with having a
half-sized shadow that he'd tried to lose her for real.

Which hadn't bothered Sophie in the slightest.
She'd doggedly pursued him each and every time,
even when she became so exhausted by her efforts
that her guards had to carry her back to the Lodge,
the big stone building that had been the Wintons'
get-out-of-town-and-clear-your-head retreat ever since
the reign of Queen Elizabeth.

But now Richard was gone, it was Sophie who
was heir to the Throne, and the Star Kingdom had
been attacked.

And the woods were no longer a place for children
to play and adults to stroll.

Woods could hide people. Woods could hide traps.
Especially the dense woods on the western side of the
island between the Lodge and the sea.

Still, the advantage of an island was that, once it

had been locked down, it tended to stay that way. Mostly, anyway. While the official announcement of the Monarch's Thanks luncheon had been made a month ago, the far quieter revelation that it would be held on Triton had only happened in the past six days. Within three hours of that news the island had been sealed off, the handful of visitors who'd been enjoying the public park sections had been escorted back to their boats and sent home, and a millimeter-by-millimeter search begun. Two days later, Felton himself had declared it clear.

But there were always ways a clever person could slip something through even the cordon into a supposedly safe place. Hence, with six hours left before the *Samantha*'s projected arrival, they were sweeping the island again.

"Major Felton?" PFC Patricia Gauzweiller's voice came over Felton's earpiece. "We may have something at the Lodge. It might be nothing, but it looks a little...odd."

"On my way," Felton said, heading off at a quick jog, his right hand resting on the grip of his sidearm. "Don't touch it."

"Roger that, Sir. Not really going to be a problem."

Felton was still frowning over that one when he reached the Lodge. Gauzweiller was standing at the southwest corner, peering up along the side of the building with her binoculars. "Where is it?" Felton asked.

"Up there," Gauzweiller said, pointing toward the roof. "At the top of the chimney. Looks like a bird's nest."

Felton focused his own binoculars on the spot. It did indeed have that nest look to it.

"Only it wasn't listed on the last report, so I thought someone should check it out," Gauzweiller continued. "You want me to take a look?"

"No, I'll do it," Felton said. Keying his counter-grav belt, he eased on his thruster and floated slowly up the side of the building, every sense alert for trouble. He reached the chimney without incident...

To discover that the mass of twigs and mud was indeed just a bird's nest.

Still, Gauzweiller was right. It should have been removed or at least noted during the earlier sweep of the island. Either someone on Felton's team had been sloppy, or Triton was home to a world-champion nest builder.

"Looks okay," he called down. Just the same, he eased his probe through the mass in a few spots, in case they had a very clever bomber on their hands. But there was nothing but nest.

"Any eggs?" Gauzweiller called back.

"Nope," Felton assured her as he carefully gathered it together for removal. If Sergeant Herzog had been assigned to the Triton detail, he mused, once this whole thing was over he would probably go over the records and find out who had let this slip through the earlier sweep. It would then have been a tossup as to whether the guilty party would suffer more from the gig or the lecture on how there was no room for sloppiness when the lives of the royal family were at stake.

A movement caught his eye, and he looked up at the blue water glistening in the early-morning sunlight. Between Triton and the distant spires of the city a couple of dozen small pleasure craft had already appeared. Some of the boaters were probably hoping for a glimpse of the King as the *Samantha* passed by, while others were simply out for a leisurely Sunday morning cruise or some casual fishing. Many of them, Felton suspected, were there for all three reasons.

They were going to be disappointed. Two of the Coast Guard's cutters had already appeared on the horizon, plowing through the waves toward the scattering of boats. Each craft would be hailed, each passenger checked against the Manticoran citizen lists, and everyone ordered clear of the corridor the *Samantha* would soon be taking to the island.

It was a task that by its very nature generated civilian disappointment and anger, and Felton didn't envy the cutter crews their duty. But it had to be done. With Triton Island locked down, the critical part was to keep anyone from approaching the yacht.

Still, the cutters had had lots of experience at that task. They were hardly going to screw up today.

0800 Sunday

Embarkation for the Monarch's Thanks three hours away. Passage through this part of Jason Bay approximately four and a half hours away.

THE MARITIME ENTHUSIASTS OF THE GREATER Landing area were not happy.

Lieutenant David Bozwell, commander of the CGC *Jackstraw*, couldn't really blame them. Triton Island was the royal family's retreat, and the Palace almost never announced their visits early enough for citizens to get out on the bay in time to watch *Samantha* plying the waters.

Bozwell wished the Palace had kept its corporate mouth shut this time, too. His best guess was that the King knew how confused and worried his subjects were and wanted to offer them the chance to line the route, possibly to cheer him on and show their support, possibly just to watch as he and the heroes of the Battle of Manticore passed by.

Still, it had raised the security issues an order of magnitude. None of the King's Own liked it. Sergeant Herzog had been especially loud on the subject, fuming over the stupidity inherent in telling potential assassins exactly where to find the entire flipping royal family, in one sinkable spot, for what amounted to a flipping publicity stunt.

What made it worse was that whatever PR advantages the king had hoped for were going to be largely negated by the security requirements. Most of the citizens who'd come out for the procession had gotten up at the crack of dawn in order to get here. A lot of them had rousted their children out of bed for the occasion, which in Bozwell's opinion was on a par with winning a space battle all by itself.

They weren't happy at being told to head back to Landing or get themselves a minimum of five kilometers away from the *Samantha*'s route. Bozwell wasn't any happier at being the one who had to deliver those orders.

But at least the job was almost done. Only five more boats were still within the safety zone, and two of them were in the *Argus*'s patrol area. Three more unpleasant confrontations for Bozwell and the *Jackstraw*, and they could move on to straight perimeter patrol.

Unfortunately, this next encounter was likely to be one of the more aggravating ones. The *Happily Ever* was a big boat, a sailing cabin cruiser of the kind favored by people who weren't necessarily rich but wanted everyone to think they were. In Bozwell's experience, most of that sort liked to project that same elitist attitude toward everyone around them, including authority figures.

This one was certainly playing the nouveau riche role to the hilt. As the *Jackstraw* approached, Bozwell could see a half dozen figures lounging in deck chairs on the fantail. Right at the stern, nestled against the low railing, were a cooler full of ice and colorful drink cans and a squat grill loaded with freshly-caught fish. The wind shifted momentarily, bringing Bozwell a whiff of the smoke from the grill: Graeling sea trout, he tentatively identified it, with way too much spice sauce for that kind of fish.

All six boaters were watching the *Jackstraw* now as it cut through the water toward them. One of the men, Bozwell noted, had a particularly apprehensive expression. That must be the owner, listed in the records as a Mr. Basil Moore, wondering if his precious boat was about to be rammed.

Luckily for him, the *Jackstraw*'s helmsman knew his business. At the last second the cutter's engines shifted into reverse, bringing the vessel to a smooth halt. A final twitch of the wheel, and the cutter ended up angled a meter off the *Happily Ever*'s stern. If Moore wasn't impressed, Bozwell thought, he really ought to be.

"Ahoy!" he called as he stepped out of the wheelhouse onto the *Jackstraw*'s deck. "Sorry to bother you, but—"

"What the hell are you doing?" Moore cut him off angrily. Not impressed, apparently. "You trying to run us down?"

"Not at all, sir," Bozwell said, keeping his tone the respectful politeness required by the CG manual. "We're clearing out this sea lane in preparation for the *Samantha*'s crossing later this morning. I'm afraid I have to ask you to move away."

Most of the people Bozwell had talked to this morning had reacted with surprise, disappointment, or annoyance. Moore reacted like a rich kid with a new toy. "Like hell you are," he bit out. "This is Jason Bay. It belongs to everyone on Manticore. The King wants to go for a cruise? Fine—he can have one boat's width of space, just like everyone else."

"I'm sorry you feel that way, sir," Bozwell said. The rest of Moore's party, he noted peripherally, were starting to look uncomfortable. One of the women, sitting directly behind her host, quietly and discreetly moved to a chair farther out of any potential lines of fire. Apparently, Moore had something of a temper. "And under normal circumstances, you would indeed have claim to freedom of the seas. But not today."

"Really?" Moore scoffed. "What makes today so special? Because a bunch of pampered politicians and stuffed uniforms want to burn a few extra tanks of hydrogen just so they can have lunch sixty kilometers from the great unwashed public?"

"No, sir," Bozwell said, really regretting that the manual's rules of conduct were so specific. "Today is special because there are extra safety considerations."

"Oh, *safety* is the issue, now?" Moore demanded. "Fine. Let me tell you about safety." He waved a hand in a wide, sweeping arc. "We've been watching you. There was a nice, compact group of boats out here, and you've spent the last hour or so scattering them to the four winds. Now, what happens if one of them has a problem? What if one of them starts to sink? Will you or your buddy be able to get there in time? Or are you just going to hope and pray that they have enough counter-grav belts for everyone and don't get dumped into the water before they can activate them?"

"We appreciate the risks involved whenever someone takes a watercraft out onto the high seas," Bozwell said. He could feel a subtle vibration in the deck beneath his feet: the measured pace of heavy footsteps coming his way from the wheelhouse. "But we can only do what we can with the limited resources we have."

"So what you're saying is—?"

"Beg pardon, Lieutenant," a deep voice interrupted.

And out of the corner of his eye Bozwell saw Sergeant Brian VanHoose step from the wheelhouse.

Only out of the corner, because most of his attention was focused on Moore.

He wasn't disappointed. The majority of Sphinxians were by nature and necessity big people, but even on that scale VanHoose was a *big* Sphinxian. As he hove into view Moore's eyes went wide, and he started to take a reflexive step back before he caught himself. His eyes flicked up and down VanHoose's bulk, finally settling on the deadpan face and half-lidded eyes that fooled people into thinking there wasn't a lot going on behind them.

Which was always a mistake. VanHoose might look like a genial giant idiot, but he had a knowledge of regs and orders that was second to none.

"Yes, Sergeant?" Bozwell said blandly. "You have a thought?"

"It seems to me, Sir, that the gentlemen and his

companions have been drinking," VanHoose said, just as blandly. "Reg gamma-four-oh-six, subsection three, paragraph four, says that if a boater is impaired the Coast Guard is required to take possession of his or her vessel and bring it safely into port."

"I do believe you're right, Sergeant," Bozwell said, frowning in thought. "Well, I'm sure that won't be a problem. I can handle the rest of the security sweep on my own while you bring the *Happily Ever* back to Landing."

Moore finally found his voice. "Wait a second," he said, a hint of nervousness starting to crack his arrogance. "No one's impaired here."

"I don't know," Bozwell said, eyeing the cooler. "I see a *lot* of beer in there. Sergeant, do the regs specify how much alcohol is required for impairment?"

"We could break out the breath analyzer," VanHoose said. "But you know it's been on the fritz lately."

"Besides, alcohol affects people in so many different ways," Bozwell pointed out. "If I let you take command of this vessel, will you promise to be more careful than the last time?"

"Hey, that fireball wasn't my fault," VanHoose protested. "The tank regulator was cracked. If I hadn't bumped the dock it would have just gone kablooie somewhere else."

"*Bumped?*" Bozwell echoed. "Is that what you call it? *Bumped?*" He lifted his hands. "Never mind—we don't have time for this. Sergeant Brian VanHoose, as per Regulation whatever it was, I authorize you to—"

"Okay, okay," Moore said quickly. "We'll go."

"In good time, right?" Bozwell said.

"As fast as we can," Moore promised, his face looking like an angry sea.

"Good," Bozwell said. "Sergeant, take us to the next vessel, please. Good day, Mr. Moore."

A minute later the *Jackstraw* had left the *Happily Ever*'s side and was speeding through the low waves toward the next boat in line.

Speeding just a tad too quickly, perhaps.

"You realize," Bozwell said, peering aft through the wheelhouse door at the *Happily Ever* rapidly receding in the distance, "that you dumped their entire fantail when you took off."

"No big loss," VanHoose said, waving a hand in dismissal. "That was about the cheapest cooler on the market—I've got one myself; they're only a couple of dollars. And they've already had enough beer."

Bozwell took another look behind him at Moore, frantically digging into the water off the stern of his yacht. VanHoose was right—the cooler had been a cheap foam job, and a man at Moore's level of snobbery really needed to upgrade. "And the grill?"

"Too much sauce on the trout," VanHoose declared. "I did everyone a favor."

"Ah," Bozwell said. Somehow, he doubted Moore would see it that way.

0900 Sunday
Embarkation for the Monarch's Thanks two hours away. Passage into the Triton Island approach four hours away.

"BRAVO-SIX CLEAR," A MUFFLED VOICE CAME in Sergeant Sara Felton's earpiece. "Moving on to Bravo-seven."

"Copy," Sara said. Back in the old days, the odd thought struck her, her voice had sounded exceedingly strange to her as it bounced back from a diving helmet's faceplate. Now, after ten years of service, she didn't even notice.

Which was just as well, because right now she needed every gram of brainpower focused on the job at hand. At last report, Triton Island and Landing were secure, and the sea lane between the two was rapidly becoming so.

Time for the area beneath the surface to be likewise.

"Sara?" the voice of Sara's cousin, B.A., came in her ear. "How's it going?"

"We're getting there," Sara said. Out in the world, of course, they had to be *Major Felton* and *Sergeant Felton* to each other, which was a never-ending source of private amusement among their fellow teammates. On a private com like this, they could be more informal. "The approach line has been checked and cleared, and we're about three-quarters done with the rest of the seabed. How about you?"

"We found a bird's nest in one of the chimneys," B.A. said. "Aside from that, we're good."

Sara grunted into her helmet. "Good thing Herzog's not there. *Someone* would be in for a coal-raking."

"Agreed. Maybe I'll mention it to him next week. It can be entertaining when he spins up."

"As long as you're not the one he's spinning up on," Sara said. "Tell me again why they couldn't just have lunch at the Palace?"

"It's politics," B.A. said. "The King needs to get out and show that he's not afraid of anything. And, by extension, that no one else should be afraid of anything, either."

Sara wrinkled her nose. But he was probably right.

Grand gestures were part of high office, and King was as high as anyone could get. "I just hope everyone appreciates it."

"The ones who matter do," B.A. assured her. "The rest probably never even notice us."

"Part of our job."

"Yep," B.A. agreed. "Listen, do me a favor, will you? One of the approach sensors seems to be winking a little. When you finish your current sector, will you go take a look? It's probably nothing, but I'd feel better if you checked it out personally."

Sara smiled as she tapped for a readout. "No problem, Cuz. Number 44?"

"That's the one," B.A. confirmed.

Ten minutes later, Sara was at the problem sensor.

"Well, for starters it's leaning sideways," she reported as she hovered beside the slender two-meter-tall rod-and-bulb device sticking up from the sea floor. "About forty degrees off vertical. I don't see any damage to the bulb or signs of tampering, though. Probably just got pushed over by crawlers digging into a grub nest."

"Probably," B.A. agreed, sounding a bit doubtful. "We'll swap it out anyway. I'm sending Keating down with a new one—she's suiting up now. Wait there until she arrives and help her install and network it."

"Right," Sara said, shifting her light to the next sensor in the lane. "Let me know when she's in the water. I'm going to give the next couple in line a quick look."

Sara hadn't found any other problems in the sensor line by the time PFC Bridget Keating arrived. Together they swapped out the sensor, networked the replacement with the others, and ran a quick diagnostic. Once B.A. confirmed the system was back to full green, Keating headed back to shore and Sara returned to her check of the Triton Island shallows.

B.A. was right, Sara knew as she resumed her part of the search. If all went well, most of the people who would soon be boarding the *Samantha* would never be aware of the work that had gone into keeping them safe.

CHAPTER TEN

BACK WHEN HE WAS A HIGH-SCHOOL sophomore, Travis had once accidentally been assigned to a senior-level class. It had taken the office three days to get it all sorted out and transfer him back to the proper class.

The classwork itself hadn't been too bad. What had made those three days so rough was the sense of being horribly out of place. He was two years behind everyone else, without any social contacts or context, and had no idea how he was supposed to interact with anyone.

He hadn't thought about the stress of that time in years. Not until he found himself aboard the Royal Yacht *Samantha* with the exact same stress.

And for exactly the same reason. Travis was a lieutenant. Everyone else aboard in uniform was lieutenant commander or higher, their tunics dripping with medals and ribbons and fancy braid and dress swords everywhere.

Once again, he was a sophomore among seniors.

"You okay?" Lisa murmured from beside him.

164

Travis took a deep breath, shaking off the feeling. High school was a long ways behind him, after all. And here, at least, he had Lisa to provide moral support. "Just a little overwhelmed, Ma'am," he said. "Still not sure what I'm doing here."

"You're obeying orders, right?"

"Well, yes," Travis conceded. "But I'm still wondering—"

"Lieutenant Long?" a voice called from behind him.

Travis turned, some of the fresh spike in his tension bleeding off at the sight of a familiar face. It was Captain Allegra Metzger, who'd been his XO on *Guardian* during the Secour Incident. "Yes, Ma'am," he said, giving her his best salute.

"I'd heard you were going to be aboard," Metzger said, returning the salute and giving Travis an unexpectedly warm smile. "Congratulations on your excellent work aboard *Casey*. That was a wonderfully inspired idea."

"Thank you, Ma'am," Travis said. "I was just lucky I came up with it in time."

"Careful, Lieutenant," Metzger warned, her smile taking any bite out of the words. "Your captain doesn't like his officers using that word."

Unbidden, and probably improper—Metzger *was* a superior officer, after all—an answering smile touched Travis's lips. "You mean *lucky*, Ma'am?"

"That's the word." Metzger shifted her eyes to Lisa. "Commander Donnelly," she greeted the younger woman. "You're looking well."

"Thank you, Ma'am," Lisa said.

"And ditto what I said about Lieutenant Long's maneuver," Metzger continued. "Your coordination with the MPARS corvettes was equally inspired, and obviously just as successful."

"Thank you, Ma'am," Lisa said again. "Though if we're keeping score, I have to point out that Mr. Long's battlecruiser trumps our little destroyer."

"Point," Metzger agreed. "Too bad no one paints kill silhouettes on their ships the way stingships do. Maybe we should adopt that custom. Have either of you met the King yet?"

Travis blinked, the sudden change of subject catching him completely off-guard.

"Ah . . . no, Ma'am. Uh—" He looked helplessly at Lisa.

"No, we haven't, Ma'am," Lisa said more calmly.

"Then it's time you did," Metzger said. "Come on—I'll introduce you."

She headed off, weaving her way through the small knots of conversation that had formed all along the *Samantha's* deck. Travis watched her go, a sudden panic freezing his brain. She was going to introduce him to the *King*?

He started as Lisa slipped a reassuring hand around his upper arm. "Come on, Travis," she murmured. "You lived through a space battle. You can live through this."

The King was in another small gathering of people, their faces all earnest and thoughtful. Travis recognized one of the women: Princess Elizabeth, the King's half-sister. The other three, two men and a woman, were dressed in civilian clothing, and Travis had the nagging feeling that he should know all of them by sight, too.

But it was too late to back off and try to gather more intel. Metzger had already passed the pair of bodyguards at this end of the group, and the King had already broken off his conversation and had smoothed out some of his seriousness as he looked with interest at the newcomers, and Travis would just have to go through with it and do the best he could.

The brief etiquette text he'd read had warned that a guest should always allow the King to speak first. Fortunately, that hurdle was quickly and easily crossed. "Captain Metzger," the King said, smiling and nodding in greeting as Metzger approached. "Good to see you again." He nodded to Lisa and Travis. "Would you care to introduce your colleagues?"

"I would be honored, Your Majesty," Metzger said, giving him a brief bow. Straightening up again, she half turned and gestured to Travis and Lisa. "May I present Lieutenant Commander Lisa Donnelly, currently of His Majesty's Ship *Damocles*; and Lieutenant Travis Uriah Long, currently of His Majesty's Ship *Casey*. Commander, Lieutenant: His Majesty, King Edward."

"Commander Donnelly," the King said, inclining his head to her. "And Lieutenant Long," he continued, shifting his attention to Travis.

And it seemed to Travis that there was a sudden new interest glistening in the King's eyes and face.

"I've read about your actions and the actions of your ships during the Battle of Manticore," the King continued. "The Star Kingdom is in your debt."

"Thank you, Your Majesty," Lisa said, bowing to him the way Metzger had.

"Thank you, Your Majesty," Travis said, following her cue.

"Allow me to introduce some of Manticore's other defenders," the King said, gesturing to his conversational companions. "This is Davis Harper, Duke Burgundy, the

Star Kingdom's Prime Minister. Beside him is James Mantegna, Earl Dapplelake, the Minister of Defense. And the lady is Clara Sumner, Countess Calvingdell."

Travis suppressed a wince. Who was also the *former* Minister of Defense, having been tossed out four T-years ago when Edward ascended the Throne and reinstated Dapplelake in that post.

And here she was now, talking with her replacement and the man who had kicked her out of her job.

Travis wasn't good at reading people's emotions, especially when those people were on their best behavior. But he had no doubt there was some serious tension going on beneath the surface.

"Pleased to meet you," Burgundy said as the other two murmured agreement. Apparently, the protocol was for him to speak for all three of them.

"Pleased to meet you, Your Grace; My Lord; My Lady," Metzger responded, nodding to each in turn. "And if I may be so bold, may I express our gratitude for the work that all of you have done in giving the Navy the people and tools necessary to defend the Star Kingdom."

"Thank you, Captain," Burgundy said gravely. "In retrospect, I'm only sorry we didn't push harder."

"But I think it's safe to say that the Cabinet's priorities are going to reflect that new focus in the very near future," Dapplelake added.

Travis winced to himself. *Now what?* Was he supposed to say something? *What* was he supposed to say? What kind of small talk did you make with the King? *Thank you for inviting us aboard, Your Highness? I think you're doing a good job? I like your tie?*

The King's eyes shifted to something behind Travis.

"If you'll all excuse me," he said, starting toward the gap between Metzger and Travis, "I have a small matter to attend to."

"Of course, Your Majesty," Dapplelake said, again apparently speaking for the group. Travis quickly stepped aside, the King and two more of his body-guards swept past, the King sending a final smile in Travis's direction as he left.

"Again, congratulations," Burgundy said, craning his neck as he looked at someone further along the deck. "If you'll excuse me, there's someone else I need to speak to."

"Of course, Your Grace." Metzger gestured to Travis and Lisa, and the three of them turned and headed in the other direction.

And with that, it was suddenly over.

Beside Travis, Lisa seemed to wilt a little. "Well," she said.

"Well what?" Metzger asked, sounding amused.

"Just *well*, Ma'am," Lisa said. "I've—first time I've ever met royalty."

"Well, I suggest you get used to it, Commander," Metzger said. Travis threw her a sideways look, but the amusement he thought he'd heard earlier was gone. "You're a rising star, and nowadays that suggests you'll eventually find yourself up to your collar in politics."

"Wonderful," Lisa muttered.

"Fortunately, that's still a ways in your future," Metzger soothed. "Right now, Cazenestro and Locatelli have that role sewed up. But they won't be around forever; and when they go, it'll be up to officers like you." She shifted her gaze to Travis. "And you, too, Lieutenant," she added.

"I hope not, Ma'am," Travis said. "If Commander Donnelly isn't up to it, I'm certainly not."

"You will be," Metzger assured him. She raised her eyes to the horizon, where only the tallest buildings of Landing were still visible in the distance. "But as I said, that's the future. For now, I believe they're setting up an appetizer bar at the stern. Let's show the politicians and MPARS officers how to do a *proper* reconnaissance in force."

☆   ☆   ☆

Sophie was standing half-concealed in one of the cabin hatchway alcoves, partially shielded from the brisk sea wind, when Edward reached her.

To find that his half-seen glimpse a moment ago had been correct. The Crown Princess wasn't alone.

Apparently, she'd brought a date.

Edward clenched his teeth. Of all places, and of all times.

And of all people.

Sophie smiled at him as he approached. Her smile slipped, just a bit, as she saw the look on his face, but she had it back in place by the time he reached the happy couple. "Hello, Father," she greeted him, ducking her head in respect. "There's someone I'd like you to meet." She took the arm of the young man at her side, easing him just a bit closer to her. His face, Edward noted, wasn't nearly as calm and controlled as Sophie's. "This is Peter Young, eldest son of Hadrian Young, Earl North Hollow."

"Your Majesty," Young gulped, bending deeply at the waist as if hoping a sufficiently deep bow would render him invisible.

Edward could only wish that was true.

"Yes, I know," he said, nodding curtly to the boy. "A word, Sophie. If you'll excuse us, Mr. Young?"

"Of course, Your Majesty," Young said. He bowed again, then eased gingerly past Edward and hurried away down the deck at a quick, stiff-backed walk.

Edward looked back at his daughter. Her eyes were apprehensive, but her jaw was set firmly. Silently, he motioned to the cabin door behind her. Her lip twitched, but she obediently reached behind her back, found the knob, and opened the door. A moment later, they were alone in the cabin, the door once again closed against possible interruption.

"Let me guess," she said with a sigh. "I should have asked your permission to bring a date along."

So *she* thought of it as a date, too. Wonderful.

"But I *did* clear it with Colonel Jackson," she went on. "And North Hollow has been doing good work with the Survivor's Fund that Aunt Elizabeth set up—"

"Sophie," Edward said, holding up his hands, palms toward her. "This isn't about Peter Young, or even Sophie Winton. It's about Crown Princess Sophie."

Sophie frowned. "Excuse me?"

"In case you've forgotten," Edward said, "let me remind you that the Constitution stipulates that the monarch must marry a commoner."

Her eyes widened with surprise and a hint of outrage. "Dad, I'm not planning to *marry* him," she protested. "It's *one* casual date."

"And every marriage on Manticore started with one casual date," he countered. "What happens if one of these casual dates turns into something more? Are you ready for the heartbreak of having to say good-bye to him?"

"So what, I should never have any friends with titles?"

Sophie bit out. "*Friends* sometimes turn into husbands, too, you know."

"Which is why you have to guard your friendships, too," Edward said gently. "I'm sorry, Sophie. I really am. I never meant for this to happen to you. But this is the reality, and you're going to have to accept it."

Sophie looked away. "It's not fair, you know," she said in a low voice. "None of it."

"Once you're Queen you can try to get the Constitution changed," he said. "But I'll warn you, it'll be an uphill battle."

"Yeah."

For a moment the cabin was silent. Then Sophie took a deep breath. "Well, at least you're not going to make him swim home," she said with a touch of the old Sophie sense of humor. "That was how you looked when I first saw you." Her eyes narrowed slightly. "You *aren't*, are you?"

"Of course not," he assured her. "But that does bring up another point. Everyone aboard is all right and will understand. But there will be people at the dock when we return who may not. There will probably also be some watching who revel in spreading rumors and innuendo. I'd rather not pump hydrogen into their bonfires, if you know what I mean."

"So you *do* want him to swim home."

"No, but it wouldn't hurt to put him in one of the aft cabins when we get close to Landing," Edward said. "I'll instruct Major Fergueson to let him out once the rest of us have disembarked and are on our way to the memorial service."

"Right," Sophie said. "Like having Peter skulk around under the radar isn't going to raise some eyebrows."

"Only if the eyes beneath those eyebrows actually see him. If we do this right, they won't."

"I suppose." Sophie sighed again. "Okay, I'll tell him."

"Thank you." Edward started to turn back toward the door, then turned back. "Oh, and he *will* be in the cabin *alone*."

"Dad!" Sophie said, sounding thoroughly scandalized. "I *said* it was just casual."

Beneath his feet, Edward felt the slight change in vibration as the *Samantha*'s engines slowed. Right on schedule. "Right," he said. "I forgot."

"Well, don't." Sophie wrinkled her nose. "Aunt Elizabeth said there were costs to being Crown Princess. This was one she didn't mention."

"I know," Edward said. "And again, I'm sorry." He lifted a finger. "But there are some advantages to being the Monarch," he said. "Namely, getting to do things that everyone else tells you you're not supposed to."

"Right," Sophie said, frowning slightly. "Like what, drinking red wine with fish?"

"Like this." He crooked the raised finger back toward the door in invitation. "Come on. I'll show you."

☆   ☆   ☆

Travis had spotted the boats approaching rapidly from astern shortly after they cleared the horizon. He'd pointed them out to Lisa, and they'd had a short discussion on whether or not they should alert anyone. But then Lisa noticed that the King's Own at *Samantha*'s stern were also watching the approaching watercraft and were showing no signs of alarm. A few minutes later, as the approaching vehicles resolved themselves into a pair of sleek hydroplane racing boats, *Samantha*'s engines changed pitch, and the yacht began slowing to a stop. Again, the guards showed no concern, and Travis put it behind him.

Until he spotted Princess Elizabeth standing by the rail staring at the approaching boats.

And the King's sister did *not* look happy.

"Over there," Lisa murmured, pointing at an empty section of railing as some of the other guests began wandering curiously sternward. "Come on."

"What?" Travis asked, hurrying to catch up as she headed off. "Why?"

"I want to see what's going on," Lisa said over her shoulder. "Snap it up—the King and Princess Sophie are on the way."

They were in Lisa's chosen place by the portside rail—downwind from Elizabeth, Travis noted, where the presumed upcoming royal conversation would carry well—when King Edward and Crown Princess Sophie reached Princess Elizabeth.

Apparently, the warning Travis had read about letting the King speak first didn't apply to family.

"You aren't serious," Elizabeth said in a low voice.

"I'm very serious," Edward assured her. "And really, you're worrying about nothing."

A couple of people in civilian clothing, apparently realizing they were in the eavesdropping zone, moved politely away from the rail. Lisa, behind Travis, nudged him to move a little closer.

"The sea is smooth, the wind is perfect," the King continued.

"And at three hundred kilometers an hour it doesn't take much of a wave to—"

"And this is the last time."

Elizabeth broke off.

"What do you mean, the last time?"

"Just what I said: the last time," the King repeated. Travis could only see half his face, the other half blocked by his sister's head, but he looked very serious. "At least, for a long while. Sophie understands that in her new role as Crown Princess she has to give up this kind of activity. I thought that as a gift to her she and I could have one last outing before putting the hydroplanes away. *And* the hang gliders, *and* the eddy-spinners, and all the rest of the excitement in her life."

"Now you're just trying to make me look bad," Elizabeth said. "So you're not going to be doing your usual racing thing?"

"No racing," Edward assured her. "Just a father and daughter getting out on the water to feel the wind in our faces. Actually, I'm thinking we'll just go on ahead and make sure everything's ready for the luncheon."

"You won't be doing any crazy stunts?"

"Well, *I* won't," Edward said. "Sophie, are you planning any crazy stunts?"

"No, Your Majesty," Sophie said solemnly.

"The King's Own has cleared the whole area?"

"Out to five kilometers."

"The boats have been thoroughly checked out?"

"Two times each, by two different techs."

"And you'll keep it under two hundred KPH?"

The King and Crown Princess looked at each other. "If it'll make you feel better, yes," the King agreed.

Elizabeth's shoulders heaved in a silent sigh. "And I can't stop you anyway, can I?"

"Please, Aunt Elizabeth," Sophie said. "Can you just be happy that I'm getting one last ride before I have to be all upright and proper?"

"And boring?" the King murmured.

Elizabeth shook her head. "You two are hopeless," she said. "Fine. But if I have to watch this, Sophie, don't expect me to come watch your next hang gliding, too."

"Fair enough," Sophie said. "Thank you."

"Now that that's settled," the King said, "it's time to get suited up. Your gear's in Cabin Three, Sophie. Last one in their boat is—"

"Edward?" Elizabeth interrupted, her voice ominous. "You said no races."

The King frowned briefly, then smiled and inclined his head. "I did, didn't I," he agreed. "Fine. Sophie, last one in their boat is last one in their boat. Good enough?"

"You know, even a King isn't supposed to mock his younger sister," Elizabeth said. "But fine. Go suit up, Sophie. Just promise me that when you get to Triton you make sure your father doesn't eat *all* the crab cakes."

"I will," Sophie promised. She gave her aunt a quick hug, then hurried forward along the deck.

"You be careful," Elizabeth said, almost too quietly for Travis to hear. "And keep her careful, too."

"I will," the King said, taking her hand. "And I promise: it *will* be the last time. At least until she's Queen and can drive you crazy with these things without my help."

"Yes, that makes me feel *so* much better."

The King gave her a final smile, then headed off after his daughter.

Lisa tapped Travis's arm, and together they drifted away from the rail.

"What do you think of *that*?" she asked.

Travis shook his head. "I don't like it."

"It *is* a little risky," Lisa conceded. "There are a lot of things that can go wrong when you're traveling that fast."

"I'm sure they know what they're doing," Travis said. "I just don't think it fits the proper mood of the day. This is supposed to be an afternoon of gratitude, with an evening of solemn remembrance following it. Doesn't seem right for the King to head off on a hydroplane jaunt as if this was just another afternoon's outing."

"Maybe," Lisa said, a bit doubtfully. "But then, he *is* King. He kind of gets to do whatever he wants."

"I suppose. But as King, shouldn't he also do what's good and proper?"

"I suppose." Lisa pondered a moment. "Tell you what. When you get to be King, you can make out a list of good and proper things for future kings to follow."

Travis frowned sideways at her. Was she mocking him?

Probably. But that was all right. Somehow, jibes from her didn't hurt. "Great idea," he said. "I'll start campaigning for the job tomorrow."

"Sounds good," Lisa said. "For now, let's just campaign for a few of those little nut clusters on the appetizer table."

Travis craned his neck. Those clusters *did* look good. "Is that an order, Commander?"

"Absolutely, Lieutenant." She nodded toward the table. "I'm going in. Cover me."

CHAPTER ELEVEN

AS EDWARD HAD EXPECTED, NOT EVERYONE approved of his decision.

No one said anything, of course. He was the King, and unless a decision impacted national security or national finances no one else could claim a vote in the matter. But it was evident in their expressions which ones were neutral, which ones were mostly positive, and which ones were flat-out against it.

Edward's wife Cynthia was studiously neutral on the whole thing. Like Elizabeth, she didn't personally care for that kind of sport, but long experience had taught her that it was a necessary stress release for both her husband and her daughter. She'd also learned over the years that both of them knew what they were doing, and that objections didn't get her anywhere anyway.

Which was a lesson the rest of them would do well to learn, too. Edward was the King, he wanted to do this for his daughter, and they were therefore going to do it. Period.

Still, as the two hydroplanes pulled away from *Samantha*'s side he couldn't help but feel a twinge of sadness. If this was Sophie's last outing for the next twenty or thirty T-years, it needed to be Edward's last, as well. A King's responsibility was to lead by example, especially within his own family.

The one upside of the whole thing was at least Elizabeth wouldn't be giving him That Look anymore whenever he wanted to do anything even remotely dangerous. It was a look she'd figured out when she was eight, and she'd only improved on it since then.

And of course, since her husband's tragic and violent death four T-years ago, her fears for her brother's safety had come with an extra edge of guilt and grief attached. Edward would be just as happy to never see That Look, in that context, ever again.

"So how does this work again if we're not racing?" Sophie's voice came through his earpiece. "I forget."

"We just ride elegantly and genteelly across Jason Bay," Edward said, settling himself snugly in his cockpit seat and peering through the bars of his safety cage. Fifty meters in front of him he could see Sophie strapped into her own seat, her red wetsuit/life vest combo brightly visible through the cage bars.

"*Genteelly* means *fast*, right?"

"Up to two hundred KPH, yes," Edward said. "We promised Aunt Elizabeth, remember?"

"I suppose," Sophie said, a bit of grump in her voice.

"And no donuts, bouncers, or bootleg turns, either," Edward admonished.

"Yes, yes, I know." Sophie huffed out a sigh. "She can really suck the fun out of everything, can't she?"

"Sure can," Edward said. "It'll serve her right if

you decide *not* to take her name when you become Queen."

"*What*?" Sophie gasped indignantly. "She *told* you that?"

"It might have come up in casual conversation," Edward said, smiling. "Or it could have come from one of your bodyguards."

"They wouldn't dare."

"No, probably not," Edward conceded. "But take that as a handy tip for the future: if you're in public, everything you say could eventually become public knowledge. You'll want to remember that."

"Oh, I'll remember it, all right," Sophie growled. "And if I *do* take her name, I'm going to spell it wrong. So there."

"Yes, that'll certainly fix her," Edward agreed. The row of diagnostics on his display turned green—"Okay, my self-check is done. Yours?"

"Not quite—there it goes. All green, and the tanks are full. Ready to be genteel?"

"Ready," Edward said. "And remember: under two hundred."

With a roar and a surge of foam from their underwater jets, they took off.

It was, indeed, a glorious day for a ride. Edward began with a wide circle around *Samantha*, keeping a close eye on Sophie's style and precision as she matched his maneuvers. It had been awhile since they'd taken the hydroplanes out, and it was easy to get rusty on something that demanded this much skill and concentration.

But Sophie was keeping up with him just fine, and her turns and bounce adjustments showed no signs of hesitation or over-correcting. And keeping their speed well below the jetboats' full three-hundred-KPH capability would help a lot, too.

"So are we just going to rock the yacht and see if we can dump the appetizer table?" Sophie asked as they finished their third circle.

"Just making sure we had our sea legs back," Edward assured her. "You got Triton locked on your nav display?"

"Yep," Sophie confirmed. "I make it eighty-seven klicks straight ahead. Half an hour if we dawdle."

"Or if we head straight there," Edward said. "Remember, we've got a five-klick lane to play with."

"I like how you think," Sophie said. "So once we're out of Aunt Elizabeth's sight . . . ?"

"We still don't do donuts," Edward said firmly. "And go easy on the turns. Aunt Elizabeth might not be watching, but the King's Own has three stingships overhead. And she *will* be able to pull the recordings afterward."

"Right," Sophie said. "So what are we waiting for?"

"Nothing I know of," Edward said. "Go for it."

And with a vibrating bounce as her hydroplane kicked off the waves, Sophie did exactly that.

Edward smiled as he fell into position five hundred meters behind her and a hundred to the side. For all her grousing about Aunt Elizabeth's restrictions, Sophie was keeping her speed well under the agreed-upon limit, running between one-seventy and one-ninety. Her turns were conservative, too, less like her favored hard-point zigzags and more the kind of amiable S-turns a less experienced hydroplaner would prefer.

But with all that, she was still clearly determined to get the most out of this last adventure. She was running back and forth between the edges of their lane, making only slow progress toward the island, getting as much water time as possible without actually turning back toward *Samantha*.

Which she could certainly do, of course. They had the time, and as Sophie had already noted their hydrogen tanks were full. In fact, once they finally reached Triton, Edward had every intention of running them a few rings around the island before they finally came in to dock.

Samantha was just out of sight over the horizon behind them, and the tallest of Triton's trees were just peeking over the water ahead of them, when Sophie's hydroplane did a sudden small yaw to starboard. The glitch barely had time to register in Edward's brain when the boat made another, even larger yaw back straight and then to portside—

And before Edward could even gasp, his daughter's boat overcorrected, flipped over sideways, and roll-bounced violently across the water.

No! The word screamed through Edward's mind. Dimly, he was aware that voices were shouting through his earpiece—the King's Own in the aircars, arrowing down toward the boat still bouncing its tortured way to a stop.

But they would never make it in time. Even as Edward kicked his own speed to full power and chased after her he could see the torn section of hull near the fuel tanks. If the tanks had ruptured, and if hydrogen was accumulating inside the hull...

Sophie's hydroplane had finally come to an upside-down halt, the torn hull bobbing forlornly amid the low waves, by the time Edward reached it. A hard bootleg turn and a few seconds of full power from his jets, and he was floating beside her.

The boat was a wreck.

Sophie was nowhere to be seen.

"She's still in there," he snapped into his mic as he popped off his restraints and slammed open the side of his cage. The voices were shouting in his ear again, ordering him to stay where he was, but they were too far out and he was five meters from his daughter and *damn* his own stupidity and pride in letting them do this in the first place. He slapped at the side of his helmet, sealing the neckpiece and starting the emergency oxygen flow, and dived over the side.

The sudden slap of cold water was a shock to his skin and heart and limbs. He barely noticed. A few quick strokes took him alongside the hydroplane, and a surface-dive took him beneath the waves and under the edge of her hull.

In the faint light from the still-glowing monitors and status board he could see Sophie. She was upside down in her cage, still strapped into her harness, not moving. Her neckpiece had deployed properly, and he could see from the indicators that her oxygen tank had gone active and was feeding air to her.

But that emergency equipment had now become a two-edged sword. The bubbling of hydrogen from the ruptured fuel tanks had been joined by a trickle of bubbles from Sophie's own oxygen supply. If the mixture reached any of the hydroplane engine's hot surfaces, the whole thing could go up in a massive fireball.

Someone in the aircars must have spotted the bubbling, too. The voices were shouting in Edward's ear again, ordering him to get out.

But he was here, and they weren't, and he might have only seconds to get Sophie out. He swam to the cockpit, pried open the cage, and unfastened her restraints.

He was maneuvering her out of her seat when the hydroplane exploded.

☆   ☆   ☆

The only warning that something was wrong was when *Samantha's* engines abruptly surged to power, sending the passengers bouncing into each other, the rails, and the deck furniture.

Travis's first thought was that the King's Own aircars and high-cover stingships overhead had detected some incoming threat that the yacht was running from. A look upward seemed to confirm that: the handful of guard vehicles had broken formation and were racing ahead toward the island at full speed. Clearly, something deadly serious was happening.

And then, through the low roar of the wind and the hiss of *Samantha's* prow slicing through the water, he heard the distant crack of an explosion.

"We're not going back," Lisa murmured, gripping his arm with one hand and the rail where they'd been thrown with the other. "They're heading forward, and we're heading forward."

Travis felt his stomach tighten. She was right. And if the aircars were running toward the source of the danger—and *Samantha* wasn't running the opposite direction—

"Come on," he said, grabbing her hand.

Together they hurried forward, weaving their way through other civilians and Navy personnel who had come to the same conclusion. They were still twenty meters back from the bow when Travis caught the glint of metal as a couple of aircars converged over the water.

In the direction the King and Crown Princess had gone.

Someone gasped. Someone else cursed. Then all was silence. More aircars converged on the scene, and stingships dropped from the sky like hunting ospreys, as the *Samantha* continued speeding forward,

But it was too late. Deep within Travis was the cold, bitter certainty that it was too late.

"Travis?" a voice murmured, jolting in the taut silence.

He turned to look. Lisa was standing beside him, her body pressed close to his side, her hand gripping his. Her eyes glistened with tears as she gazed out at the sea ahead.

Her face blurred, and Travis realized that his eyes had gone moist, as well.

And then, somewhere ahead, someone started crying.

☆ ☆ ☆

Elizabeth had been on the bridge, clearing up a small snafu with the chefs at the Lodge, when the report of the catastrophe came in. Five seconds later, she had ordered the *Samantha* to full speed and called for the King's Own to bring Cynthia immediately to the bridge.

The King's wife had just arrived, her face flushed with fear and horror when the aircars began their desperate convergence ahead.

"Oh, God," Cynthia murmured, her eyes transfixed on the horizon as Elizabeth hurried to her side. "Oh, God. Elizabeth—please, God."

It's all right, were the first soothing words that sprang to Elizabeth's mind. "I'm here, Cynthia," she said instead.

Because it wasn't all right. There was no way in heaven or hell that it was all right.

And they both knew it.

They stood there together, clinging silently to each other, as the reports came in.

One of the hydroplanes, totally destroyed.

The other hydroplane, superficial blast damage only.

For a few minutes Elizabeth dared to hope. Cynthia's pleadings to God began to take on a tentative hint of gratitude.

But there was to be no hope that day. Five minutes later, the final, horrible news arrived.

Crown Princess Sophie. Dead.

King Edward. Dead.

Beside Elizabeth, Cynthia turned into her sister-in-law's arms and collapsed in complete and unrestrained sobbing.

Elizabeth held the other woman close, her own heart shattering within her. A hundred memories flashed across her eyes: memories of her brother and niece, of laughter and anger and love and tears. Memories that would now forever be darkened.

And as Cynthia's tears flowed in bitter grief, Elizabeth wondered why she herself wasn't crying.

Hadn't she loved her brother and niece? Of course she did. Didn't she love Cynthia enough to share in the other woman's anguish? Of course she did.

A whiff of moving air touched her cheek. Colonel Petrov Jackson, head of the King's Own, was standing beside the two of them, his face carved from granite.

"Yes, Colonel?" Elizabeth asked. Her voice, too, seemed to be under the same inexplicably superhuman restraint as her tear ducts.

"Major Felton has been alerted, Your Highness," he said quietly. "The Lodge is being prepared, unless you would prefer we return to Landing."

Elizabeth swallowed hard. Why was this *her* decision?

Because apparently it was.

"We'll continue to Triton," she told him. "It's closer and . . . more private. You'll see to . . . you understand? Whatever arrangements are necessary?"

"I understand, Your Highness," Jackson said. "Is there anything I can do for you?" His eyes flicked to Cynthia. "For either of you?"

Elizabeth reached up to stroke Cynthia's hair. "No, thank you," she said. "Maybe later."

"Yes, Your Highness." Something unreadable flickered across Jackson's face. "Your Majesty," he corrected with a slight bow. Turning, he headed toward the com board.

Leaving his final words whispering through Elizabeth's mind.

Your Majesty.

And *that*, she realized suddenly, was why she wasn't crying.

Edward's wife could mourn her late husband. Sophie's mother could mourn her late daughter. The Star Kingdom could mourn them both.

But not Elizabeth. Not yet. Not as deeply as she wanted.

Because a Queen's life was not her own.

There was no longer an Elizabeth Winton-De Quieroz. There was only Queen Elizabeth the Second.

And she had never felt more alone in her life.

CHAPTER TWELVE

IT WAS, ELIZABETH WINTON-DE QUIEROZ REFLECTED as she watched the enormous wall screen Archbishop Bradford had arranged for her, a suitably historical moment. Of course, she'd never liked history the way Edward had.

And she'd never in her worst nightmares expected she and her brother would both be making it this way.

Her eyes prickled. They had a way of doing that whenever she thought about her brother and her niece, and she'd thought about them a lot in the last few days. She knew from painful, dreary experience that eventually her eyes would stop burning every time she thought of them. Just as she knew a time would never come when she stopped weeping in her heart.

Now there's *a dreary thought*, a voice remarkably like Edward's said in the back of her brain. *Way to go, Beth.*

Her lips twitched in a somewhat watery smile and she made herself draw a deep breath as she listened to the magnificent organ music pour from the wall screen's speakers. The enormous cathedral her father had commissioned sixteen years earlier was a sea of color, especially to the left of the nave in the pews reserved for the peers of the realm on this day.

Her lips twitched again as she remembered her grandmother's somewhat caustic comments when the peerage first began the fad of dressing in their house colors on formal occasions. The original Elizabeth Winton had possessed a less than awestruck attitude where the Star Kingdom's aristocracy was concerned.

For that matter, she'd had her reservations about the entire reason there was a "Star Kingdom" in the first place. Elizabeth had read her grandmother's journal when she was much younger, and she knew neither her grandmother nor her great-grandfather had really favored the notion of an explicit aristocracy, far less a hereditary monarchy. She was certain revisionist historians would ultimately conclude such family reservations were nonsense, no matter what Elizabeth Winton might have written in her journal, given the power the new constitution had invested in the Winton family.

But Elizabeth had known her grandmother. She knew that the constitution's preservation and institutionalization of the original shareholders' privileged positions against a flood of new Manticoran citizens was the only thing which had enabled Roger and Elizabeth Winton to win approval for the subsidized immigration desperately needed to rebuild after the Plague Years.

Just as she knew her grandmother was the one who had insisted that the heir to the throne must marry a commoner, not a descendent of that newly created aristocracy. In public, that Elizabeth—who was subsequently to be crowned Queen Elizabeth the First—had argued passionately in favor of its symbolism.

But her journal showed the deeper thoughts and fears lurking beneath the surface. Elizabeth the First had hoped that the requirement would foster the alliance between Crown and Commons she believed necessary in order to prevent the Star Kingdom's aristocracy from turning into one of the oligarchies which had pillaged the people of so many star systems since the beginning of the Diaspora.

And while the Princess Royal who was about to become Queen Elizabeth the Second might not be the historian her brother had been—or that her father was—she'd read enough history to be damned grateful for her grandmother's foresight.

Elizabeth I would have had a few tart comments for what she would undoubtedly have called "all the hoopla" presently awaiting her granddaughter. But the current Elizabeth didn't much care about that bit. Elizabeth I's coronation had been a modest affair, really—not surprisingly, since she'd come to the throne well before the end of the Plague Years. People had had other things on their minds in 47 AL.

But that was then. This was now. People had other things to worry about today, too, things that had nothing to do with uncaring microbes or diseases. They needed reassurance.

And so, she admitted, did she.

Of course, the other reason Elizabeth I's coronation was so simple might be because no one had built the Cathedral yet. Not until King Michael had the Throne and the family had enough attention to spare for this kind of project.

Not that either Roger or Elizabeth I would have disapproved. Whatever the latter would have said about the hoopla.

The Constitution expressly prohibited any official state religion—that had been another point which had drawn her grandmother's strong support—but the Winton family had been Catholics since well before the colony ship *Jason* ever left the Sol System. They still were, and that faith ran deep, which was why Michael Winton had built a cathedral out of the family's private purse. It had taken centuries to complete many of the great cathedrals back on preindustrial Old Terra, but with the Star Kingdom's modern technology the entire job had been completed in only six T-years.

There'd been some criticism on the public boards, of course. Some protested that a church built by the ruling house would automatically be seen as creating a de facto state religion, whatever the Constitution said and regardless of who actually paid for it.

That argument had struck Elizabeth as pretty silly. The House of Winton had never been shy about publicly acknowledging its faith, which surely came closer to creating such a religious bias than the act of building a cathedral. King Michael, certainly, had been more amused than anything else by the arguments, at least in private. She remembered the time he'd informed Duke Burgundy, with an absolutely straight face, that he should just tell the critics that building cathedrals was what Catholic monarchs did, and it was not Michael's place to defy tradition.

Officially, the magnificent structure was simply Landing Cathedral, although it was almost universally, if informally, known as King Michael's Cathedral. In fact, Elizabeth suspected the "official" name would only last until her father's death.

If that was the case, she could only hope and pray that it would be Landing Cathedral for as long as God would allow.

Her eyes were prickling again. With a sniff, she ordered them to stop.

And then, the organ music crested and the antechamber's door opened.

It was time.

☆   ☆   ☆

Elizabeth followed the crucifer down the endless nave through the swelling voices of Landing Cathedral's choir. The Constitution might ban any official state religion; it did not ban public religious expression on the part of the Star Kingdom's monarch. Crown Prince Michael Winton had made that point clear at his own coronation, and Crown Prince Edward, despite pressure from some quarters to moderate his father's stance had, instead, become the first Manticoran monarch to be crowned in his father's newly built cathedral. Now Crown Princess Elizabeth would become the second.

In only four T-years.

She was not going to break with the tradition her father and her brother had created, and so she processed through the cathedral, through that magnificent outpouring of music and voices, preceded by the crucifer, thurifer, and candle-bearers, with her grandmother's Bible clasped in her hands.

The long train of her mantle glided across the polished marble floor behind her. Her formal coronation robes glittered with embroidery and gem work, and the slight weight of the coronet she'd always avoided wearing rested heavily upon her head.

Not as heavily as the crown about to replace it, though. Her grandmother had attempted to avoid official Manticoran crown jewels and state regalia, but that was one fight she'd lost, and a State Crown had been the first on the list to be made.

She would have given everything she possessed to be somewhere else, watching her brother still bear the crown she wished so desperately she could have avoided.

The journey down the nave took forever, yet ended far too soon. The other members of the procession spread away from her, leaving her alone before the small group of men and women awaiting her.

Archbishop Wallace Bradford, as the Archbishop of Landing, stood in the host's position at the center of that group. He was flanked by the other acknowledged senior spiritual leaders of Manticore: Rabbi Malcham Saltzman, Imam Acharya Hu-Jiang, and Guru Bagaskro Shrivastava. Bradford raised his hands in benediction, joined by his fellows, as Elizabeth reached the polished sanctuary rail and went to her knees on the embroidered kneeler. The music crested, then died.

The cathedral was silent in the anthem's wake. Bradford let that silence linger for perhaps fifteen seconds. Then he stepped half a pace forward and raised his voice, looking out across the packed pews.

"We have come together for a solemn occasion of state," he said into the quiet. "We are a diverse people. We know God in many ways, and under many names. Some doubt His existence; some deny His existence, and that is, perhaps, as it should be in a kingdom dedicated to freedom of conscience and thought. Yet Crown Princess Elizabeth is a woman of faith. For her, this is a spiritual as well as a secular occasion, for on this day she takes a groom, the people of Manticore. She has chosen, as her brother before her, to celebrate that publicly under the eyes of God, as well as under the auspices and requirements of our Constitution. She bids you now to join her in that moment and asks that all of you, whether present in this cathedral or attending electronically, join her in the common dedication of our hearts, our minds, and our courage in preserving the Star Kingdom of Manticore and always and forever holding it—and her—accountable to its people."

He paused once more, then held out his hands to Rabbi Saltzman, Imam Acharya, and Guru Shrivastava. They joined him, and he raised his voice once more.

"Lord of all Creation, we call upon You, by whatever name and in whatever fashion You are known to us. We ask You this day to witness Your daughters and Your sons, and especially this, Your daughter Elizabeth, as she takes up the mighty task to which she has been called. It is a sobering, grueling, often frightening task, and she is only mortal. All mortals are fallible, and all mortals sometimes know fear, but she comes to You with a simple request this day, and we share it with You in her name. Be with her, we pray. Bless her, strengthen her, and give her always the power to look within her heart and find there the love for her people, the strength to serve their needs above any other calling, and the will and the courage to fight tirelessly for that which she knows is right. She asks this in Your name, and we ask You to hear her prayer for all of us, as well. Amen."

A rumble of answering amens came back from the crowded cathedral, and all four of the spiritual leaders reached out in unison to lay their hands briefly upon Elizabeth's head. Then they stepped back and Adelaide Summervale, Duchess of Cromarty, and Kenneth Pavón, Speaker of the House of Commons, took their place. Cromarty bore the Scepter, while Pavón carried the velvet cushion upon which the bejeweled Crown of State glittered.

"We stand in the name of the Peers and Commons and all the subjects of the Star Kingdom of Manticore," Cromarty said. She was an elderly woman, growing frail, and her voice seemed fragile in the wake of Archbishop Bradford's powerful, well-trained baritone. But she was also the ranking member of the Manticoran peerage, the senior member of the House of Lords.

"As our Constitution requires, we have come to hear the coronation oath of our new Monarch," Pavón took up the discourse. He was barely half Mansfield's age, and his voice, though not the equal of Bradford's, rose clearly. "In return, as representative of Peers and Commons, we have also come to pledge to her our fealty, on behalf of all the Crown's subjects."

He paused for a moment, then looked down at the woman kneeling before him.

"Elizabeth Antonia Adrienne Winton-De Quieroz," he intoned.

There was a slight, almost imperceptible stir from the pews. There'd been pressure for Elizabeth to renounce her married surname, given that she was accepting the crown as the heir of the House of Winton, not the House of De Quieroz.

But there were some lines Elizabeth was prepared to draw with all the fabled stubbornness of her family, and this was one of them. Carmichael De Quieroz might not be physically present in Landing Cathedral today, but he would always be with her.

"You are attested, acknowledged, and proved as the rightful Heir to the Crown of Manticore in direct inheritance from your father Michael and your brother Edward. Do you now, before this company and all the people of the Star Kingdom of Manticore, take up the Crown?"

"I do," Elizabeth said, with a clarity and strength she hadn't been at all sure she would be able to produce.

"Will you honor, respect, administer, and enforce the Laws and Constitution of the Star Kingdom of Manticore?" Cromarty asked.

"I will," she replied.

"Will you bear true, unflinching, and just service to the people of the Star Kingdom of Manticore and to your subjects, of whatever degree?" Pavón asked.

"I will."

"Will you protect, guard, and defend the Star Kingdom of Manticore and all its citizens against all threats, foreign and domestic?"

"I will." This time Elizabeth's voice came out hard, cold, and she sensed a shiver of mingled dread and satisfaction as it swept through the cathedral.

"Do you undertake these promises willingly, fully, and without reservation of thought, word, or intention?"

"I do."

Pavón and Cromarty moved a pace apart and Bradford stepped forward between them, taking Elizabeth I's Bible from her granddaughter's hands and holding it. Bracing herself, Elizabeth reached out and placed her right palm upon it, looking up as the Duchess and the Speaker placed their right hands atop her own.

"I, Elizabeth Antonia Adrienne Winton-De Quieroz," she said, "being of sound mind, do swear that I will faithfully honor and discharge every pledge I have made this day to the People and Constitution of the Star Kingdom of Manticore. I take up the Crown in the name of those oaths, with the acceptance of my subjects, and under the authority of the Constitution, and I swear that the Star Kingdom's laws will be fairly and impartially administered, that its Constitution will be honored and obeyed, and that its people will be protected from any foe, so help me God."

The last four words weren't legally part of the official Coronation Oath, but Elizabeth Winton-De Quieroz was the fifth Manticoran monarch to say them, and she meant every one of them. She wondered if her father and Edward had been as conscious as she was in that moment of just how badly she would need His help.

The other hands left hers, and the archbishop looked down at her for a moment. Then he rested one his own hands lightly on her head and closed his eyes in a brief, silent prayer of benediction before he handed the Bible back to her.

"In the names of the Peers and Commons of the Star Kingdom, and as the joint custodians of its Constitution, we hear and accept your oath," Cromarty said as Elizabeth took back the Bible. A moment later she felt a sudden lightness as Archbishop Bradford lifted the formal coronet of the Crown Princess from her head.

"And, in the names of the Commons and Peers of the Star Kingdom, we swear and avow our loyalty, our service, and our homage, under the Constitution," Pavón said. "In token of which, we Crown you Queen of Manticore."

The Crown of State didn't really weigh thirty kilograms. Elizabeth knew that. As it came down upon her head, though, what she knew didn't matter beside the reality of all that crown represented.

"We surrender to you this Scepter," Cromarty said, "the symbol and sign of the power and authority which are yours as the Star Kingdom's chief magistrate, head of state, head of government, and commander in chief."

Elizabeth laid the Bible on the sacristy rail as the duchess extended the Scepter of State in both hands. She felt the warmth of Cromarty's grip on the scepter's staff as she accepted it, and her eyes stung as she remembered how her father had explained its symbiology to her the day before his own coronation.

"It's a mace, Beth," he'd said, his voice somber and his expression grave. *"It looks pretty, but that's what it is—a weapon. Something to use to smash heads and break skulls. An emblem of the raw power that comes with a crown. I never wanted it, but I think that's the way it's supposed to be. Something you do because you have to, because someone has to do it, because it's your job, and that makes it your duty, as well. I know Edward isn't looking forward to it, either, but he's a good kid and he's going to turn into a better man someday. Be there for him when this gets too heavy, honey. Trust me, he'll need you."*

I'm here, Dad, she thought as she felt the Scepter's weight. *I'm here for him, and God I wish he was still here himself. Now it's your turn to be here for me.*

"I accept this Scepter—"

Despite all she could do, the words came out husky, and she paused and cleared her throat.

"I accept this Scepter," she repeated, her voice strong and clear once more, "in the name of the people of Manticore. May I always wield it with justice, tempered by mercy."

"Rise, then," Pavón said, and she was surprised by how steadily and smoothly she stood, despite the sense that her knees should be shaking.

"Turn," he said, and she turned to face those packed pews, those watching cameras, and all the millions of Manticoran citizens behind the silent lenses. In that moment, as everyone in the Cathedral stood to face her, she felt the weight of all those individuals' massed hopes, desires, and needs pressing down upon her.

"People of the Star Kingdom!" Cromarty's fragile voice was suddenly as strong and clear as Elizabeth's own had been "I present to you, Her Majesty, Elizabeth the Second, Queen of Manticore. God save the Queen!"

Elizabeth's eyes widened slightly as the duchess appended the last four words. They were also not part of the formal coronation proceedings—

"*God save the Queen!*" a thousand voices rumbled the response without a trace of hesitation.

And Elizabeth Antonia Adrienne Winton-De Quieroz, Elizabeth II of Manticore, saw all those bright colors wash together through the sudden veil of her tears.

BOOK TWO

1544 PD

CHAPTER THIRTEEN

BEING THE MANAGER ON ONE OF Solway's orbiting warehouses, Greez Paco reflected as he walked along the curve of the spin ring between the neatly stacked crates, didn't pay very well. Being first assistant manager paid less. Being second assistant manager paid even less.

Being second assistant manager in a warehouse used by the Red Hand pirates, on the other hand, paid *very* well.

"Yes, I have them," Paco confirmed into his uni-link as he stopped beside a set of six three-meter-tall crates. "Transshipment from Beowulf, en route to Haven."

The man at the other end of the call snorted. "Of course they are," he said. "Machine parts, right?"

"Machine parts it is," Paco confirmed. Sure they were. Just like the man he was talking to was a purser on a legitimate freighter. "I assume you want to dock and check out the boxes before I load them into your container?"

"Before *we* load them," the man corrected, his voice going a little less friendly. "Something wrong with your memory?"

"No, no, of course not," Paco said hastily. "I just thought—I sent you that new directive about outsiders using the station's gantries, right?"

"Yeah, you sent it," the man said. "Do you think we care?"

Paco winced. "No, I just—okay, sure. I'll be waiting at the gantry to unlock it when you get here. I just thought—"

"Don't think," the man cut him off. "It's not good for you. Just do what you're told, and be happy."

"Sure," Paco said. *Don't think, don't ask; and look the other way.* That was what the man had told him ten T-years ago when the Red Hands' relationship with this particular warehouse began, and the orders hadn't changed.

The man had never told Paco his name. Paco sometimes wondered what it was, but never for very long. Wondering wasn't good for you, either.

"The shuttle will be there in twenty minutes," the man continued. "You just make sure everything's ready when it gets there."

"Sure," Paco said. "I'll go double-check the datawork right now."

"You do that. And watch those crates. Watch them *real* close."

The connection went dead. "You bet," Paco muttered into the empty ether. Keying off his end, just to be sure, he headed toward the Third Quadrant terminal to make sure everything was in order. The last thing he wanted was for some last-minute wrench to be thrown into the operation.

He'd gone three steps when he heard a faint noise from somewhere behind the crates.

He stopped short, straining his ears. He'd managed to put everyone on jobs in the ring's other quadrants, precisely so that there *wouldn't* be anyone snooping around when the Red Hands came to collect their cargo. A rat, maybe, or some other small animal that had somehow found its way up from the surface?

Only one way to find out. Reaching into his pocket, he pulled out his little Coltline 3mm and walked silently back to the line of crates. He thumbed off the gun's safety and eased around the corner.

To find an old woman in a warehouse jumpsuit kneeling on the deck in the lane between the crates, her head bowed, her eyes closed, her hands clasped in front of her.

"What the *hell* are you doing?" Paco snarled.

The woman jerked with surprise, her eyes snapping open. "I'm sorry, sir, I'm so sorry," she gasped as she scrambled to her feet. "Please—I did not mean to intrude."

"Yeah, sure," Paco said, frowning as he stepped up to her. She wasn't nearly as old as he'd thought, he saw now, probably no more than her late forties or early fifties. She had a proper ID badge clipped to her jumpsuit's breast pocket, but he couldn't recall seeing her here before. Her accent was odd, too: a bit like Havenite, but with something else mixed in. "Who are you?"

"I'm Elsie, sir," she said, reaching for her ID badge. Fumbling for it, rather—her hands were trembling too violently for her to work the clip. It made a nice counterpoint to the quivering of her lower lip, Paco thought scornfully. The woman was terrified, all right.

As well she should be. If she'd heard any of Paco's

uni-link conversation—*any* of it—she was in for the high jump. "What are you doing here?" he demanded.

"I came to pray." The woman gave up her attempt to unclip her badge and instead folded her hands together like they'd been when Paco first saw her. "The others— they laugh and make fun of me when I pray. I come here to kneel in the sunlight and speak to the Lord."

Paco glanced around. Sure enough, one of the warehouse's dingy viewports was directly across from her, the sunlight rising and waning in time with the station's rotation.

"Yeah," he said, looking back at her. "But I ordered everyone out of this area. Weren't you listening?"

"It was my break time," Elsie protested. Her hands had unclasped in her agitation and were now moving together in a sort of nervous kneading motion. "I was told—I must come in here and pray. The others, they would laugh at me if they knew."

Paco sighed. She was right about that, anyway. None of the other warehouse workers cared much for religion, of any sort, and they could be pretty nasty to anyone who did.

But even though Paco agreed with them, he had a sister who'd gone all in a few years ago. Under normal circumstances, he probably would have bent the rules and let Elsie go with a warning to never ignore his orders again.

Unfortunately, the situation here wasn't normal.

"I understand," he said. "But you've disobeyed a direct order, Elsie. We have to go put it on the official record."

"I understand," Elsie said, her shoulders slumping as she bowed her head. "Must we do it now?"

"*Right* now," Paco said, scowling. *Damn* her, anyway. Now he was going to have to figure out how and where to hide a body until the Red Hands left with their crates. He couldn't very well shove her out a lock—things that were together in orbit tended to stay that way. Better to let the pirates deal with her, somewhere between picking up their cargo, ferrying it to their hidden ship, and heading out to the hyper limit. They would have a whole universe worth of empty space to drop a body in.

On the other hand, asking for a favor like that could be a very bad idea. If he let it slip that someone had overheard their conversation there was a good chance he would join her in the long float into infinity.

He would just have to lock her in the office for now, give the Red Hands their stuff, and then figure out what the hell to do with her.

At least she would have her religion to comfort her when she saw death coming. Maybe there was even a God out there somewhere who would actually take her in or something.

"Let's go," he said, gesturing with the gun. "The office is this way."

"Yes, of course," she said, her shoulders still slumped with dejection. She stumbled toward him, her feet dragging on the floor. As she passed, her foot caught on something, and she started to topple forward. Reflexively, Paco reached out and grabbed her arm with his free hand to steady her.

The last thing he saw before the lights went out was her other forearm as it slammed into the side of his head.

☆   ☆   ☆

She had the crates lined up in the staging area when the shuttle arrived. The men who came out of it were large, rough-looking, and well-armed.

And suspicious. Highly suspicious.

"Who are you?" the one in the lead demanded as he strode up to her.

"Elsie Dorrman," she said, tapping her ID badge. "Paco's a bit indisposed, so he sent me to meet you."

"Did he, now," the man said, flicking a glance over her shoulder. "And you are...?"

"I already told you: Elsie. I'm Paco's partner."

"He never mentioned a partner."

She shrugged. "I'm new."

"How new?"

"Oh—" She consulted her chrono. "As of fifteen minutes ago. That was when Paco found out, anyway. I've known for a year."

"Yeah?" The man's hand dropped to the butt of his sidearm.

"Oh, relax," she said scornfully. "The crates are right here, with whatever you've got in them; *you're* here; and your ship's location could be pulled from the nav log in two minutes. If I was a cop or part of a rival gang we wouldn't still be talking."

"Sure," the man said suspiciously. "Bosc? Check the seals on the crates, will you? Then open one."

It took them three minutes to check all the seals, then pop one open and paw through the upper layer of contents. During that entire time the man just stared silently at the woman. Rather like some first dates she'd had, she thought dryly.

"Looks good," Bosc reported. "Nothing missing or tampered with. You want me to seal it back up?"

"Yeah, and then get everything aboard." He cocked his head. "I assume you unlocked the gantry so we could use it?"

She waved toward the big crane hanging from the ceiling above the crates. "Help yourself."

One of the other pirates was already in the control booth, and she watched in silence as he snagged the first crate and lowered it into the container. "So I guess we're dealing with *you* now?" the boss asked as the second crate began its own journey downward.

"If you want to keep using this warehouse, sure," she said. "If not, that's okay, too. I figured this to be just a one-off until I got a whiff of who Paco was dealing with. If you want to keep going, just let me know—you can keep using Paco's uni-link number." She held out her hand, palm upward. "But whatever you decide, I'll take my payment for this job now."

For another long moment, he just gazed at her. Then, snorting a little chuckle, he pulled out a chip and tossed it toward her. "You've got brass, Elsie—I'll give you that. We'll be in touch. Maybe."

"I'll look forward to it," she said, deftly catching the chip and slipping it into her pocket. "Maybe."

He gave her a tight smile and turned back to the shuttle. Ten minutes later, with all six crates safely inside the container, they sealed the hatch and headed back to their shuttle. She watched through the side viewport as they maneuvered to the container, wrapped the locking arms around it, then headed out.

She watched until the glow of their drive had disappeared from the small viewport beside the hatch. Then, she retraced her steps back into the main part of the warehouse, heaving a sigh of relief. It had been touch-and-go there, first with the embarrassing foot scuff that had alerted Paco while she was sealing the last crate's hidden compartment, and then with the hastily improvised role she'd had to throw together to play for the pirates.

But it had worked. So far.

And now, in the relative anonymity of the warehouse, she finally pulled out her uni-link and keyed it on. "Owl One to Owl," she said tersely. "Owlets have left the nest. Mouse hunt is on; repeat, mouse hunt is on."

"Mouse hunt, copy," the woman on the other end said, just as tersely.

"I'll be there in fifteen," the woman said, peeling off her jumpsuit with one hand to reveal the innocuous civilian clothing beneath it. "Out."

Two minutes later, she was in the lift heading for her shuttle. The Solway authorities would be highly displeased if they knew she was here, and even angrier if they knew she and her colleagues were about to dig into the kickback structure that had served them so well with so many pirates, marauders, and under-the-radar mercs over the years.

But she wasn't worried. The Republic of Haven Navy didn't answer to anyone on Solway. SCAFE, the 303rd Special Commando Assault Force, Expeditionary answered to only one person.

And the Red Hands were going down today. Major Elsie Dorrman, hand-picked for this job by Brigadier Jean Massingill herself, was absolutely damn sure of that.

☆   ☆   ☆

It took the RHNS *Terrier* almost two hours after making it past Solway's hyper limit and into the Alpha band to find *Bloodlust*.

"Finally," Ambassador-at-large Louis Joffre said from behind Massingill's station when CIC finally confirmed that the ship in the distance was indeed their target pirate vessel. "I was afraid they'd gotten away."

"There was never any chance of that," Massingill assured him, keeping her own relief out of her voice. Elsie Dorrman was adept at everything having to do with cargoes, pirates, and bureaucracies, and Lieutenant Bastonge's forty-man platoon was one of the best teams in the 303rd, but in any military operation there was the chance that something would go horribly wrong.

In this case, that clearly hadn't happened. *Bloodlust* was sitting quietly in the middle of nowhere, her wedge down, her nodes cold. With a couple of nodes out of commission, and her hyperdrive having presumably succumbed to Bastonge's doorbuster—

The com pinged. "Owl Two to Owl," Bastonge's voice came from the speaker. "Mouse is trapped. Repeat: mouse is trapped."

—and with *Bloodlust*'s com system successfully tapped into, the 303rd was officially in the catbird seat.

Massingill smiled, her first genuine smile since the team arrived in Solway space six days ago. "Owl copy," she said. "Stand by."

"So that's it?" Joffre asked. "It's over?"

"It's about to be," Massingill assured him. "Com?"

The com officer nodded. "Ready, Ma'am."

Massingill adjusted her uniform collar with one hand and tapped the mic switch with the other. "Pirate ship *Bloodlust*, this is Brigadier Jean Massingill aboard the Republic of Haven Fast-Transport Ship *Terrier*. I'm the commander of the men who have infiltrated your ship and disabled your impellers and hyperdrive." She considered. "Actually, considering the firepower my commandos brought aboard, your hyperdrive probably isn't so much disabled as it is a collection of charred metal shavings on the deck."

She paused, waiting for the usual outrage and denials. But the *Bloodlust*'s captain had apparently decided to skip that page.

"So here's the deal," she continued. "You'll immediately shut down your reactor, just to make sure nobody tries anything rash. Then you'll gather your crew in your impeller rooms and prepare to receive boarders. *More* boarders, I should say."

"This is Captain Blaine of the *Cornucopia*," a dark voice came. Apparently, he'd finally found the standard script. "I don't know who you think you are, *Terrier*, but the Solway Enforcers are *not* going to be happy at this flagrant abuse of their jurisdictional authority. In point of fact, it is *you* who are committing piracy—"

Massingill let him finish his rant. Sometimes they believed their protests meant something. Usually they just wanted to get it on someone's record.

Eventually, he ran dry. "I appreciate your legal and ethical concerns," she said. "Let me point out the concerns you *should* be thinking about. With no impellers, you're not going anywhere. With no hyperdrive, you're stuck in the Alpha band while not going anywhere. Basically, you're not going anywhere. Not before you run out of air or starve."

She paused, waiting for more protests. But they didn't come.

Not really surprising. By now Blaine would be fully aware of the damage his ship had sustained, and knew that if *Terrier* took off he and everyone aboard was dead.

"So here's the deal," Massingill said. "You can die, or you can surrender and let us take you in tow to Haven."

"What about your men?" Blaine bit out, pulling out his final card. "You going to leave them to die, too?"

"Oh, I'm sure they've already picked out which shuttle they'll be leaving in," Massingill said. "None of that will change your own end game. You surrender, or you die, and either way, the Red Hands' piracy stops forever."

"And if we accede to your outrageous demands?"

"Your piracy still stops," Massingill said. "But you'll still be alive."

"At least until the show trial has concluded?"

"There may not be a trial," Massingill said. "There are always pretrial interrogations, and often pretrial deals to be made. In particular, we're very interested in the details about your work with three other groups who've been working the Beowulf-Haven trade route."

"I have no idea what you're talking about."

"Oh, I'm sure it'll come to you," Massingill said. "I hope so, anyway. Because if you can't tell us anything, there'll be nothing to do but move on to that show trial you mentioned." She touched a switch on her board. "I'm launching my shuttles now. I suggest you prepare to receive them. Peaceably, of course."

"Of course," the captain said bitterly. "What other choice do we have?"

"Dying before dinner time," Massingill said pointedly. "Good day, Captain. I'll look forward to meeting you in person soon. Massingill out."

She keyed the switch and turned to face Joffre. "*Now* it's over," she told him.

"Good," Joffre said, puffing out a sigh of relief. "Though he's right on one point. We could still be in trouble if Solway Enforcement catches us."

"They won't," Massingill assured him, suppressing the impulse to roll her eyes. Back on Haven she'd argued long and hard against Joffre's presence aboard her ship. Given that there was no way the local authorities could tumble to her team's presence in the system, let alone catch them in the act of nailing the Red Hands' main ship, there was no reason to saddle her with a diplomat.

But the upper brass—more likely the politicians above them—hadn't seen it that way. They'd insisted that Joffre come along as an official Havenite representative, just in case Massingill troubled any waters that needed to be soothed.

A complete waste of time, as it turned out, most of that time Joffre's. But the man had been decent enough company on the voyage, and he mostly reserved his questions for when Massingill wasn't in the middle of something important.

Still, having a politician tag along on a purely military mission wasn't a precedent she particularly liked. Hopefully, once the analysts in NavInt finished sorting through the leads, and the 303rd had stomped all the pirates and pirate bases they were able to locate, the political aspect would be filed away and forgotten.

"I hope not," Joffre said. "As long as we have a moment, may I ask you a question?"

Again, Massingill managed not to roll her eyes. "Of course."

"I believe I heard somewhere that you grew up on Manticore," Joffre said. "I was wondering—"

"Actually, my husband and I grew up on Earth,"

Massingill said. "We were recruited by Manticore twenty-five T-years ago, then emigrated to Haven ten T-years ago. That should all be in my file."

"Ah," Joffre said. "My apologies. That will teach me to read past the summary page. I was just wondering what you thought about the Star Kingdom's recent one-two punch."

Massingill turned away from him, not wanting to trust herself to hold a neutral expression. The sudden, violent attack on Manticore, followed by the equally sudden and violent deaths of King Edward and Crown Princess Sophie. The news had arrived at Solway a few weeks before the *Terrier*'s arrival, and there was still a sort of distant numbness in Massingill's brain whenever she thought about it.

She had also spent a fair amount of that time planning how she would present a recommendation to her superiors that the Republic reach out to the Star Kingdom. She wasn't sure what form that assistance should take: military aid, investigative aid, or heightened patrols in that area.

But it was going to be tricky. Nouveau Paris didn't like sticking its nose into other nations' affairs, nor did it like overstretching its resources, and any flavor of aid to Manticore could be perceived as both. The message to Solway had included few details, but Massingill could read between the lines and it was painfully clear that if Tamerlane had enough of a reserve force for a second attack, there would be virtually nothing Manticore could do to stop it.

"I think the Manticorans are a lot tougher than anyone realizes," she told Joffre. "I'm also confident that the government will be able to come together and work through whatever Constitutional issues the death of the King and the Heir Apparent have created."

"Yes," Joffe murmured. "There's an old saying about that. Something about a ship and a raft, but I don't remember the details."

"'A monarchy is a merchantman which sails well, but will sometimes strike on a rock, and go to the bottom,'" Massingill quoted. "'A republic is a raft which will never sink, but then your feet are always in the water.' I don't remember the source."

"I'm impressed," Joffe said. "I really am. I had no idea you were a scholar."

"I'm not," Massingill said. "Alvis ran into that quote when we were first considering emigrating to Manticore. I know they're not the only monarchy out here, but it was still a bit of a concern for us. But they seem to have it under control."

"Well, let's hope they haven't struck a rock on this one," Joffe said. "They've been decent allies and friends over the years. I don't necessarily agree with their system of government, but I'd hate to see it collapse."

"Agreed." Massingill raised her eyebrows. "Perhaps you'd be willing to put that sentiment into action."

"What sort of action?" he countered, his expression shifting into the genial mask of a man who knows he's about to be asked for a favor.

"Nothing drastic," Massingill assured him. "I know you have a number of high-level contacts in the government. I thought you might be willing to suggest to them that Haven and Manticore work together on whatever follow-up investigation or action is required."

"Meaning you want Nouveau Paris to commit ships to Manticore's defense?"

"It wouldn't take much of a force," Massingill said. "And it wouldn't be for very long. Manticore has a strong industrial base, and I'm guessing they'll be able to repair the damaged ships within a few months. I imagine they're also pulling their mothballed vessels back to active duty as quickly as possible."

"Mm." Joffre pondered a moment. "That assumes the Manticorans would be willing to allow a group of foreign warships in orbit over their capital. They might not; and if they weren't, our ships would have made a long trip for nothing."

Massingill felt her lip twist. But he was right. She'd known Admiral Locatelli back in the day, and First Lord Cazenestro had always seemed like a reasonable sort. But the final decision on these things rested with the monarch, and the brand-new Queen Elizabeth was a complete unknown. "You're right," she conceded. "I suppose we have to wait for them to ask."

"That's generally best," Joffre said. "Unfortunately, the time delay means that, even if they asked tomorrow, we couldn't get them any help for nearly a year. Which is, of course, precisely the timeframe when they would most likely need us."

"True," Massingill said reluctantly. "I'm just hoping Nouveau Paris sent something as soon as they learned of the attack—if Manticore sent word to Solway they surely sent word to Haven. My fear is that they're still dithering about it."

"I realize politics can be frustrating," Joffre said. "But knee-jerk reactions without proper consideration can be just as catastrophic. I note that when we pinpointed Solway as one of the Red Hands' transfer points you didn't just load up and charge into battle.

You paused to think and plan and reconnoiter before you made your move." He gestured toward the display. "And we see how all that prep work paid off."

"I suppose," Massingill said. "Not quite the same as loading a few ships we don't need for our own defense and sending them to aid a friend."

"Ah—but what if we *did* need them for our defense?" Joffre countered. "What if the people who hit Manticore are a new Brotherhood sort of group? In that case, sending a pair of our battlecruisers away might just make the difference between victory and annihilation."

Massingill scowled. Far-fetched to an extreme . . . but far-fetched didn't necessarily mean wrong.

And he was right. The Republic of Haven Navy's first responsibility was to defend the Republic of Haven. If push came to shove, Manticore was on its own.

"But I'll give you this much," Joffre continued. "If and when Manticore requests aid, of whatever sort, I'll make sure that request is given Nouveau Paris's full attention. If we can assist without endangering our own people, I'll push hard to make it so. Fair enough?"

"Fair enough," Massingill said. The words were relatively meaningless, of course, given the uncertainties of who and what Manticore was up against. But at this point words were all she was going to get.

Maybe later the situation would change. If so, she would be ready to remind Joffre about this conversation.

"Brigadier?" the com officer spoke up. "Sergeant Cochran reports his shuttle has docked. Sergeant Gnoli is about two minutes behind them; both leaders prepping for simultaneous boarding."

Massingill took a deep breath. Time to get her

mind back into this particular game. "Inform Lieutenant Bastonge," she ordered. "He may want to move out while the Red Hands have their attention split. Especially since letting them see what's left of their hyperdrive might help them make up their minds."

"Yes, Ma'am."

"And warn the boarding parties to be careful," she added unnecessarily. "The pirates could still decide to be stupid today."

CHAPTER FOURTEEN

PRIME MINISTER BURGUNDY AND CHANCELLOR OF the
Exchequer Breakwater were waiting when Elizabeth
arrived in the Palace conference room. The two men,
standing on opposite sides of the long table, turned in
unison as the door opened, bowing at the Sovereign's
approach.

"Your Majesty," Burgundy greeted her for both of
them.

"Your Grace; My Lord," Elizabeth greeted them in
return, wondering uneasily what was going on. After
the last chaotic two T-months, at least she no longer
felt as if she'd fallen into a drug-induced dream—or
nightmare—whenever someone called her *Majesty*.

The job that went with the title, though, was a
different matter entirely, and she especially hated
walking into a situation cold. All Burgundy had said
in this case was that Breakwater wanted to talk about
some matters that were about to be brought before
the Lords and to give her advance notice.

That alone wasn't particularly worrisome. Breakwater

was one of several Cabinet ministers who liked to get the Queen's input or approval on a given piece of legislation before bringing it into the public eye. Elizabeth had wondered about that until Burgundy suggested that it was all part of the process of getting a feel for Manticore's new queen. The same ministers had done the same to Edward when he ascended the Throne, he told her, and assured her the private audience requests would eventually fade away.

What concerned her was the fact that Burgundy had insisted on accompanying the Chancellor on this one. That automatically raised it above the usual testing-the-water meetings that she'd become used to.

Elizabeth had always known that politics was a complex and arcane profession. She'd just never realized how deeply nuanced it was.

Getting thrown headfirst into the deep end of the pool hadn't helped, either. Edward had been careful to keep Richard up to speed on matters of state, and in the brief time that Sophie had been Crown Princess he'd started the same process with her.

No one had ever thought Elizabeth might need those briefings, including Elizabeth herself. That, among many other things, would have to change.

But she had a few months under her belt now, and was finally starting to get the hang of this. Hopefully, whatever Breakwater was about to pitch would be something she already knew how to handle.

"We appreciate your seeing us on such short notice," Burgundy continued as Elizabeth seated herself at the head of the table. Once she was settled, he also sat down, taking the seat one chair down the table to her right, where he would be close enough for easy conversation but not so close that he was encroaching on her personal space. Breakwater, probably following the same logic, took the seat opposite him. "As I mentioned earlier, Earl Breakwater has two matters he wished to bring to your attention."

"Understood." Elizabeth focused on Breakwater. "Go ahead, My Lord."

"Thank you, Your Majesty," Breakwater said gravely. "Let me be brief. Regarding the first matter, I wanted you to know that some of the Lords will be proposing a resolution tomorrow calling for the official censure of Commodore Rudolph Heissman for his failure to properly protect Crown Prince Richard during the Battle of Manticore."

Elizabeth flashed a glance at Burgundy. The prime minister's jaw was set, his face wooden.

"That's very interesting, My Lord," she said to Breakwater. "Particularly since the Navy has already cleared him of any wrongdoing in that matter."

"The Navy naturally has their own agenda," Breakwater said. "And yes, I've heard their argument that there was no time for Prince Richard's ship to decelerate and escape before the attackers arrived." He lifted a finger. "But there *was* time to order the same split-tail maneuver that Heissman eventually ordered for all of his remaining ships. If *Hercules* had done that as soon as Heissman knew the size of Tamerlane's force, it would have been well out of missile range by the time the force arrived."

"And it would have cost Heissman the use of one of his ships for that battle," Burgundy pointed out.

"Which may or may not have made a difference," Breakwater said. "Ultimately, it was *Casey*'s actions alone that made the difference in that particular action."

"There was no way for Heissman to know that would be the case," Elizabeth pointed out. "His job—*and* Richard's—was to put themselves in harm's way for the sake of the Star Kingdom."

"Perhaps," Breakwater said. "At any rate, Your Majesty, the point is that I wanted you to know about the resolution in advance so that the...reminder...of your nephew's demise wouldn't come as a surprise."

"I appreciate your concern, My Lord," Elizabeth said, letting just a hint of sarcasm color her otherwise very proper Official Tone. Breakwater could talk all he wanted about how *some* of the Lords would be bringing up this matter, as if his own heart was innocent and his hands pure as the drifting snow. But she knew better, and from the expression on Burgundy's face it was clear that he did, too. Breakwater was a power broker, and an ambitious one, and his fingerprints were all over this.

As to how she would handle it...well, that was going to take some extra study. "You said there were *two* matters?"

"Yes, Your Majesty," Breakwater said. Out of the corner of her eye, Elizabeth saw Burgundy's expression go even tighter. "This one's a little more...delicate, shall we say?"

"Get on with it," Burgundy growled, and Breakwater inclined his head.

"Very well. As you may know, Your Majesty, the Constitution requires the Sovereign to be married to a commoner. At this point, your marital status does not conform—"

"Excuse me, My Lord," Elizabeth cut him off, her stomach suddenly tightening. "If you're suggesting what I think you're suggesting, you'd best tread *very* lightly."

Breakwater spread his hands.

"I make no suggestions of my own, Your Majesty," he protested. "I merely point out what others are already whispering: that their Sovereign is out of compliance with the Constitution. I'm sure you don't want to add any further uncertainties to an already uncertain time..."

He continued on. But Elizabeth could no longer hear him. All she could hear was Carmichael's voice, her eyes filling with his face, her skin tingling with his touch. His smile... his frown... his voice... his laughter...

"We're done here," she said abruptly.

She had the vague sense that Breakwater was in the middle of a sentence. She didn't care.

"You will leave now," she said, hearing the quavering in her voice and not caring about that either. "Both of you."

She was vaguely aware of Burgundy saying the usual farewells, and then of the two of them standing up and passing on either side behind her toward the door.

She saw none of it. Her head throbbed with a kaleidoscope of her life with Carmichael. The love, the comfort, the tears, the horror of his death...

Slowly, the memories ebbed, gradually and reluctantly like a receding tide, back into the recesses of her mind. She'd thought she'd done such a good job of burying those images away in the four and a half T-years since he was snatched so suddenly away from her.

And yet, all it had taken to bring them flooding back was a single gut-wrenching comment.

She swore, softly, feelingly. When she'd ascended

the Throne, as custom dictated, the entire Cabinet had submitted their resignations. At Burgundy's suggestion she'd reinstated all of them, with the goal of maintaining as much continuity as possible in the political arena until the shock of Edward's death had time to settle.

Breakwater had been among the reinstated group. Now, she was wishing she'd kicked him the hell out.

Theoretically, it still wasn't too late to do that. She could call Burgundy back right now and ask him to form a new government without Breakwater.

In practice, unfortunately, it wouldn't be that easy. Breakwater had a large following among the Lords, and throwing him out without cause would not sit well with them. They weren't a majority, as near as she'd been able to calculate, but they might have enough swing to force a no-confidence vote and bring down any government Burgundy tried to form without their leader. With the Star Kingdom's citizens still twitchy from the events of the past few months, that would probably cause more harm than good.

Besides which, Breakwater was a good Chancellor. Everyone, supporter and opponent alike, agreed on that. He managed the Star Kingdom's money in a quiet, efficient, and exemplary way.

And really, up to now he'd mostly behaved himself. There'd been a few critical speeches, most of them centered around the kinks still being worked out in his new MPARS training center. But even the speeches had been reasonably mild in tone, more informative than incendiary. For the past couple of months Elizabeth had almost forgotten that she needed to be on her toes around him.

All that had now changed. Because just like the Heissman resolution, this suggestion of noncompliance clearly wasn't coming from others in the Lords. This was being created, nurtured, and driven by Breakwater himself. With a single back-stabbing gut punch, Breakwater had ended whatever truce had existed.

Mentally, she shook her head. *Back-stabbing gut punch*. She really needed to work on her metaphors. Even the ones that never saw the light of day.

Slowly, she got to her feet and turned around. Adler and Penescu, her two bodyguards, stood silently on either side of the doorway, waiting patiently for their Sovereign to either go elsewhere or give them new orders. Despite her own proximity to the throne, she'd never had to deal with the all-pervasive—and highly intrusive—security which surrounded the Queen of Manticore every minute of her life. That was yet another thing she hated about this job.

They'd heard every word, of course. Distantly, she wondered what they thought about her reaction.

"Well, that was interesting," she said. She wasn't sure whether the Queen should exchange idle conversation with her guards, but she'd started out that way from the beginning and saw no reason to change. "Back to the office."

The guards exchanged glances.

"Your office, Your Majesty?" Penescu asked.

"Yes," Elizabeth said, frowning at him. "Why, is there a problem?"

Another set of glances.

"Prime Minister Burgundy indicated that he'd wait in the library," Adler said, her forehead creased slightly. "He said you'd want to see him."

Elizabeth pursed her lips. Technically, inviting himself to a conversation with his Queen—as opposed to asking for an audience—was seriously overstepping the privilege of both rank and position.

But now that Adler mentioned it, she rather wanted to see Burgundy, too. At least for long enough to ask if he'd known in advance about Breakwater's bombshell.

"Well, then," she said. "Let's not keep him waiting."

There were several comfortable chairs and sofas in the Palace library. She found Burgundy seated in the one that faced the wall-mounted Royal Seal.

Seated across from him, directly under the seal, was former King Michael.

Elizabeth hadn't seen much of her father for the past two weeks, though he and Elizabeth's mother Mary had visited almost daily during the first month after the accident. Occasionally, Edward's widow Cynthia had joined them as well, as the broken remnants of the family talked and mourned together.

But Cynthia had now gone back to her own family, and Michael and Mary had sequestered themselves in the Tower—*in seclusion*, the official notices called it. Part of that, Michael had explained to Elizabeth, was the need for private mourning, while part was to avoid distracting the nation from its new sovereign by allowing images of its former one wandering the Palace to get out.

Though that might no longer be the problem he thought it was. Michael had aged a great deal since the accident, to the point where a casual observer might fail to recognize him at all, certainly not at first glance.

But while his face was more lined and his hair had gone thin, his eyes were as bright and alert as ever.

"I take it there was more, Your Grace?" Elizabeth asked as she walked into the room.

"Your Majesty," he said, scrambling to his feet and bowing to her. "I'm sorry—I expected you to be longer...No matter. I just wanted to offer my apologies for the...well, for all of it, I suppose. I'm so sorry."

"As well you should be," Elizabeth said, more harshly than she'd intended. "Did you know about this in advance?"

"Easy, Elizabeth," Michael said quietly. "None of this is his fault."

Elizabeth grimaced. He was right.

"I know," she said. "My apologies, Your Grace."

"No apology needed, Your Majesty," Burgundy assured her. "And to answer your question, no, I didn't know." His lip twitched. "At least, not far enough in advance. I did know about his first point, which was why I wished to accompany him in the first place. We were already on our way into the Palace when he told me what his *second* point was going to be. Which," he added, his expression darkening even more, "made me even gladder that I'd come along."

"I see." The emotional tsunami had faded far enough now for Elizabeth's rational mind to start operating again. And the first rational question needed to be— "Does he have a case?"

"I don't know, Your Majesty," Burgundy he admitted. "The Constitution states unambiguously that the heir to the throne must marry a commoner. Unfortunately, whether that means you *have* to marry, or whether it simply means that *if* the heir marries, he or she must marry a commoner, is somewhat less clear. And the language does specifically refer to the *heir* to the throne."

"Well, I'm not the *heir*," Elizabeth said more than a bit bitterly.

"I know, Your Majesty," Burgundy replied gently. "The problem is that the peers Breakwater was referring to are construing the language rather more broadly than I believe it was ever meant to be construed. They're taking the position that the provision is intended to assure that any future monarch has at least one parent from outside the aristocracy. The reason the Constitution requires that the heir must marry a commoner is to bring about that specific end. And, unfortunately, the marriage requirement is combined in the same clause of the Constitution as the requirement that any new monarch must be the *heir of the body* of the previous monarch unless the monarch dies without issue."

"You're saying that that's one interpretation of the Constitution?"

"Yes, Your Majesty." Burgundy inclined his head slightly. "A countervailing interpretation is that although the *heir* is required to marry a commoner in order to ensure that, as the Constitution itself says, 'Crown and Commons are perpetually wed,' extraordinary circumstances, such as your own, aren't actually covered. That's my own opinion of what the drafters intended, as a matter of fact."

"The problem is that the Constitution's still in what you might call its infancy," Michael added. "Or at least its adolescence."

"Exactly," Burgundy said, nodding. "Your brother, King Edward, was actually the first heir to the Throne to marry *anyone* since its ratification. Your grandmother and your father were both already married before the

Constitution was drafted. The truth is that, as yet, no reigning Monarch has ever married, so that means we're in what the lawyers like to call 'a gray area,' and there are likely to be plenty of people wanting to push constitutional interpretation *their* way, for a whole range of reasons. We're already seeing plenty of debate over 'strict constructionism' and 'living document' reinterpretation to suit points people think weren't adequately covered or in which circumstances may have changed."

Elizabeth looked at her father.

"My reading is the same," Michael said, nodding. "We can call in a legal scholar to get something more definitive, but I'm betting we'll get conflicting views. Of course, neither Davis nor I are constitutional lawyers, but we *were* both there when it was written. I'm afraid I wasn't paying as much attention to it as he was, and I *should* have been, since it was going to have such an impact on our family. My own memory is that Davis is right, but he's also right that God knows a profitable business has grown up already around interpreting constitutional law. Frankly, I'm strongly in favor of supporting the 'strict constructionist' school."

"As were your grandmother and your great-grandfather," Burgundy said. "They were damned insistent that if the Constitutional Convention was going to fundamentally rewrite the way we governed ourselves, then the rules it set forth had to *be* the rules, not something we decided to change any time they got a little inconvenient."

"Exactly," Michael agreed. "I remember Mom—your grandmother—saying that the very best thing we could do as a family and as future monarchs was to put as much grit into the system as we could because, more than anything else, it was going to be our job to maintain stability. Having said that, though, we probably do need to start looking into current expert opinion on it."

"That won't be necessary," Elizabeth said. "Because I'm not going to marry again. Not yet. *Absolutely* not simply because someone else tells me to."

"Understood, Eli—" Burgundy glanced at the guards at the door. "Your Majesty," he corrected himself.

Elizabeth felt her throat tighten. Even a man old enough to be her grandfather, a man who'd watched her grow up, and who'd held her hand through this whole horrific crisis, now couldn't bend enough to be her friend instead of her subject.

Edward had sometimes talked about how lonely the Monarch could be. Elizabeth had usually dismissed such comments as over-dramatic grumbling. Little had she known.

"More concerning to me," Michael said, "is the question he *didn't* bring up. Namely, what happens with the line of succession?"

Elizabeth stared at him. She'd been so preoccupied with Breakwater's marriage thing that the succession hadn't even occurred to her.

"Your father's right," Burgundy agreed soberly. "Your three stepchildren aren't eligible—they're not your biological offspring and the Constitution definitely *does* specify that the crown can pass only to the heirs of your great-grandfather King Roger. With Richard, Sophie, *and* Edward gone—" He shook his head. "We may be on the edge of more than just a constitutional crisis here, Your Majesty. We could conceivably lose the whole Winton line." He lifted his hands, palms upward. "And *then* what?"

"Unless I remarry," Elizabeth murmured.

"Unless you remarry."

"Or find another solution," Michael said.

Abruptly, Elizabeth noticed that she and Burgundy were both still standing.

"We need to discuss this further," she said, gesturing the Prime Minister back to his chair. "Do you have time now?"

"I always have time for my Queen, Your Majesty," he said.

"I think my schedule's clear, too," Michael added dryly.

Unbidden, a smile touched Elizabeth's lips. Even unnaturally aged with grief, her father had the ability to lighten her mood.

"Thank you," she said. "Thank you both." She walked over to her father's couch and sat down beside him. "Let's start by pulling up a copy of the Constitution. After that, we'll want a sampling of relevant commentary for the past sixty T-years."

"And perhaps speak—privately—with the handful of writers, like Davis, who are still around," Michael said.

"Yes, excellent point," Elizabeth agreed. "We need to know what the document says, what the writers *meant* it to say—" She smiled briefly at the two men, but the smile faded quickly "—and what the experts *think* it says."

CHAPTER FIFTEEN

GENERAL HAUS HADN'T BEEN HAPPY THAT neither Llyn nor any of the others of his team would be going to Barca with them. But he'd accepted the second payment with mostly good grace and headed back to the Grand Duke with the goodies.

Now it was time to head over to Telmach and see how many of Gensonne's people were still breathing.

Of course, given the number of battlecruisers the damned Manticorans still had, the entire Volsung force could still be alive. If Gensonne had realized his pre-battle intelligence was off and had run for it without firing a single shot, none of them would have gotten so much as a scratch.

But if there *had* been a fight, especially given the Manticorans' obviously minimal losses, he could have gotten hammered pretty damned badly. And if that had happened, it was unlikely he'd blame anything but his faulty intelligence for it. Given that, and given Gensonne's reputation and temper, a slower, more careful approach was called for.

"Sir, we've received a transmission from Posnan Customs," Katura reported. "A stock-sounding welcome to their system and a list of the services they offer."

"Along with the associated prices, I see," Llyn said dryly, running an eye down the list.

In his limited experience with the Silesian Confederacy, the main sport was attempting to gouge everyone in sight, on every good and service imaginable.

Not that there was much of either in a backwoods place like this. Still, what *was* available was definitely being overcharged for.

Unfortunately, they had a monopoly. If you didn't want to pay their prices, you had to go elsewhere... assuming you had the range to do that.

"Nice to see Silesia maintaining its new-frontier charm," he continued. "Go ahead and transmit our greetings and compliments, Captain, and put in an order for a complete refueling when we reach the station."

"Sir, we don't have to do this," Katura protested. "We have more than enough fuel."

"I know," Llyn said. "But if the Manticorans pounded hard enough on Gensonne, he might have stopped on his way back to Telmach, or to wherever his real shipyard is. Posnan, Silesia, and Saginaw are his three most likely choices and we just happen to have an asset on the Obrączka refueling station."

"Really?" Katura asked, clearly surprised. "I didn't know we had anyone here."

"He's mostly an independent stringer, but he's always been reliable. He gets a cut on purchases we make at his station, and whenever he refuels one of our ships we let him add five percent to the invoice without squawking."

"I assume no one in Accounting ever sees that five percent?"

"Exactly," Llyn said. "We don't have the same arrangement in Silesia and Saginaw, which is why I sent Vaagen and Rhamas to poke around there. *Banshee* and *Shrike* are better equipped for poking around on their own than we are."

"I see, Sir," Katura said. He seemed a bit surprised by the depth of the explanation—Axelrod operatives weren't in the habit of sharing need-to-know information. But he'd been so clearly unhappy with the decision to detach *Banshee* and *Shrike* that Llyn had decided he deserved a bit more background.

Still, Llyn couldn't argue the point that splitting an already small force was never a good idea.

"I still don't know why Gensonne would bother to stop off here," Katura said. His tone was less unhappy than it had been, but he clearly remained far from completely mollified by Llyn's explanation. "If he made it this far, he could certainly make it the rest of the way to Telmach."

"Unless he expected the Manticorans to be on his tail," Llyn pointed out. "In that case, he might stop by one of these other systems to make a few large purchases and try to throw off any pursuit."

"You think he's that clever?"

"Not really," Llyn conceded. "But he could have gotten himself killed in the battle and left someone smarter in charge. Regardless, it's worth checking out."

There was a barely-heard sigh.

"Yes, Sir."

Llyn smiled. Katura was a good pilot, and a highly competent associate. It had been totally the luck of the draw that he'd been available when Llyn needed a crew after stealing that courier ship on Casca.

But then, luck had always been one of Llyn's best assets.

Some black ops agents, Llyn new, believed themselves to be infallible and had no patience for anyone else's ideas or suggestions. But Llyn had seen that kind of hubris backfire too many times. Encouraging Katura's questions and input meant another set of eyes and an additional brain on tap, and that was almost always a good thing.

At least until the operation commenced. At that point, Llyn required instant, unquestioning obedience.

He hadn't had a chance yet to test Katura and his crew under fire. But that moment would come.

"Sir?" Katura's voice came again, breaking into his thoughts. "Take a look at the tactical."

Llyn swiveled around to that display. It took him a moment to spot the flashing icon the captain had highlighted, just over three light-minutes distant from *Pacemaker*.

"I see it," he said. "What about it?"

"It just changed vector, Sir," Katura said. "It *was* headed for Piec. Now, it's not."

Llyn frowned as he considered the data codes beside the icon. The transponder beacon identified it as an Andermani freighter, the *Hamman*, and its current acceleration was a comfortably conservative eighty gravities. Three light-minutes was closer proximity than one might normally expect here in Posnan, but that was only because traffic was so sparse. It wasn't so much a matter of their finding themselves in close physical proximity as it was the oddity of two ships arriving at such a backwater system so close to simultaneously.

The Posnan System was unusual among inhabited star systems in several ways. The most striking was that it contained not one but two gas giants inside its 18.92-light-minute hyper-limit. The outer of the two was Obrączka, *Pacemaker*'s destination. Piec, the inner giant, was just outside the relatively cool G7 primary's habitable zone, but the planet itself was hot enough—the name meant "Furnace"—to bring the surface temperatures of its moons up to near-terrestrial levels. Two of them, Kuźna and Palenisko—"Forge" and "Hearth"—were both massive enough to generate atmospheres, hydrospheres, and respectable gravities and warm enough to support life. Both were tide-locked to Piec, though, and their short day-night cycles took some getting used to. They were the only habitable real estate in the system, so it wasn't surprising that the ship Katura had highlighted had been headed there.

Obviously, the other vessel's hyper astrogation hadn't been perfect. It seldom was, really, especially over lengthy distances. Astrogators tried to hit as close as possible to a least-time course to destinations inside a star's hyper-limit, but it wasn't uncommon to emerge from hyper as much as two or even three light-minutes from one's intended alpha translation. Katura was one of the better astrogators Llyn had worked with, and even so, *Pacemaker* had emerged from hyper a good twenty light-seconds from his intended locus. At the moment, Piec and Obrączka were approaching conjunction, both on the same side of the primary with Piec's smaller orbital radius catching up on Obrączka from behind. It would be some months yet before they aligned perfectly, but it wasn't too surprising that ships heading for either of them should emerge from hyper in fairly close proximity.

Except that if Katura was right, the Andermani had just changed course.

"She not only changed heading, Sir, but she also just brought up her wedge to do it," Katura continued. "I ran back the record, and it turns out she shut down her impellers for about thirty-nine minutes before she brought her wedge back up and changed course."

Llyn looked at the time cut on *Hamman*'s vector change. The freighter's impeller signature had indeed disappeared from *Pacemaker*'s tracking systems at the time Katura had specified.

Perhaps more ominously, that had been just over two and a half minutes after *Hamman* could have detected and read *Pacemaker*'s transponder.

"Maybe it's a technical problem," he suggested. "Obrączka is closer than Piec if she's got problems."

"I don't think so, Sir," Katura said. "To reach her current point, assuming she's held constant acceleration since crossing the limit, she would have been in-system for over an hour before we arrived, and she was only about six and a half hours from Piec. She can cut about three hours off that by making for Obrączka, but if she had some sort of engineering problem and it was severe enough to make it necessary for her to change course to save that short an amount of time, she ought to be broadcasting a distress signal. Only she isn't."

Llyn gazed at the display, an unpleasant feeling creeping up his back. The timing here was suspicious, to say the least. Of course, there were always two or three possible explanations for anything.

Still, he'd learned over the years to trust his instincts, and Katura seemed to have excellent instincts of his own. If the captain didn't like this . . .

"Sir, she's changing vector again," Katura said.

"I see it," Llyn said, feeling his eyes narrow. The freighter had executed a slight yaw turn, adding another small sideways component to its original Piec-bound vector. "Get me a new projection."

"Working on it, Sir, but that yaw was so slight... here we go...hell."

"Indeed," Llyn agreed, the unpleasant creeping feeling on his back breaking into a full gallop.

Two vectors extended themselves across the display. One was *Pacemaker*'s, headed for orbital insertion around Obrączka. The other was *Hamman*'s, which was now headed *toward* Obrączka but not directly *to* Obrączka. Instead, its new course would intersect *Pacemaker*'s just over seven million kilometers short of the planet.

And if both ships maintained current profiles, their velocities toward the planet would match almost exactly when *Hamman* crossed *Pacemaker*'s track at a range of less than half a million kilometers. *Hamman* would be on a heading slightly away from Obrączka at a fairly shallow angle, but her crossing velocity when she intersected *Pacemaker*'s course would be less than two hundred kilometers per second.

The freighter was hunting *Pacemaker*.

She was being subtle about it, with a small enough deviation from a direct course to Obrączka that System Patrol probably wouldn't notice and wonder what she was up to. Or, for that matter, small enough to be plausibly explained if System Patrol *did* ask what she was doing.

But she *was* hunting *Pacemaker*.

Llyn shifted his eyes to the status board. *Pacemaker* was still running the Barcan beacon they'd used back at Manticore, mainly because they had it and there was no reason to put together a new throwaway ID.

So who the hell out here would want to bother a nondescript Barcan courier ship?

And then, abruptly, he got it.

"You think it's a pirate?" Katura suggested.

"It's not a pirate, Captain," Llyn said grimly. "I wish to hell it was.

"It's Gensonne."

☆   ☆   ☆

"*Gensonne?*" Katura repeated disbelievingly. "What's he doing on a freighter?"

"I seriously doubt that's *just* a freighter," Llyn ground out, thinking hard.

"But why would he be running an Andermani ID?"

"You know anyone around here who'd mess with an Andermani?" Llyn countered. "Makes for great camouflage. Especially since the conventional wisdom is that Andermani freighters are routinely armed."

Katura grunted. "Terrific."

"I wouldn't worry too much about it," Llyn said, more confidently than he actually felt. "By the time they cross our course, they'll be too close to Obrączka for them to try anything blatant."

"Unless System Patrol doesn't want to mess with them, either."

"System Patrol knows its job better than that," Llyn said, frowning at the tactical display while he tried to get inside Gensonne's head.

As he'd pointed out to Katura, they'd be within little more than half a light-minute of Obrączka—basically shouting range—by the time their courses intersected. Unfortunately, shouting range wasn't remotely the same as *shooting* range. Given their new vectors, the freighter would pass within seven million kilometers of the planet before her current heading took her back out across the hyper-limit at a fairly shallow angle, so even if there were System Patrol units in Obrączka orbit, they'd be millions of kilometers outside missile range of the intercept point. Even if they were inclined to intervene, they wouldn't be able to unless they got underway in the next forty-five minutes or so.

Worse, to get to that range in time to do anything about it they'd have to pile up so much delta-V that they'd go right past *Pacemaker* and *Hamman* on opposing vectors with a closing rate of over eleven thousand KPS, which would take them through their entire engagement envelope in barely forty-five seconds. Unless they had enough cause to simply blow the freighter out of space as they passed, there was no way they could stay in engagement range long enough to do any good or, for that matter, even overtake *Hamman* before her vector took her back across the hyper-limit and safely out of both their range and their jurisdiction.

Pacemaker, on the other hand, was headed directly into the system, and she'd built too much velocity to simply stop and go back the way she'd come. She was still forty minutes short of her own turnover point for a zero-zero orbital insertion at her destination, but if *Hamman* was serious about intercepting her—and willing to be more obvious about it—she could change course enough to catch *Pacemaker* closer to the courier boat's turnover point, before she was able to generate much velocity back towards the limit. The crossing rate would be higher, but *Hamman* could do it.

And if she had any appreciable acceleration left in

reserve, she could do it even sooner . . . or at a lower crossing rate, which would leave her within theoretical missile range longer.

"All right," Llyn said slowly. "If we maintain profile and he holds his current acceleration, he'll get within four hundred and fifty thousand kilometers of us at closest approach. Correct?"

"Yes, Sir."

"So what happens if we *don't* make turnover? If we just keep accelerating straight in-system past him?"

"Depends on whether or not he really is a freighter," Katura said. "If eighty gravities is his maximum safe acceleration, then his maximum acceleration with a zero margin on his compensator is only a hundred. But from his wedge strength and his current acceleration, it looks like he's probably somewhere around a million to one-point-five million tons. If he is, and if he's got a military-grade compensator, he could conceivably hit twice that. He could come within twenty or thirty gravities of us, anyway."

"And that means?"

"That means he could add velocity a lot faster than a freighter could, and at the moment, he's got the base velocity advantage. He'll still have it when we hit our turnover point, too. If he can hit within . . . call it twenty-eight gravities of our acceleration, he can still catch us by simply delaying his own turnover point."

"And we make turnover *before* he does," Llyn said, wincing.

"Exactly. He'd have time to adjust if we didn't."

Llyn stroked his lip thoughtfully. On the other hand, if they continued to accelerate and *Hamman* adjusted to intercept them short of Obrączka, Gensonne would be forced to break profile as an innocent freighter. At the moment, he *could* be headed for Obrączka. His astrogation would be a little off, but he'd have plenty of time to correct it and no one would be worrying about it yet.

For that matter, even when he crossed *Pacemaker*'s projected track, his velocity away from Obrączka would be so low that it would add only about ninety-five minutes to an orbital rendezvous with the planet. But if he altered that profile in obvious response to *Pacemaker*'s maneuvers, he'd risk inspiring suspicion in any System Patrol unit in Obrączka's vicinity soon enough it might actually be able to intervene after all.

Still, Gensonne or not, it had to be a commercial hull. It was headed for Piec, which meant it was headed towards System Patrol. Surely they wouldn't take kindly to a warship falsely identifying itself as a freighter, and a warship couldn't pretend to be anything else once it got into visual observation range. So whatever it was, at least it wasn't a cruiser or a destroyer.

Unfortunately, one of Llyn's intelligence sources had warned that Gensonne might have a couple of armed freighters. Out here, where naval patrols were few and far between, armed merchantmen were hardly uncommon, and Posnán System Patrol probably wouldn't turn much of a hair over one as long as it behaved itself.

Especially if it claimed to be Andermani. Gustav Anderman was a tough-minded old buzzard, and he'd made it a point to ensure that everyone—especially including pirate gangs—knew his freighters were as well-armed as many a warship. He was also the sort of man the Posnán authorities wouldn't care to annoy without very good reason.

More to the point, if *Hamman* had any weaponry at all, then it was automatically superior to *Pacemaker*, which didn't mount even a single popgun.

The bottom line was if Gensonne managed to get into missile range with minimal difference between their vectors and demanded *Pacemaker* heave-to for a rendezvous, *Pacemaker* would have no choice but to obey. And since they'd still be seven million kilometers from Obrączka, Gensonne could then drop his mask, seize or destroy Llyn, and be gone before anyone in Posnan could do a damn thing about it.

Unless there was enough difference between their vectors that *Pacemaker* could somehow squeak into Obrączka orbit—or at least break past *Hamman*—before Gensonne overhauled her.

"Try this," he said. "Assume he wants to intercept us seven million klicks short of Obrączka. We make turnover, all fat, dumb, and happy, and both of us maintain our current profiles until he makes turnover for the intercept. If we then stop decelerating and kick back up to maximum safe acceleration in-system, can he intercept us at his current acceleration rate?"

"No way," Katura said, not even bothering to run the numbers.

"Assume his maximum acceleration is two hundred gravities and he cranks it that high."

"In that case . . ." Katura paused, crunching the numbers. He eyed the results a moment, then shook his head.

"If we go back to two hundred sixteen gravities at the point he makes turnover, our starting velocity relative to Obrączka will be forty-eight hundred KPS higher than his," he said. "If he flips back and goes to two hundred gravities at that point, we'll pass over two million kilometers clear of him and our velocity advantage at that point would be about eleven KPS higher than it was when we both resumed acceleration."

"So he couldn't bring us back into missile range even at two hundred gravities?"

"No, Sir. He'd have to be able to pull at least two hundred and thirty-two to manage that, and our velocity advantage would still be over forty-two hundred KPS. So even at that acceleration he'd only be able to keep us in missile range for a bit under three minutes."

"I like the sound of that," Llyn said softly, still gazing at the display. If they pulled this off, he knew, Gensonne would be furious.

Sometimes, the universe gave out bonuses.

☆   ☆   ☆

The two ships continued on their respective vectors for another hour. After forty minutes, *Pacemaker* made turnover, beginning her steady deceleration toward Obrączka orbit. Twenty minutes later, right on schedule—and still close enough to a routine zero-zero entry into Obrączka orbit to pass cursory inspection from System Patrol—*Hamman* flipped, as well.

Llyn watched the plot for a second or two, imagining Gensonne's expression as the Volsung watched the rabbit hopping steadily and leisurely straight into the fox's jaws. He looked at Katura and nodded.

"Let's do it, Captain."

"Yes, Sir." Katura's gestured to his helmsman. "Execute."

"Yes, Sir," the helmsman repeated. A moment later, *Pacemaker* had flipped over and once again begun accelerating.

Llyn watched *Hamman*'s icon. For a moment, nothing changed. Then the freighter's wedge disappeared; and when it reappeared the ship was also again accelerating toward the hoped-for rendezvous.

"His acceleration's increasing," Katura reported.

"Not surprising," Llyn replied calmly. At least it wasn't surprising for Gensonne. Most captains would have realized at this point that *Pacemaker* had already escaped, but Gensonne wasn't going to give up on the possibility. He would resume his pursuit until his astrogator finished crunching the new numbers and hesitantly explained that—

"Sir," Katura said, an edge of disbelief in his voice. "The freighter—"

"I see it," Llyn murmured, watching the vector projections change yet again. *Hamman* hadn't accelerated to the two hundred gravities he'd told Katura to assume. Instead, it had increased its pace to two hundred and *forty* gravities.

Which meant...

"How long can he keep us in missile range if we both maintain present accelerations?" he asked.

Katura was already running the numbers. "He's bought himself another twenty-four seconds," he said, clearly still not believing it. Even assuming a military grade impeller, the freighter must have reduced her safety margin almost to zero to produce that kind of acceleration. No captain wanted to take his command *that* close to the edge of destruction without a damned compelling reason.

"He must want us even worse than I expected," Llyn said, keeping his own voice calm. In point of fact, if Gensonne wanted them that badly he was likely to go ahead and fire off a few missiles no matter what Posnan might think about it.

And in that case, the less time he had in which to do the firing, the better.

He took a deep breath. "Redline our compensator," he ordered.

Katura turned to face him, his mouth slightly open. "Excuse me?"

"You heard me," Llyn said. "Let's see how badly he really wants to dance."

Katura looked at him another moment, his face unreadable, then nodded to the helmsman.

"Zero compensator margin," he said. "Take us to two hundred and seventy gravities."

The helmsman swallowed visibly. "Yes, Sir," he replied.

Llyn made sure his own expression remained no more than calmly attentive as the courier boat's acceleration sprang upward by over fifty gravities. He wasn't any happier about doing this than Katura or the helmsman.

But now, given their new acceleration rates, *Pacemaker* would never enter *Hamman*'s missile envelope at all. In fact, she would pass beyond *Hamman*'s maximum missile range just over two minutes before the freighter arrived. Gensonne couldn't possibly overtake him, not even if he was prepared to stay at a zero safety margin. And assuming Gensonne retained a single gram of common sense—

"*Hamman* is decreasing acceleration, Sir," Katura announced suddenly. He stared at the display another moment, then turned back at Llyn. "She's back down to a hundred gravities."

Llyn watched the projected vectors, now diverging more and more broadly, feeling the tension draining out of him. Gensonne had gotten the message, and apparently even the Volsung was unwilling to hold his ship on the edge of disaster when he couldn't catch his quarry anyway. Which meant that Llyn didn't have to keep *Pacemaker* at that edge, either.

"There's a game people have played for centuries, Captain," he said to Katura. "Back on Old Terra, they called it *chicken*. Apparently, even Admiral Gensonne can recognize when it's time to quit playing."

"As you say, Sir," Katura replied.

"Run us down to two hundred thirty gravities," Llyn continued. "Keep us just enough above the standard safety margin that he'll remember we can run away faster than he can chase us."

"Yes, Sir. Two-thirty gravities it is. And if I may again suggest . . . ?"

Llyn chewed the inside of his cheek. The fact that Gensonne had been headed in-system probably meant he'd just arrived and that none of the rest of his ships were already in Posnan. It was always possible that that wasn't the case, but it seemed most likely.

Still, if there *were* other Volsung ships in-system and *Pacemaker* continued to Obrączka, those other Volsungs would know precisely where to find her.

They must also know that a quiet hijacking would be a lot less noticeable than a mid-space interception. A few boarders aboard the courier boat, a quiet change of command without all the hubbub of missile exchanges, and it was likely no one would even notice.

Best not to tempt fate, he decided.

"All right, Captain," he said out loud. "Plot us a course to the hyper-limit that bypasses Obrączka. I think we've already overstayed our welcome."

☆ ☆ ☆

Thirteen hours later, without further incident, *Pacemaker* was back in hyper.

"I had Thom and Seikor do a complete check of everything," Katura said as he accepted a cup of tea from his boss. Normally, Llyn didn't mix much with his officers and crew, but the captain had earned a little extra socialization. "The nodes came through without any damage. The compensator took some stress, but nothing seems damaged. I've ordered a recheck anyway, just to be on the safe side."

"Considering the reason we're out here, I don't think a safe side really exists," Llyn pointed out. "But, yes, go ahead."

"I will, Sir." Katura hesitated. "You really think that was Gensonne?"

"Gensonne or his people," Llyn said, pouring a second cup for himself. "Why? Don't you?"

"I don't know," Katura said, gazing thoughtfully into his cup. "I never met the man. But from the way you've talked about him, he seems more of a hit-it-with-a-hammer type. The freighter's commander seemed... more subtle, somehow. Certainly more clever."

"You don't get to Gensonne's level without a certain animal cunning," Llyn reminded him. Still, the captain had a point. "But if it wasn't Gensonne or one of his men, who else could it have been?"

"Maybe someone with a beef against the Grand Duke?" Katura suggested. "We *were* still running that Barcan ID."

"There's that," Llyn conceded. "Though we're a pretty long haul from Barca."

"If the Grand Duke was in the market for anything questionable, Silesia is a place he might go shopping without awkward questions being asked," Katura pointed out.

"There are closer places to Barca for that sort of thing," Llyn said. "And if it really *was* an Andermani freighter, we run into the question of why they'd be interested in Barcan ships in the first place."

"True," Katura acknowledged. "Could it have been the Manticorans?"

"Running Andermani IDs?" Llyn shook his head. "Not a chance. The Andermani would skin them alive if they caught them at it. Besides, our people looked into Manticore's intelligence apparatus, and it's a complete joke. They wouldn't have the faintest idea even where to start looking."

"They might get better," Katura warned. "They're pretty motivated right now."

"Motivation doesn't equal competence," Llyn said. "Trust me: the people running their Office of Naval Intelligence are moss-bound political appointees. Gensonne's got a better chance of dying from old age than from Manticore tracking him down."

"Maybe." Katura eyed him thoughtfully. "I trust that by the time *we* track him down you'll have a plan for confronting him?"

"Oh, I have a plan, all right," Llyn assured him. "As a matter of fact, I've got four of them."

"Depending on what we find at Telmach?"

"On what we find, and maybe *who* we find," Llyn said, nodding. "And as always, what will ultimately get us what Axelrod wants."

CHAPTER SIXTEEN

BACK IN HIGH SCHOOL, TRAVIS MUSED, if someone had told him he would someday be a teacher he would have laughed in the other person's face. More probably, given what Travis was like in high school, he would have silently disagreed and walked away. Teaching was something that had never occurred to him as a possible future profession.

To be sure, he'd had a taste of the job over the past two years simply owing to the fact that he was a Navy officer. There was always someone under his command who needed instruction on how a procedure had to be implemented, or how some bit of equipment had to be properly repaired or pounded into submission.

But until the aftermath of the Battle of Manticore, when *Casey* was in for repairs and Travis was summarily tossed into the new MPARS section of the Academy, he'd never been on the teacher's side of an actual classroom.

Rather to his shock, he'd discovered he liked it.

There was the mental challenge of having to boil

down lesson material into a lecture that was as simple, focused, and informative as possible. There was the quiet personal confirmation of his own knowledge when he was able to answer a question that he'd never consciously thought about before. And there was the deep satisfaction of seeing a student's eyes light up as a new concept or technique suddenly clicked.

On top of that, teaching meant order. There was organization and structure. Even better, it was Travis himself who got to define how that structure was established and implemented. That alone was worth its weight in spare parts.

Best of all, Lisa was two floors up in a classroom of her own.

Her presence at the MPARS Academy was a nice plus for him. Not so much for her. Like Travis, she'd been assigned teaching duty while *Damocles* was undergoing repairs. Unlike Travis, she hated the job.

It wasn't that she wasn't good at it. Travis had taken advantage of a canceled class of his own to sit in on one of hers, and in his opinion she was better than fifty percent of the instructors he'd had at Casey-Rosewood, and with more patience than any of them.

The problem was that while he enjoyed the structure and discipline, all she could see was that she was stuck in a building on the ground instead of traveling in a ship out in space.

But there was nothing for it. *Damocles* had taken far more internal damage from the loss of her missile launcher than anyone had realized at the time, and the Navy's lack of proper service, construction, and maintenance infrastructure had exacerbated that problem. Adding in the fact that Dapplelake and

Breakwater were once again locking horns, this time for the money and access to repair facilities for the Navy and MPARS ships, meant Lisa was likely to be teaching for at least a few more months.

It was an almost-amusing irony, one which Travis carefully kept to himself, that he was actually adapting to a new situation faster and better than she was.

But aside from her frustration—or perhaps in some ways because of it—she and Travis had become closer over the past few months. Closer than Travis had ever expected. Closer, sometimes, than he was entirely comfortable with.

But it was good. It was very good. And it mostly seemed right.

If the deaths of King Edward and Princess Sophie had shown anything, it was that life was incredibly precious and heartbreakingly uncertain. It was both foolish and dangerous to let time slide away.

Travis didn't know exactly where the relationship was going. But for now, he was content to work alongside her, spending lunches and weekends together, and let the future take its own course.

Which was why the fresh orders were a kick to the gut.

"I don't understand, Sir," he said looking up from his tablet at MPARS Academy Commandant Allen Innes.

"Seems pretty self-explanatory to me," Innes countered tartly. "You're to hand off your notes to your replacement and report immediately to your new assignment."

Travis looked back at his orders. Unlike all the rest of the orders he'd been issued, this one was maddingly vague.

Admiralty Building. Suite 2021. Smack in the center of floors eighteen through twenty-two.

BuPers territory.

The Navy had taken him from his ship and put him in a classroom. Now, just as he'd learned that he was a damn good teacher, they were kicking him even farther downstairs to desk duty.

And not just any desk duty, but the most boring desk duty imaginable.

"Has my work been unsatisfactory?" he asked.

"I don't know how to answer that, Lieutenant." The commandant gestured toward Travis's tablet. "All I know is the order says immediately, and in my experience Admiral Dembinski hasn't issued any extra patience to her people. You have your notes?"

Silently, Travis pulled the data chip from his tablet and handed it over.

"Very good, Lieutenant." Innes hesitated. "For whatever it's worth, Long, your students seem to learn a lot in your classes. Good luck to you."

"Thank you, Sir," Travis said, suppressing a sigh. Innes was sorry to see him leave, but apparently not sorry enough to fight to keep him. He'd hoped, with the aftermath of the king's death winding down, that his tennis-ball journey from assignment to assignment might be over.

Unfortunately, it looked like it might be. After all, conventional wisdom was that BuPers was where careers went to die.

Still, the Admiralty Building was currently also host to the MPARS offices and classrooms, which meant Lisa was still just a lift ride away. Granted, it would be a longer lift ride, and they were likely to be on different schedules, but he was sure they could work it out. Maybe careers weren't as important when a person had friends.

On the other hand, now that he was in BuPers, maybe she would see him in a different and less flattering light. In fact, maybe she would break off the relationship completely.

He was already junior to her in rank. Now that he was in a dead-end job, maybe she would rethink everything.

What a hell of a way to start a Monday.

The lift doors opened, breaking his downward spiral of thought. Taking a deep breath, he stepped out onto the twentieth floor. He glanced at the directory, confirmed that 2021 was to the right, and turned in that direction.

"Well, hello, Sir," a familiar voice came from behind him. "Fancy meeting you here."

Travis turned around, his stomach knotting. Chomps Townsend. Of course. After all, the best way for the universe to make a bad day even worse was to throw a man who hated him into his path.

"Petty Officer Townsend," he greeted the other in turn, keeping his voice steady as he turned around. "Sorry—*Chief* Townsend," he corrected himself as he noted the insignia on Chomps's left sleeve.

He frowned as his brain caught up with the oddness of that fact. Six months ago, during the invasion scare, Townsend had been a mere petty officer first class. Now, suddenly, the man had been promoted to chief petty officer? *And* he was back in Navy uniform after getting kicked to MPARS?

Unlike Travis, someone had clearly taken Chomps under his or her wing.

Though who that could be wasn't at all clear. Chomps's shirt color was a nondescript gray, and his shoulder patch indicated a shore assignment.

"Yes, Sir," Chomps said, grinning widely as he strode towards Travis. "And back in the RMN, I trust you noticed."

"I did, Chief," Travis said, his heart sinking. Chomps back in the Navy, and promoted to chief. Heading up the ladder while Travis was headed down. "Congratulations."

"Thank you, Sir. What brings you up here, if I may ask?"

"New assignment," Travis said, determined not to let his envy show.

"Ah," Chomps said. "You wouldn't be heading to Room 2021 by any chance, would you?"

Travis frowned. How in hell could Chomps have known *that*?

"As a matter of fact, that *is* where I'm reporting," he said.

"What a stroke of luck. That's where *I'm* heading, too. May I accompany you, Sir?"

Travis's sighed. The universe, prolonging the agony. "Of course, Chief," he said. "What's your business with BuPers, if I may ask?"

"We're getting a new officer in my department," Chomps said as they resumed walking, the CPO pacing along at Travis's side. "I need to pick up the data work."

"Ah," Travis said. For a fleeting moment he wondered if he was that officer. "What department are you in?"

"Oh, it's something new that the Admiralty's thrown

together," Chomps said. "It's a little complicated. A little political, too, I'm afraid."

Travis made a face.

"Yes, I know how that works."

"Yes, Sir." Chomps gestured. "Here we are, Sir."

Travis nodded. *Room 2021*, the ID plate said. There was no secondary plate giving the name of the officer in charge. That was unusual, and probably not good.

"Here we are, Sir," Chomps prompted again.

"Right." Taking a deep breath, Travis pushed the door open.

Beyond the door was a small anteroom with a desk, two guest chairs, and a single potted plant on the stand beside a plain door at the back of the room. Seated behind the desk was a young woman in civilian clothing. Standing behind her, peering over her shoulder at something on her computer display, was—

Travis stiffened. Was that really—?

"Good morning, Lieutenant Long," Lady Calvingdell said briskly, straightening up and giving Travis a quick once over. "I'm Countess Calvingdell. You may remember me from that dreadful day on *Samantha*."

With an effort, Travis found his tongue.

"Yes, My Lady," he said, ducking his head in a bow. "It's nice to see you again."

"Likewise," she said. She cocked her head for a moment, apparently studying his expression. "Should I assume that you weren't overly enthralled with your orders to BuPers? And should I further assume that your enthusiasm level hasn't scaled new heights at finding yourself face-to-face with the woman who was tossed out of office as Minister of Defense and replaced by Earl Dapplelake?"

Travis winced. What was he supposed to say to that?

"Well, yes, My Lady."

"Good," she said briskly. She eyed his expression and smiled slightly. "First, some record-clearing. The official story that I was tossed out of office is the tale we *wanted* everyone to hear. In point of fact, I quietly resigned in order to take over this brand-new agency. From your record, it appears you might be a good fit for it. So, of course, you had to disappear into the bowels of the bureaucracy."

Her smile brightened at his perplexed expression and she glanced over his shoulder at Chomps.

"It's your doing that Lieutenant Long is here, Chief, and I know you're dying to tell him. Have at it."

"Yes, My Lady." Chomps turned to Travis, an extremely self-satisfied smile of his own on his face. "Welcome to my new home, Travis. And *your* new home, if you want it. Welcome to the Special Intelligence Service."

☆   ☆   ☆

For maybe half a dozen heartbeats Travis just stared at him, years of history rewinding at furious speed as the universe seemed to do a complete about-face around him. If Chomps was telling the truth—and if today wasn't his first day on the job—

"The computer hack aboard *Phoenix*," he murmured. "You were never brought up on charges because there *weren't* any charges."

Chomps looked at Calvingdell, his smile going even broader. "I told you he was quick, My Lady."

"That you did," Calvingdell agreed. "Very good, Lieutenant. Continue."

Travis frowned. "Ma'am?"

"You're playing out Chief Townsend's revised history," she said. "Let's hear some more."

"Yes, Ma'am," Travis said, feeling uncomfortably like a trained animal being asked to perform. "There weren't any charges because it wasn't a hack in the first place. You were...what? Supposed to check on incoming freighters?"

"That, and anything else that came into the system," Chomps said, nodding. "It was our first—Lady Calvingdell's first, I should say—experiment with an agent-aboard program. One of my duties was to sift through everything we got from incoming ships and run an extra set of eyes over it for discrepancies, contradictions, omissions, and any other oddities I might notice. Captain Castillo and the rest of the senior officers were fully aware of all this, of course."

"Which is also why *I* didn't get more than a slap on the wrist for failing to properly report it?" Travis asked.

"Exactly," Chomps said. "Commander Sladek had to say *something*—he couldn't have you getting suspicious, after all. But he could hardly put any major disciplinary action on you, given that it *was* a fully-authorized activity."

"Which isn't to say Sladek didn't also slap *Townsend* down for taking you into his confidence in the first place," Calvingdell put in.

"Oh, he did, all right," Chomps said, wincing at the memory. "After that, it was Lady Calvingdell's turn."

"Is that why you transferred him to MPARS?" Travis asked as another piece of the puzzle fell into place. "As a punishment for talking to me?"

"Oh, that wasn't a punishment," Chomps assured

him. "I was already slated for a stint there." He cocked an eyebrow at Calvingdell. "Though possibly not quite so soon. No, Lady Calvingdell wanted me to rub shoulders with a lot of different people, in both services, with an eye toward spotting and recruiting promising talent."

"Such as yourself, Lieutenant," Calvingdell said.

"Okay," Travis said, frowning. There was something here that still didn't make sense. "But why a new department? Doesn't ONI already handle intel?"

"It does, after a fashion," Calvingdell said. "And a lot of our work to this point is officially under ONI's charter. Townsend's work aboard *Phoenix*, for example. Unfortunately, ONI is so hidebound, ingrown, and politicized that we decided it was useless for what we need."

"These days it's mostly just a handful of mossbacks pondering diplomatic reports," Chomps said. "And in their spare time leafing through Solarian weapons brochures saying *ooh—shiny* at all the cool hardware that Breakwater will never let us buy."

"It was determined that we needed a new start," Calvingdell said. "So I was publicly kicked out of office, quietly gathered a few good people around me, and started ramping up operations here."

"Casca," Travis said, looking at Chomps as one more piece suddenly fell into place. "Lisa said your computer hack there was under Lady Calvingdell's orders."

"Yes, it was," Calvingdell confirmed. "At the time, understand, it was just a one-off—I'd brought Townsend's uncle aboard as an advisor, and he recommended his nephew as someone aboard who could handle the job. As it turned out, the incident more than proved he was someone I wanted to take on permanently." She cocked her head. "As are you, Lieutenant. *If* you want the job."

Travis pursed his lips, his eyes running up and down Chomps's uniform. To his mild surprise, the other caught the implied question.

"You'll still be in the Navy," he said. "Not just as a cover, either—you'll still be doing all your normal shipboard work. This will just be an extra duty that only the senior officers know about."

"Understood," Travis said. With the mystery that had been Chomps starting to unravel, his brain shifted from past to future. "You sound as if you already have a mission in mind, My Lady."

"We do," Calvingdell said. "Flora?"

The young woman at the desk, who had yet to say a word, stood up and stepped back out of the way. "This is Flora Taylor, by the way," Calvingdell added as she sat down in Flora's vacated chair and gestured to Travis. "We call her the Gatekeeper. Her job is to smile and redirect those who don't know what's going on here and pass in those who do."

Travis nodded to Flora as he walked around the end of the desk. Flora nodded back, offering him a small, polite, and precisely proper smile in return.

A woman who understood and followed official etiquette. Travis liked her already.

"There wasn't a lot of debris left from the battle," Calvingdell said. Travis reached her side, to see that she'd pulled up a data list. "And of course, what was there was scattered across several million cubic kilometers of space. It's taken the Navy—*and* MPARS *and* every tug and mining ship we were able to press into service—this whole time to collect enough to find some clues." She lifted a finger. "Understand that what I'm about to show you is classified as need-to-know."

On the other side of the desk, Chomps stirred. "Excuse me, My Lady...but, uh, Lieutenant Long hasn't yet agreed to join us."

"I know," Calvingdell said. "It's all right."

"Yes, My Lady," Chomps said stolidly. "May I remind the Countess that she raked me over the coals for telling him things he wasn't authorized to know?"

"Reminder noted," Calvingdell said. "That's the advantage of being the one in charge, Chief: you get to bend the rules when you deem it necessary." She gave Travis a puckered smile. "Lieutenant Long isn't the type to blindly jump into something just on someone else's say-so. Especially when the say-so is coming from a disgraced former Defense Minister and a petty officer who blames him for getting him kicked over to MPARS."

"Ah—yes," Chomps said, nodding. "I'd forgotten what a disreputable bunch we were."

"Exactly." Calvingdell gestured to the display. "So. Take a look, Lieutenant. Tell me what you see."

Gingerly, Travis leaned over her shoulder, trying to ignore how close he was standing to a member of the nobility and a more or less complete stranger. The list turned out to be a rundown of various retrieved parts that had been in good enough shape to identify and, in some cases, ascertain their point of origin.

A lot of it was Solarian. No surprise there, given how much the League dominated shipping and shipbuilding. There was a surprising amount of Tahzeeb material, which hinted that at least a couple of Tamerlane's ships might have come from that system.

But even more intriguing...

"What are these?" he asked, pointing to a group of objects midway down the list. "Are they gravitics array components?"

"Indeed they are," Calvingdell confirmed. "It must be years since you had to deal with a gravitics inventory list. You have an excellent memory."

"When the Navy drums something into you, it stays drummed," Chomps said. "Anything in particular about those components that intrigues you, Travis?"

Travis shot a look at the other. A petty officer wasn't supposed to use that kind of familiarity with an officer, not in front of a civilian.

Calvingdell apparently spotted the look as it went by and correctly gleaned the thought behind it. "Please excuse Townsend, Lieutenant," she said. "We're more informal in here than we are out in public. And of course, the two of you have a certain amount of history together. You were about to tell us the significance of these components?"

"Yes, My Lady," Travis said. He *had* known Chomps since boot camp, after all. In private settings that allowed more familiarity. "A lot of systems in this region, even those who can build their own ships, still get their impellers from the League or Haven. So those components and spare parts won't tell us much. But gravitics arrays are something almost anyone can make, and more cheaply than importing them. So it seems reasonable to assume those would be items Tamerlane could buy closer to home."

He pointed over Calvingdell's shoulder. "If the analysts are right about those bits coming from the Silesian Confederacy, I would say that's where we should start looking for him."

"Very good, Lieutenant," Calvingdell said. "That's exactly the conclusion we came to. Anything else?"

Travis chewed at the inside of his cheek. Silesia was a good lead, certainly. But it never hurt to have a second string to their bow.

And if he was clever, maybe he could do Lisa a favor along with it.

"It looks like you also found some parts that came from Haven," he said. "If the Havenites can pull any serial numbers or other ID off them, we might be able to backtrack those purchases."

"That's rather a long shot," Calvingdell said doubtfully. "It's also something of a two-edged sword, if you'll excuse the mixed metaphor. The fact that a fair amount of material came from Haven *might* imply the attackers were based somewhere in that area. Nouveau Paris won't like that implication."

Travis suppressed a smile. Perfect. "Maybe we can make it more informal," he suggested. "We could send someone who can ask for an unofficial favor."

"You have someone in mind?" Chomps asked, an odd tone in his voice.

"Lieutenant Commander Lisa Donnelly," Travis said. "During the Secour Incident she worked with Colonel Jean Massingill, who emigrated to Haven afterwards."

"Oh, she didn't just *go* to Haven," Calvingdell said dryly. "She more or less conquered it. Your Colonel Massingill is now Brigadier Massingill, who created, organized, and now commands SCAFE, Haven's own Special Forces division."

Travis felt his eyes bulge. He hadn't heard any of that.

"That's . . . impressive, My Lady," he said. "It should

also make it easier for Massingill to pull whatever strings are needed to get those fragments analyzed."

"Provided she remembers Manticore fondly enough to call in a favor or two," Calvingdell said. "She might not. In light of that, it might serve us better to pull someone a bit more senior from the Secour thing to make our pitch. Commodore Eigen, for instance, or Captain Metzger."

"I doubt the Navy would let either Eigen or Metzger go for that long," Chomps warned.

"And the more senior the officer, the more official the pitch would look," Travis added. "We were trying to avoid that, right?"

"Though if we wanted a more senior officer, you could arrange for Donnelly to be promoted to Commander and put in *Damocles*'s XO slot," Chomps suggested.

Travis winced. Much as he appreciated Lisa's abilities, promoting any officer too quickly was potentially setting her up for failure. All he'd really been angling for was for Calvingdell to expedite *Damocles*'s repairs and get Lisa out of that hated classroom. Chomps, unfortunately, had gotten a little too enthusiastic.

Calvingdell apparently thought so, too. "Not a good idea," she warned, shaking her head.

"She's got all the necessary experience, My Lady," Chomps persisted. "More than that, she has the respect of *Damocles*'s officers and crew." He lifted a finger. "And unless I'm mistaken, *Erinye*'s Captain Timberlake recently announced his retirement. *Damocles*'s current XO, Commander Shiflett, could easily be moved into that slot."

"Yes," Calvingdell murmured, looking back and forth

between them. "I'll look into it." She cocked an eyebrow. "You two *do* work and play well together, don't you? Of course, you're missing the other obvious candidate: Lieutenant Long himself. I understand your contribution to the Navy response at Secour was quite pivotal."

"But if he goes to Haven, he won't be able to go to Silesia with me," Chomps protested. "I thought that was the plan."

"You assume Mr. Long will join us," Calvingdell said. "As you pointed out earlier, that hasn't been established."

"Sure it has," Chomps said. "Right, Travis?"

"It's... interesting," Travis said. "But are you just going to...? I mean, isn't there some test or something I have to take?"

"You just took it," Calvingdell said, gesturing to the display. "Your record shows you have an eye and a mind for picking out details and coming up with ideas. Furthermore, Chomps informs me that you're quick on your feet and, if properly motivated, can tell a convincing lie. Something about chocolate chip cookies, I believe."

"Yes, My Lady," Travis admitted, feeling his face warming. It had been a long time since he'd thought about that incident.

"So," Calvingdell said briskly. "Here's the deal. Once you sign on, there'll be six weeks' of training—not really long enough, but that's all the time we have before *Casey*'s upgrade is finished and she's ready to head out to Silesia. Chomps will be aboard as a Chief, and he'll continue your training—"

"Excuse me, My Lady?" Travis interrupted, frowning. "We'll be taking *Casey*?"

"Indeed," Calvingdell said. "In case you'd forgotten—or more likely never knew—part of the original plan for *Casey* was to send her around the region as an example of Manticoran shipbuilding skill. A chance to drum up future business, and possibly give certain parties a reason to excavate a money pit to develop our own impeller ring industry."

"Sounds expensive," Travis said, frowning.

"As I said: a money pit."

"But is there really that much call for that kind of work out here?"

"That's what this goodwill cruise was supposed to ascertain," Calvingdell said. "That's also why you'll have a passenger: Countess Acton's assistant manager Heinreich Hauptman. He'll be handling the sales pitches along the way."

"Purely coincidentally, of course, he also has contacts with some of the shipyards and supply people there," Chomps added. "That's the real reason he's coming along. You and I will be looking into inventory lists; he'll be our intro vector for getting our hands on them."

"Does he know what we're really doing?"

"Yes, he's been fully briefed," Calvingdell said. "But that's him. We're talking about you. Bottom line, Lieutenant: are you in? Yes, or no?"

Travis took a deep breath. A lot of good men and women had died in the Battle of Manticore. If there was a chance he could help track down the perpetrators and bring them to justice...

"Yes, My Lady," he said. "I'm in."

"Excellent," Calvingdell said, standing up and offering Travis her hand. "Welcome aboard. Flora, if you'd let them in?"

"Yes, My Lady." Flora glided back to the desk—Travis hadn't noticed until that moment how graceful the young woman's movements were—and tapped a few computer keys.

Chomps gestured to Travis and circled the desk to the door beside the potted plant. He turned the knob and pushed open the door.

To reveal a much larger room than Travis had expected. One section was packed with computer desks, a handful of which were occupied by men and women gazing intently at the displays. On the other side of the room were a trio of lab tables with various high-tech devices gathered around them, with more men and women working there. At the very back was an open space, currently unoccupied, filled with mats like the ones in the hand-to-hand combat training areas at Casey-Rosewood.

"Sorry about the mess," Chomps apologized as he led the way toward the rows of desks. "This is supposed to be just our analysis area, but the three other rooms we're supposed to get aren't ready yet, so everything's been crammed into here."

"How big a department is it going to be?" Travis asked.

"At least a couple more big rooms," Chomps said. "Personnel-wise, so far we've got a couple of dozen. Ultimately, Calvingdell wants Delphi to get this whole floor and enough people to fill it. But we'll see."

"Delphi?" Travis echoed.

"That's what we call the place," Chomps explained. "Shaves a whole syllable off *Ess-Eye-Ess*, plus it has a nice classical ring to it."

He stopped at one of the computer desks and

pulled out the chair. "There's a lot of reading to get out of the way, so we'll start you on that. So. How does our Lisa like teaching at MPARS?"

Travis's first reaction was to blink at the abrupt segue. His second was to bristle at Chomps's casual familiarity. *Our Lisa?* Where did he get off talking about *our* Lisa?

His third was to belatedly realize he was being tweaked.

"Not really, no," he said. "All things being equal, Lieutenant Commander Donnelly would rather be aboard a ship."

"Oh, she's *Lieutenant Commander Donnelly* now?" Chomps asked, giving Travis a sidelong look. "My mistake. I thought she was your special friend."

"She's a friend, yes," Travis said firmly. "But just a friend. And she's definitely not *your* special friend."

"Of course," Chomps grinned. "Regardless, whoever she is or isn't, I think we've convinced Her Ladyship to send her to Haven." He shrugged. "Personally, I'd rather teach than go on a multi-month voyage with nothing but talking at the end of it. But to each their own."

"Let's hope there's more than just talking," Travis said. "If this lead fizzles, do we even *have* anything else?"

"Oh, yes," Chomps said, his voice gone suddenly dark. "You remember that little incursion we had awhile back? Count Ernst Bloch and his Merry Men of Barca?"

"Of course."

"Well, our dear Count made a mistake," Chomps said. "Amid all the double-talk he was pitching, he smiled."

Travis frowned. What was he talking about?

And then, abruptly, he got it. *Smiled* . . .

"You're joking."

"Not at all," Chomps assured him. "It was the same smile. The exact same ice-fish-cold smile.

"Count Bloch was our Cascan mass-murderer. *And* the one who offed your Secour pirate in his cell on Haven."

"The man gets around," Travis murmured. "So that NAVSAT thing was you?"

"It was Lady Calvingdell, actually," Chomps said. "But yes, it was my suggestion. We set up the satellite to spout complete gibberish, hoping Bloch would interpret it as an encrypted transmission and see if he got spooked. He did, which helped cement the conclusion that he was up to something."

"Your smile thing wasn't sufficient?"

"Strangely enough, no," Chomps said. "But I think the Admiralty is fully on board now. Of course, that doesn't mean we'll have a plan if and when he comes back."

"So how is he connected to Tamerlane?"

"No idea," Chomps said. "But finding out is very high on our things-to-do list." He gestured again to the desk. "Anyway, here's where you start. Sorry we can't just send it to your tablet, but this is stuff we don't want floating around the ether. Punch in your ID, set up your encryption, and start reading."

With a nod, Chomps headed across the room toward the work tables.

Hunching his shoulders, Travis sat down. There was still a lot about this whole thing that made no sense at all. But at least Delphi and the Navy were starting to make a collection of puzzle pieces. With enough pieces, and enough people working on them, hopefully they could come up with an answer.

And as to Lisa...

He glowered at Chomps's back. *She's* not *a special friend*, he insisted silently. *Not the way you think. She's not.*

Glowering at the display, he keyed in his ID and got to work.

CHAPTER SEVENTEEN

DUCHESS NEW BERN, FIRST LORD OF Law, set her tablet on the table in front of her. "That's the situation, Your Majesty," she concluded. "The original wording simply doesn't make a compelling case one way or the other. My apologies that the situation isn't more definitive."

"I see," Elizabeth said, keeping her voice even. Out of the corner of her eye she saw Burgundy shift uncomfortably in his seat on the opposite side of the table. Clearly, he'd hoped the situation would be more definitive, too.

Or maybe he was regretting that he and the other Framers hadn't taken the current possibility into account. "And your personal opinion, Your Grace?" she added.

"I have no *opinion*, Your Majesty," New Bern said primly. "My job is to strictly follow the law."

"I understand," Elizabeth said. "Let me put it another way. If you were the Justice hearing the case, how would you decide?"

"I would decide based on whatever was best for the Star Kingdom," New Bern said. "I believe that's the burden on all who serve our star nation."

"Excuse me?" Burgundy spoke up, his voice harsh. "Your job is to determine what the law *is*, not interpret it according to your own personal feelings."

"And I will continue to do that job," New Bern said frostily. "But Her Majesty asked me a hypothetical question with regard to an unclear law, and I answered."

"Of course," Burgundy said, mollifying his tone a bit. But Elizabeth could see the flash in his eyes that showed he understood exactly where New Bern was coming from.

Only in this case, unfortunately, he was wrong. New Bern was usually an ally of Breakwater's, and thus could be expected to follow the Chancellor's lead on most matters of policy. Here, though, her friends and quiet allegiances didn't really come into the calculation.

Because Elizabeth had waded through the Constitution, plus a raft of concurrent documents and discussions, plus the later writings of each of the Framers, *and* had quietly interviewed the handful of men and women who, like Burgundy, had been involved in the process.

And she'd come to the same conclusion New Bern had. Both sides of the marriage question could be reasonably supported, and both sides could be reasonably attacked.

Still, the idea of the First Lord of Law talking about what was best for the Star Kingdom . . .

"It seems to me that the marriage question is relatively minor," Burgundy continued. "The far more urgent problem is that we currently have no legitimate heir to the throne. And if you'll forgive my bringing up a painful subject, we've already seen with your brother and niece how that can end in disaster."

"And not just for the Winton line," Elizabeth said, a fresh trickle of old pain whispering through her. "I'm not sure what would happen to the Crown and the Star Kingdom."

"Your father still has two sisters and a brother," Burgundy pointed out.

"But all of them are in their seventies or eighties and in questionable health," New Bern said.

"And none of them have children who would be Constitutionally suitable heirs to the Throne," Burgundy conceded.

"No, I suppose not," Elizabeth murmured, eyeing her Prime Minister closely.

And not liking what she saw.

As far back as she could remember, Burgundy had always seemed old. Granted, when she was a child *everyone* over fifteen T-years had looked that way. But as she grew up, and her parents and brother changed, Burgundy didn't. His hair had slowly gotten thinner, and a few splotches had appeared on the backs of his hands, but otherwise he seemed to be treading water, age-wise, as if he was going to forever stay the same.

Until now. Now, like a collapsing star, he seemed to be falling in on himself.

His body and face had grown thinner. He moved more carefully, as if concerned about his bones and uncertain of his balance. He leaned forward in conversations, as if worried that he could no longer see or hear everything that was going on.

Elizabeth didn't know for sure when the rapid decline in Burgundy's health had begun. But her gut suspicion was that it had been triggered by the deaths of her brother and niece in the waters of Jason Bay.

Burgundy had had high hopes for the Star Kingdom under Edward's leadership. Edward had talked to Elizabeth about it, and she'd seen some of it in action for herself. The Prime Minister had acted as traveling blocker, cutting through the political noise and doing what he could to smooth the path for his King.

And then, in an instant, it had all been taken away.

A part of Elizabeth wondered if she should feel insulted that Burgundy apparently thought she was such a lost cause compared to Edward that he might as well give up. But she knew that wasn't the case. Burgundy was simply *old*, and it had only been his affection for the King that had kept the weight of all those years at bay.

Now, the King was gone, and the years were finally winning.

"I know you don't want to hear this, Your Majesty," Burgundy said. "But it has to be said. You need an heir, and the Constitution strongly implies that the father must be a commoner. The simplest solution—"

"I'm not going to remarry," Elizabeth interrupted. "Not under this kind of duress."

"Your Majesty—"

"I said *no*."

Burgundy pursed his lips, a muscle in his cheek tightening. "All right, then. Let me suggest the following. I'll make up a list for you of suitable . . . consorts, shall we say . . . should you decide to go that direction at some point in the future," he finished hurriedly, as if expecting her to cut him off at the knees.

For a moment, Elizabeth was tempted to do exactly that. But this was Burgundy. Even if she violently disagreed with him, he'd earned the right to be respected. "I can't prevent you from doing what you want in your spare time," she said instead. "Thank you both for your time. You may go."

"Your Majesty." New Bern stood up, bowed low, and strode past Elizabeth's chair to the door.

Elizabeth remained seated at the table. So, to her complete lack of surprise, did Burgundy. They sat together in silence, listening to New Bern's footsteps as she passed between the guards flanking the door and out into the Palace corridor. The guards closed the door behind her—

"She has got to go," Burgundy bit out when the door had closed behind her. *"Whatever's best for the Star Kingdom?* Seriously? She's supposed to be a *jurist*, for God's sake."

"There are five years yet in her term," Elizabeth reminded him tiredly. "Leave her be. We have more important matters hanging over us."

"I know." Burgundy took a deep breath, visibly pushing his frustration at New Bern aside. "First of all, I want to apologize for that suggestion of possible consorts. I hope you weren't offended."

"It *did* come across as a bit cold-blooded."

"I didn't mean for you to take it seriously," he hastened to add. "I knew New Bern would report all of this back to Breakwater, and I wanted him to think that we were...you know...doing something. Of course I would never actually do you such an insult."

Elizabeth sighed.

"Perhaps you should."

His eyes narrowed. "Your Majesty?" he asked cautiously.

"Perhaps you *should* make me a list," she said. "It's a reasonable enough step for me to take."

"But if you—" He broke off, and a tight smile creased his lips. "So that Breakwater will think you're giving in to his demand?"

"Or at least that I'm considering it," Elizabeth said. "Unfortunately, the demand isn't his alone. But yes, it should quiet his bloc for a while. Especially since I can drag out the whole process until we can come up with a better solution."

"Yes, Your Majesty." Burgundy hesitated. "Assuming there *is* such a solution."

"There is," she said firmly. "And we *will* find it."

"I hope you're right." Getting his hands on the edge of the table, Burgundy carefully pulled himself to his feet. "With your permission, Your Majesty, I'll get started on that right away."

"Thank you, Davis," she said. "It's comforting to know that you, at least, will always be standing firmly at my side."

"Always, Your Majesty," he promised. With one hand still gripping the table, he bowed low. "I'll let you know when the list is ready. It may take a few days."

"Take whatever time you need," Elizabeth said. "I'll look forward to meeting with you again when you're ready."

"Thank you," he said. "I'll let you know."

Walking with a curiously stiff-legged gait, he passed

behind her along the same path New Bern had just taken, between the guards and out the door.

Elizabeth never saw him again.

☆   ☆   ☆

It happened three days later, just before dawn.

The head of the Queen's Own, Major Jackson, with Elizabeth's rest in mind, waited another two hours before informing her. By the time she arrived at Burgundy's office, the doctors had already come and gone, taking the body with them.

"What was it?" she asked as she stood beside the Prime Minister's desk, her mind numb, her eyes trying to see her friend and advisor sitting in the empty chair.

"The doctors said it was a heart attack, Your Majesty," Burgundy's personal secretary, Louisa Geary, murmured. Three hours after finding him, the tears were no longer flowing, but her eyes were still red. "It was . . . we knew it would happen one day. We just . . . you're never ready for something like this."

"I understand," Elizabeth said, a dark sense of guilt digging into her heart. Burgundy's office staff had clearly known he had heart problems. Why hadn't she?

Or had that fact been reported to her and she'd simply forgotten it amid the press of other business?

The Star Kingdom as a whole was the Queen's primary business. But what was the point of protecting her star nation if the individual people didn't matter to her?

She raised her eyes from the desk and the chair and slowly looked around the room, pausing on each of the mementos arranged on the rows of display shelves. Burgundy had lived a long and productive life, serving four monarchs. It was a legacy he and his family could be proud of.

Distantly, she wondered if anyone would ever match that record.

"Your Majesty?"

Elizabeth started, only then realizing she'd gone into introspective mode. She usually tried to avoid doing that in public. "Yes, Ms. Geary?"

The secretary was holding out a data chip. "I took a moment earlier to check His Grace's most recent work before you arrived," she said. "I thought there might be something vital that needed to be given to Parliament or—" She broke off, blinking back a fresh welling of tears. "The most recent file was labeled *For The Queen*. It was... I think he must have been working on it when..." She trailed off.

"Thank you," Elizabeth said, gingerly taking the chip. Was this what she thought it was? "Thank you, too, for everything you did for him over the past... how many years have you been with him?"

Geary gave a little sniff. "Twenty-three, Your Majesty."

Twenty-three years. Exactly half of Elizabeth's life. And she hadn't even known *that* about Burgundy and his people. "You should probably go home and rest," she told Geary. "If anyone needs you, I'm sure they'll know where to find you."

"Thank you, Your Majesty," Geary said with another sniff. "If it's all right, I'd rather stay. There's... I need to start organizing his things. His family... and someone else will be moving in here soon."

Someone else will be moving in here. "Of course,"

Elizabeth said between suddenly stiff lips. That aspect hadn't even occurred to her.

And why would it? She'd never had to worry about the makeup of Parliament or the Cabinet. Even in the months since she'd ascended the Throne her only real decision had been to reappoint everyone in the Cabinet who'd been there under her brother.

Now, suddenly, the position of Prime Minister had to be filled.

And the Queen was the one who had to choose a candidate to offer to the House of Lords.

Her first, reflexive thought was that she needed to talk to Burgundy. Her second, gut-wrenching thought was the fact that she would never talk to him again.

And there was no one else in the cabinet, or in politics in general, who she could trust to guide her through this.

In fact, there was only one person on Manticore, period, who she could trust.

She waited until she was back in her aircar heading back to the Palace. Then, her heart pounding, she keyed her uni-link.

Her father answered on the first ping. "Hello, Elizabeth," he said, his voice sounding even more raspy than usual. "How are you holding up?"

"Not too well," Elizabeth admitted. "I assume you've heard the news?"

"About Davis?" There was a barely audible sigh. "Yes. I gather you want to talk?"

"Very much," Elizabeth said. "Are you available?"

"Always," Michael assured her. "I'll be waiting in the Sanctum when you get back."

"Thank you," Elizabeth said. "And also . . . I'm sorry

if this isn't very regal. But right now, I really need a hug from my father."

"That's good," Michael said gently. "Because I could really use a hug from my daughter, too. I'll see you soon."

☆   ☆   ☆

The man Gensonne had chosen to be the public face of the Volsung Mercenaries was, in Llyn's opinion, something of a mixed bag.

On the one hand, he was big, bluff, and bearded, a look that put him midway between merc and pirate. Given that the Volsungs' work similarly straddled that line, it gave prospective customers a good idea of what to expect.

On the other hand, a public liaison ought to at least make a pretense of being helpful. And Lieutenant Commander Syncho wasn't even trying.

"No," he said, shaking his head even more firmly than he had the first two times he'd delivered himself of that same negative. "I have no idea where Admiral Gensonne might be. Probably out on a job somewhere."

Which was compete nonsense, Llyn knew. Gensonne wasn't off on any money-making venture. He was either tucked away in his secret shipyard, licking his wounds and trying to put the pieces of his fleet back together, or he was sitting there glowering, having been run out of the Manticore system without firing a single shot.

Or was on his way back from Posnan, having failed in his effort to catch Llyn's ship there.

"Can you at least give me a hint?" he persisted.

"How many times do I have to say it?" Syncho demanded. "I'm not telling you anything. And if you ask me, friend, you've got a lot of nerve showing up here after what happened at Manticore."

"Do I, now," Llyn said. Unfortunately, that answer didn't really eliminate any of the choices.

The polite approach had gotten him nowhere. Time to switch tactics.

His backup was out in the anteroom, and he could theoretically call them in at any time to help tighten the screws on Syncho. But Syncho's own backup was out there, too, glowering suspiciously at the visitors, and taking them out would make enough noise that even Syncho would figure out what was going on.

So fine. Llyn would just have to do this himself.

"Fine—let's talk nerve," he said. "I'm not asking anymore, I'm demanding. Tell me where he is."

Syncho's face darkened. "Or what?" he growled.

"Or I stay right here." Llyn reached across the narrow desk with his left hand and slapped his fingertips on the top of Syncho's computer display. "*Right* here." He tapped the display again, harder this time. "Until you reach into this little magic box—" *tap-tap* "—and tell me—" *tap-tap-tap* "—where the hell Gensonne is."

"Stop that," Syncho snapped, reaching up to slap away Llyn's fingers.

Llyn twitched his hand back, just far enough to avoid Syncho's. Syncho withdrew his hand, and Llyn again reversed direction, slapping his left fingertips again on the top of the display.

"You don't like this?" he asked, tapping the display again.

"Damn you—*stop* it!" Leaning forward, Syncho

darted out his hand, this time grabbing for Llyn's hand instead of just trying to slap it away. Again, Llyn twitched his hand back just out of Synch's reach.

And then, even as Syncho stretched further forward, trying to close the gap, Llyn snapped out his right hand and caught Syncho's wrist. Throwing on a quick finger-lock with his left hand, he yanked the trapped arm toward him.

Syncho was caught completely by surprise. His first reflexive move was to try to pull back; but he was seated, and Llyn was standing, and Llyn had a two-handed grip and far better leverage. Llyn continued to pull, stretching the arm and bowing Syncho over at the waist until Syncho's elbow was directly over the top of the monitor.

And even as Syncho slammed his left hand down on the tabletop in an attempt to regain his balance and resist Llyn's pull, Llyn rotated the merc's arm over and set his elbow down on the top of the monitor. Leaning forward, he shifted from a backwards pull to a downward push.

Syncho cursed again. But this time the fury had an edge of fear to it. With the full weight of the merc's body now concentrated on his elbow, all Llyn had to do was add a few kilos of his own weight to his end of the lever and the joint would snap like a dry stick. Desperately, Syncho scrambled to his feet, kicking back his chair in his haste, trying to relieve the pressure and delay his imminent crippling.

And as his belt and the attached holster cleared the edge of the desk, Llyn released his left-handed finger lock, reached over the desk, and deftly plucked Syncho's handgun from the holster. He shoved backward with his right hand, releasing Syncho's wrist, and took a quick step backward.

And with that, he had Syncho exactly where he wanted him.

"Not a word," Llyn said quietly. He nodded toward the door behind him. "Not unless you want your men out there to die."

For a long moment he thought Syncho was going to try it anyway, and to hell with the consequences. But the man wasn't as stupid as he looked. He stood where he was, his hands chest-high, his open palms toward Llyn, his lips pressed together into a thin line.

"Good," Llyn said. "Back up a bit more, if you would. Let's say all the way to the wall."

Silently, still keeping his hands visible, Syncho complied. "So what now?" he asked quietly. "You shoot my knees and elbows and crotch until I talk?"

"Oh, please," Llyn protested. "We of the Solarian League like to think we're more civilized than that. On the floor, facing the wall with your hands behind your head, fingers laced. I'm sure you know the routine."

He waited until Syncho had complied. "As I said, I'm sure it's all in the magic box here," he continued, circling to the other side of the desk. He reached for the keyboard with his free hand—

And paused, his lips puckering. The computer, which had been on earlier, was now off. "Deadman switch?" he asked.

"Foot pedal," Syncho said. "Activated when someone we don't know comes in for a chat. Or someone we don't trust."

"I'm guessing that's me," Llyn said, peering under the desk. There was indeed a small foot switch down there.

Clever. "Like I said, magic box," he said. Keeping one eye on Syncho, he started unplugging the computer. "I figure everything I need is in here."

"You'll never get it out."

"I think I will," Llyn assured him. "I know a magician who loves cracking magic boxes. Be sure to say hello to Admiral Gensonne the next time you see him. Or not—I'll be there in person soon enough."

"Oh, don't worry," Syncho growled. "He'll be waiting."

"You misunderstand," Llyn protested. "He's going to be happy to see me."

"You think that, huh?"

"I know it," Llyn assured him. He pulled out the sensor in his pocket, which he'd turned on just before entering, and checked the analysis readout. Smiling in satisfaction, he put it back in his pocket and swapped it out for a book reader he'd bought on his way over to the Volsung office. "Now, I'm leaving you a little deadman device of my own," he said, placing the reader on the edge of the desk closest to Syncho. "It's a neuro toxin dispenser. In one hour the internal fuse oxidizes and the thing becomes harmless. Until then, move in this direction and you won't have to worry about what you're going to tell Gensonne about this little incident. Under the circumstances, I suggest you have yourself a nice nap."

He pulled out his uni-link, tapped the signal key, and waited the twenty seconds it took for the noise coming from the anteroom to fade back to silence. Then, keeping his gun pointed at Syncho, he backed out of the office.

The six Volsungs who'd been playing guard were

scattered around the room, none of them seriously marked, all of them still breathing. That was good, and per Llyn's specific orders to his three-man team. Gensonne wouldn't take kindly to having more of his people killed, after all, especially not by Llyn himself.

A moment later he and the team were back on the street. Fifty-five minutes later, without further incident or any indications of pursuit, they were back aboard *Pacemaker*.

☆   ☆   ☆

Captain Katura wasn't impressed.

"You realize they're going to have at least three layers of encryption on this thing," he pointed out as Llyn set up the Volsung computer in *Pacemaker's* wardroom. "Plus passwords, biometrics, and possibly a rolling code."

"There's no rolling code," Llyn said. "Those need to run a periodic synch signal, and I checked for that before I left the office. As for passwords and biometrics, they can be hacked, altered, or worked around."

"There's still the multiple encryptions."

"There's a lady aboard named Hester Fife," Llyn said "You may not have seen much of her—she tends to be something of a recluse. But she's a genius with such things. I'll turn her loose on the computer while we wait for Syncho or one of his comrades to go tearing off to warn Gensonne that I'm on his tail."

"And when he does, *Shrike* or *Banshee* will track him?"

"Exactly," Llyn said. "Naturally, Syncho will see that he's being followed and either take a completely roundabout route or else just head off in the opposite direction. But that's all right, because both captains have been instructed to break off pursuit after two days and return here."

"All right," Katura said slowly. "But if you're not expecting Syncho to lead you to Gensonne, and you're not even going to stick with him long enough to know for sure . . . ?"

"I'm buying time." Llyn tapped the computer. "Time for Hester to crack this thing. If we *don't* follow Syncho, he'll go straight to Gensonne and give him his account of what just happened. I'd rather my version be the one Gensonne hears first."

"So we make him either evade or try to lure our ship away," Katura said, nodding. "And even when it breaks off, he won't be absolutely sure he hasn't just been handed off to someone else."

"Exactly," Llyn said. "Especially since he'll also wonder if we have some exotic Solarian tech that will let us follow him without being seen. I figure four days for Hester to get in, and we'll be ready to go."

"I hope you're right, sir," Katura said, still clearly not convinced.

"I am." Llyn shrugged. "And if it doesn't work, we'll just come back and go with Syncho's suggested approach."

"Which was?"

"I believe it started off with a bullet to the knee."

CHAPTER EIGHTEEN

RECENTLY, WINTERFALL HAD NOTICED, IT DIDN'T seem to take much to set Breakwater off. Today, unfortunately, was no exception.

Especially since the announcement from the Palace was probably not what he'd expected.

"Harwich," Breakwater snarled, pacing back and forth across his office like a Kodiak Max on stimulants. "Of all people. The entire House of Lords to choose from, and she pushes *Harwich* to be PM?"

"He seems a reasonable choice to me," Winterfall said cautiously. Probably not what Breakwater had expected. Definitely not what he'd wanted. "He *did* vote with us in the last three MPARS funding debates."

Breakwater's eyes might have flashed at Winterfall's use of the word *us*. "That's not the point," the Chancellor growled. "Of *course* he voted with us—he votes for *everything* that builds Manticore's industrial base. The point is that he's stolid, unimaginative, and completely unequipped to maintain the political balance that's a big part of the Prime Minister's job.

And how in the world did he manage to put together a majority?"

"Maybe political balance isn't what the Queen is looking for," Winterfall suggested. "And maybe he has a majority *because* she made it clear she favored him."

This time, Breakwater's eyes definitely flashed. "Of *course* that's what happened," he said. "Elizabeth is making her move. This is her first salvo in an all-out attack on us."

And there it was: the landing pad where Breakwater's strange flights of fancy always seemed to end up these days. The Chancellor was convinced that the Queen was out to get him—him personally—and no amount of evidence or logic to the contrary seemed to matter.

"You could fight it," Winterfall pointed out. "If you call in enough favors, you might be able to pull back enough of his majority to push him out again."

"I'm tempted," Breakwater rumbled. "Don't think I'm not. But better to save our ammunition for later." He snorted. "In fact, that may be exactly what she's hoping we'll do. Flush out all our supporters so that she knows who to target before she starts trotting out her pet projects for Harwich to push through."

"Or maybe she has something else in mind," Winterfall suggested. "Maybe she's not so much moving Harwich *into* the PM position as she is moving him *out* of the Minister of Industry slot."

"If she thinks—" Breakwater broke off, his forehead furrowing. "That's a very interesting thought, Gavin," he said in a more subdued tone. "*Very* interesting. Who do you think she might want to put in his place?"

"Depends on her ultimate goal, I suppose," Winterfall said. At least he'd distracted Breakwater from his paranoid rant. "If she's focusing on building the Merchant Marine, she might put Countess Acton in. I know she's been working with Heinreich Hauptman to develop contacts and supply sources in Silesia, Haven, and the League. Not counting places like Casca and—"

"No," Breakwater interrupted, his pacing coming to an abrupt halt. "Not the Merchant Marine. I'll be damned—she's going for Edward's crazy scheme."

"*King* Edward?"

"He was only Crown Prince then, but that's him," Breakwater said. "He had this insane idea of turning Manticore into the major shipbuilder in the region. *Complete* ships, all the way up to building our own impeller rings."

"I thought that was extremely hard to do."

"Extremely hard, and extremely expensive, both in dollars and man-hours," Breakwater said. "It'll suck up resources and people like a black hole."

"Is there really enough demand out here for ships that we would ever turn a profit?"

"I seriously doubt it," Breakwater said, starting up his pacing again. "Let me think—let me think. He was going to send—right; he was going to send *Casey* around to all our neighbors as an example of what we could do."

"But *Casey*'s impellers and fusion plant are from—"

"Yes, yes, of course they are," Breakwater cut him off again. "That wasn't the point." He inhaled sharply. "Oh, hell. *Casey.*" He waggled a finger at Winterfall. "Look her up—right now. Is she still undergoing repairs?"

"Let me check, My Lord." Winterfall sat down at Breakwater's desk and keyed the computer. A quick search—"Yes, she is," he confirmed. "The work's projected to be finished in about a month."

"What's her schedule after that's done? Is anything posted?"

"Nothing public," Winterfall said, skimming down the page. "Let me dig a little deeper."

"Try the private records."

"I am, My Lord." Winterfall called up the special files, wincing a little. Those records were highly restricted, for Cabinet ministers' eyes only, and Winterfall wasn't even supposed to see them, let alone be able to access them. Breakwater had given him the access codes months ago for another project, and had never bothered to change them. Probably because he was relying less and less on his own staff for this kind of work and more and more on Winterfall.

Once, Winterfall would have taken that as a compliment, an indication that Breakwater was grooming him to one day take his place at the head of his group of like-minded Lords. Now, he was more concerned that such confidence was merely because he was one of the few people Breakwater still felt he could trust.

Which made no sense. Others of the group were just as loyal to the Chancellor and his political point of view as Winterfall, at least as far as he knew.

But then, most of the Lords didn't think the Queen was out to get them.

Did Breakwater think *everyone* except Winterfall was against him, too?

An entry caught his eye. "Here it is, My Lord," he said. "*Casey* is slated to leave in just under a month for an extended voyage of—" He blinked. "Of the Silesian Confederacy."

"*Silesia*?" Breakwater strode over and stopped behind him. "What in the world do they want in Silesia?"

"I don't know," Winterfall said grimly, "but it looks like you may be right about the late King's idea." He pointed a finger at the display. "Look who's scheduled aboard as a passenger."

"Hauptman," Breakwater murmured. "Acton's errand boy. The perfect person to pitch Manticore's future shipbuilding capabilities."

"Is that such a bad thing, My Lord?" Winterfall asked, looking up at Breakwater out of the corner of his eye. He didn't want to be perceived as arguing the point. "Being able to build our own ships without having to buy those components from elsewhere would make us more secure."

"You're not seeing the full picture, Gavin," Breakwater said, resting a hand heavily on Winterfall's shoulder. "Let's assume Hauptman gets ten orders for Manticoran-made ships. Hell—let's say he gets a hundred. How much of our resources will be immediately dedicated to the new impeller and reactor industries?"

"I don't know. A fair amount, I assume."

"A *fair amount*?" Breakwater echoed irritably. "I daresay an *extreme* amount. Resources that would necessarily be taken away from the construction of new MPARS ships and the maintenance of all the old ones." He snorted. "That goes for the Navy's ships, too. Of all times to be tying one hand behind our backs, a period in which the Star Kingdom may be invaded again without warning is the absolute worst."

"I understand," Winterfall said, keeping his voice calm and soothing. On the other hand, wouldn't having a ship-building facility of their own make it *easier* to build more MPARS ships? And, moreover, to build them in whatever configuration they wanted? Surely

Breakwater could see that. Was he so focused on the near-term detriments that he couldn't even see the long-term advantages?

"Good," Breakwater said. "Because there's more. Suppose you were the League and you heard we were starting our own impeller facility. Would you be inclined to sell us any more impellers? Or would you figure that this market was closed and move on to greener pastures?"

"I assume I'd keep selling until the market went completely dry."

"*If* they're good, upstanding business people," Breakwater said. "But what if they're vindictive types who would prefer to watch us swing in the wind while we bring our facilities up to speed? Remember, it'll be years before the first impeller ring comes off the line, and years more before we see any kind of profit."

"Seems a bit counter to their best interests," Winterfall said.

"Is it?" Breakwater countered. "A clever League manufacturer might conclude that we would fail, and when we came crawling back in a few years he could charge double price for his product."

"*If* he was the only manufacturer. There are several."

"Most of whom are controlled by a handful of Transstellar corporations," Breakwater said. "Technodyne, Shadwell, Axelrod, Timmerman, maybe one or two others. If one of them cuts us off, the others might take the cue and either follow suit or else immediately raise their prices." He snorted. "And no impellers also means no expansion of MPARS. *Or* the Navy."

"Yes," Winterfall murmured, his stomach knotting. Certainly a passionate argument.

Only as far as he could tell, it was also a ridiculous one. The Transtellars did too much other business with Manticore and the other systems in this region to bother blacklisting the Star Kingdom. Besides, even if they lost *all* their impeller ring sales out here—which was never going to happen—they were raking in plenty of profit from their other divisions.

"So the bottom line is that we have to stop this," Breakwater concluded. "Suggestions?"

Winterfall pursed his lips, gazing at the data. Assuming that Breakwater's paranoiac scenarios were genuinely on the line, if *Casey* headed off on schedule, there was a chance that one of them would come to pass.

What if she *didn't* leave?

Or if she did leave, what if she didn't look nearly as good as she did now to prospective buyers?

They couldn't do any damage to the ship herself, of course. That would be utterly irresponsible, not to mention flat-out treasonous.

But maybe a little tweaking of the personnel...

"*Casey's* under the command of Commodore Heissman," he said. "A certified war hero."

"Especially since that censure motion went nowhere," Breakwater growled. "Yet another setback we can lay at Harwich's feet."

"Yes," Winterfall continued hurriedly. The last thing he wanted to listen to was another tirade. "That status makes him the kind of person foreign officials love to throw state dinners for. In fact, they'd probably arm-wrestle each other for the privilege of hosting him."

"I see where you're going," Breakwater said. "Whereas if the Navy put a nobody in his place...?"

"Hauptman can still preach the wonders of Manticoran shipbuilding," Winterfall said. "But he won't have nearly so prominent a pulpit."

"Excellent, Gavin," Breakwater said warmly. "Most excellent." He gestured to the computer. "Proceed."

Winterfall blinked up at him.

"Excuse me, My Lord?"

"Proceed," Breakwater repeated. "Make it happen." He glanced at his chrono. "I need to meet with Castle Rock and Chillon. Go ahead and use my office. By the time I get back, I expect the plan to be in motion."

Winterfall sighed. At least the Chancellor wasn't expecting to read about Heissman's firing on the news tonight.

"Yes, My Lord."

A minute later he was alone, staring at the display, wondering how in the world he was going to pull this off. He hadn't been exaggerating about Heissman's heroic stature. Getting him fired would be next to impossible.

So he wouldn't. He would get him promoted.

Winterfall paused, a momentary doubt flickering through him. But the hesitation passed. He wasn't doing this for himself, he reminded himself firmly, or even for Breakwater. He was doing it for his star nation.

Obviously, he couldn't go through any of Breakwater's usual associates. The Chancellor had stayed in the background during the whole censure debate, but no one had been particularly fooled. Likewise, he couldn't go to any of Breakwater's opponents, or even neutrals—every one of them would smell a rat.

But Breakwater also had some associates outside of the Lords. Winterfall had only met a couple of them, and they'd struck him at the time as being a bit on the shady side. But a couple of those had contacts within the Navy and even among certain of the Lords. The right word dropped in the right ear from someone who had no connection whatsoever with the Chancellor should do the trick.

Flexing his fingers, he got to work.

☆　　☆　　☆

When Travis was ten T-years old, his uncle had once taken him to a stage magic show. Part of the magician's routine had involved yanking a tablecloth out from under a quartet of dinner settings, complete with filled wine glasses, without disturbing any of it.

Right now, he felt exactly like one of those wine glasses.

"With all due respect, My Lady," he said looking up from his tablet, "this is a bad idea."

"I agree," Calvingdell said sourly. "But it's out of my hands. Cazenestro and Locatelli think it's a terrific idea, and signed off on it before I even knew it was in the works."

"Can't you go to them now, My Lady?" Travis persisted. "Not only was Commodore Heissman the ideal man to lead the mission, but shuffling the top command tier of a ship this close to sailing is never a good idea."

"Believe it or not, Lieutenant, there *are* a few people outside the Navy who get that," she said. "I like to think the Queen and I are among them."

"And the Prime Minister?"

Calvingdell's nose wrinkled. "If not, he'll learn," she said. "Baron Harwich is a decent enough man, if a little tunnel-visioned. Unlike some others I could name, I think he was an inspired choice for PM." She waved a hand impatiently. "The point is that it's too late for him or Dapplelake to intervene now. A sudden rescinding of Heissman's promotion and cancelling the formation of *Swiftsure*'s task force would raise eyebrows, questions, and suspicions, none of which we can afford right now."

Travis looked back down at his tablet, silently seething. After all the time at MPARS, and then this Delphi training regimen he'd been put through, he'd been eagerly looking forward to serving under Heissman again.

Only now Heissman was out. Promoted to Admiral, which he certainly deserved, and being prepped for command of a new Navy task force, which he also deserved.

But the timing of the whole thing stunk. Delphi was running very much under the radar, at Calvingdell's insistence and the Queen's consent, but the First Lord and System Commander were of course in on the secret. If one of them had thought to run this by Calvingdell before they made their decision, this whole thing might have been caught in time.

But they hadn't, and it was too late now.

"I don't think I know this Captain Clegg," he said, looking up from the tablet. "What's she like?"

"Solid," Calvingdell said. "Competent, smart, dedicated, and ready for action. Not a particularly good people person, though. A bit thorny, I'm told."

"Terrific," Travis said under his breath. "Exactly what we want for *Casey*."

"Oh, the feeling is mutual," Calvingdell assured him. "I also gather she considers *Casey* a step down from her previous post aboard *Vanguard*, which isn't helping her mood any."

"What if Admiral Eigen asked to keep her?" Travis suggested. "Maybe then we could get someone else."

"You've got it backwards," Calvingdell said. "Eigen's the one who recommended her for the post in the first place."

"You sure he's not trying to get rid of her?"

Calvingdell shook her head. "He's on record as saying she's the best captain he's ever worked with. In fact, it's right there in his recommendation that he hates to lose her, but that *Casey* deserves the best, and he wants us to have it."

"Ah," Travis said. "Well . . . hopefully, she'll warm up to us."

"She will," Calvingdell assured him. "I'll do what I can to put all this in a better light when we have our little talk later this week." She waved a hand. "Oh, don't look so glum. Commander Belokas is unfortunately still at the MPARS academy, but at least you'll still have Woodburn on the bridge and Norris in Engineering. Between the three of you, there should be enough command continuity to carry the rest of the ship."

"I hope so," Travis said, frowning. The note about Clegg's appointment as Captain hadn't included the rest of the ship's roster. Odd. "You said Commander Woodburn would be remaining as Tactical Officer?"

"Actually, he's been promoted to full Commander and will be taking over the Executive Officer position from Commander Belokas," Calvingdell said, a small smile playing at the corners of her lips. "The Tactical Officer slot is to be filled by—let me see—oh, that's right: a Lieutenant Commander Travis Long. Did I forget to mention you've also been promoted?"

Travis felt his mouth drop open. According to the

usual advancement timetable, he wasn't due for a promotion for at least a couple more T-years. "My Lady?" he managed.

"You heard right, Commander," Calvingdell said, smiling openly now. "Congratulations. You deserve it."

"I—thank you, My Lady."

"And with that, the good news of the day is over," Calvingdell said. "You've got less than a month before you sail, so get back to work."

Travis was halfway back to the main Delphi room when a thought occurred to him. Namely, that his new promotion would make it easier to pull rank aboard *Casey* if the mission required it.

Was that the only reason he'd been promoted so far ahead of schedule?

For a moment the warm glow faded a little. But only a little, and only for a moment. Whatever Calvingdell's ulterior motives might have been, the fact remained that he was now a lieutenant commander.

And as someone had once told him, the best of all good fortunes were the ones that benefited everyone. He would do his best to make sure that *Casey*, and everyone aboard her, benefited from his promotion to Tactical Officer.

He only hoped that Captain Clegg would eventually feel the same way about her new position.

☆　　☆　　☆

Joshua Miller was fifty-two T-years old, with a face that was pleasantly craggy and a body that had once been lean and well-muscled but had started running a bit to fat over the past few years as more of his time shifted from running his farm to sitting in the House of Commons. His clothing was neat but not expensive, as befit a man of the soil who had steadfastly refused to let his work in the city permeate his views, values, habits, or temperament.

He was also about as ill at ease as anyone could possibly be, though he was trying very hard not to show it.

Neither of which was really surprising. It was not every day, after all, when a lowly Member of Parliament was invited to the Palace for lunch with the Queen.

"I hope you enjoy what the chef has prepared," Elizabeth said as she picked up her napkin and set it in her lap, pretending as she did so that she was paying more attention to it than she was to Miller.

A forlorn hope, probably. Like the two men she'd had to lunch in the weeks before him, Miller was paying acute attention to everything she was doing. Wondering, no doubt, exactly what he was doing here.

Which, unfortunately, put him in good company, because Elizabeth herself really didn't know. All she knew was that his was the third of seven names on the list Burgundy had left her.

His name, and *only* his name. There had been no detailing of qualifications, family, genetic profile, or anything else that might have put him on Burgundy's radar as a suitable consort, as the late Prime Minister had so delicately put it.

The other names had been similarly plain and unadorned. Presumably Burgundy had planned to add in those details later, either on the document itself or in a face-to-face with his Queen.

Unfortunately, he'd done neither. And now all Elizabeth had was a set of enigmas.

She'd done her own homework, of course. She'd

looked into each of the seven men, reading through their public profiles and digging as deeply into the more private data lists as she could without feeling like a voyeur. She had stacks of facts and figures, but no real feel for the men behind them.

Hence, these one-on-one lunches.

"I'm sure it will be wonderful, Your Majesty," Miller assured her, carefully laying his own napkin across his lap. His motions, Elizabeth noted, were an exact mirror image of her own. Observant, and not taking any chances with unfamiliar protocol.

"According to my spies, you like Chicken Kiev," Elizabeth continued. "The Palace chef has a slightly different variant than what you're probably used to."

"I'm sure it will be wonderful, Your Majesty," Miller repeated. He hesitated, then dared a small smile. "Though all your spies had to do was ask for the recipe. I'm sure my cook would have been delighted to share it."

"Next time," Elizabeth promised. And he had a sense of humor, too. "I hope this version will be satisfactory."

"I'm sure it will," Miller said. "It won't be the first variant on familiar cuisine that I've tried during my years in Parliament."

"I'm sure it won't," Elizabeth said, a little ruefully as memories came back. "I remember the first time I tried San Giorgio cuisine. It was quite a shock to my taste buds."

"You don't have to tell *me*," Miller said dryly. "My first stab at Gou stew, I was convinced the cap had fallen off the spice jar while the chef was sprinkling it into the pot. I can't even smell it without my mouth starting to tingle." His face went suddenly rigid again. "Your Majesty," he added hurriedly.

Elizabeth sighed inwardly. Once again, the all-but-impenetrable barrier that existed between Sovereign and subject. She'd never liked it much when she was merely Princess Elizabeth; now that she was Queen Elizabeth, there were times when she absolutely despised it. A picture flashed to mind: her newly chosen royal consort on their wedding night, calling out her name in passion and then adding *Your Majesty*.

Angrily, she shook the completely improper image away. This wasn't courtship. It was just the very beginning of a possible dating period. They were here to share a meal and learn a little about each other, and that was all.

Her stomach tightened. No. This wasn't even dating. It was, fundamentally, the vetting of a farmland stud animal.

"My experience wasn't quite that bad," she said. "But there are definitely some dishes and spices I've learned to graciously decline. Fortunately, that shouldn't be a problem today."

"I'm sure it won't, Your Majesty." Miller hesitated. "If I may ask, and please forgive the bluntness . . . but why exactly am I here?"

It was the obvious question, and both of Miller's predecessors had also asked it. Fortunately, having now gone through the routine twice, Elizabeth had a stock answer ready. "Before his sudden death, Prime Minister Burgundy made up a short list of names that he labeled only *For The Queen*," she explained. "Your name was on that list."

Miller seemed to draw back. "Really," he said, his

voice odd. "That's very strange, Your Majesty. May I ask what the list was for?"

"A good question," Elizabeth said. "Unfortunately, I don't have an answer. That's why I invited you here today. Can you think of any reason Duke Burgundy would have wanted to bring you to my attention?"

"Not really, Your Majesty," Miller said, frowning at the table's centerpiece as if the answer might be hidden among the flower petals or the stem weavings. "At home, I'm a moderately successful farmer and rancher; here in Landing I'm a somewhat less esteemed MP who's known mainly for his inability to know when to keep his mouth shut. I can't see either of those items lifting me out of the mass of far more distinguished men and women."

"Don't sell yourself short, Mr. Miller," Elizabeth admonished him mildly. "Duke Burgundy put you on the list for a reason. We just have to figure out what set of abilities and interests he was selecting for."

"Well, I wish you good luck, Your Majesty," he said. "I'll also think about it, of course, and I'll certainly stand ready to help in any way I can. But right now, I'm completely at a loss."

"I suppose we'll just have to work on it together." Elizabeth tapped the call button. "In the meantime, we also have a Chicken Kiev to work on. And while we eat, perhaps you'll be good enough to tell me about yourself."

The two previous lunches had been pleasant enough. So, too, was this one. And it definitely made for a nice change from business lunches with various Lords, industrialist groups, or even close associates like Dapplelake.

Still, in the end it was a wash. Miller was a decent enough man, with a quick mind and a good sense of humor, at least what little of it he dared to let show in front of his Queen. But there was no chemistry between them that Elizabeth could sense. Nothing that might make Joshua Miller suitable to stand beside her as the Queen's Consort.

Certainly not with the memory of Carmichael still so painfully fresh in her heart and soul.

But of course, the Constitution never mentioned chemistry. All it specified were the rules of the Monarch's union, and the children of that union.

And as lunch ended, and Miller went on his way, she found herself wondering distantly if she'd suddenly been transported back to the pre-Diaspora middle ages.

CHAPTER NINETEEN

IN LLYN'S LINE OF WORK, IT was vital to understand the people he dealt with. Unfortunately, no matter how carefully he planned or how insightful his assessments, some of those people occasionally surprised him.

Syncho, it turned out, was among that group.

Or at least at the edge of it. There were two ships in orbit when the *Pacemaker* headed out: a courier ship and a midsized freighter. Llyn had assumed that the courier was the Volsung ship; instead, it was the freighter that took off before Llyn was halfway to the hyper limit.

And it was going fast, burning space at probably ninety percent of the ship's capability.

On paper, at least, the freighter appeared to be the property of the system governor. But a little digging through the records revealed that it had just been transferred to him by anonymous parties, undoubtedly the Volsungs. Apparently, Syncho had borrowed it back for the purpose of running a message to Gensonne.

Whether or not he had permission to commandeer it was, of course, a different question. Llyn guessed the governor and Gensonne would be having words somewhere down the line.

Still, the subterfuge was a waste of effort. Llyn had carefully bracketed the system with his three ships, and while Syncho's vector was clearly designed to make sure *Pacemaker* couldn't change course to intercept him, *Shrike* was already in position to follow.

When Syncho finally escaped into hyperspace, he had a tail.

The tail, as per Llyn's orders, had returned to Telmach four days later, with Captain Vaagen reporting on Syncho's efforts to lose him or at least draw him away from the Volsung base. But again, the merc's efforts went nowhere. By the time *Shrike* returned, Hester had hacked, sliced, tweaked, and frauded her way through every one of the captured computer's security barriers and reached the precious data within.

And Llyn finally had the location of Gensonne's secret base.

Walther was only eight light-years from Telmach, containing a single habitable planet that no one yet had seen fit to develop or even inhabit. Apparently, that was a pattern in Silesia: someone would stake claim to a planet or system, just to have their ownership on record, and invest in a few hundred colonists or an orbiting frigate to make the claim viable. Later, if the owner felt like it, he might put some real time and money into developing the place.

How Gensonne had gotten permission to park himself and the Volsungs' orbiting base here Llyn didn't know. Best guess was that he'd done the owner some off-the-books favor, probably involving violence and firepower.

Gensonne's main stock in trade. The question right

now was whether the Volsungs were about to trot out some of that same merchandise.

"Anything new on the ship out there?" Llyn asked.

"Almost within decent sensor range," Katura said. "You *did* say you had a plan for this reunion, correct?"

"I have four of them," Llyn assured him. "Depending on the scenario we end up in."

"Yes, Sir," Katura said, not sounding completely convinced.

Llyn couldn't really blame him. Until they had more data, there were so many possibilities and variables.

Still, Llyn had a fair amount of experience with this sort of thing. He was pretty sure he had everything covered.

Scenario One: The Volsungs ran when they saw the Manticorans' firepower and are undamaged. Plan A: Regroup and discuss how to hit them again.

"Sensor data's coming in now from *Banshee*, Sir," Katura said. "It's definitely a battlecruiser, though still no ID. Captain Rhamas reports that the dorsal radiator vanes are non-functional and that the starboard sidewall is having some issues with flickering."

"Thank you," Llyn said, rubbing his cheek. *Banshee*, traveling parallel to *Pacemaker* and a thousand kilometers above it, had far better sensors and analysis equipment than Llyn's simple courier ship did. He couldn't verify *Banshee*'s conclusion, but he also had no reason to doubt it.

And Rhamas's analysis was quite telling. A radiator problem could be internal, but adding in a flickering sidewall strongly suggested battle damage. Odds were that the battlecruiser approaching them was one of the ships Gensonne had taken to Manticore.

So much for Scenario One.

The question now was why Gensonne had sent a damaged ship to meet Llyn. To underscore what had happened there? "Still no response to our hail, I assume?"

"No, sir," Katura said. "Do you want me to send it again?"

"No, let's try something new," Llyn decided. The standard hail was pretty generic. Time to perhaps sweeten the pot a bit. "Put a com laser on him. Let me know when it's ready."

Scenario Two: The Volsungs were hit hard and retreated. Gensonne or his replacement is ready to try again. Plan B: Regroup, repair, rearm, and discuss how to hit the Manticorans again.

"Ready, sir."

Llyn tapped the key.

"This is Jeremiah Llyn calling for Admiral Gensonne," he said into the mic. "I'm bringing your second payment, ready for delivery. I assume you're our escort?"

He stopped, waiting for the short time delay—

"Llyn, you have one *hell* of a nerve coming here," Gensonne's voice boomed from the speaker.

"Ah—Admiral," Llyn said calmly. "I thought that was probably you. You're very quick off the blocks—we only entered the system a hundred forty minutes ago."

"Don't be so surprised—I knew you were coming," Gensonne growled. "While you were busy following the freighter, Syncho signaled one of my other ships in the system, which slipped away right under your nose and brought me the news that you were back. Give me one good reason I shouldn't blow you out of the sky."

"I'll give you two reasons," Llyn said, feeling sweat gathering under his shirt collar. He'd expected Gensonne to be angry, but there was a viciousness in the mercenary's voice that went far beyond anything he'd been prepared for. "One: as I said, I'm carrying your second payment for what you did at Manticore. Two: I want to talk to you about resetting for another try at them—"

"What we *did* was mostly get our butts kicked," Gensonne shot back as the first part of the message did its turnaround. "Thanks to you and your useless data on their fleet. That little expedition cost me two of my battlecruisers, and I swear to *God* that I'm taking it out of your hide."

Llyn waited another second, just to make sure he'd gotten the whole tirade. "I understand your anger," he said. "That brings me to point two: I want to discuss how our second approach will be different and more successful."

"If you think I have any interest in working with you ever again, you're badly mistaken," Gensonne ground out.

"I'm hoping I can change your mind," Llyn said. "We first need to talk about what happened at—"

"Are you listening?" Gensonne cut him off. "We're out. We'll take our payment, and *you* will take a hike. Where's our cargo?"

"As I said, we have it," Llyn said with a sigh. All the work of setting this up, now straight down the drain.

So much for Scenario Two.

Scenario Three: The Volsungs were hit hard. Gensonne or his replacement is unwilling to try again. Plan C: Pay them off and begin search for a new mercenary group.

"I mean which of your ships is it on?" Gensonne asked.

A small red flag popped up in the back of Llyn's mind. He tapped the mute key—

"Katura, signal *Banshee* to double-check all sensors," he said. Gensonne had known Llyn was coming in, and he'd known where they were coming in from, which meant he'd had a pretty good idea where *Pacemaker* and *Banshee* would enter the system. "I'm looking for a ship lying doggo, probably somewhere behind us."

"Yes, Sir," Katura said, keying his com.

Llyn hit the mute key again. "As you requested, it's in the form of equipment and tech," he told Gensonne.

"I know that," Gensonne said impatiently. "I asked which ship it was aboard."

"Sir?" Katura murmured tensely.

Llyn gestured him to be silent. "*Pacemaker* is a courier ship," he said. "*Banshee* is a freighter. See if you can figure it out."

"*Thank* you," Gensonne said, his voice icy.

Llyn hit the mute button again. "You were saying, Captain?" he invited.

"I was going to say, Sir, that that might not be the best thing—" Katura broke off as a warbling alarm filled the bridge. "Missile trace!" he snapped.

Llyn swallowed hard as the trace appeared on the tactical. It was a missile, all right—the acceleration profile made that abundantly clear—coming as expected from somewhere aft of them.

So much for Scenario Three.

Though it was a very *slow* missile, at least by modern standards, with an acceleration coming in under two thousand gees. That probably gave it more range before its impellers burned out; on the flip side, the lower acceleration also gave Llyn nearly four minutes to figure out his response.

Still, a missile was a missile, and as such was a highly expensive piece of military hardware. What did Gensonne hope to accomplish by throwing that kind of money at him? Especially since all *Pacemaker* had to do was pitch wedge, and the missile would shatter against her stress bands.

Unless Gensonne had something else up his sleeve.

"Sir?" Katura prompted tensely. "Do we pitch wedge?"

Llyn stared at the trace. At this distance it was impossible to tell which of the two Axelrod ships the missile was aimed at. Assuming Gensonne still wanted his payment, and given that he'd just told the self-styled admiral it was aboard *Banshee*...

"Order Captain Vaagen to pitch wedge against the missile," he told Katura.

"Yes, Sir. And us?"

Llyn pursed his lips. "I think, Captain, it's time for another round of chicken." He braced himself. "Strike our wedge."

He turned to see Katura's mouth drop open. For a moment the two men stared at each other. Then Katura closed his mouth again, and nodded. "Helm: Strike wedge," he ordered. He lowered his voice. "I hope you know what you're doing, Sir."

Llyn nodded. So did he.

He hit the com button again. "Admiral Gensonne," he said.

"I'm here," Gensonne said. "I see you've struck your wedge. Are you surrendering?"

"If I am, are you calling off your attack?"

"I don't know," Gensonne said. "How much groveling are you prepared to do?"

"No groveling," Llyn said. "But there *is* one more factor you need to consider. I told you earlier there were two reasons why you shouldn't blow me out of the sky. There are actually three."

"A second *and* a third payment?"

"In a sense," Llyn said. "I liked your idea of infiltrating the Manticore system using ships coasting with their wedges down. I liked it so much, in fact, that I decided to use it on you."

There was a short pause, longer than the simple time-delay.

"What are you talking about?" Gensonne demanded cautiously.

"I'm talking about my other ship," Llyn said. "The one that came in quietly several days ago. The one that will shortly be coming into missile range of your base.

"The one that just saw my wedge go down, and assumes I've been destroyed."

This time, the pause was longer.

"You're bluffing."

"I'm *bluffing*?" Llyn scoffed. "Is that the best you can come up with? That I'm *bluffing*?"

"You might as well be," Gensonne shot back. "You really think my base isn't fully prepared to repulse an attack? We have ships at the ready, plus station-mounted autocannon and counter-missile banks. Your missiles and ship won't even get close."

"Who said I was targeting your base?" Llyn countered. "You *do* realize the Eridani Edict only applies to *inhabited* planets, right?"

"You—" Gensonne broke off. "You're not serious."

"Oh, I'm *very* serious," Llyn assured him. "Granted, I don't know exactly what would happen if my ship fired a full load of missiles into the planet's surface with their wedges still active. Or, for that matter, what would happen if the missiles hit after the wedges have burned out."

"Damn it, there are people down there," Gensonne snapped. But there was a little less bite to his tone. "There are dependents, troops—"

"Not officially," Llyn reminded him. "On paper, Walther is completely uninhabited. Good luck making any claims or accusations stick. As I was saying, I'm guessing we're talking torn-up crust and explosively ejected atmosphere, both of which will have a serious effect even at the distance your base is orbiting. But that's just an assumption. Shall we invoke the name of science and find out for sure?"

There was a long, hissing sigh. "I'm not convinced anything would reach the base," Gensonne said. "But point taken. I assume you have a way of calling him off?"

"Of course: raising my wedge again," Llyn said. "So shall we end this nonsense? I still have a proposal for you, and I'd like to present it without death hanging over either of us."

Another long pause. "Fine," Gensonne said. His tone was still angry, but there was a new mix of caution and surliness added in. "Don't worry about the missile—it's an old practice missile I picked up awhile back. Antique, plus no warhead. I just wanted to make a point."

"That you didn't need me?" Llyn suggested.

"That you mess with the Volsung Mercenaries at your own risk," Gensonne said darkly. "That includes your bosses. And trust me, I never forget. Whatever you're offering, whatever you think you can do to make me forget all this, that won't happen. Ever."

"I'll keep that in mind," Llyn said, his eyes on the missile trace. It was still incoming.

"So are you going to raise your wedge?" Gensonne prompted.

"Once the missile is gone," Llyn said.

There was another pause...and then, on the display, the missile vanished as someone on the battlecruiser sent the self-destruct code.

"Thank you," Llyn said. "That makes things much more civilized. Actually, this whole incident segues rather nicely to my comment earlier about planning our next attack. As you've just demonstrated, your missiles are a hodgepodge of ages, styles, and efficiencies. I'm thinking that what we need to take down Manticore is something a bit more up-to-date."

"*How* up-to-date?"

"Very," Llyn assured him. "Shall we discuss the details at your base?"

"Assuming it's still there?"

Llyn gestured to Katura, who gestured in turn to the helmsman. On the status display, *Pacemaker*'s wedge reappeared.

"Your base will be fine," Llyn assured Gensonne, eying their relative vectors and running a quick mental calculation. "Looks like you'll arrive a few hours behind us. You might want to send word back regarding my accommodations. Nothing fancy—I'd be happy to just make myself comfortable in your office, if you'd like."

"We have more than enough room for you to have a place of your own."

"Good," Llyn said. "I also suggest you have someone assemble the files of the battle for me. I need to know exactly what happened, and if I go through them now you won't have to sit around later with your feet up while I read."

"You'll have them." Gensonne paused. "Just remember who it is you're dealing with."

"Of course," Llyn said. "Don't you forget, either."

"I won't," Gensonne said softly. "Have a safe journey, Mr. Llyn. I'll look forward to hearing about these missiles."

"I'm sure you'll find the conversation most interesting," Llyn said. "I'll see you back at your base."

He gestured, and Katura keyed off the com.

For a long moment Llyn stared at the tactical, watching as his ships and the Volsungs all reshuffled or refined their courses. Yes, he had no doubt that Gensonne would jump at the chance to get hold of some modern missiles. No doubt that he would do whatever was necessary to gain such a prize.

No doubt that he would follow any of Llyn's instructions to the letter.

Scenario Four: The Volsungs were hit hard. Gensonne or his replacement is swearing vengeance.

Plan D: Kill them all.

CHAPTER TWENTY

GENSONNE'S PEOPLE WEREN'T THRILLED at the prospect of having a houseguest. Particularly not a houseguest that the majority of them seemed to blame for the faulty intel that had handed them a resounding defeat at Manticore. They were even less thrilled by Gensonne's order to hand over all the records of that battle.

But they were professionals, of a sort, and they knew an order when they heard it. They didn't obey willingly, but they *did* obey.

Not that Llyn blamed them. Before he was even halfway through the battle's timeline, he could see why they didn't want him seeing it.

The thing had been a disaster from square one. The idea of splitting the force into two waves was reasonable in theory, but the minute Gensonne lost his first battlecruiser he should have tightened up the formation. A single wave would probably have meant fewer Manticoran ships destroyed, given the speed at which the two forces would shoot past each other and the subsequently short combat window. But even that was a fool's misreading of the mission's objective. As in chess, the goal was to checkmate the king—in this case, literally—not simply destroy as many pawns, knights, and bishops as possible.

The frustrating part was that even after Gensonne's failure to make sure a wounded enemy ship was dead, the error that had cost him a second battlecruiser, he still could have pulled it out. He had the numbers, the arsenal, and the expertise to reach Manticore orbit and call on King Edward to surrender.

As for the Manticorans' final ploy, that had clearly been nothing but a bluff. Unfortunately for Gensonne, by that point he was so rattled that he'd fallen for it, flat on his face. And in the process, he'd handed Manticore the victory.

By the time Gensonne made it back to the Volsung base and summoned Llyn to his office, Llyn had gone through the records twice and had a solid grasp of the mistakes that had led to the fiasco.

The Volsungs' mistakes he would need to downplay. There was no point in coming off as too critical, given that he needed Gensonne to trust him. The Manticorans' mistakes he could likewise ignore in his upcoming analysis.

But he had made careful note of them. They would be something he would discuss with whatever group ended up taking the Volsungs' place.

"First of all, under the circumstances, I think you and your men did a tremendous job," he told Gensonne. "You had the Manticorans outnumbered and outgunned, and it was pure bad luck that forced you to retreat."

"Bad *luck*?" Gensonne ground out. "That's what you call losing two battlecruisers and a destroyer? Bad *luck*?"

"Call it incredibly good luck on the Manticorans' part, then," Llyn amended with a shrug. Still, he could see in Gensonne's face that he'd hit the right angle. The Admiral was already strongly inclined to blame his defeat on the fortunes of war. All Llyn had to do was keep reinforcing that idea.

"Damn straight," Gensonne said bitterly. "You don't have cruisers and destroyers taking out battlecruisers. Not without the Lady solidly in your corner."

"Absolutely," Llyn agreed. "Plus a couple of bad decisions on your late captains' part." When luck could only support half the load, he'd found, the rest could usually be handled by shifting blame, especially to people who couldn't shift it back. "Captain Blakeley should never have let himself get close enough to an enemy for the kind of sucker punch that took him out. Captain De la Roza similarly should have confirmed all damaged enemy ships were out of the fight before moving in."

"The heat of battle," Gensonne said, scowling out at the universe. "And overconfidence."

"Exactly," Llyn said. "As for the two Manticoran battlecruisers you saw heading into the battle—"

"Yes, let's talk about those," Gensonne interrupted. "Those damn ships weren't even listed in your supposedly up-to-date intel."

"With all due respect, Admiral, they *were* on the list," Llyn countered mildly. "They simply weren't listed as *functional* warships."

"They sure the hell looked functional to me."

"I agree they were flying. But flying alone doesn't make for a warship." He gestured to his tablet. "And having reviewed your records, I'm even more of the opinion that they were paper tigers. No weapons, no defenses, probably not even full crews. Had you stood your ground, I believe it would have taken no more than a single missile to destroy each of them."

"You believe whatever you want," Gensonne said stiffly. "You weren't there. You didn't see them."

"No, I didn't," Llyn conceded. Though he *had* seen them shortly afterward, of course.

But there was no point in rubbing Gensonne's nose in the fact that the Barcan follow-up team had had to abort because of the Volsungs' failure. Time to back off. "But what's done is done. Let's focus on the future."

"Yes, let's," Gensonne said. "Starting with these new missiles you mentioned." He cocked his head. "And maybe a few new ships to go with them. *Big* ships, like top-of-the-line battlecruisers."

Llyn shook his head. He'd prepped hard for this conversation on the trip in from the confrontation, and Gensonne was running exactly true to form.

"I've already told you the League's view of that," he said, putting some regret into his voice. "They have a monopoly on the most modern warships, and fully intend to keep it that way."

"I'm sure they do," Gensonne said contemptuously. "I'm also pretty sure that Axelrod doesn't give a damn what the League wants or doesn't want."

It took every bit of Llyn's self-control to keep the reaction to that name off his face. *God*—how could Gensonne have figured it out? "Axelrod?" he asked, allowing a slight frown to crease his forehead.

"Axelrod of Terra," Gensonne said, smiling in the mocking way people smiled when they were trotting out knowledge of someone else's deepest secrets. "Your bosses. The ones who want to take over Manticore."

For a split second Llyn thought about denying it. He'd worked so incredibly hard to keep even a hint of Axelrod's involvement out of this.

But he knew that look. Knew it all too well. Somehow, Gensonne had discovered the truth, and nothing Llyn could say would convince him otherwise.

No matter. He'd already decided that Gensonne and his men had to die. Now, he simply had to extend that scorched-ground destruction to their entire base and records, too.

"Fine," he said with a casual shrug. "But even Axelrod can't make battlecruisers appear out of thin air. Besides, new missiles on your current ships should be more than enough to take out the RMN."

"Really," Gensonne said, eyeing Llyn closely. "All right. I'm listening."

"I'm talking about Hellflares."

"Are you, now," Gensonne said, his expression still hard and suspicious.

But Llyn had caught the subtle widening of Gensonne's eyes, and the equal loosening of his lips. The man was hooked, all right. All Llyn needed to do was be careful how he reeled him in.

"I am," he confirmed. "AKM six-three-four, to be exact. Maybe some thirty-eights, too, depending on what my man was able to get his hands on."

"I thought Hellflares were on the Class-AA list."

"Everything in the 600 block is, yes," Llyn said. "Again, I don't know what my buyer is bringing. But either one will let you cut through the Manticorans like they were tissue."

"Wait a minute," Gensonne said, frowning. "Did you say your buyer already *has* them? As in bought and paid for?"

"Bought and paid for, shipped and presumably ready to install," Llyn assured him. "That's the reason I came here to see you myself—it was supposed to be a surprise." He lifted his hands. "Surprise."

"And it's not even my birthday," Gensonne said sarcastically, his eyes hard on Llyn. "Why didn't you say something about this when you were threatening to destroy my base?"

"What, on an open com line?" Llyn countered. "Violations of League Class-AA interdictions are hardly a topic for idle conversation. All it would take is one of your men running his mouth at a bar on Telmach to put us all away forever." He gestured to his tablet again. "Besides, I needed to look over the record of the battle and make sure you were competent enough for a second go at Manticore. Now I am."

"We're honored," Gensonne said, his expression still hard. "When are they supposed to get here?"

"For starters, they're not coming *here*," Llyn said. "You don't have the equipment to handle the upgrades. I've arranged—"

"*What* upgrades?" Gensonne demanded. "I've already got launchers."

"Not for Hellflares you don't," Llyn said patiently. "These will require modifications to your launch systems to handle the new plasma feeds, and a whole new targeting and telemetry system to interface with the new seeker software."

Gensonne was still maintaining that hard, suspicious expression. But his eyes were starting to glaze over with the look of a man who's just met his own true love.

"And you're *giving* these to us?"

"I'm giving you the *missiles*," Llyn corrected. One never wanted to make things *too* easy for a mark. "I'm afraid you're going to be on the hook for the launcher upgrades."

"And how damn pricey is that going to be?"

"Don't worry, your second payment should cover it," Llyn said. "Unless you'd rather let your crew spend it all on beer and night ladies."

"I think they'll understand the priorities involved," Gensonne said with a sort of grim amusement.

"And there are going to be a few other restrictions," Llyn continued. "You understand that we can't just let weapons like this go wandering off without someone keeping an eye on them. Any mission you run with them will be under my watch, or the watch of one of my colleagues."

"So what, we're now a wholly-owned subsidiary of Axelrod?"

"Let's just say that you'll be our go-to for anything involving serious muscle," Llyn said. "That doesn't mean you won't be able to take on other jobs, just that we'll have first priority on your time."

"Mm," Gensonne murmured, and once again Llyn saw the subtle shift of his expression. If Axelrod wanted to keep tabs on the missiles, Llyn or someone like him would always be at Gensonne's side as advisor and supervisor.

And hostage.

"That's assuming you don't mind going back to

Manticore first and feeding them the same dirt sand-wich you had to eat," Llyn added.

Gensonne's face darkened a moment. Then his expression cleared, and he actually smiled.

"You have an interesting way with words," he said. "Fine, you've got yourself a deal. What's first on the list?"

"You'll start by unloading the *Banshee*'s cargo," Llyn said. "While you do that, I'll prep *Pacemaker* to head to Haven."

"*Haven*?" Gensonne asked, his eyes narrowing. "You're delivering illegal missiles to me at *Haven*?"

"Not at Haven, at Danak," Llyn hastened to assure him. "Much more quiet, out-of-the-way place. The government has a shareholder interest in the industrial consortium that's developing Danak, and releasing the missiles requires a signoff from the consortium office in Nouveau Paris."

"So there's going to be a data trail?"

"With missiles, we have no choice," Llyn said. "Don't worry, none of it will lead back to you or me."

"Or Axelrod?"

Llyn felt his throat tighten. "Or Axelrod," he said. "And just to be clear, no one is going to release the missiles to anyone who arrives without his visit having been prescheduled by the office in Haven, so we'll need to make sure we give *Pacemaker* time to get to Haven and then back to Danak."

"I see," Gensonne said. His eyes, Llyn noted, were still narrowed. "And I suppose you'll have to go ahead personally to work out all that paperwork?"

"Why, are you afraid I'll cut and run?" Llyn lifted a hand before Gensonne could answer. "Relax. *Banshee* and I will be with you the whole way."

"You're actually going to rough it in a *freighter*?" Gensonne said, some of his tension fading.

"Why not?" Llyn dared a small smile. "Even Axelrod's freighters are quite comfortable. Unless you want to clear out space for me in *Odin*."

"I don't think that would be a good idea," Gensonne said, his voice going grim. "A lot of the men lost friends on *Tyr* and *Thor* and *Umbriel*. Some of them probably blame you and your half-assed intel for those deaths."

A shiver ran up Llyn's back. That was a part of his creative bookkeeping he hadn't considered. "Murdering me in my sleep wouldn't get you those missiles."

"Some people don't think that far ahead."

"Understood," Llyn said. "In that case, I'll *definitely* be flying aboard *Banshee*."

Actually, he would have preferred *Pacemaker* even more than *Banshee*. But *Pacemaker* was faster, and could arrive at Haven with more time to get things rolling.

Besides, parking a freighter as heavily armed as *Banshee* over Haven would be begging for official inspections and lots of official frowns, none of which he wanted.

"Anyway, once *Banshee* is unloaded, you'll need to prep your big ships for travel," Llyn continued. "You have, what, two battlecruisers and six heavy cruisers?"

"Plus two light cruisers, seven destroyers, and three frigates," Gensonne said. "We've got another battlecruiser coming, but it's still five to ten T-months down the line."

"I don't think we can wait for it," Llyn said, carefully hiding a grimace. So there was another big warship on the way. Damn.

"I could leave word for it to follow us."

"No, we can't afford to let the missiles sit around that long," Llyn said reluctantly. He would have preferred to have all of Gensonne's jumbo eggs in the same basket, but there was nothing for it. "A quick in and out is the best way to keep this under everyone's radar."

"I suppose," Gensonne said reluctantly. "How many Hellflares are your people bringing?"

"Enough," Llyn assured him. "Especially since only the battlecruisers and heavy cruisers will be able to handle the upgrades, so we only need to supply eight ships. How fast can you have them ready to go?"

"Fast enough," Gensonne said. "Three, maybe four weeks," He frowned. "You know, Danak is still too damn close to Haven for my liking. Isn't bringing a pair of battlecruisers into Havenite space going to get us noticed?"

"Not really," Llyn soothed. "Danak may be physically close to Haven, but it's not part of the Commonwealth. They're trading partners, but not yet real allies. That's why we're bringing the missiles there in the first place: they're close to Haven, they've got a well-equipped shipyard, but they also have no official ties or obligations. Equally important, they know when and how to keep their mouths shut."

Which was also why Axelrod had set up a contact house there, complete with a legitimate name and background. Llyn's masters would not be happy if he burned that contact, but they'd understand if he had to do that.

"If you say so," Gensonne growled. "Just remember that if anything goes wrong, you'll be under the same guns we are."

"Which is yet another excellent reason why nothing will go wrong," Llyn said. "And just to muddy the waters a little more, we won't be going in as the Volsungs. Everyone will have fresh IDs, the finest Danak has ever seen."

"Good." Gensonne gave a little chuckle. "Do me a favor, will you? When you make them up, put in something that shows an Andermani affiliation."

"Whatever you want," Llyn said, frowning to himself. *Andermani.* Did that mean that the freighter he and *Pacemaker* had run from in the Posnan system had indeed been one of Gensonne's? Or had it genuinely been Andermani, and there was some subtext going on here that he was missing? "Before I transfer to *Banshee,* I need to record a message for Captain Katura to deliver to the consortium office on Haven," he continued as he stood up. "If he gets back to Danak with the paperwork ahead of us, he can make sure the missiles and electronics are properly prepped so that the work can begin the minute your ships hit orbit."

"Sure," Gensonne said. "Your shuttle will be ready by the time you reach the dock. I'll give orders for both your ships to be fueled and have my men check on their other supplies."

"Thank you," Llyn said. "I'll tell my captains to expect a screening. Good day, Admiral." He turned to the door—

"One other thing," Gensonne called from behind him. "Your so-called third ship, the one you told me out there was ready to unload its missiles into the planet. Was that a bluff, or is something actually there?"

With his back to Gensonne, Llyn permitted himself a small, grim smile. *Shrike*, with its wedge down and

its smart skin rigged for full stealth, was still coasting undetected through the Walther system. It was a
wild card, one that Llyn had every intention of using
to its fullest.

"There's one sure way to find out," he said over
his shoulder. "Good day, Admiral."

☆   ☆   ☆

Two days later, *Pacemaker* left orbit and headed
for Haven.

Llyn watched on the Volsungs' main tactical display as the ship accelerated toward the hyper limit,
a hard knot in the pit of his stomach. With Captain
Katura on his way, the die was cast and the plan set
firmly in stone.

Llyn had thought it through as best he could. But
the uncomfortable fact remained that the scheme
had been conjured up on the spur of the moment,
relatively speaking. That kind of haste, he knew all
too well, could leave any number of unnoticed flaws
and unconsidered contingencies in its wake.

But for good or bad, he had no choice but to
see it through. Gensonne knew about the Axelrod
connection, and for that bit of cleverness alone the
self-proclaimed admiral had to die. Along with anyone
and everyone else he might have told.

In other words, the entirety of the Volsung Mercenaries.

Getting Gensonne to split his force had been the
first step. Sending *Pacemaker* and Katura's secret
message to Haven was the second.

And for the third...

Casually, Llyn let his eyes drift to the point on
the tactical where Captain Rhamas's calculations said

Shrike should currently be located in its hyperbolic orbit through the system. Nothing. As per the tight-beam orders Katura had sent on *Pacemaker*'s way out of the system, Captain Vaagen would continue to let his ship coast, with none of the Volsungs the wiser, until he reached the hyper limit at the other side of the system.

By then, of course, the Volsungs' mightiest warships would be gone. The handful of light cruisers, destroyers, and frigates Gensonne would leave behind would undoubtedly never notice *Shrike*'s hyper footprint as it headed out for its own rendezvous.

The Volsung Mercenaries were on borrowed time. They just didn't know it.

CHAPTER TWENTY-ONE

"SO THERE IT IS," ADMIRAL LOCATELLI said briskly. "Do you have any questions?"

Captain Clegg looked down at her tablet, her pulse thudding in her ears. Did she have any *questions*?

Damn right she had questions.

What idiot thought it was a smart idea to send one of the Navy's most advanced warships way the hell over to Silesia for who knew how long on this fool's errand?

Who had signed off on the plan to put a civilian aboard a military mission?

And worst of all, was she really supposed to take orders from a Tactical Officer and a Chief—a *Chief*!—if one of them decided it was necessary?

"No questions, Sir," Commander Alfred Woodburn said from Clegg's right.

"None here, either," Lieutenant Commander Jeffrey Norris added from her left.

Clegg pursed her lips. So her new Exec and Chief Engineer were going to wimp out? Fine. She could carry this one herself.

"Yes, Sir," she said. "I have a few."

Locatelli glanced at Lady Calvingdell, seated quietly at his left, and seemed to settle himself more sedately in his chair. "Proceed, Captain."

"Let's start with a few concerns, Sir," Clegg began, choosing her words carefully. "Personnel and chain of command are the two biggest. You said SIS is a largely civilian organization, Yet this mission is under their auspices instead of ONI's?"

"The relationships here are a bit complicated," Locatelli conceded. "Part of that's due to the fact that SIS is freshly-minted and no one is yet entirely sure how it fits into the existing structure. But be assured that ONI—and System Command—are going to be solidly in the loop."

"It's actually a bit more complicated than that," Calvingdell spoke up calmly. "For the moment, anyway, ONI doesn't know SIS exists."

Clegg shot a look at Woodburn. "Excuse me?" she said.

"There are certain political aspects that still need to be worked out," Locatelli said reluctantly. "As far as ONI is concerned, the underlying purpose of your voyage is to use *Casey's* new sensor suite to check out the various vessels and defense stations you'll be encountering, with an eye toward friend-or-foe analysis. That data will be Chief Townsend's responsibility as head of the new department of Signals Intelligence. At the same time, he and Mr. Long will be working the third layer: to gather information that will hopefully bring us to Tamerlane and the group that attacked us."

"I see," Clegg said. Not that she did, really. This whole cloak-and-dagger thing was bizarre, not to mention ridiculously complicated. "And aboard *Casey* it'll just be the three of us, along with Long and Townsend, who are in on this?"

"And Mr. Hauptman, yes," Calvingdell said. "The current Special Intelligence Service chain of command runs through me to the Minister of Defense." She looked at Locatelli. "With System Command also in the loop, of course."

"I see, My Lady," Clegg said.

"And I see you have more reservations," Calvingdell added.

Clegg took a deep breath. Since she'd asked...

"You spoke just now of chain of command," she said. "There's also the fact that the orders you're giving me are vague and open-ended. Furthermore, ultimate authority is vested, not in the Captain, but in two crewmembers who are unaccountable to anyone aboard the ship." And crewmembers, she added silently, whose actions could be disavowed with the flick of a stylus.

"It's not quite that bad, Captain," Calvingdell said. "Authority is invested in Lieutenant Commander Long only in certain very specifically defined aspects of the mission. Certainly not in any situation that would endanger the ship."

"I understand, Sir," Clegg said. "That doesn't mean he might not make a catastrophic error somewhere along the line that then puts the ship in an untenable position."

Again, Locatelli and Calvingdell looked at each other. "You are the commander and ultimate authority aboard *Casey*, Captain," Locatelli said. "If Long or Townsend seeks to invoke these secret orders, and you don't think it's justified or safe, you can certainly override them."

"And face whatever consequences might come of that?"

Locatelli smiled faintly. "Or face the consequences of letting them go ahead," he said. "That's the bottom line for every captain on an extended mission."

"If it helps, we wouldn't have chosen Long and Townsend if we didn't think they were smart and level-headed enough to know their limits," Calvingdell said.

"Just as you wouldn't have been given this ship and this assignment if everyone from Admiral Eigen on up didn't think you were an outstanding commander and could handle any situation," Locatelli added.

Despite her reservations, Clegg felt a brief warmth trickle through her. She'd hated to leave *Vanguard*—hated even more leaving Bertinelli in pole position to take command someday—but Eigen had been absolutely glowing about both her abilities and how *Casey* was the fast-track to admiral and possibly even beyond.

Of course, Eigen hadn't mentioned she was going to be saddled with a cloak-and-dagger contingent for her first time out. But then, he probably hadn't known that himself.

"So," Locatelli said into her thoughts. "Was there anything else?"

Concerns about the workability of her mission. Convinced the command structure was too complicated and likely to go flying off in all directions. Concerns about having spies aboard. Concerns over having a civilian aboard.

"No, Sir," Clegg said. "I think that's all. Thank you."

"Then I'll let you get back to your duties," Locatelli

said, all brisk business again. "You have three weeks, and I have no doubt there's still a lot of work to be done."

"Yes, Sir, there is," Clegg agreed. She stood up, her two colleagues standing with her. "I trust Commander Long and Chief Townsend will be presenting themselves aboard ship at their earliest convenience?"

"They will," Calvingdell promised. "They're undergoing some last-minute training of their own, but they'll be aboard shortly."

"Good," Clegg said. *They'd better*, she added silently.

"Then good day to you all," Locatelli said. "And if I don't see you again before you sail, good luck."

Clegg waited until she and her two senior officers were back in their aircar before speaking. "Comments?" she invited.

"I think it's all a crock, Ma'am," Woodburn said. "I don't know how anyone can tell a Silesian quad from a Havenite quad. Or whatever."

"There are ways," Norris said. "I'm more interested in this Long character. I've read the reports, Alfred, but you actually worked with him on the bridge. What's your assessment?"

"He's clever, in his way," Woodburn said. "He can also be a pain in the butt when it comes to regs, though he's getting better at that. I suppose if Calvingdell had to grab someone for this, she could have done worse than Long." He snorted. "No guarantees on Townsend, though. Everything I've heard suggests he's a *royal* pain in the butt."

"Hauptman can be that way, too," Norris said. "Though he *does* know a hell of a lot about ships and shipbuilding."

"Well, it looks like we're stuck with them," Clegg said reluctantly. "I'll be counting on you gentlemen to help me ride herd."

"Absolutely, Ma'am," Woodburn promised. "Back to the ship?"

"Back to the ship," Clegg confirmed. "As our System Commander said, we have a lot of work to do."

☆   ☆   ☆

For once, and against all past performance, the weekly Cabinet meeting had been calm. Maybe even—if one dared use the term—friendly.

Breakwater and Dapplelake hadn't gotten into any arguments. Education Secretary Broken Cliff had merely asked for more money instead of demanding it. Prime Minister Harwich was settling nicely into his job of riding herd on the proceedings without being perceived as leaning too hard on any person or faction. It was as if the Battle of Manticore, followed by the unexpected deaths of the King and Crown Princess had finally effected a change in Manticoran politics.

Elizabeth didn't believe it for a minute. In her experience, it was the times when things were going smoothly when one needed to be extra alert.

Sometimes, though, the surprises still came from unexpected directions.

Her first indication that something was amiss was as she approached the Royal Sanctum—the Palace staff's term for her private office—and saw Colonel Jackson standing stiff guard outside the door. Normally, she seldom saw the commander of the Queen's Own except on special occasions, given that he was usually buried away in his office or out overseeing the advance security sweep of some area she was scheduled to visit.

"Your Majesty," he said as she approached, bowing his head toward her. "Your visitor is here."

An unpleasant feeling tingled the hairs at the back of her neck. *Visitor*? She wasn't expecting anyone.

But there was something in Jackson's face that strongly suggested she not ask about it even in the relative privacy of a Palace hallway.

"Thank you, Colonel," she said instead. He opened the door as she approached, and she stepped through.

To find her father waiting on the couch in the conversation area. "Hello, Elizabeth," he said. "How are you doing?"

"Much better now," Elizabeth said, picking up her pace as she crossed the room. No matter how many times he dropped in to see her, it never seemed like enough. "You're looking good, Dad."

"I'm looking old, you mean," he corrected as she reached him and flung her arms around him. "Easy—easy. I'm much more breakable than I was in the pony-ride days."

"Oh, come on—you're as strong as an ox," Elizabeth scoffed as she hugged him.

But he was right, she realized with a sinking feeling. She could feel the thinness of his body, and sense the frailness there. He was only eighty-seven, but his aura was that of a man in his nineties. Clearly, the past few months had been harder on him than she'd realized.

"What brings you here today?" she said as she extricated herself carefully from his hug. "Can I get you some tea? Scones? The baker found the recipe they were using when you were a boy, if you want a taste of history. How about lunch? We could have an early lunch."

"No, thank you," Michael said. "I had a good breakfast, and I'll be returning to the Tower before lunch. Mostly I'm here to deliver some news." His face hardened a little. "*And* a warning."

"I see," Elizabeth said. She took his hand, and they sat down on the couch together. "Shall I call in Colonel Jackson?"

"No, it's not that kind of warning," Michael assured her. "You're not in any physical danger, at least as far as I know."

"That doesn't sound very definitive."

"Interestingly, that's the same word Jackson used while he was walking me to the Sanctum."

"He takes his duties very seriously," Elizabeth said.

"Yes, he does," Michael agreed quietly. "I'm sure he still blames himself for the accident."

Elizabeth's stomach tightened. The public report on the disaster had glossed over the details, merely stating that Sophie's jetboat had suffered a malfunction.

But Elizabeth and the top government officials knew the entire truth. Sophie had run into something floating just below the surface of the water, possibly a piece of a cheap cooler. The object had jammed into the screen of the starboard jet intake, blocking some of the flow just long enough to decrease the thrust from that jet and start the boat into a slight yaw. A split-second later, as the object disintegrated and the intake cleared, the resulting counter-surge had reversed the direction of the yaw, kicking the boat in the other direction. Both effects were small; but in combination, and at the speed the boat was making, it was enough to destabilize the craft and send it into a devastating crash.

Protected by her safety cage, Sophie might still have survived if the leaks from her fuel and emergency oxygen tanks hadn't mixed near a damaged and sparking circuit. But they *had* mixed, and they'd ignited, and the resulting explosion had killed her.

And the King, more intent on rescuing his daughter than saving himself, had joined her in death.

"It wasn't his fault," Elizabeth murmured.

"I agree," Michael said. "But as I say, I doubt he does. He's aged a lot in the past few months." He waved a hand. "But that's neither here nor there. My point is that our good Lord Chancellor of the Exchequer and a couple of his friends came to see me about an hour ago."

"Really," Elizabeth said, wrinkling her nose. Jackson would have any information that was relevant to her, of course, and normally it would have been passed on to her staff at tomorrow morning's briefing. Apparently, this was important enough for her father to short-circuit the process by bringing it straight to her.

And if there was one person in particular besides Breakwater who seemed determined to be a permanent thorn in her side—"Let me guess. Was one of those friends Winterfall?"

"I knew you were going to ask that," Michael said. Apparently, he'd noticed the young baron's annoyance factor, as well. "And oddly enough, no, Winterfall wasn't among them. This time Breakwater just brought Castle Rock and Tweenriver. In a nutshell, they wanted me to consider the idea of taking back the Throne."

Elizabeth stared at him. "Taking back—? Is that even possible?"

"I have no idea," Michael said. "But I'm guessing

not. Oddly enough—or maybe not so oddly—when we were assembling the Constitution, we never considered adding a provision for an abdicated King to change his mind."

"Do you want me to screen New Bern and ask her to do a quick write-up?"

"I don't think that would be a good idea," Michael said. "The fewer people who know about this, the better." His lip twitched. "Especially considering Breakwater's alleged reason for broaching the subject in the first place."

Elizabeth closed her eyes. "The marriage thing."

"And your lack of an heir." Michael hesitated. "And to be perfectly honest, Elizabeth, he *does* have a point."

"Fine—I'll get one," Elizabeth ground out. "Carmichael left some frozen sperm. I can have that brought in—"

"Except that Carmichael was a noble," Michael interrupted gently. "The Constitution says that—"

"I know what the Constitution says," Elizabeth cut him off. "And I am *not* going to get married again—or have someone else's baby—just to cover some half-assed rule that never anticipated my situation."

He tilted his head a little. "Really? Constitutions and laws are established precisely because you *don't* want everyone simply claiming unique circumstances in order to justify doing whatever they want. You know that."

Elizabeth clenched her teeth. But he was right, of course. "Why does Breakwater have such a hat-hornet about this in the first place?" she growled. "For all he knows, if I die without an heir maybe they'll make *him* King."

"Don't even joke about things like that," her father said severely. "That's also not in the Constitution—I think we all assumed the Winton line would last forever. You dying without an heir would precipitate a major Constitutional crisis. So don't do it."

"Right. I'll try."

"Good," Michael said. "As to why he's hammering on the subject...well, I get the distinct feeling you've proved a disappointment to him."

"A *disappointment*?"

"As in not being nearly as malleable as he expected," Michael explained with a small smile. "He probably figures a doddering old fool like me will be easier to manipulate, so he's trying to banish you to the doghouse until you learn your lesson." He shrugged uncomfortably. "And, yes, probably have a baby or two."

Elizabeth looked down at her hands, still holding her father's. Prim, proper, and serene, the way she assumed a Queen ought to look.

Only what she really wanted to do with those hands was throttle the life out of Breakwater.

"What are you going to do?" she asked, looking up at her father again.

"Do?" Michael shrugged. "Not really much I *can* do. I'm certainly not going to petition Parliament to give me back the Kingship, and without my cooperation Breakwater's campaign goes nowhere. Not unless he wants to make this whole thing public."

"Which he won't," Elizabeth said. "He wouldn't dare risk looking like he was bullying the Queen."

"Not directly," Michael said. "But that doesn't mean he won't try an end run of some sort. I'd look for him to try to tarnish your image somehow with either the

Parliament or the people. Maybe try to hang some fiasco or perceived fiasco around your neck."

Elizabeth swallowed. SIS, and its complete disconnect with ONI, most of the Navy, and even Parliament. If Breakwater ever got wind of what Calvingdell was doing, he would have an absolute field day with it.

And if he managed to connect it with *Casey's* upcoming trip to the Silesian Confederacy...

"I gather there *is* something going on that he could use against you?"

Elizabeth snapped her thoughts and attention back to her father. "What do you mean?"

He had a disturbingly knowing expression on his face. "Oh, come on, sweetie," he protested. "Just because I'm out to pasture doesn't mean I can't sniff out the piles of manure." He considered. "That didn't come out nearly as clever as it sounded in my head. Forget that. The point is that I can feel when something's going on. Somebody suddenly seems to have misplaced all the money that was allotted to them. Someone starts gathering people around them with no clear announcement as to the whys or wherefores. Or someone who's been loud and critical suddenly shuts up."

"I was unaware that anyone out there was shutting up," Elizabeth said dryly.

"There are a couple," Michael said. "Joshua Miller, for instance, used to get up in the Commons all the time to rail at the Lords. Lately, though, he seems to have gone strangely quiet."

Elizabeth felt her cheeks warm, grateful as always that the ebony Winton skin was way too dark to show any actual blushing. She'd officially seen Miller only twice: that one exploratory luncheon, and then a week later when he brought by some honey for her from his farm in Friedman's Valley.

But there'd also been that secret meeting, the one where Elizabeth had sent Adler to bring him in late at night through the service tunnel where no prying eyes might catch a glimpse of him.

Adler wouldn't have talked, of course. Miller definitely wouldn't have. Still, Elizabeth would have to double her efforts to make sure their future meetings were kept even quieter.

"I've told you before that I want to stay hands-off on all this," Michael said quietly. "You need to be the Queen, and you especially need to run the Star Kingdom without me hovering behind you. That's why I haven't asked to sit in on security briefings and have resisted my penchant for prying into the affairs of mice and men."

"I appreciate that, Dad." Elizabeth forced a smile. "Though if they're going to hoist you on their shoulders and carry you back to the Throne—"

"Don't even joke about that," Michael growled. "That's absolutely *not* going to happen."

"Got it," Elizabeth said. "Thank you for the warning."

"No problem," Michael said. He stood up, again moving carefully. "I'm heading back to the Tower. Please remember that you can call on me any time."

"You have to go right now?" Elizabeth, automatically standing as well. She didn't have to, but it felt right. "You could stay for lunch."

"Tempting." Michael stood up, again moving carefully. "But people go all nosy and speculative even when I just visit you for a few minutes or stop to play with my grandchildren. Something momentous like lunch is bound to get tongues wagging."

"And we certainly don't want anyone misinterpreting things," Elizabeth agreed. "But we *could* have lunch served in here. No one else would have to know."

"I suppose we could," Michael said. "I don't know, though. Is there anything more we need to talk about?"

Elizabeth's mind flashed to Joshua Miller. She so wanted her father's advice . . . and if there was one person in the Kingdom she could trust, it was surely him. "Nothing we *need* to, no," she hedged. "But there's a topic or two you might find interesting."

"Really." Michael studied her face, then resumed his seat. "In that case, yes," he said, smiling up at her. "I'd love to have lunch."

CHAPTER TWENTY-TWO

LISA HAD FINISHED SETTING THE TABLE, and was doing a final check on the chicken casserole when the doorbell chimed.

She frowned. Travis hadn't said anything about possible visitors tonight. And he wasn't the type to have friends who dropped in without screening first.

Could he have forgotten his key? That was even more unlikely than unannounced visitors.

The chime came again. Wrinkling her nose, she pulled off her apron, draped it over the kitchen desk, and headed across the apartment. Still hoping it was just Travis with a misplaced key, she unlocked the door and pulled it open.

She'd never officially met the man standing outside. But she knew his face. Knew it *very* well. "Yes?" she said guardedly.

"Hello, I'm Gavin Vellacott," he said, his forehead creasing as he looked at her. Obviously, he hadn't expected to find anyone except Travis in Travis's apartment. "Travis's half-brother." His frown flicked over Lisa's shoulder to the living room behind her. "Is he in?"

"No," Lisa said shortly. Travis hadn't talked about his brother much, but she knew enough to suspect that an impromptu meeting between them wasn't a situation he would greet with enthusiasm. "Perhaps you could screen him later, My Lord."

"Please; just Gavin," Winterfall said, a tentative smile trying to gain a foothold on his lips. "This isn't anything like official business. Do you expect Travis soon, ah—?"

Lisa sighed. She didn't mind being firm, but she really shouldn't be rude. "Lisa," she identified herself.

"Pleased to meet you," Winterfall said with a polite nod. "Yes; Travis's special friend. I've heard of you. Do you have any idea when he's due back?" He sniffed. "Dinner time, for example?"

"I really don't know," Lisa said. "As I said, you'd do better to screen him."

Winterfall shook his head. "I'm sorry to intrude, Commander. But what I have to say needs to be said in person." He hesitated. "I'm walking on thin ice here as it is."

It was probably a ploy, Lisa knew. Almost certainly a ploy. Winterfall was in the Lords, and was one of Breakwater's allies on top of it. Both of those strongly implied he was a master of manipulation.

But recognizing a ruse wasn't the same as resisting it. And she'd already conceded to herself that she didn't want to be rude. At least, not without a good reason.

And so far, at least, Winterfall hadn't given her one.

"Fine." She stepped out of the doorway and gestured him inside. "He should be here soon. And to answer your implied question, no, I'm not Travis's *special friend*. I'm just a friend."

"My mistake." Winterfall walked past her, glancing around as he headed for the couch. "Nice place. I wouldn't have thought my brother had such good taste."

"There are a lot of things about Travis you don't know," Lisa countered. In point of fact, Travis *didn't* have much taste, at least when it came to home furnishings. The basic furniture here was his, dating from before they'd gotten to know each other, but she was the one who'd suggested most of the handful of pictures and accent pieces.

Which she had a strong suspicion Winterfall had already figured out. Damn him.

And Travis *wasn't* a special friend. He just *wasn't*.

"Touché," Winterfall admitted. "I'm sure you know that he and I haven't been . . . well, close."

"Some might put it even more strongly," Lisa said. "You haven't exactly been there for Travis, you know. And don't even get me started on your mother."

"I'm painfully aware of that," Winterfall said heavily. "Though I'll admit that it was just . . . well, just before we lost the King, in fact, that I really understood how distant they'd become."

"You took your time."

"I'm aware of that, too," Winterfall said. "Sadly, I can't do anything about our mother. But I'm hoping Travis and I, at least, can rebuild some bridges."

"Really." Lisa studied his face. His expression wasn't nearly as open as it might have been. He might pretend he was bridge-building—might even believe it—but the manipulation was still lurking beneath the surface. "Starting tonight?"

Winterfall's lip twitched. "Well, no, probably not," he said reluctantly. "Tonight's conversation may not be—"

He broke off at the sound of a key on the lock. Lisa stood up, taking a deep breath.

The door opened and Travis walked in.

He spotted Lisa first, and his face softened in the small but deep smile he always greeted her with. It was a smile of calm and closeness, an expression that told her that in her presence he had everything he needed: friend, confidante, and ally against the turmoil of the world outside.

And then Winterfall stood up, and Travis's eyes shifted to his brother.

The smile vanished.

Travis's eyes flicked again to Lisa as he stepped inside the apartment, then back to Winterfall as he closed the door behind him. "Hello, Gavin," he said, his tone the one Lisa had heard him use with unknown or unfriendly superior officers. "This is a surprise."

"I know," Winterfall said, "and I apologize for dropping in unannounced. But as I was just explaining to Commander Donnelly, there's something I need to talk to you about. Something very much private and off the record."

"I see." Travis hesitated another moment, then continued toward them. "How off-the-record are we talking about?"

Winterfall's eyes flicked to Lisa. "No one has sent me, if that's what you mean," he said, looking back at Travis. "In fact, no one even knows I'm here."

"Okay," Travis said. "Our dinner's almost ready, so keep it brief."

Winterfall inclined his head. "Of course. In ten days

you and *Casey* are scheduled to leave Manticore for a mission to the Silesian Confederacy. I've come to ask you, for the sake of the Star Kingdom, to make sure that mission fails."

"What do you mean?" Travis's voice was calm enough, but to Lisa's eye it looked like his face paled a little.

"I know about your agenda," Winterfall said. "But you have to understand that trying to set up those kind of facilities will drain away resources that are vital to rebuilding the Star Kingdom's defenses. Not just the Navy and MPARS, but also—"

"Wait a minute, wait a minute," Travis interrupted, looking thoroughly confused now. "What facilities? What are you talking about?"

"I'm talking about drumming up enough ship orders to justify creating our own impeller industry," Winterfall said. "You don't need to play coy—I've seen the report. I know it sounds good on paper, and it might even be something we'll want to do some day in the future."

"But not now?" Travis suggested. His face, Lisa noted, had regained its color.

"Exactly," Winterfall said. "Right now, all our military resources need to be focused on rebuilding the Navy, MPARS, our fixed defenses—the stuff we'll need in the next few months or years. With all due respect, having our own impeller factory isn't part of that list."

"And you got all this from secret Parliament files?" Travis asked.

"Yes, I already said that," Winterfall said, a hint of impatience in his tone. "Look, I know you can't confirm or deny—" He broke off, his face going rigid as his eyes swung to Lisa. "Oh," he murmured.

"Indeed," Travis agreed. "I don't know if you're supposed to have access to that information, Gavin. But Commander Donnelly here *definitely* isn't supposed to have it."

"No, no, of course not," Winterfall said, his face rigid. "Damn it."

"Okay, relax, it's not as bad as you think," Travis said, holding out a calming hand. "I think we can all agree to forget this ever happened. *I* won't tell; *you* certainly won't tell; and since reporting it could get Commander Donnelly bounced from her own upcoming mission, *she* won't tell." He nodded behind him. "But I think you'd better go."

"Yes," Winterfall said. He took a deep breath. "But think about what I said, will you? It doesn't have to be anything blatant or overt. Just a little nudging the wrong direction—"

"Good-bye, Gavin."

Winterfall pursed his lips, then nodded. "Good-bye, Travis." He nodded to Lisa. "Commander Donnelly. Safe voyage to you." He looked at Travis. "To you both." Walking past Travis, he opened the door and disappeared out into the night.

"Well, *that* was different," Lisa said as Travis closed the door and locked it.

"And you thought we were just having a regular dinner and normal conversation," Travis agreed dryly. "He just pop in on you?"

"A couple of minutes before you got here," Lisa said, bracing herself. If there were going to be recriminations for letting him in, this would be the time for it. "I'm sorry if I handled it wrong. I didn't think I just should slam the door in his face."

To her relief, Travis just nodded. "No, no, you did fine," he assured her. "I was just . . . really surprised to see him."

"I was, too, if that helps any," Lisa said. "Uh . . . that thing he was talking about. I know I'm not supposed to know the details of *Casey*'s mission. But since he was the one who talked, can you at least tell me if was he right about this being a shipbuilding mission?"

"You heard what he said," Travis reminded her. "I really can't talk any further about it."

"Right," Lisa said. It had been worth a try, anyway.

And it wasn't like she didn't have secrets of her own. *Damocles*'s upcoming trip, after all, wasn't just the good-will mission that Cazenestro had pitched to Parliament and the public. Captain Marcello was taking some of the battle debris to Haven, with the hope of persuading them to do an off-the-books analysis.

But there was more even than that. The secret Parliamentary files the Cabinet ministers could access included all of those details. What they *didn't* include was the fact that if the Haven analysis pinpointed Tamerlane's true identity and location, Captain Marcello was authorized to open discussions on a joint Havenite/Manticoran military response.

It wasn't like the two star nations hadn't worked together before. What made this different was that it would be an official agreement, documented and signed, as opposed to something thrown together on the spur of the moment in the face of imminent need.

The tricky part was that, for the moment at least, the Queen and Prime Minister Harwich had decided that it would he handled on a purely military level, with the rest of Parliament cut out of the loop. Even

Foreign Secretary Susan Tarleton, who was supposedly in charge of such matters, was being kept in the dark.

To Lisa, the whole thing seemed like a ticking bomb. She could understand Harwich's desire to keep politics out of this, especially given Breakwater's all-but reflexive opposition to anything involving the Navy. But if an agreement *was* reached, the *ex post facto* revelation would create an outraged backlash that might sweep away even some of Harwich's strongest supporters.

But the decision had been made, and far above Lisa's rank and authority. As *Damocles*'s XO, her duty was to support it, and her captain, and let the chips fall where they may.

At least the mission had gotten her out of that frustrating MPARS academy. Another few months there, and she'd have been ready to claw her way straight through the classroom wall.

"But I *can* confirm that dinner smells wonderful," Travis continued. "Your chicken, rice, and broccoli casserole; right?"

"Right," Lisa said, putting thoughts of missions and politics and relatives aside. In ten days, she and Travis would be leaving Manticore in different ships, heading in not-quite opposite directions, and they wouldn't see each other again for at least a year, possibly more. This might be their last quiet time together, and she was determined to make the most of it. "And if I don't get it out of the oven soon, it might start smelling not so wonderful."

"Got it," Travis said, resting his hand on the small of her back as they headed together toward the kitchen.

They were halfway there when another thought suddenly occurred to Lisa.

"Those secret files," she said. "Is your brother supposed to have access to those?"

"I doubt it," Travis said. "As far as I know, only the Cabinet ministers get to see them. Breakwater must have given him access."

"Is that legal?" Lisa asked.

And instantly wished she could call back the words. Travis's long-standing reputation for strictly following the book...

"Probably not," he conceded, and she could hear the fresh tension in his voice as the fingers resting against her back went stiff. "In fact, almost certainly not."

"He probably looked it up for Breakwater," Lisa said quickly. "He's kind of an appendage of the Exchequer these days, anyway. Or maybe he was reading over Breakwater's shoulder."

"Maybe."

"What I'm saying is that it's nothing you need to report."

Travis was silent for another couple of steps. Lisa held her breath...and then, she felt his hand relax a little. "I suppose," he said. "Civilian matters. None of our business, really. Besides, he's totally got the wrong end of the stick."

"Really," Lisa said, intrigued. "So which end is the right end?"

"Don't you start, too," Travis chided. "You're Navy. *You* I'd have to lock up."

"And then you wouldn't get any dinner, because I'd take the casserole with me."

"And *you* wouldn't get any salad," he countered. "Because I think that's my job tonight."

"It would only be trouble," Lisa concluded.

"Exactly," Travis said. "So you don't ask about mine, and I won't ask about yours. Did you remember to grab extra croutons when you were out?"

It was only later, as Lisa was drifting off to sleep, that Travis's odd comment suddenly came back to her. *Don't ask about mine, and I won't ask about yours.*

Had that just been a throwaway line, something to seal off the end of their banter? Or did he somehow suspect that *Damocles* had a secret mission of her own?

No. It had surely just been banter.

Because he couldn't know. There was absolutely no way he could know.

☆   ☆   ☆

"Acceleration, two point zero KPS squared," Commander Woodburn reported. "All systems showing green."

"Acknowledged," Captain Clegg said formally. "Keep an eye on the forward sensors. They seemed a bit twitchy during the last trial run."

"Yes, Ma'am," Woodburn said. "At least the Beta nodes seem to have settled down. Jeffrey did good work there."

"It's Commander Norris's *job* to do good work."

Out of the corner of his eye, Travis saw Woodburn wince. "Yes, Ma'am."

Mentally, Travis shook his head. The officers and crew were trying, in most cases trying very hard. But Clegg wasn't making it easy on them.

Part of it was the stress of taking over command of a ship with a largely established crew, of course. Travis had seen that plenty of times in his career, and it was always a bit bumpy.

But more than that was the chip she seemed to

have permanently bonded to her shoulder. Which in turn, he suspected, was probably due to the presence and secret authority of Travis and Chomps.

To be honest, her skepticism might well be justified. Travis couldn't speak for Chomps, but after a mere six weeks of training he felt wholly unprepared for this job.

But then, why shouldn't he? Not only was this new territory for Travis, it was new territory for the Star Kingdom as a whole.

As a boy, he'd read occasional novels about Solarian League Special Agents: spies, counterspies, intrigue, danger, action—the whole gamut. But those had been stories. This was real. And whatever he did, or whatever he failed to do, there would be real-world consequences for his star nation and his people.

He had six weeks of training. He had Chomps. He had a trunkful of specialized equipment. And he had a senior officer cadre that was ambivalent, and a captain who was openly antagonistic.

Two and a half months to Silesia, followed by however long it took to track down Tamerlane, followed by another long trip home.

And no Lisa the whole time.

Silently, Travis let out a sigh. It was going to be a *very* long tour.

☆　　☆　　☆

"Acceleration one point six five KPS squared," Lisa reported. "All systems showing green."

"Acknowledged," Captain Marcello said. "So, XO. How does it feel to be back in space?"

"It feels wonderful, Sir," Lisa said, glancing around *Damocles*'s bridge. It was literally like coming home again.

"Our gain is certainly MPARS's loss," Marcello said dryly. "I'm told you did a fine job at the Academy."

"I wouldn't go *that* far, Sir," Lisa demurred. "Fair to middling at best."

"Begging your pardon, Ma'am, but I have to agree with the Captain," Lieutenant Commander Wanda Ravel, the new Tactical Officer, spoke up diffidently. "I have a nephew who was in one of your classes. He said you did an exemplary job."

"See?" Marcello said, gesturing back toward Ravel. "I told you. As I always say, quality rises to the top."

"Thank you, Sir," Lisa said, smiling as she threw a sideways look at Ravel. The woman was a new addition to *Damocles*'s bridge: formerly Assistant Tactical Officer on HMS *Salamander*, she'd been transferred to *Damocles* to fill Lisa's previous position.

The woman was playing it cautious, Lisa could tell, still a bit uncertain of where she fit into the camaraderie of a long-established crew. But she was already far more relaxed than Lisa herself had been when she first came aboard. She would do fine.

The real question was how well Lisa herself was going to do.

Executive Officer. It was a slot every Navy officer eagerly looked forward to: the last step on the way to commanding a ship. And if anecdotal evidence was to be believed, not a single officer ever felt quite ready to take on the job.

But she would make it. She had a captain who trusted her, officers and crew who respected her, and long T-years' worth of training and experience under her belt.

And she had four and a half months before they

reached Haven. Four and a half months in hyperspace in which to settle into the job.

True, it would be a year or more before she saw Travis again, and that was a depressing thought. But it was really the only downside to this whole thing.

She smiled to herself. This was going to be a good tour.

☆   ☆   ☆

In perfect synch—near perfect, anyway—the two Volsung battlecruisers and six heavy cruisers translated up into the Alpha band.

In the center of the formation, tucked away neatly between the battlecruisers, was *Banshee*.

"Llyn?" Gensonne's voice crackled over the speaker. "Everything all right there?"

"Everything's fine, Admiral," Llyn assured him. "Nice translation, by the way. Well-coordinated."

"I don't know why you'd expect anything less," Gensonne said with obvious pride. "We're going to open up the formation a little. You just stay put—we'll spread out around you."

Llyn smiled tightly. In other words, Gensonne still harbored the suspicion that Llyn was going to cut and run at the first opportunity, leaving the Volsungs to head to Danak alone. Wrapping him up in the center of the formation was the admiral's unsubtle way of dissuading him from such thoughts.

A completely pointless exercise. A senior Axelrod agent would never simply cut and run. Especially not when the plan was going smoothly.

And this plan was going *very* smoothly. Four weeks ago *Pacemaker* had left for Haven, carrying both the message Gensonne *thought* Captain Katura was going to deliver to Danak and the message Katura was *actually* going to deliver. Three days ago, *Shrike* had completed its invisible hyperbolic drift through the Walther system and past the hyper limit, and was even now proceeding to make contact with a small Black Ops force which should be gathering for another mission. Llyn had been involved in the early planning stages for that one, and while it had been years in the making it could probably afford to pause long enough to deal with the Volsung base. That would ultimately be the local Axelrod agent's call, but Llyn was pretty sure the data he'd sent would make a compelling case.

The final die was cast. The game was in motion. In five and a half months, when Gensonne's fleet reached Danak, the Volsungs would be destroyed.

And best of all, Llyn's work was essentially done. All he had to do now was sit back and enjoy the show.

He smiled to himself. This was going to be an excellent tour.

BOOK THREE

1544 PD

CHAPTER TWENTY-THREE

JACQUES CORLAIN WAS A BIG BLUFF, round-faced man with a hearty laugh, who was currently single but had left two ex-wives in his wake. Like Joshua Miller he was a member of Parliament. Unlike Joshua—

Elizabeth smiled politely at the man across the table as he hit the punch line of his latest story. Unlike Joshua, pretty much everything.

Miller was quiet and observant. Corlain was casually domineering and seemed mostly to focus on himself, to the point where he hadn't even noticed when Elizabeth set her napkin on her lap. Miller had a quick, concise mind, and had talked about himself only to the extent of answering his Queen's questions. Corlain took forever to get to a point and would launch into a story or belabor a fact about his life at the drop of a fork. Miller was a staunch supporter of the Crown. Corlain seemed to have run for Parliament solely for the purpose of having a permanent platform for bashing two or three of the Lords he'd locked horns with over the years.

And whereas Elizabeth would be more than happy to invite Miller to another lunch, she had no intention of ever again eating at the same table with Corlain. His casual approach to talking with his mouth full alone guaranteed that.

The dessert was long gone by the time he finished his final, somewhat pointless story. "And now, I really should get back to Parliament," he said, brushing off his mouth and setting his napkin beside his plate. At least he hadn't simply dropped or thrown it. "We've got an appropriations vote coming up, and there's no way I'm letting them simply kick it up to the Lords and take the rest of the afternoon off. The Constitution gives the Commons *some* say in these things, and by Go—by thunder, we need to take that responsibility seriously."

"I'm glad you feel that way, Mr. Corlain," Elizabeth said politely, though the thought of being trapped in the Commons through one of his speeches threatened to curdle the milk in her tea. "I've noticed that many of your colleagues seem to enjoy the privileges of being an MP without wanting to perform the associated work."

"Way too many of them," Corlain agreed. "Don't worry, Your Majesty, I'm working on them." He paused, his forehead wrinkling. "I guess I just leave now?"

"Whenever you're ready," Elizabeth confirmed with her final courteous smile of the afternoon. "Thank you for coming."

"Thank you for feeding me, Your Majesty," Corlain replied, getting to his feet and bowing to her. "Someone will show me out, right?"

"There's a guard waiting outside the dining room."

"Right." Corlain's eyes flicked over her shoulder,

and he bowed again. "Thank you again, Your Majesty. Maybe I can return the favor at the Commons dining room someday."

"Perhaps," Elizabeth said. "Good afternoon, Mr. Corlain."

She waited two minutes after he left, just in case he'd buttonholed someone outside the door and had stopped to deliver one final story. Then, with a sigh, she stood up and headed for the door.

Adler and Penescu were waiting with their usual quiet all-but-invisibility. "Any messages come in while we were eating?" she asked as she came up to them.

"Nothing that would justify interrupting you for, Your Majesty," Penescu said. He looked sideways at Adler. "Believe me, we tried to find one."

"I appreciate that," Elizabeth said with a smile. "But as I told Mr. Corlain, there are certain tasks that come with positions of authority. This was one of mine."

"Yes, Your Majesty," Adler said. But her eyes seemed troubled as they flicked to the far end of the table and Corlain's discarded napkin. "May I ask, Your Majesty, how many more of these you're planning to do?"

"Are you concerned about my security?" Elizabeth asked mildly.

"No, Your Majesty," Adler said. "Just—" she pursed her lips, apparently wondering how far even a close bodyguard dared to go "—just your sanity."

"Oh, come now," Elizabeth chided. "Most of them haven't been *that* bad."

Still, Adler had a point. She'd been working her way through Burgundy's list as slowly as she could reasonably do so, pretending she was ruminating and thinking deep thoughts, but actually simply stalling her way through the process while she worked on another solution. On the surface, she supposed, the chronic hesitation *could* be interpreted as having been caused by stress.

"No, most of them haven't, Your Majesty," Penescu said. "But if I may be so bold, Sergeant Adler has a point. Our job is to protect you, and Colonel Jackson has always maintained that protection includes more than just your physical safety."

"The Colonel is probably right," Elizabeth said. "Don't worry, this was the last one."

"Yes, Your Majesty," Penescu said. "Where to?"

"My office."

Because unfortunately, a Queen's duties weren't limited to entertaining potential suitors in order to satisfy the demands of a sixty-T-year-old document whose creators clearly hadn't thought it through.

She'd had private meetings with some of those creators over the past few weeks, sometimes asking their opinions, sometimes verbally punching them in the arm for causing her so much grief. It had been interesting, but had led nowhere.

Meanwhile, there was also a *lot* of datawork to slog through.

"Prime Minister Harwich will be coming by at four to report on the Navy funding debate," she told her guards as they walked down the ornate hallway leading to her office. "After Breakwater's news channel interview last night, I'm guessing the debate will be a lively one. Please make sure the chef has some of those turnovers His Lordship likes to go along with his tea. He'll probably need them."

☆   ☆   ☆

"We are, of course, pleased to welcome a representative of Her Majesty's government to Saginaw," Governor Karl Olbrycht said, his voice and face about equally strained. "All the same, I have to say that this is extremely irregular. One doesn't drop by a foreign system without at least a modicum of advance notice."

"This *is* your advance notice, Governor," Clegg said, fiddling uselessly with the controls of her day cabin's com display. At *Casey*'s current distance from the planet Olbrycht's transmission was a bit sketchy anyway, and ever since the refit the feed from the bridge had consistently had problems.

But there was privacy here that the bridge didn't afford. Travis wasn't sure why Chomps had insisted on that kind of seclusion, but he'd been willing to bow to the other's gut and more extensive training.

Clegg wasn't nearly so happy with the suggestion. But at least she hadn't argued the point. Much.

She also hadn't argued against Travis, Chomps, and Hauptman being in here with her. But she hadn't been happy about that, either.

"We're still six hours out," she continued, "plus probably another two while we settle into orbit and secure from the long voyage. Plenty of time for you to arrange whatever entry formalities you think necessary."

There was a short time delay—"That's not really the point, Captain," Olbrycht protested. "We need to arrange the proper meetings, dinners, and events. It's not every day that we get a visitor from outside the Confederacy."

"I'm sure it isn't," Clegg agreed. "But it's really not necessary. We're mostly here to talk to your ship people: builders, equippers, shippers, and possibly some members of your Navy."

"Really," Olbrycht said, his voice cooling noticeably. "May I ask why exactly you want to examine them?"

"I said I wanted to *talk* to them, not *examine* them," Clegg said with clearly strained patience. "Queen Elizabeth is starting to upgrade and expand the Manticoran shipbuilding business, and we're here to see what kind of ships the Silesian Confederacy might be interested in ordering from us."

"I hardly think we would need to go all the way to Manticore to purchase ships," Olbrycht said. "We have three such facilities of our own within our borders."

"But nothing with its own impeller fabricators," Hauptman put in, floating up beside Clegg. "Within a couple of years, that's a service Manticore may be able to provide."

Olbrycht peered owlishly at him. "And you are?"

"Heinreich Hauptman," Hauptman identified himself. "I've done a bit of business with Ms. Simone Sei and her Eiderdown Cocoon Ship Systems. Enviro stuff, mostly, but I've also bought some of their food-prep equipment. My employer, Countess Barbara Acton, is using them on her long-range freighters and some of her new mining ships."

Olbrycht's eyes had dropped to something off-screen after Hauptman identified himself, probably checking his database. Now, he looked up again.

"Yes—Mr. Hauptman," he said, his frown clearing and his voice regaining its earlier warmth. "Ms. Sei has mentioned you, very favorably, I might add. Her reports indicate you gave her a few suggestions that have markedly improved Eiderdown Cocoon's product line."

"One or two suggestions only, Governor," Hauptman corrected modestly. "I'm looking forward to actually meeting her. It's the main reason I asked Captain Clegg to make Saginaw the first stop on our tour."

"I'm sure we can arrange a meeting," Olbrycht said. "And perhaps a tour of Eiderdown Cocoon, if you have time."

"I would love a tour," Hauptman said. "Perhaps my colleagues and I can do that while Captain Clegg discusses possibilities with the representatives from the Navy."

"I think that would be possible," Olbrycht said, his eyes going back to Clegg. "Though again, I really don't think we're in the market for imported warships."

"Perhaps a look at *Casey*'s capabilities will change your mind," Clegg said. "I presume that we're now cleared for approach?"

"Yes, of course, Captain," Olbrycht said. "We'll look forward to seeing you. And I'll be sure to contact Ms. Sei on your behalf, Mr. Hauptman."

"Thank you, Governor," Hauptman said. He looked at Clegg, his eyebrows raised in silent question.

To Travis's mild surprise, Clegg took the cue and the implied order without argument. "We'll see you in a few hours, then, Governor. *Casey* out." She slapped the key that cut off the com.

"I think we're in," Hauptman said, turning to Travis and Chomps. "First thing—"

"Before we go any farther," Clegg interrupted, "I'd like a little amplification on these *suggestions* Olbrycht says you gave this Simone Sei person."

"Oh, calm down, Captain," Hauptman said, his smooth cultured voice of a moment ago switching back to his usual gruffness. No matter how often Travis heard the transformation, it never ceased to startle him. "I didn't give away any trade secrets. Certainly nothing the Star Kingdom has claim to. They were just a few thoughts on how to modify the shape of a component or two to better fit the space we wanted to put them into."

"How about *our* manufacturers?" Clegg countered. "We make some of that same stuff, you know. Did you give *them* the same suggestions?"

"I tried," Hauptman said stiffly. "No one was interested." His lip twitched. "Though to be fair, that wasn't entirely their fault," he added in a slightly less argumentative tone. "Most of Manticore's production line goes to Navy and ore processing ships. Miners and freighters have different requirements."

"I think the bottom line here, Captain," Chomps cut in, "is that we've got the openings we wanted. You, Commander Woodburn, and Commander Norris will have an opportunity to be wined and dined by Governor Olbrycht and his cronies, while Commander Long, Mr. Hauptman, and I will get access to Sei's factory and records."

"While you do the *real* work, in other words?" Clegg demanded sourly.

"Hey, it's not like we could have gotten here without you," Hauptman said. "Hell of a walk from Manticore."

"Actually, Ma'am, we're going to be depending on you and the other senior officers a lot," Chomps again intervened, this time throwing a warning look at Hauptman. "If Tamerlane is working out of Silesia, *someone* in the Confederacy has to know about them."

"Someone at a high level," Travis put in.

"Exactly," Chomps agreed. "You and the others will be in a much better position to draw conversations in the right direction, maybe get someone who knows what's going on to drop the hints we're looking for. Commander Long and I don't have that kind of access."

"We'll really be doing the same job, Ma'am," Travis added "It's just that we'll be looking at the hardware side of things, while you tap into the people side."

"And no doubt, all of our work and sacrifice will be well documented," Clegg said, clearly still irritated. "Never mind. We all have our orders. I'm sure we'll all carry them out to the fullest of our abilities." She looked pointedly at Hauptman.

"Absolutely," he assured her. "I'm as much under orders as you are."

"See that you remember that." Clegg eyed him another moment, then looked back at Travis and Chomps. "And now, you're all cordially invited to get out of my cabin. I believe you, Long, are still on the bridge; and you, Townsend, probably have some ensign's nose to wipe or some spacer's butt to kick." She looked at Hauptman again. "And *you* just stay out from underfoot. Dismissed."

☆　　☆　　☆

Simone Sei was a nice counter-balance for Governor Olbrycht: easy-going, gracious, and genuinely enthusiastic about having visitors come to call.

She was also, sadly for her, far too trusting of those visitors.

"I have to say, Ms. Sei, that this place is fantastic," Hauptman boomed as she finished the tour of the busy assembly floor and headed back toward the little private office tucked away in one corner of the building. "I always pictured it as being smaller, more cramped, and a lot more automated."

"The secret of our success," Sei told him. "Also why we were able to make use of your reshaping suggestions a couple of years ago. With assembly machines you have to redo all the configuration equipment and spatial dimensioners when you change the shape of a component. With people, all you have to do is lay things out, figure out the new assembly pattern, and then just tell the workers to do it that way." She opened the office door and gestured her three visitors inside.

Travis glanced casually at the furniture arranged in a semicircle around the desk, a small bit of his tension fading away. Their pre-landing check of the social nets, plus the bits and pieces they'd seen on the way from the spaceport, had indicated that the current rage in interior décor here was for spindly, fragile-looking chairs. He and Chomps had counted on Sei being right on fashion's cutting edge, and it turned out they'd been right.

Perfect.

"We've started offering custom designs for everyone now, not just Manticore," Sei continued as they filed in. "It takes a little longer, but it's very handy for people who've gotten hold of older ships, or ships with odd configurations who want to upgrade the enviro systems. Some of those hulls had equipment tucked away into the strangest places."

"I know what you mean," Hauptman said. "We don't get nearly as much traffic in the Star Kingdom as you do, but we've had the occasional freighter or courier that's blown a component or two and needs a quick repair or replacement. Some of those take real ingenuity to fix."

"We've had a lot of the same challenges," Sei agreed.

"Please; sit down. I'll have someone bring us some tea. I think you'll like the brand I use; it comes from an island in the South Sea—yes, Chief Townsend?"

"Sorry, Ma'am," Chomps said hesitantly, his massive hand half raised like he was asking a question in class. "But I don't think your chairs are going to be strong enough for me."

"Oh—yes," Sei said, her face reddening a little. "I'm so sorry. You were walking so far behind us most of the time that I almost forgot about your, uh—"

"We call it being *heavy boned*, Ma'am," Chomps said with a grin. "No need to be tactful—we're used to needing special furniture and equipment whenever we're off Sphinx. Is there somewhere I could grab something more substantial? If not, I could sit on the floor, or just stand."

"That would hardly be polite, now, would it?" Sei said, heading for her desk. "The staff lounge around the corner has some small couches. I'll get a couple of men to bring one."

"It would probably be better if I went along," Chomps suggested. "Make sure we get one that fits me. And there's no need to bother anyone else—I can carry it if you can show me where it is."

"All right, if you're sure," Sei said, looking a bit doubtful.

"I'll be fine," Chomps assured her. "Can you show me where it is?"

"Certainly," Sei said, reversing direction back toward the door. "Follow me. Mr. Hauptman, Commander Long—if you'll have a seat, we'll be back in a minute."

"Yes, Ma'am," Chomps said, heading after her toward the door.

And as he brushed by Travis, he surreptitiously pressed a data chip into his hand. A moment later, the two of them were gone, Sei's chattering voice fading into the background hum of the floor's general conversation.

"Watch the door," Travis ordered Hauptman as he circled the desk to the computer. The tension was back, his heart pounding, his hands shaking. His first real act of espionage...

"You sure you know what you're doing?" Hauptman murmured as he stepped to the door and leaned casually against the jamb.

"We're about to find out," Travis said. Still, Chomps had had plenty of time out there to casually watch over the workers' shoulders at their computer setups. Assuming he'd spotted all the proper cues as to which operating system variant they were using, he should have picked the correct hack-chip to give Travis before he and Sei went furniture hunting.

Fortunately, Sei's computer was already running, with meant Travis wouldn't need to bypass any passwords or first-level barriers. Mentally crossing his fingers, he plugged the chip into the slot.

For a couple of seconds nothing happened. Travis kept one eye on the display and the other on Hauptman in the doorway, feeling his already racing heart picking up speed. The chip ought to get them past the kind of simple security that most people typically used with non-critical systems like this. If Eiderdown Cocoon's customer and invoice lists were similarly unprotected—and again, there was no particular reason Sei would bother loading on extra layers—this should work.

Hopefully, it would. The pieces from the invaders' enviro systems had been the clearest sign of Silesian involvement with Tamerlane, even clearer than the gravitic components Travis had first spotted. Even better, Hauptman had been eighty percent certain at least one of the systems had come from Eiderdown Cocoon. Getting hold of the customer lists would give them a solid first pass at the name and system they were hunting for.

If it *didn't* work, he and Chomps would have to fall back on a more intrusive and dangerous midnight black-mask job. Clegg would no doubt be thrilled by that one.

And then, to Travis's relief, the display cleared and a long list of files appeared.

"Got it," he muttered to Hauptman, keying for a copy.

"You copying the whole database?" Hauptman asked.

"Right," Travis said. "Easier to sift it out aboard ship than try to find what we want here and now."

"Well, snap it up," Hauptman warned tensely. "They're coming."

"How soon?"

"Ten seconds?"

Travis looked at the display, ran a quick estimate. Not enough time. "Get over here," he muttered, hurrying around the end of the desk. "As soon as the download's complete, pull the chip. I'll try to slow them down."

He headed out onto the floor. Chomps and Sei were coming, all right, Sei walking at Chomps's side as he lugged a small couch toward the office. They were three seconds from the door when

Travis reached them. "Here, let me help," he offered. He stepped directly in front of Sei, forcing her to come to an abrupt halt. "Sorry," he apologized. "I can take that," he continued, blocking her path while he reached around to try to get a grip on the couch frame nearest to her.

"That's all right, Sir—I've got it," Chomps assured him, swiveling the end around to further block Sei's path.

Travis was ready, backing away and to the side, again getting between Sei and the office door. She tried to back up and get around him.

But Chomps was on to the game now, swinging the end of the couch further around, adding it to the blockage. "Really, Sir, I've got it."

"Stop *moving*," Travis said with feigned frustration.

"For heaven's sake, Commander, let him have it," Hauptman chided from the office doorway. "What's the matter with you?"

"Fine," Travis growled, stepping back. "Sorry, Ma'am," he added as Chomps again lined up the couch with the doorway.

"That's all right," Sei assured him. Together, she and Travis stood aside as Chomps maneuvered the couch inside.

And as they rejoined their host, Hauptman pressed the data chip into Travis's hand.

☆   ☆   ☆

The rest of the afternoon and evening went by quickly and comfortably. With the job finished, and Travis finally able to relax, he discovered that their hostess was delightful company, with a sharp wit he'd completely missed while his mind was spinning with details and fears about the job. She gave them tea, and when the floor shut down for the day she gathered a handful of her top people and trooped the whole crowd off to a nearby restaurant. Most of the conversation centered around Eiderdown Cocoon and the details of their equipment and operation, information that mostly went soaring over Travis's head. Fortunately, Hauptman was more than able to handle the Manticoran side of the discussion.

Which was fine with Travis. The food was exotic, but good, and it was nice to just sit back and have an evening where he didn't have to worry about anything.

By the time Commander Woodburn screened that he and Clegg were finished with their own round of talks and that it was time to head back to the ship, he was almost sorry he had to say good-bye.

Two hours later, he and Chomps were deep in the files from Sei's computer, looking for her list of customer names.

Three days after that, as the officers continued their official meetings, get-togethers, and dinners on the planet below, and the crew continued to spend their time and money on slightly less formal shore-leave activities, they had what they'd come for.

☆　　☆　　☆

"So this is it?" Clegg asked, frowning at the list Chomps had pulled up on her office computer display.

"It is, Ma'am," Chomps confirmed. "Sei's customer list, and the first step to backtracking Tamerlane's supply line."

"And how many more do we need before we can end this?"

Chomps glanced at Travis, his face settling into a

mask. "I don't know, Ma'am," he said. "In this kind of search you don't know when you're there until you're there."

"And of course you're now biting at the bit to get going."

Chomps looked at Travis. "We understand that there are other factors, Ma'am."

"Glad to hear it," Clegg said severely. "Because while you're playing spy, the rest of us are on an actual, honest-to-God goodwill tour. That means we have to stay at least a week at each system to keep up appearances." She shifted her gaze to Travis. "Meanwhile, I thought you were going to ride herd on Hauptman."

"Yes, Ma'am, we are," Travis said. "Is there a problem with him?"

"Not from *his* point of view," Clegg said. "He's socializing and racking up points with everyone down there he can find. He's also making offers and talking contracts that he can't possibly fulfil."

"We'll talk to him, Ma'am," Chomps promised.

"So you said we're going to be here another four days, Ma'am?" Travis asked.

"Or possibly longer," Clegg said, turning up the voltage in her glare. "Unless you're planning on taking command of my ship."

Travis winced. That *wasn't* where he was going. "No, Ma'am, of course not," he floundered. "I just thought—"

"You thought that showing the flag is only third on our priority list?" Clegg cut him off. "That once you and Hauptman have what you need we should wave good-bye and go find some other dot that needs connecting?"

"I think what Commander Long was trying to say—" Chomps began.

"If I were you, I'd stay out of it, Chief," Clegg cut him off. "Unless you were given magic mind-reading powers, you can let Mr. Long figure out how to explain things on his own."

The intercom pinged. "Captain?" Woodburn's voice came. "We may have a situation here."

"Oh, we definitely have a situation," Clegg growled. Reaching over, she slapped the switch. "Clegg. What's the problem?"

"We're being hailed, Ma'am," Woodburn said. "An Andermani freighter, *Hamman*. The commander—"

"An *Andermani*?" Clegg echoed in clear disbelief. "What would one of them want with us?"

"You can ask him yourself, Ma'am," Woodburn said. "Their commander, Captain Charles Kane, would like to speak with you."

"What about?"

"I don't know, Ma'am," Woodburn said. "All he would say was that he wished to speak to *Casey*'s captain."

Clegg shot a look at Travis.

"Fine," she said, waving Travis and Chomps to the door. "I'll be right there."

"Thank you, Ma'am. And you might want to bring Commander Long with you."

Clegg stopped in midstep. "Excuse me, XO?"

"I know, Captain," Woodburn said hesitantly. "But there's something about Kane that seems a little off. I'd like to get the TO's assessment."

"Fine," Clegg said between clenched teeth. "We'll *both* be right there."

Three minutes later, they reached the bridge.

"Is he still there?" Clegg demanded as she pulled herself along the handholds.

"Yes, Ma'am," Woodburn said, quickly unstrapping from the CO station. "They're cutting across the system—doesn't look like they were planning to stop here. They started their deceleration about an hour after they would have picked up our ID beacon."

"Sounds like we've piqued their interest," Clegg said. "Let's find out why."

She gestured toward the com station.

"Hot mic, Captain."

"Captain Kane, this is Captain Trina Clegg," Clegg called. "I understand you asked to speak with me. Are you having some kind of problem?"

"No problem, Captain," a melodious, almost singsong voice came. "I understand that the Star Kingdom of Manticore recently battled an invasion force led by a man who called himself Admiral Tamerlane. I also understand that your ship, HMS *Casey*, was instrumental in Tamerlane's defeat. Am I correct on both counts?"

"You are," Clegg said, shooting a frown at Woodburn. "And this is important to you why?"

"I have an interest in military matters," Kane said. "A hobby of sorts, as it were."

"A hobby," Clegg said flatly.

"One that is shared by many in the Empire," Kane said. "We also understand what it is like to be attacked without provocation, and thus have high regard for those who successfully stand against such aggression."

"We're glad you approve," Clegg said with just a hint of sarcasm. "Is there anything more we can do for you?"

"As a matter of fact, there is," Kane said. "I was hoping you would have an hour or two to join me aboard *Hamman* for a meal."

Travis eyed Clegg out of the corner of his eye. For possibly the first time since they'd met, the Captain seemed completely surprised. "That's very generous of you," she said. She shot a speculative look at Woodburn. "Is this invitation for myself alone?"

"Oh, no, not at all," Kane assured her. "Bring as many of your officers as you'd like. The more I can learn of your part in the Battle of Manticore, the better."

"Our part was to take out one of Tamerlane's battle-cruisers," Clegg said pointedly. "At close range, I might add."

"So I've heard," Kane said. "I admit that to be the aspect that most fascinates me."

"Yes," Clegg said. "A moment, please." She gestured to the com officer, and the mute indicator came on.

"You're not seriously considering going, are you, Captain?" Woodburn asked anxiously. "That's a foreign vessel, from a star nation we know very little about."

"But we *do* know that Emperor Gustav seems to have a code of honor," Clegg pointed out.

"A *mercenary's* code of honor."

"But a code of honor just the same." Clegg gestured to the display. "I also seem to remember reading that Andermani freighters were routinely armed. It might be instructive to see just how that armament is laid out." She looked at Travis. "I'm thinking our TO might like to have that closer look, as well."

Travis felt his stomach tighten. Absolutely her TO would like a closer look at that ship, both as Tactical Officer and as a Delphi agent.

But to walk into an unknown ship, with an unknown crew and unknown motives, was a scenario that sent a shiver up his back. As far as he knew, the Star Kingdom didn't even have official diplomatic relations with the Andermani.

Accepting Kane's invitation would be risky. The question was whether the potential benefits outweighed those risks.

Clegg was still waiting for a response.

"Yes, Ma'am," Travis said. "I'd very much like to see that ship."

"Then it's settled." Clegg gestured again to the com officer.

"A moment, Captain," Woodburn put in, throwing a gesture of his own at the officer. "Shouldn't you take at least another three or four officers with you?"

"What for?" Clegg countered. "He said he was interested in *Casey*'s role in the battle. I believe you and Long were the only officers on the bridge at the time."

"Then you should let me go with you as well, Ma'am," Woodburn said doggedly. "If there's trouble, I don't want the two of you facing it alone."

"I appreciate the offer and the concern, XO," Clegg said. "But I'm not expecting trouble." She raised her eyebrows. "And if there *is*, I'd rather you be here on *Casey*'s bridge. Where you can show him what real, genuine trouble is."

Woodburn's lips settled into a thin, compressed line, but he nodded. "Yes, Ma'am."

Clegg again gestured to the com, and the mute indicator disappeared. "Captain Kane, my Tactical Officer and I would be honored to accept your invitation," she said. "It looks like you were just passing through. Do you want to come here to orbit, or shall we come out to meet you?"

"Perhaps we can compromise," Kane suggested. "I'm sending you my deceleration profile. Are you available to come out and meet us? If not, we can adjust our schedule to meet you in orbit."

"Accommodating type," Woodburn said under his breath.

"I'd hate to make you go to that much trouble," Clegg said. "We should be able to meet you halfway. I'll turn you over to my Exec to coordinate the most convenient zero-zero."

"Thank you, Captain," Kane said, and there was no mistaking the delight in his tone. "I will look forward to our meeting. And to our meal, whichever meal it turns out to be. Do you have any preference as to the cuisine?"

CHAPTER TWENTY-FOUR

FOR MOST OF *CASEY*'S APPROACH, *HAMMAN* looked more or less like a perfectly normal freighter. It was only as they settled into a zero-zero within convenient shuttle range that the differences became apparent.

"Still has the standard rotational hab ring, I see," Clegg commented, hovering over Travis's shoulder. "What kind of armament are we talking about?"

"I'm seeing two launchers," Woodburn said, "plus the associated targeting sensors. Looks like multiple autocannon installations, too."

"When Gustav arms his freighters, he doesn't fool around," Clegg murmured. "Twin launchers?"

"Singles," Woodburn said. "They look similar to the old Mark Two we carry on the *Salamanders*."

"High-end military grade, in other words," Clegg said thoughtfully. "I definitely want to see the inside of this thing. Speaking of which, I suppose we should get started."

Pushing off one of Travis's handholds, she floated to the command station behind him. Woodburn remained where he was, in a spot where he could keep an eye on the helm and com stations, while still getting a good view of Travis's tactical displays. Travis glanced over his shoulder and saw Clegg make a final adjustment to her uniform collar and then gesture to the com rating. The other tapped a few keys, and Kane's face appeared on the display.

"Good evening, Captain Kane," Clegg greeted him. "We're ready to come aboard. Are there any special instructions or protocols we need to follow?"

"You mean are there any anti-intruder traps or docking codes?" Kane asked, looking amused. "No, nothing like that. Come aboard at your convenience."

"Thank you." Clegg gestured the image away. "Time to go, Long. You ready?"

Travis took a careful breath. "Yes, Ma'am."

"Good. Let's do this."

Clegg had had Woodburn settle *Casey* in at a fair distance from the Andermani, and between the undocking procedure, the shuttle trip itself, and the redocking the whole thing took nearly half an hour. Clegg didn't speak during that entire time, except to give the coxswain occasional directions. Whether she was deliberately ignoring Travis, or was deep in thoughts of her own, he couldn't tell. For his part, he alternated his attention between the navigational sensor displays and the view out the viewport and kept his mouth shut.

As Travis had expected, Kane was waiting for them just inside the airlock hatch.

"Welcome, Captain Clegg," he said, smiling expansively. "It is indeed an honor to have you aboard my humble freighter. I do wish you'd allow me to offer you more than a light breakfast."

"Light breakfast will be fine, Captain," Clegg assured him. "An interesting ship you have here."

"I know, I know, it's not exactly the norm for cargo transport vessels," Kane said ruefully. "But the Empire has enemies, and the Emperor believes in being prepared for all eventualities." He raised his eyebrows a bit. "As, clearly, does the Star Kingdom of Manticore. My congratulations on your fine leadership and tactics during the recent battle."

"Thank you," Clegg said again. "But I fear you may be laboring under a misconception. I wasn't *Casey*'s commander during that action. That was Commodore Rudolph Heissman, who's since been transferred to a new post."

"Oh?" Kane sounded surprised. "My apologies for the error. I had assumed the winning team—but of course he would have been promoted after such a success. Congratulations on inheriting his ship."

"Thank you," Clegg said yet again. "Allow me to introduce my tactical officer, Lieutenant Commander Travis Long. He *was* part of the team that took out Tamerlane's battlecruiser."

"Indeed," Kane said, eyeing Travis closely even as he inclined his head in greeting. "At any rate, Captain, breakfast is ready. If you'll follow me, please?"

The trip from the shuttle to the breakfast table was an interesting one. The spin section seemed bigger than that of most merchant ships, Travis noted as they walked, though it was only sparsely occupied. Perhaps there were passenger sections Kane wasn't taking them through, or maybe there were special holds for cargo that did best in gravity. Travis had read about planets that specialized in shipping exotic pets across the galaxy, though he suspected a lot of planetary authorities frowned on letting in non-local fauna.

And of course, there would be extra crew necessary to handle all the weaponry bristling from the freighter's hull.

"I'm a little surprised that your armament is so transparent," Clegg commented as they walked.

"Hardly a mystery," Kane said. "Emperor Gustav's philosophy is that a man-of-war should not conceal his identity or his capabilities, either from enemies or potential friends."

"Certainly makes things easier," Clegg agreed, looking sideways at Travis. "I wonder which category the Star Kingdom is in."

"The Emperor doesn't share his foreign policies with the Merchant Marine," Kane said dryly. "Or with such humble military reservists as myself."

"You were in the military, then?" Clegg asked.

"Many aboard are such," Kane said. "The merchant fleet is in many ways the armed auxiliaries of the Imperial Andermani Navy, though I prefer to avoid uniforms and military formality for our day-to-day activities. Still, to address your comment, simple logic suggests that Manticore is neither friend nor foe to the Empire. Emperor Gustav never sought conquests in the first place, but merely defended his people against outside aggression."

He gave Clegg a wry smile. "And no offense, Captain, but I also suspect the Star Kingdom is too small and much too far away to intrude upon the Emperor's attention."

"But I assume the Emperor also recognizes that there are times when intelligence must be gathered in a covert manner?" Clegg suggested.

Kane frowned.

"I beg your pardon?"

"Normal freighters run pretty tight schedules," Clegg said. "Yet you were willing to pause for several hours while we made rendezvous with you."

"Very astute, Captain," Kane said, inclining his head to her. "May I suggest in turn that the possibility of an intelligence mission would not likely be the first guess of a naval officer...unless such missions were uppermost in her mind because she herself was on one?" He raised his eyebrows.

Travis felt his stomach tighten. But Clegg just waved a casual hand. "I'm sure you understand that I can't talk about *Casey*'s mission or orders."

"Of course not," Kane said. "But perhaps we can talk in hypotheticals."

They reached a hatch and Kane tapped the release. It slid open, and he gestured his guests inside.

The compartment turned out to be a small wardroom, complete with a serving area, coffee and tea urns, and several tables and chairs set out in a neat row. One of the tables had place settings laid out at each of the seats, and there was a platter of pastries in the center.

"I'm sorry I can't offer you more companionship," Kane said as he gestured toward the table. "But as you suggested, downtime is a freighter's bane. We're thus taking the opportunity to do some badly needed maintenance, which is occupying the rest of my crew." He gestured to the urns. "I assumed you both would enjoy tea, but we also have coffee if you'd prefer."

"Tea is fine, thank you," Clegg said. She sat down in the chair at his right and nodded to Travis to take the one to his left. "You said something about hypotheticals?"

"We'll get to that in a moment," Kane said, stepping to one of the urns and drawing a cup of tea. "But first, I would very much like to hear about your battle."

Clegg gestured to Travis.

"Go ahead, Commander."

Travis knew very little about the battle aside from *Casey*'s own role and the official accounts that had been released to the public. Still, even with those limitations it took him two cups of tea and one and a half pastries to get through it.

Kane, his eyes firmly fixed on Travis the whole time, barely even touched his tea.

"Interesting," he murmured when Travis finally finished. "Particularly the tactics."

"We were just in the right position at the right time," Travis said, feeling his cheeks warming. Even the simple Andermani freighter captain appreciated his contributions more than the Royal Manticoran Navy did.

"What?" Kane said, frowning briefly. "Oh, I see. No, I wasn't talking about *your* tactics, Commander, clever though they were. I was referring to Tamerlane's."

"You know him?" Clegg asked, her voice carefully neutral.

"Not by that name, no," Kane said. "The Star Kingdom's official statements on the battle were quite limited, and there was only so much I could glean from them. But I found this so-named Tamerlane's chosen ruse to draw you into his range interesting. In fact, now that I've heard about it, I feel more certain than ever of his true identity."

"May I ask which side of Tamerlane's signature style you were on?" Clegg asked pointedly.

Kane smiled again.

"You mean is he a friend or a foe? At various times, both. Right now, he's very much a foe of the Empire."

"I thought the Emperor didn't share his policies with you," Clegg reminded him.

"Warfare is my hobby," Kane reminded her right back again.

"Right—I forgot," Clegg said. "So who *is* Tamerlane, anyway?"

Kane puckered his lips.

"I think he's a man named Cutler van Tischendorf, who now goes by the name Cutler Gensonne," he said. "I cannot yet confirm it, but I think the indications are strong."

"And you think he's in Silesia?" Clegg persisted.

"We have certain evidence pointing to the Confederacy." Kane gestured to her. "I imagine you, too, have some evidence of your own? Hypothetically speaking of course."

"I'm afraid you have things a bit confused, Commodore," Clegg said. "We're not here to hunt down our invaders. We're here to try to drum up ship orders."

"To drum up *what*?"

"It doesn't make much sense to me, either," Clegg conceded. "But there are influential voices on Manticore who think we should be manufacturing our own impellers. The only way to make that even marginally affordable is to build a lot more ships than we ourselves have any use for. Hence, this trip."

"A *sales* journey?" Kane said, clearly still not believing it. "Undertaken by your most advanced warship?"

"That's exactly why *Casey* was chosen," Clegg said. "She's the best showcase we've got for our shipbuilding skills."

"Ah." Kane's eyes flicked back and forth between his guests. The earlier brief confusion was gone, and he had the look of a man who was again reading between the lines. "But of course, if you should happen on information concerning Tamerlane, you'd be sure to take notice of it? I'm sure the Empire would pay handsomely for such information."

"I wish we could help you," Clegg said. "But *Casey's* mission is simply to find interested customers. I'm sorry."

"As am I." Kane gave a philosophical shrug. "Well. At least I was able to hear a firsthand account of the battle. Allow me to escort you to your shuttle, and we can go our separate ways."

"Thank you again for your hospitality, Captain," Clegg said, standing up. "Perhaps we can return your generosity in the future." She gestured to Travis. "Commander?"

And, to his surprise and dismay, Travis realized that he was at a crossroads.

Clegg was his commanding officer. The oath he'd taken when he joined the Navy required him to obey her lawful orders, and she was now ordering him to leave with her.

But he worked for Lady Calvingdell, too, and *she'd* ordered him to do everything possible to find Tamerlane.

Kane had information that could be crucial in that search. He might be willing to give up that data for the right price. But if they left now...

"Commander?" Clegg repeated, and this time there was an edge to her voice.

Calvingdell wasn't here, she wasn't in the RMN chain of command, and her orders had been general and nebulous. Clegg was right here, she *was* in the chain of command, and her implied order was as clear as hard vacuum.

Regulations said that a CO's direct order was always to be obeyed. *Always.* There might be times when two lawful orders conflicted with one another, and the Navy had a rule for that, too. In that instance, the *most recently-given* lawful order was to be obeyed.

And Clegg had just given him the most recently-given lawful order he was likely to get.

Regulations were why Travis had joined the Navy in the first place. The network of structure and order that those regulations created had been vitally important to him in his late teens and early twenties. He couldn't just set them aside, not even for a higher purpose.

But he had to. Manticore had been attacked. Many good men and women had died, and the entire Star Kingdom had been threatened. That was why he and Chomps had been inserted into *Casey's* crew in the first place. It was why he was *here*, and he had the chance to avenge that attack, perhaps even make sure it never happened again.

And he was the only one who *was* here. The *only* one who could do that.

Which left him no choice. No choice at all.

"What about a trade?" he asked, not moving from his chair.

Both of them looked at him, Kane with mild surprise, Clegg with disbelief.

"Excuse me?" Kane asked.

"You said you'd pay for information about Tamerlane," Travis said, his heart pounding. The rapidly growing incredulity and anger in Clegg's face was a blazing fire that he could feel burning into his heart and mind.

This was not the way he liked to do things. This was not the order and discipline he found comfortable.

But he'd made his decision. There was nothing to do now but continue.

"Instead of payment," he said, "how about a trade?"

"You said your mission was to solicit ship sales."

"*Casey's* mission is," Travis said. "*My* mission is to track down Tamerlane."

Kane's eyes flicked to Clegg, back to Travis.

"You're Naval Intelligence, then?"

"I have multiple duties," Travis said, hoping that would be interpreted as an affirmative. There was absolutely no way he could justify telling a foreigner about Delphi.

"And when you find him? What are your plans then?"

Travis looked at Clegg. She had the air of a very angry predator about her.

"We find out why we were invaded," Travis said, looking back at Kane. "We hopefully also find out whether he was working on his own or was hired by someone else."

"Your turn, Captain," Clegg said, her voice under rigid control. Still furious, probably, but aware that her choices were to back Travis's play or sink it and choosing the former. For the moment, at least. "You know more about this than you pretend. Who are you?"

Kane shrugged.

"Cards on the table, then. Very well. I'm part of a mission to bring Gensonne and his activities to an end. That's all you need to know." He smiled slightly at Travis. "It's probably more than I—more than either of us—should have said."

"Fortunately, as we agreed earlier, this is all hypothetical," Clegg said. "So who exactly is Gensonne?"

"Cutler Gensonne was one of the Emperor's chief captains," Kane said, sitting down again and gesturing for Clegg to do likewise. "He was rising nicely through the ranks when ... well, let's just say he fell from the Emperor's favor. He left the Empire and disappeared.

"Then, a few years ago, we began to hear rumors that he'd resurfaced, working with or possibly commanding one of the less-than-reputable mercenary groups."

"Sounds like Tamerlane's group, all right," Travis murmured.

"It could be," Kane agreed. "We've been tracking mercenary movements and operations as best we could, focusing especially on post-battle repair and replacement purchases and looking for unidentified credit lines and payment deposits. Andermani ships have standing orders to make informal surveys of any system we enter, paying special attention to ships running questionable or suspicious IDs or seem out of place." He smiled thinly. "A Manticoran warship in Silesia, for example."

"May I ask how long you've been hunting him?" Travis asked.

"Actively, not until quite recently, I'm afraid." Kane shrugged. "At the time he left Imperial service, his rumored activities were far enough from New Berlin that we decided he was someone else's problem."

"Such as ours?" Clegg asked pointedly.

"I'm sure there was no intent on the Emperor's part to allow him to prey on others," Kane said. "It was mostly that the distance made a direct response impractical. At any rate, later information suggested he might be assembling a force large enough to return and challenge the Emperor. That, of course, the Emperor could not permit."

"So you were sent to hunt him down," Clegg said.

"Exactly," Kane said, nodding. "Recently we've heard rumors of a man matching his description having been seen in Silesia, so this is where I began my search."

"Hell of a haystack."

"True. But we've had some success. We've largely eliminated the larger systems as his base, and cleared most of the likely smaller ones, as well. But as you say, the Confederacy is a huge haystack. Any assistance you could give us would be greatly appreciated."

Travis looked questioningly at Clegg. "Captain?"

"Are you invoking Special Order Seven?" she countered coolly.

Travis winced. *Special Order Seven*: the one that permitted Travis or Chomps to effectively take command of the ship. Clegg had reportedly argued vehemently against it in her consultation with Locatelli and Calvingdell, and Travis was himself rather of two minds about it.

The entire notion of Special Order Seven cut directly against the Navy's entire tradition. It also seriously compromised the chain of command, which was vital to a ship's efficient operation or even its survival. The idea of overriding his own commanding officer offered more ways to create dangerously untenable situations than he could count. Worse, while Clegg might have a thorny personality, she was obviously a highly capable, highly professional captain, while Travis was only a lieutenant commander.

He didn't want to override her. In fact, he himself had argued against Special Order Seven when Calvingdell first explained it to him.

Because the Navy was right: command authority aboard a starship, especially one deployed far from home, simply could not be divided between two people.

Clegg probably didn't know that he'd felt that way, and probably wouldn't believe it if he told her. But the truth was that he would much prefer offering suggestions to his captain and having her agree with him.

On this point, clearly, she didn't. Travis wondered how much of that was because this particular exchange was a bad idea in her coldly considered, professional opinion, and how much of it was because of her totally understandable resentment at being put in such a position.

But whatever she might think, he had a job to do, and his superiors in Delphi had been very clear about the reasons he'd been given Special Order Seven. He might not agree with all of them, but he couldn't pretend they hadn't been explained to him in detail.

"I suppose I am, Ma'am," he told her. "But just—"

"Then this is your show, Commander," she cut him off. "Carry on."

Travis swallowed. It looked like she was even more pissed off by Special Order Seven than he'd feared. That did not bode well for the rest of the voyage.

But it was too late to backtrack now. "Yes, Ma'am," he said, turning back to Kane. "Captain, I take it you haven't seen any of the communications Tamerlane had with our forces before the battle?"

"That's correct," Kane said. "We have only the data the Star Kingdom released to the general public, which we obtained via our people in the Republic of Haven. No communications were included, between or among any of the parties."

"Do you have a picture of Gensonne I could see?"

"Of course." Kane pulled out a tablet. He punched a few keys, frowned at the result, then punched a few more. He did something with the screen, then reversed it and offered it to Travis. "The one on the left is his last picture before leaving the Empire. The other is a more recent picture from a Silesian security camera that is claimed to be him."

Travis felt his stomach tighten. The first picture was probably twenty years out of date. The second was blurry almost to the point of being unrecognizable.

But between them, there was no doubt.

"That's him," he confirmed, offering the tablet to Clegg. "That's Tamerlane."

"I agree," Clegg confirmed, peering at the images. "He's aged pretty well, all things considered."

"The Emperor's wish is that he not age much more," Kane said grimly. "Thank you, Captain; Commander. At least we now know that we're on the right track." He raised his eyebrows. "Is there anything more you'd like to share?"

"What are you offering in return?" Clegg asked.

Kane's lips puckered again.

"I can give you our accumulated data on Gensonne and his possible Silesian connections," he said. "Largely rumors and unsubstantiated pictures like that one, unfortunately. I can also include our assessments of where he and his mercenaries *aren't* located, along with some of our credit and purchase data, though much of the latter is somewhat out of date."

"That would be very helpful," Travis said.

"Also very generous," Clegg added. "Not to question your authority, Captain, but are you authorized to share all this information with us?"

Kane smiled.

"I hear two questions, Captain. The first is if I will be in trouble with my superiors for handing over Imperial secrets. The second, given Question One, is if you can trust my information to be accurate, or if I might give you useless or even falsified data."

"You have a blunt way of putting things," Clegg said. "But let's say those are my concerns. How do you address them?"

"The first is quite simple," Kane said. "I've been given an assignment—to locate Gensonne—and as long as I don't put my ship and crew at unnecessary risk, I have wide latitude and discretion." He shrugged. "It's true that the Empire and Star Kingdom are hardly allies. But I can't see how the location and activities of a common enemy could qualify as state secrets."

Travis suppressed a grimace. Though Countess Calvingdell might have a somewhat different opinion of what constituted a state secret. The post-battle debris analysis that had brought *Casey* to Silesia in the first place came to mind, as well as the data he and Chomps had stolen from Sei's records.

But the Andermani had clearly been on Gensonne's trail far longer than Delphi had. Whatever trade they made here, Manticore was almost certainly going to come out ahead in the deal.

"Your second question is a bit more delicate," Kane

continued. "Perhaps I could best express my position in the following way. Our most recent information lists the Royal Manticoran Navy's assets at approximately twenty ships, including five battlecruisers. Tell me: how many of those ships would fall into Gensonne's hands if he attacked again and forced a surrender?"

Travis felt a shiver run through him. Gensonne had attacked with three battlecruisers, two of which had been destroyed in the battle. Even if he had a second or third tucked away somewhere in reserve, a successful capture of Manticore and the Navy could conceivably double the size of his fleet.

And if he was holding a grudge against Gustav Anderman, the Empire might well be his next target.

"I see your point," Clegg murmured. "You said we weren't the Empire's allies or enemies. However, we *are* someone's potential shopping center."

"Well put, Captain," Kane said. "You see now that we have strongly interlocking interests in this matter. I put it to you: what use would it be for me to deliberately offer you bad or useless information?"

"Indeed," Clegg said. "Thank you for your candor. How do we do this?"

"I presume you didn't bring your data with you," Kane said. "I'll therefore prepare a data chip you can take with you, and you can transmit your information to me after your return to *Casey*. Will that be acceptable?"

"Yes, very acceptable," Travis agreed. "Thank you."

"You're more than welcome," Kane said. "Oh, and if you have a full report of the battle, please include that as well. It could be useful to see if Gensonne has picked up any new tricks along the way."

"Of course," Travis said.

"Excellent," Kane smiled. "And while the chip is being prepared, we should have enough time for a final cup of tea."

☆　　☆　　☆

"No," Clegg said flatly. "Out of the question."

"But I made a promise Captain," Travis protested. "Our data in exchange for—"

"I *know* what your deal was," Clegg cut him off. "And I'm telling you that I will not release the full record of the battle to a foreigner."

"But it shows Gensonne's tactics capabilities. They need that information before they go up against him."

"I'm sure it would be valuable to them," Clegg said. "I doubt that it would be *vital*. The problem is that it also gives them details of *our* tactics. Plus details of our ships, our organization, our com patterns, our sensor capabilities—pretty much everything about us. Giving that kind of information to a foreign naval officer, retired reservist or otherwise, is not in the best interests of the Navy or the Star Kingdom."

Travis swallowed. Caught up in the moment back on the *Hamman*, the fact that those details would be in the complete files hadn't occurred to him. "Captain—"

"Stow it and listen," Clegg growled. "Special Order Seven is a terrible idea, and you've just demonstrated why. With your lack of experience, coupled with your tunnel vision on this Tamerlane hunt, you completely failed to think through the logical implications of your blithe promise to a foreign officer. I strongly suggest that you rethink your position, Commander...because special orders or not, if you insist on overruling my considered judgment of what constitutes the Star

Kingdom of Manticore's vital strategic interests, there *will* be consequences."

With an effort, Travis unclenched his jaw. She was right, all the way up and down the line.

But on the other hand—

"Ma'am, you have a valid point," he said, keeping his voice as emotionless as he could. "You're right, I didn't think through all of the implications."

Clegg raised her eyebrows. "*But*...?" she prompted.

"But Captain Kane gave us exactly the data he promised," Travis continued. "Chief Townsend has verified that. And whether I screwed up or not, he's expecting us to transmit the data we promised in return. If we renege on that promise—on *my* promise—we'll risk losing any future cooperation with the Andermani, not just Kane but all the rest of them."

"The Andermani Empire is a hell of a long ways away," Clegg said icily. "The odds that the Star Kingdom will need their cooperation for anything anytime soon strike me as pretty damn remote."

Still, Travis could hear a shade of new thoughtfulness in her tone. She'd seen the implications of giving Kane too much data; maybe she could also see the implications of annoying even a distant neighbor.

"I'm not thinking of the Star Kingdom as much as I'm thinking about us," Travis said. "What if we need them again before we find Gensonne? We still don't have any clue as to why he picked Manticore to attack, and we desperately need to know that. The Andermani want him as badly as we do, and they've got a lot bigger navy than we do. If we want to take Gensonne off the board before he attacks us again, the best way to do that is to give them everything we—" He hesitated. "Everything we *reasonably* can. Captain."

For a long moment Clegg just stared up at him from her desk, her forearms planted on the arms of her chair, her eyes dark. "Fine," she said at last. "Then I'll just say one more thing. Special Order Seven is a bad order. But it *is* an order, issued by lawful national command authority. and if you insist on invoking it, as an officer of the Royal Manticoran Navy I'm bound to follow it. I'll follow it under the most strongly-worded protest, but I *will* follow it. But know this."

She paused, and her eyes went even darker.

"When we return to the Star Kingdom, I will make it my personal crusade to make sure that an officer whose judgment was sufficiently flawed to use his authority in this way never, *ever* finds himself in a position to do so again. Do you understand?"

"Yes, Ma'am. I do." It took every ounce of strength for Travis to get the words out. But he did, and to his surprise his voice was even steady.

"Very well," Clegg said. A trace of respect might have flickered in Clegg's eyes, but it was gone almost before it registered. "In that case—"

"Excuse me, Captain," Chomps spoke up.

He was standing off in a corner of the office, busily working at his tablet. He hadn't said a word since Clegg had hauled them in here, and Travis had assumed that he was simply keeping his head down and letting his superior take the brunt of Clegg's broadside.

But now, as the big Sphinxian looked up calmly in the face of Clegg's glare, Travis realized that hadn't been the case.

"What?" Clegg demanded.

"A thought, Ma'am," Clegg said. "What if we edited out all of the RMN material? In other words, we cut out everything except the invaders' attack and their defensive maneuvers. We don't have to show anything of our own tactics."

"Except that those maneuvers will still be shown on Manticoran displays," Clegg shot back, "which will be fed by Manticoran sensors and compiled and sifted by Manticoran CIC and bridge personnel."

"All of which can also be cut out," Chomps said. "I can strip out the data on Tamerlane's ships and build what amounts to a simulation. I can't disguise our ability to collect and resolve data, not if we want to give him anything useful about the battle, but I can strip out every com protocol, every order, every ship-to-ship transmission, every weapon launch on our side. They'll have to see our missiles coming at Tamerlane's ships, but, really, Captain, I'm pretty sure they already have all of the performance specs on our missiles. It won't be a complete read on the battle, but if we combine it with what Delphi's been able to sift out of the debris and the customer lists we got on Saginaw, the Andermani will probably accept it as a good-faith effort to keep our word. And, as Commander Long says, it will put that information into the hands of the most powerful navy in the region. A navy that already wants Tamerlane's head."

Clegg eyed him another moment. Looked at Travis; looked back at Chomps. "How long will it take you to make me a sample?" she asked.

"I've got one right here," Chomps said, stepping forward and handing her the tablet. "It's only about three minutes worth—the idea didn't occur to me until you brought us in here. The original record's on the left; my scrubbed version's on the right."

Clegg accepted the tablet, and with a final look at Travis settled down to read.

Travis looked sideways at Chomps, but the other's eyes were fixed on the captain. Briefly, he wondered if he dared ask Clegg permission to look at Chomps's work over her shoulder, but knew instantly that would be a very bad idea.

And so he stood at attention, feeling the sweat trickling down his back, for one of the longest three-minute chunks of his life.

Finally—finally—Clegg looked up again. "Interesting," she said. She fingered the tablet a moment, sent another pair of hard-eyed looks at each of them, and then handed the tablet back to Chomps.

"You'll take this immediately to Commander Woodburn," she said. "He will supervise the operation, and advise you of whatever proprietary data can and cannot be included in the packet. I will personally review it afterward, and if—*if*, I say—I am entirely satisfied with the end result, it will be transmitted to *Hamman*. Do you think you can get it finished before they leave the system?"

"Easily, Ma'am," Chomps assured her. "Probably even before we make it back to orbit."

"Then go." She sent one final look at Travis. "Both of you."

☆　　☆　　☆

"Ten minutes to orbit," Commander Woodburn announced.

"Very good," Clegg responded.

Typically, a warship's bridge was a quiet place, where

extraneous conversation was very much frowned upon. At this particular moment, though, as *Casey* returned to Saginaw to resume their show-the-flag social events, her command deck was even quieter than usual.

And Travis couldn't help the feeling that everyone was staring at him.

Which wasn't exactly the case, of course. Aside from Woodburn and Clegg herself, no one on the bridge knew what had happened earlier in the captain's office. Still, some of the others had undoubtedly picked up on the fact that Clegg was less than pleased with her tactical officer. No doubt the rumors about how he'd managed to blot his copybook this time were already flying.

And that didn't begin to cover what would happen when they got home.

Travis had played the scene over and over in his mind, as he'd run the scene aboard *Hamman* over and over. Whatever his failings, whatever the consequences, he was still convinced he'd done the right thing.

And if he was summarily kicked out of the Navy, at least he'd be able to look into the mirror and—

"Ma'am," the com officer said suddenly. "We've received a transmission from *Hamman*. It's for you, from Captain Kane."

Clegg looked up from the message board she'd been reading, her forehead creased slightly. "Send it to my station," she ordered. "Long? With me."

"Yes, Ma'am," Travis said, unstrapping and pulling himself over behind her chair. At least whatever Kane was about to say, whatever outrage he might be about to dump on them in regards to the scrubbed battle data, the entire watch wouldn't get to hear it.

He settled into position, and Clegg tapped the key. The display cleared, and Kane's face appeared.

Travis frowned. If the Andermani was angry, it certainly didn't show.

"Captain Clegg," he said, "I would very much like to thank you for the generosity and completeness of the information packet you shared with me. I'm sure that when you integrate our two sets of data, you'll see several interesting correlations between what you've discovered here in Silesia and what we already knew. I'm confident that will be very valuable to both of us in our missions.

"I didn't anticipate the full depth of some of your more, shall we say, unofficially gathered information." He smiled faintly, inclining his head. "Very efficiently done. My congratulations to those involved.

"But far and away the most useful of all is the tactical data on the attack. Additional congratulations are in order for whoever prepared it. It must have been quite a challenge to excise so much background data while at the same time preserving the details of the battle." His smile grew both more pronounced and more ironic. "I rather wondered how your Commander Long would approach that aspect of the exchange."

For a fleeting instant Travis wondered if Clegg would turn around to look at him. She didn't.

Kane's smile faded. "I don't know whether or not you've had a chance to look at my *Tarnung* data file. I suspect not, with your attention on your overt mission to Saginaw. But I urge you to do so as soon as you can. It contains a list of ship profiles, both physical and electronic and gravitic, and includes sensor recordings of what *might* have been one of Gensonne's ships. One of those recordings, which came from the same star system where the picture of Gensonne which I showed you was taken, is particularly interesting, because that ship is effectively identical with *Tamerlane's* flagship."

Travis huffed out a silent breath. So there it was. Tamerlane and Gensonne—

"Which I believe conclusively demonstrates that your Tamerlane and my Gensonne are indeed the same individual," Kane continued. "Which means you and I—and the Star Kingdom and the Empire—share a common enemy. Which brings me to the most important reason for this transmission."

He paused. Again, Clegg kept her eyes on the display.

"It is unlikely that *Hamman* and *Casey* will cross paths once again," Kane said. "However, I can reveal to you now that there are other Imperial vessels in Silesia seeking Gensonne. If, should you encounter any of them, you would be good enough to share an additional copy of your data with them, I would be extremely grateful. Furthermore, sharing a recording of this message will constitute my authorization, as a member of the SMS reserve, for them to cooperate fully with you. That cooperation includes reasonable joint military support against Gensonne, should the opportunity arise."

Clegg stiffened in her chair. Travis could still only see the back of her head, but it didn't take any skill at body language to see that she was as astonished by the offer as Travis himself was.

"This man is a danger to my Emperor, a danger to your Star Kingdom, and—based on the information already available to us—a mass murderer," Kane said, his voice going cold. "He is, in fact, a criminal against humankind in general, and my Emperor would account it an honor to assist anyone in his destruction.

"Thank you again, Captain Clegg, and good hunting to you. Kane out."

The transmission ended. For a long moment neither Clegg nor Travis said anything.

Travis wasn't sure, at this point, if there was anything to say.

"Orbit achieved, Captain," Woodburn announced.

His voice seemed to break a spell. "Thank you," Clegg said.

"And may I remind the captain that she has a dinner engagement in three hours," Woodburn added.

"Thank you," Clegg said again. She took a deep breath.

And finally turned to look at Travis. Her face was composed, but there was a glint in her eye that Travis had never seen there before. "Have my shuttle ready in one hour," she added to her XO. "Until then, I'll be in my office. Commander Long, you and Chief Townsend are invited to join me."

CHAPTER TWENTY-FIVE

THE HOUSE OF LORDS, LIKE ANY other living, breathing thing, had its moods.

Sometimes it was angry. Sometimes it was smug. Occasionally, as when it sat helplessly on the sidelines during the Battle of Manticore, it was fearful.

Today, as near as Winterfall could judge it, the mood was anticipatory.

The problem was he couldn't see anything that was driving it.

There were no major votes on the day's agenda. No one had announced a forthcoming bill. None of the usual firebrands were slated to address the assembly, Breakwater included.

So what were they all anticipating?

He puzzled at it most of the morning, checking news feeds and screening associates who also had their ears to the ground. None of them had the slightest clue. Most of them hadn't even noticed the calm-before-the-storm feeling.

It was after lunch before he finally realized that

what he'd thought was a general mood was really only Breakwater's mood, and the mood of his inner circle.

A circle which, on this point at least, apparently didn't include Winterfall.

That was new. And it bothered him more than he wanted to admit. For years he'd been Breakwater's chief confidant, sounding board, ally, and trusted errand runner. Or at least, so he'd thought.

Maybe it had all been a lie. Maybe Breakwater played that same game with everyone else, giving each of them the impression that he or she was the most important person in his circle.

In years gone by, Winterfall reflected, he might have spent the rest of the day brooding about it. But not now. Breakwater was a master of redirection; and if Winterfall's exclusion from the joke was significant, the more significant question was what the Chancellor was anticipating in the first place.

And so he resumed his digging…and finally, finally, came up with at least a possibility.

Joshua Miller, MP from Friedman's Valley, was scheduled to address the House of Commons within the hour.

That alone probably wouldn't have caught Winterfall's eye except that he vividly remembered Miller's last speech. It had been a detailed, acerbic, and mostly accurate castigation of the Lords for some of their votes on the Navy, MPARS, and the Star Kingdom's defense in general.

Winterfall had spent some time afterward going back over Miller's record. What he'd discovered was a slowly but steadily growing strength of rhetoric and support over the man's six T-years in the Commons.

He'd been a rallying point for those who felt the Lords had regained too much of the power the Commons had once wielded, as opposed to those members who simply enjoyed the stature afforded by the letters *MP* attached to their names. That group was usually content to draw their pay without having to take any serious responsibility for anything.

And then, a little over three months ago, Miller had gone silent.

There'd been some quiet speculation at the time, mostly in the Commons, as to what had happened. Some thought he'd been bought off; others thought he'd recognized the futility of railing against the dominance of the Lords and given up; others wondered if he'd suddenly developed a health problem. But the theories had all evaporated, and eventually the whispers had been buried beneath newer and more interesting gossip and forgotten.

Only now Miller was headed back to the podium. Was he planning to say something that would seriously rock the boat? And if so, what about his speech had caught Breakwater's eye?

Winterfall had switched his search to Breakwater's old files when he noticed something odd. Not only had Breakwater been closely following Miller's public comings and goings, but he'd had the same virtual trailing going on with six other men, as well. One was another MP, but the other five were private citizens. Reasonably prominent men, but private citizens nonetheless. Ten more minutes of searching failed to find any obvious link between them.

So what was Breakwater's interest?

The other lesson Breakwater had hammered into

him over the years was that there was a time for subtlety and a time for bluntness. With Miller's speech less than ten minutes away, it was time for the latter.

If Winterfall had been summarily dropped from Breakwater's close-associate list, the word hadn't made it to his secretary. Angela merely nodded a silent greeting as Winterfall strode across the outer office and pushed open the door.

The whole group was there: Breakwater; Ross Macinroy, Earl Chillon; Maria Stahlberg, Baroness Castle Rock; and Yvonne Rowlandson, Baroness Tweenriver, all gathered in the conversation area around a large display Breakwater had set up. All four of them looked up with varying degrees of surprise at Winterfall's entrance. "Gavin," Breakwater said, half rising before sitting down again. "We weren't expecting you this afternoon."

"My apologies, My Lords; My Ladies," Winterfall apologized as he walked over to them. "But I thought we should all be together to hear what Joshua Miller has to say."

A look of consternation flashed across Breakwater's face before he could smooth it over. "Of course," he said, gesturing to an empty seat beside Castle Rock. "Please join us."

"Or not," Tweenriver said disgustedly as she gestured at the display. "Looks like he's canceled."

Winterfall followed her pointing finger. A young woman was walking toward the Commons podium, the caption identifying her as Sarah Tonquis from White Sand. The rest of the caption, listing the speech lineup for the rest of the afternoon, made no mention of Miller.

"Well, *that's* useful," Chillon growled. "Any idea what he was *going* to say?"

"If we knew that, we wouldn't have had to listen to him," Breakwater pointed out, his eyes still on Winterfall. "You're probably wondering why you were excluded from our session today."

"Yes, My Lord, I was," Winterfall said, trying to read the Chancellor's mood. He didn't seem angry that Winterfall had tumbled to the private get-together, or even that he'd chosen to crash it.

"It was no reflection on you, I assure you," Breakwater said. "Well, perhaps a bit. But only as to your ability to act outraged on command."

"To act outraged?" Winterfall echoed, letting his volume rise and his pitch grow deeper and darker. "To act *outraged*? You think I'm just going to stand here and let you meet behind my back? I have rights, My Lords—do not *ever* think I don't." He paused, then raised his eyebrows. "Was that sufficiently outraged, My Lord?"

Breakwater smiled wryly. "Touché, Gavin. Very well. What do you want to know?"

"Let's start with seven names," Winterfall suggested. "Jeremy Miller, Jacques Corlain, Placido Amadeo—"

"Where did you get those names?" Chillon demanded.

"Earl Breakwater has been watching them and their movements," Winterfall said. "Which I assume you all already know."

"What *we* know isn't the question," Chillon said. "I asked how *you* knew."

"From my files, of course," Breakwater said. "Relax, Ross—Gavin's done enough work for me over the years that I've given him complete access." He smiled faintly. "Well, *mostly* complete. The answer, Gavin, is that those seven men are the names on a list the late Prime Minister Burgundy put together for the Queen."

"And the list was for...?"

"We don't know for sure," Breakwater said. "But we know he was going to suggest some possible suitors for her. Almost certainly this is at least the start of that list." His lips compressed briefly. "There are indications he was working on it when he had his fatal heart attack."

"I see," Winterfall said again, his mind racing in at least three different directions. "How do you know about the list?"

"Please, Gavin," Breakwater said with another smile. "I *do* have other sources besides you and the others in this room. The point is that we do have it." He gestured to the display. "And we were wondering if Miller was going to make some sort of announcement related to it today. Apparently not."

"I'm sorry, but I'm still confused," Winterfall said. "Why does the Queen need a list of suitors in the first place? I mean, why does she need a list from Burgundy or anyone else? Can't she come up with names on her own?"

"My Lord, this may not be the right time," Castle Rock warned.

"It's all right, Maria," Breakwater soothed. "Now that Gavin knows, he might as well know everything." He again gestured Winterfall to a seat. "We have a potential crisis facing us, Gavin. And as you know, in any crisis there are points to be made and points to be lost.

"The crux of the matter is this. Queen Elizabeth

has no heirs to the throne. To obtain an heir obviously requires her to have a child; and the Constitution states that the father of that child must be a commoner."

"Yes, I understand all that," Winterfall said. "There are certainly enough rumors flying around on the subject. But I also understand she was still in mourning for her late husband. Again, it seems to me this is something she should be able to do on her own, and in her own timing."

"We disagree," Breakwater said. "Our position is that, given the uncertainty of the future—a fact that was so recently underlined by the sudden deaths of her brother and niece—she can't risk putting off this obligation indefinitely."

"It's only been a few months," Winterfall pointed out.

"You're not thinking this through," Chillon said, his tone going a bit more severe. "Aside from the practical reasons, there are political gains to be made from this situation. We want to make sure *we're* the ones who benefit."

"Exactly," Breakwater said. "We foresee her taking one of three options. First, she will bow to our pressure and choose one of the men on that list as her new husband. That gains us little directly, but does set a precedent in her mind toward accepting advice and direction from us, which can't help but strengthen our position. Second, she will defy the call for remarriage, at which point we will declare her out of compliance with the Constitution and introduce a bill to return King Michael to the throne."

"Can he even *do* that?" Winterfall asked, frowning. "I thought abdication was permanent."

"Since it's never been done before, we don't really

know," Breakwater said. "Hence, the bill's introduction. This case is somewhat better, because we already know how easily Michael can be controlled and manipulated. Or third, Elizabeth will ask for a Constitutional amendment to allow her to use her late husband's frozen sperm to conceive a child. That's the best case of all, because she'll need our support to get the supermajority of both the Lords and the Commons she'll need to pass such an amendment."

"Support she'll need to pay for," Tweenriver said.

"In one form or another." Breakwater cocked his head. "Your job, Gavin, was to be the one who would stand before the Lords in outrage at the Queen's presumption in defying the Constitution. Since we weren't certain—before now," he added dryly, "of your histrionic abilities, we thought it best if there was some genuine surprise behind your speech."

"I see," Winterfall said, carefully filtering the outrage out of his voice. This wasn't just some other Lord or Cabinet Minister or industrialist they were talking so calmly about manipulating. This was the Queen. The *Queen*. "Does she have a deadline to make a decision?"

"Not yet," Breakwater said. "I'm going to wait another four or five weeks, make sure that the sympathy bump her brother's death gave her has well and truly worn off. After that, I'll deliver her a quiet ultimatum: betroth herself, or we'll publicly declare her out of compliance and force a decision."

"Do we have enough support to make that stick?"

"We've been counting potential votes," Castle Rock said. "A bit tricky when we can hardly broach the true subject of the question. But we think we do."

"And the Commons?" Winterfall persisted.

"The least of our considerations," Chillon said, waving a hand in dismissal. "There will be some token opposition, but in the end they'll fall into line like always."

"Unless Elizabeth chooses either Miller or Corlain as consort," Castle Rock said. "That may endear her to them somewhat. But that kind of sentimentality fades quickly. And as I said, that would establish the precedent of her bowing to our demands."

"You have to understand, Gavin, that Elizabeth is still a bit of an enigma," Breakwater said. "We have to learn more about her if we're going to know how to work her in the future. This heir business, besides the fact that it's vital to the future of the Star Kingdom, is the perfect hammer. Seeing which way the nail bends will show us how best to use the next hammer that comes into our possession."

"Of course, My Lord," Winterfall said. "So I'll eventually be giving the key address. What can I do until then?"

Breakwater glanced around at the others, his eyebrows raised. "Anyone?"

"I think everything's under control at this point," Castle Rock said. "We're mostly into waiting mode right now."

"In fact, going about your other business is probably the best thing you can do," Chillon added. "The less you're seen meeting with any of us, the more believable your outrage and passion will be when you mount that podium."

"Agreed," Breakwater said. "Thank you for coming, Gavin. I'm sorry we weren't able to tell you before, but I admit I'm rather impressed that you were able to sniff this out. Well done."

"Thank you, My Lord," Winterfall said. "And again, my apologies for intruding. I'll take my leave now."

He kept his face emotionless during the walk back to his office. Only when he was safely behind a closed door did he permit himself the scowl, and the words, he'd so wanted to express back there.

Breakwater had manipulated the Navy's victory over Tamerlane's invasion force in order to get more money and personnel for MPARS. He'd manipulated other Cabinet Ministers, the entire House of Lords, and possibly King Michael in ways that had slowly but surely added to the Chancellor's personal power and prestige.

For that matter, he'd manipulated Winterfall himself into his current position of visibility, all on the strength of Winterfall's brother joining the Navy.

But he was *not* going to manipulate the Queen. Not if Winterfall had anything to say about it.

Dropping into his chair, he keyed his computer. As Breakwater had mentioned, he had many sources, men and women whose information had proved very useful in the group's activities and maneuverings. Winterfall had never before questioned Breakwater's ethics or identities of those sources.

Time to start questioning.

And the first step was to figure out who, exactly, had known Burgundy's suitor list existed.

Clearing his mind, he got to work.

☆　　☆　　☆

It had been a pleasant enough dinner, Gensonne decided as he gazed at the tactical display, watching as his shuttle made its way back across the wavering gray and black of hyper space.

Even taking into account the company.

"Rhamas seems a pleasant enough sort," Captain Sweeney Imbar, *Odin*'s commander, commented from behind Gensonne. "He's had an interesting life, at least, if his stories are to be believed."

"I doubt that," Gensonne said. "Llyn probably made them up for him to tell."

"Maybe," Imbar said. "Still pretty entertaining. I wonder how the two of them hooked up."

"Probably over money," Gensonne said. "I noticed Rhamas's stories were pretty vague about who he was working for during any of them. I'm guessing he and his crew are just hirelings Axelrod got to fly Llyn's ship for him."

"And to run the weapons?" Imbar asked. "You *did* notice that the damn thing's armed, right?"

Gensonne glared at him. Like he would miss something like *that*. "Not going to be a problem," he assured the other. "As long as we keep him close he can't target us. Besides, he's not stupid enough to pull anything with the rest of the fleet all around him."

"Yeah, hopefully," Imbar said with a grunt. "I noticed he wasn't talking very much at dinner. You think the food disagreed with him?"

"Probably still trying to figure out how mad we are at him for his cooked intel numbers."

"Or maybe wondering how you figured out he was working for Axelrod?"

"Well, he can just keep wondering," Gensonne said. "He's kept plenty of secrets from us. We can keep a couple from him."

"Seems fair." Imbar was silent a moment. "I went back and looked at his last intel report before we headed off to Manticore. He never actually *lied* about anything."

"There are lies, damned lies, and statistics," Gensonne quoted the old saying. "Whether he lied or not, he sure as hell manipulated the truth."

"Arguable," Imbar said. "But I've been thinking. If he was right about those other two battlecruisers being unarmed—"

"Then what?" Gensonne cut him off. "We were fools to retreat?"

"No, no, not at all," Imbar said hastily. "Under the circumstances, retreat was the only reasonable move. What I'm saying is that if they were unarmed then, they can't be more than partially armed now. Especially since Manticore probably has to send to Haven or the League for more missiles."

Gensonne scratched his cheek. That was a damn good point. And if Manticore really *did* have to send all the way back to the League—"You're saying we could go back right now and take them down?"

"Probably," Imbar said. "Though now that we're on the road to Danak, we might as well stock up on Llyn's new missiles first."

"True," Gensonne said. "A shame, though, if you're right. Seems kind of a waste to spend a perfectly good Hellflare missile on an empty shell of a ship."

"We don't have to *start* with a Hellflare," Imbar pointed out. "We could use a regular missile first, and if their point defenses take it out *then* we use a Hellflare."

"We could," Gensonne agreed. "Too bad the countermeasure window is so short. I'd love to be on the com with Locatelli when the missile cuts straight through his defenses. See his face as he realizes he's about to die."

"We could target the rest of his force first," Imbar suggested. "That way you could at least watch his face while we take out each of his ships with a single missile."

"That might work," Gensonne agreed, nodding slowly. "In fact, that's an excellent idea. If we take out enough of his screening ships, he may surrender fast enough for us to take his battlecruiser intact."

"Oh, wouldn't *that* be nice," Imbar murmured. "And if we scare the King enough that he surrenders the whole planet before we have to destroy those other battlecruisers, we could double the size of our fleet."

"Exactly," Gensonne said.

Of course, after that would be small matters of arming, repairing, and crewing their captured ships. But Llyn's final payment would go a long way toward funding all of that.

And with top-of-the-line Hellflares in the launchers, Emperor Gustav would be in for a *very* rude awakening.

"There," Imbar said, pointing to the display. "Shuttle's heading back."

Gensonne focused again on the tactical. The shuttle was indeed returning, having dropped off Llyn and Captain Rhamas at their ship.

Together with a small device the shuttle's crew had left implanted on *Banshee*'s hull while its passengers were disembarking.

Llyn had promised that he would stay with Gensonne's force all the way to Danak. Gensonne was pretty sure neither of them believed Llyn would keep that promise past the point where unexpected trouble began.

Or perhaps the trouble wouldn't be unexpected at all. Perhaps Llyn was once again playing with half his cards under the table. Maybe the missiles weren't really Llyn's property, like the little man claimed, but were earmarked for someone else. That actually made more sense than Axelrod simply buying them to give away to the Volsungs. Maybe a week out from the system, when it was too late to turn back, Llyn would apologetically mention the truth and explain that Gensonne would have to take them away from their proper owners by force.

At which point, Llyn would probably try to slink out of the battle zone before things got hot, just as he'd managed to avoid the whole Manticore incursion.

If he really wanted to get away, there was probably nothing Gensonne could do to stop him. What he *could* do was make sure that Llyn's escape was a very brief victory.

His uni-link pinged, signaling a relay through *Odin's* com system, and he held it up. The message was brief: *Reset Spoilsport? Y/N*

He smiled. *Y*, he confirmed.

Spoilsport reset. Timer: 12 hours.

The timer started its countdown. Gensonne watched for a couple of seconds, then returned the program to the uni-link's background. From now on, every twelve hours from here to Danak, he would get that same prompt. If Spoilsport didn't get the proper reset code within an hour after the count ran to zero, the device would assume that none of Gensonne's ships were in relay range and act accordingly.

A starship was an amazingly sturdy thing. But even a ship as modern and sturdy as Llyn's couldn't survive a half kiloton blast going off right against its hull.

"So he's ours now?" Imbar asked.

"Yes," Gensonne said, his smile turning grim. Finally, *finally*, he had that little worm exactly where he wanted him. "He's ours."

CHAPTER TWENTY-SIX

THE PALACE, ELIZABETH'S FATHER MICHAEL HAD once warned her, was both the safest and the least safe place she could ever be.

The safest, because the Queen's Own were always standing watch around her. The least safe, because there was nothing she could do, and no person she could meet, without a good chance that someone else would know about it.

Most of those someone elses were of the Palace Guard and the Queen's Own, all of whom she should be able to trust. But even people who had pledged their loyalty and their lives to the Monarch could slip, or accidently say the wrong word, or possibly even be bribed or blackmailed.

But there were ways to lessen that danger. One was to hold any such secret rendezvous in the Royal Sanctum, which was as isolated from the rest of the Palace activities as it was possible to be. The other was to leave the arrangements to someone of proven competence and discretion.

Elizabeth had paced the Sanctum four times by the

time Adler finally slipped in through the Queen's private entrance. "Your Majesty," the bodyguard greeted her sovereign. "My apologies—there was a small holdup outside the garage entrance."

"That's all right," Elizabeth assured her. But her main attention was on the figure in the shadows. "You weren't seen, were you?"

"She's very good at her job, Your Majesty," Joshua Miller assured her, stepping into the room. "There may have been an alley cat or two who spotted us, but no one else."

"Good," Elizabeth said, breathing a little easier. If word of these clandestine meetings got out... "Thank you, Adler. You may wait outside."

"Yes, Your Majesty," Adler said, bowing again. She shot a speculative look at Miller, and then backed out of the room.

The door closed behind her, and Miller grinned. "She has no idea, does she?"

"Oh, I'm sure she knows *exactly* what's going on," Elizabeth said, wrinkling her nose. "Hard to keep secrets from your bodyguard. I just hope she knows enough of it to sit on the rest of the guards and keep them from asking questions."

"She will," Miller said firmly. "I've known people like her. She'll follow your orders to the letter *and* to the spirit, with no room anywhere for personal interpretation. And she'll trust that you know what you're doing."

"I hope you're right," Elizabeth said, crossing to the couch and motioning for Miller to sit. "On both counts. As it is, it's clear that Breakwater and his faction already have some suspicions."

"Yes, thanks to you," Miller said, a bit ruefully. "I

could feel the tension in the Lords all the way over in the Commons. How did you know that announcing I would make a speech would trigger that much reaction?"

"It was really just a guess," Elizabeth said. "A test run, if you will. In retrospect, though, it makes perfect sense. Breakwater's always known way more than he should, even when you add up all the cronies and information sources he has. And this little stunt has clinched it."

"He knows about Burgundy's list," Miller said soberly. "Which leads to the question of whether he knows what the list is."

"I don't know," Elizabeth said. "But he *does* seem to know all seven names. I had Colonel Jackson watch com and uni-link traffic when I invited Placido Amadeo over for dinner this evening."

"And Breakwater's links went ballistic?"

"Nothing so obvious," Elizabeth said, shaking her head. "But Jackson says he definitely took notice."

"More notice than a Queen entertaining a prominent shipbuilding industrialist should have garnered, I gather?"

"Yes," Elizabeth said. "I'm sure your movements are being watched, too."

"Well, if he wants to electronically look over my shoulder while I relax with couple of classic vids at home tonight, he can be my guest," Miller said.

"I hope they're at least movies you like."

"Of course. As I said: classics."

"Good." Elizabeth took a deep breath. "Well. Shall we get started?"

☆   ☆   ☆

"Ready?" Chomps's voice came softly through Travis's earpiece.

Travis clenched his teeth. "Ready," he said. *Hardly*, he thought.

And the evening had begun so well.

Mostly, anyway. He and Chomps had scouted the Volsung Mercenary office building, they'd confirmed that the known members of staff were either in their rooms in the apartment building next door or out bar-hopping, and Chomps had arranged somehow to have the local police presence harmlessly diverted elsewhere. As far as everyone on *Casey* was concerned—aside from Clegg and the senior officers, of course—the two of them had simply escorted Hauptman down to the surface for yet another sales pitch, so that part was covered.

Then had come the gearing-up. Chomps had equipped himself for the break-in with a handgun and a pair of big, nasty-looking knives, a rappel line setup, and something to bypass the office alarm system. They'd gotten across the city and successfully made it up to the roof without being detected.

The second-floor window into the Volsungs' isolated section of their office building was well protected by dual alarm systems, but Chomps was well versed in the arts of hacking, jacking, and cracking. While Travis played lookout on the other side of the rooftop, watching the building's street entrance, Chomps tackled the window. Despite the fact that the task felt to Travis like it took at least an hour, Chomps in fact had the alarms neutralized inside of three minutes.

And then, the whole thing had gone sideways.

Somehow, their earlier reconnaissance had failed to detect that the damn window was too small for Chomps's Sphinxian bulk to fit through.

Which had left them with only one option.

"Okay," Chomps said. "When I whistle, I expect you to break the all-Telmach rooftop racing record."

"You sure I can't just come back there, get your gear, and *then* we change places?"

"You want to leave either side of the building unwatched that long?" Chomps countered. "Come on, you'll be fine. The rappel line is set, and you know how to get into the harness. You *did* remember to grab your gun and knives, right?"

"Of course," Travis said.

Though that had been another sticking point. Chomps was a whiz-bang cat burglar and crack pistol shot. Travis was neither. Even more critical—at least to Travis—was the question of whether official members of the Star Kingdom of Manticore ought to be running around a foreign planet with lethal weapons in the first place.

Chomps had conceded the theoretical point—sort of—but reminded Travis that they were dealing with vicious men who absolutely wouldn't give a second thought to carrying and using lethal weapons themselves. Travis had conceded that point in turn, and the guns and knives had gone into their packs.

"Relax, Travis," Chomps soothed. "Trust me, this is the easy part."

Travis made a face. "Yeah. Right."

"Or think of it as the end part," Chomps offered. "Our final scene before we hand the whole thing off to someone else. Is that better?"

"Sure," Travis said.

Only it wasn't. And both of them knew it.

Still, he had to admit that he'd never expected them to get even this far.

The first part of the journey had been sheer leg-
and data-work. They'd dug up the ground and found
Gensonne's footprints in the sand. They'd tracked
his materiel, his men, and his money. They'd visited,
hacked, cajoled, and cross-examined dozens of men
and women, none of whom had the slightest idea that
they were even being interrogated, let alone what the
puzzle was they were supplying pieces to. And after
only two months in the Silesian Confederacy, they had
successfully tracked Manticore's attacker to his lair.

Almost.

Because while the Volsung Mercenaries' headquarters
might be here on Telmach, their ships were nowhere to
be seen. Nor were there any indications in the official
records of mysterious comings and goings that might
indicate a quiet base somewhere within the system but
beyond the hyper limit.

No, Gensonne had another base somewhere. Somewhere nearby, presumably, but another base nevertheless.

Tonight, if they were lucky, he and Chomps would
get the last piece they needed to find it.

"One more minute to pop the window latch and
you'll be set," Chomps said. "And I mean that about
breaking the speed record."

"Don't worry," Travis said. "I'll be there before
you're here."

Chomps grunted, and the earpiece fell silent. Staring down at the light traffic passing by on the street
five stories below, Travis counted out the seconds . . .

"Got it. *Go.*"

"Right." Giving the street one last check, Travis
turned from the edge and headed toward the rear of
the building in a crouched-over jog.

He reached Chomps's side of the building just as his partner came up from below. The Sphinxian rolled over onto the roof and stripped off his harness, and was halfway to the street side by the time Travis had the harness on and headed down on the motorized rappel line. By the time he reached the Volsungs' window, he knew, Chomps would be on guard duty above him.

He only hoped that no one had entered the building and office during the thirty seconds they'd left the street unwatched.

Firmly, he put that thought out of his mind. It was one thing to practice killing another human being in close-order combat. It was, he suspected, something else entirely to actually look into another person's eyes while pulling a trigger.

He really didn't want to find out for sure how different that experience would be.

The rappel line was small and compact, lowering him on a slender line that didn't look strong enough to support a child's weight. It also worked perfectly, depositing him neatly outside the second-story window Chomps had opened.

He slipped inside and unhooked his harness from the line. The room he was in seemed to be a sort of crash area, with a pair of cots on opposite sides of the room and a small table in the middle. Fortunately, no one was taking advantage of the area for a nap. Unfortunately, there were no computers, tablets, or file cabinets that might hold the data they were looking for. Keying his light-amp lenses up a notch, keeping one hand on his holstered sidearm, he crossed to the door and slipped out into the corridor.

The building was a relatively small one, and there

were only three other doors between Travis and the stairs. He paused outside each as he passed, confirming with his audio enhancer that there were no signs of activity behind any of them. He reached the stairs and headed cautiously down.

The stairway let him out into a large office which, according to the blueprints Chomps had dug out, was the main Volsung Mercenaries conference room. It looked the part, too, with a long table surrounded by a dozen chairs in the center. The main office would be next door, with another door leading out to a reception office which would normally be the first place visitors would see. Hopefully, one of those places would have what he needed.

The door into the office was unlocked. Travis opened it carefully, alert for trouble. Once again, the room was empty. He passed between a pair of large, long cupboards of some sort, with surfaces textured to look like rock outcroppings and sporting planters full of exotic-looking ferns on their tops, and headed toward the glass-and-hardwood desk in the center of the room. There were a couple of guest chairs, a few hand-painted pictures of warships on the opposite wall—

"You in?" Chomps's voice came in his ear.

Travis jerked. "Yes," he said, feeling the sudden adrenaline spike drain away. They'd had to do a couple of other break-and-enters on this voyage, but this was by far the creepiest of them. "And there's a computer on the desk."

"Great," Chomps said. "Stay put until I'm down—there may be another surprise or two on the inside of the door, and I want to be right there if you need me to help you disarm it."

"Right," Travis said, frowning. There was an odd sort of rumbling in his ear. Something interfering with the transmission? Or had the earpiece picked up a glitch?

Abruptly, a shiver ran up his back. The rumble wasn't coming from his earpiece. It was coming through his other ear.

Slowly, carefully, he turned around.

He'd been wrong about the planters' bases being cupboards. They were, instead, kennels.

And the deep rumbling was coming from a pair of large, black dogs.

Some kind of Doberman mix, his frozen mind automatically tagged them. His mother had bred a few such animals, and he remembered them being smart, powerful, and dangerous. The perfect guard animal for people who wanted to sleep well at night.

Or for people who didn't mind returning to their office to find a bloody mess.

The dogs were just standing there, staring at him, rumbling deep in their throats. Their tails were down, their ears laid back. Swallowing hard, Travis cleared his throat.

"Chomps?" he said quietly. "We have a problem."

"You can't wake up the computer?"

"Never mind the computer. I woke up the dogs."

"The—? Oh, *hell*. What kind?"

"Big and nasty," Travis said, sparing a quick glance behind the animals to their kennels. "Kennels flanking the office door. Big enough for internal heat exchangers—probably why our IR scan didn't pick them up."

"Okay," Chomps said. "Okay. Well, obviously, you're

going to need to take them out. Are they in range for a quick two-shot?"

"I don't know." Slowly, carefully, Travis eased toward the door to the outer office. If he could get to that door and put it between him and the dogs, he and Chomps would at least have bought themselves a little breathing space.

The dogs apparently knew that one. Travis was barely into his first step when the dog closest to the door took a pair of steps of his own, quick ones, angling toward the door. Travis froze, then eased the half step back. The dog stopped, and he and his partner settled back into their staring contest.

"Travis?"

"If they weren't in range before, they're even less in range now," Travis said grimly. "Besides, I don't trust there not to be a backup booby trap that a gunshot would trigger."

"Yeah, if they've got dogs, they probably have that, too," Chomps conceded. "Okay. If the gun's out, you're going to have to use your knives."

Travis winced, freshly aware of the pair of combat knives riding in their thigh sheaths. "Chomps, I can't do that. I can't kill a dog that way."

"If you don't, you're dog food," Chomps said bluntly. "You'll just have to—"

"Hold it," Travis cut him off. The dogs had apparently come to a decision, and were now walking slowly and deliberately toward him. "They're on the move," he said, backing away at the dogs' same pace, maintaining his distance. "They're pushing me back toward the far side of the room."

"No chance there's a door on that wall, I suppose?"

"Not unless it's hidden inside one of the paintings."

"What about the outer office door? Can you get to that one?"

"Already tried that," Travis said. Just the same, he once again tried to add a sideways angle to his backward motion. Once again, the dog on that side took a pair of quick steps to cut him off. "No, not a chance."

"Okay." Chomps was silent for another of Travis's steps. "You said there were pictures on the wall behind you. What else is there?"

"Nothing," Travis said.

"There has to be *something*," Chomps insisted. "Planter, statue—even a wall hanging. Anything you can use as a defense or a weapon."

"Yeah, that would be really nice," Travis growled. "But past the desk, there's nothing but rug." Though he might be able to use the computer display to fend off at least one of the dogs at a time. He added a small angle to his right, away from the door and toward the desk.

But the dog on that side was just as alert as his partner. He did the same quick two-step the other dog had just done, silently waving Travis off the desk. Travis went back to his straight-back walk, and the dogs resumed their straight-ahead stalking.

"What about the pictures?" Chomps persisted. "Are the frames heavy enough to hit the damn mutts with?"

"They look heavy, and they look bolted to the wall," Travis said, frowning as something suddenly struck him. Why *was* that section of room so empty?

The end of the office where he'd entered had the planters and the disguised doghouses. The center had the desk, with not just the computer but also a handful of objects that he guessed were mementos of the Volsungs' past glories. But the other end of the room was empty.

The end the dogs were forcing Travis into.

"Did the blueprints show a basement?" he asked.

"A—? Let me check."

Travis and the dogs had taken two more steps before Chomps answered. "There's no basement shown, but the buildings on either side have them. You see something?"

"Maybe." Steeling himself, Travis took his eyes off the dogs and gave the floor behind him a good, hard look.

There it was. It was subtle, nearly invisible, in fact, against the dark pattern of the carpet. But it *was* there.

A long stress crease two meters from the far wall and running parallel to it along the entire width of the room.

"Travis?"

"Yeah, yeah, hang on," Travis said. He threw a glance back at the dogs, confirmed they were still doing their slow advance, then looked over his shoulder at the wall behind him. The paneling was some sort of wood, he decided. Hopefully, strong; hopefully not impenetrable.

"I'm coming in," Chomps decided abruptly. "If I trip an alarm, then we'll just have to run for it."

"No, wait," Travis said. "Let me try something first."

Chomps hissed loudly into his mic. "Make it fast."

"Trust me." With a supreme effort, Travis forced his right hand to ease off its death grip on his gun and slid both hands slowly down his thighs to his sheathed combat knives. He drew them slowly, watching closely for a reaction.

The dogs' ears flattened a bit more. But neither broke step. Still backing away from them, Travis turned the knives into overhead-stab positions in his hands.

Two more steps to the crease in the rug. Bracing himself, he made a final adjustment to his grips...

And then, spinning around, he took one final step to the very edge of the crease and leaped toward the wall. A fraction of a second before he hit he swung both knives over his head as hard as he could, burying them halfway to their hilts in the wood. He slammed chest-first into the wall, the impact nearly jolting him loose from the knives before he could tighten his grip. Behind him, the dogs gave an enraged howl and leaped forward. Travis peered over his shoulder, cringing against the wall—

And as his attackers' paws hit the carpet on Travis's side of the crease, the entire section of floor between the crease and the wall swung downward, dropping them into the officially non-existent basement.

The howl of rage became a yip of surprise and dismay. Travis craned his neck just in time to see both animals tumble helplessly into a pit filled waist-high with fist-sized plastic balls.

"What the *hell's* going on?" Chomps demanded. "Travis—?"

"It's okay," Travis said, starting to breathe again. "The dogs are out of commission."

"Are they barking? I don't hear anything."

"They're not," Travis said. "Must be trained to stay quiet. Hang on."

He measured the distance across the gap with his eyes. It was uncomfortably long, but he should be able to make it. Pulling his knees up and tucking them to his chest, he braced his feet against the wall and pushed off.

Two meters was a long jump, especially backwards. But with a pair of very angry dogs floundering around in the ball pit below him, he had plenty of motivation to get it right. Even so, he barely made it, landing on his back with his legs briefly dangling into space. He clawed his way back from the edge, and scrambled back to his feet. "Okay," he breathed, trying hard not to hyperventilate. "I'll be right there."

It was clear from Travis's first glimpse of Chomps's anxious face that the big Sphinxian was practically melting down with questions. But he didn't ask them. He waited until they were back in the office, and as Travis headed to the computer he went over to the trap door for a look.

"Damn bloodless bastards," he growled. "The ball pit's a nice touch. Requires zero maintenance, and your intruder doesn't get damaged by the fall before you have a chance to question him. And *then* damage him, probably. Damn good thing you figured it out in time." He leaned a little farther over the edge. "Your mother breeds dogs, doesn't she?"

"Yes." The computer came up, and Travis fed in the first part of their worm program. "And yes, that breed is quite capable of tearing you to pieces."

"Figured as much," Chomps said, taking one last look and then joining Travis at the computer. "Let's get this done, and then get the hell out of here."

☆   ☆   ☆

The Volsungs' computer system proved harder to crack than either of them had anticipated. After half an hour of hearing the dogs growling and trying to scramble up the trap door, they decided it would be simpler—and safer—to just take the system with them.

It took several hours' more work aboard *Casey*, but in the end they found what they were looking for.

☆   ☆   ☆

"Walther," Clegg said flatly, frowning at the data. "That's not what it says here."

"No, Ma'am," Travis agreed. "But we think that's a blind, set up to send anyone who digs this far into their system the wrong direction."

"There are indications of a write-over, Ma'am," Chomps added, reaching past her to point at the appropriate places. "These two spots here are the most obvious. If you dig farther, it looks like Walther is the name that was buried."

"How do you know that's not a second blind?" Clegg asked.

"There doesn't seem to be anything deeper," Travis said. "More importantly, we also have confirmation from another direction. Governor Bilshing's private files also point us to Walther."

"He's got title to the system, and the files show he's closely associated with Gensonne and the Volsungs," Chomps said. "They're probably his go-to guys for whatever nasty things he needs done."

"Right," Travis said. Actually, that last bit was mostly speculation on Chomps's part. Still, even if some of the individual pieces were somewhat squishy, the overall picture was more than definitive. At least to them.

Unfortunately, Clegg insisted on somewhat higher standards, which meant he and Chomps occasionally had to oversell their findings a little.

"Fine," Clegg said. "So what do you propose as our next step?"

"I think we need to go to Walther and take a look, Ma'am," Travis said. "A quiet, distant look, of course—a shallow chord across the edge of the hyper limit, for instance, with our wedge down. Given a wide enough baseline, *Casey*'s sensors ought to be able to get a good feel for what's there."

"Very well, I'll give the order," Clegg said. "Dismissed."

Travis nodded. "Ma'am."

"Ma'am," Chomps echoed.

"That went well," Travis commented as they made their way down the passageway from the Captain's office. "Better than I expected."

"Don't kid yourself," Chomps rumbled. "She's hoping we're wrong."

"She seemed pretty convinced," Travis said, frowning.

"Why not?" Chomps said. "She gets paid the same whether we're showing the flag, letting Hauptman run around, or flying off on wild goose chases. She clearly thinks we've got the entirely wrong end of the stick, and is happy to give us the opportunity to poke ourselves with it."

"So that we'll go back to Manticore in full-blown disgrace?"

"Exactly," Chomps said. "We're the new kids on the block, and everyone who gets some of their territory handed over to us is going to resent that."

"How does that bother Clegg? The only toes we're stepping on are ONI's."

"Hardly," Chomps said. "We're also cutting into the Lords' and Commons' authority—all those lovely oversight committees, you know—Breakwater's purse-string control, and probably a few others I haven't thought of. Captain Clegg's particular square of turf is *Casey*, and our ability to give her orders cuts way too deep into that for her to be happy with it."

Travis thought about that. "So shouldn't her best

approach be to cooperate with us so that we succeed and she can get us off her ship?"

"Or to cooperate with us, hope that we fail, and never have to see us *or* any other Delphi people aboard her ship ever again," Chomps said dryly. "Whatever else you say about Clegg, she's definitely the long-view type."

"Well, then, let's just hope we're right," Travis said. "For our sakes *and* Manticore's."

"Right," Chomps said. "Especially Manticore's."

CHAPTER TWENTY-SEVEN

SUSAN TARLETON WAS A BIG, HAWK-FACED bear of a woman. She'd been in politics longer than Winterfall had been aware that politics even existed, with over half of those T-years spent sitting in the small side room off the Prime Minister's office, where the Foreign Secretary traditionally held court.

Which wasn't nearly as impressive as it sounded. While the Foreign Secretary position was technically a cabinet post, pretty much everyone treated her as an adjunct of the Prime Minister's office, including the Prime Minister himself. Indeed, the quiet joke was that the Foreign Secretary was really just a regular secretary, with the *Foreign* having been added to justify a salary bump.

Given all that, it wasn't surprising that Tarleton had held the Foreign Secretary position this long mainly because no one else really wanted it. Up until the Secour Incident, the Manticoran version of foreign affairs had consisted mostly of sifting through data from Haven and the League that came in on the occasional sporadic freighter or courier. But then had come Secour, and then Casca, with each incident sparking an increase in communications with foreign governments. For a while, according to rumor, there had been actually been some mild interest in ousting Tarleton so as to put someone's favorite son or daughter in what was starting to be perceived as a prestigious and important position.

But the interest had faded quickly. As soon as people realized that most of the information was military, and that the Foreign Secretary's sole task was to compile it and pass it on to the Admiralty, the Prime Minister, and the Palace, the perceived prestige evaporated and it was back to business as usual.

Especially since Tarleton's appearance and manner didn't exactly encourage encroachment on her turf.

All of that ran through Winterfall's mind as he approached her desk, adding to his apprehension.

Which made her response to him that much more unexpected.

"Of course I know you, My Lord," she said, nodding her head respectfully. "What can I do for you?"

"I've come on an errand from Chancellor Breakwater," Winterfall told her, mentally crossing his fingers. "I need to find a document that Duke Burgundy was preparing at the time of his death. It was a response to Earl Breakwater's suggested budget for MPARS."

"All such documents would be under the care of Prime Minister Harwich now," Tarleton pointed out.

"Yes, I know," Winterfall agreed. "And in fact the Prime Minister has already submitted his response to the Exchequer and the Palace. But His Grace had spoken to Earl Breakwater about some private suggestions he was going to make, and it was thought they would be a valuable addition to the government's considerations." He gave her a sad half-smile. "You worked more closely with His Grace than anyone else in the government," he added. "I'm sure that you, even more than the rest of us, appreciated the depth of his mind and the uniqueness of his vision and ideas."

"Indeed," Tarleton said, and Winterfall thought he could see a brief shine of gathering tears in her eyes. "I'm sure Earl Breakwater would agree that the current Prime Minister is hardly in Duke Burgundy's class."

"So do we all," Winterfall said with a commiserating nod. "Breakwater locked horns many times with Burgundy, but always considered him an exceedingly worthy opponent."

"Indeed," Tarleton said again. "I wish I could help you, My Lord. Unfortunately I have no way to access His Grace's files or documents."

"But Prime Minister Harwich is still using that same computer, isn't he?" Winterfall asked, frowning. "Surely Duke Burgundy's private records were merely partitioned out of reach of standard access."

"Of course," Tarleton said patiently. "But those areas can only be reached via His Grace's passwords. I don't have those."

"There's no backdoor or universal access?" Winterfall pressed, crossing his mental fingers a little harder. Tarleton was his very last chance. "I understood that every computer in the Lords had something like that for use in emergencies."

"Of course there are universals, My Lord," Tarleton said. "But they require an order from the Queen's Bench." Her eyebrows went up, making her look now more like an owl than a hawk. "Do you have such an order?"

"No, though I'm sure we could get one," Winterfall said, putting a note of frustration into his voice. "It's Breakwater's own document, after all, just with the Prime Minister's notes and comments. But the Chancellor was hoping we could get those notes today, so that we could incorporate them into the final version of the proposal before tomorrow." He shook his head. "He is *not* going to be happy."

Tarleton pursed her lips. "Breakwater sent you personally?"

"He did," Winterfall confirmed.

"And he really needs the document by tomorrow?"

"It would make our presentation that much more complete and balanced."

Tarleton's lip might have twitched on the word *our*. "If you'll wait here a moment, My Lord, I'll see what I can do," she said, pushing back her chair and standing up. "It's possible Prime Minister Harwich has some access codes that will work. Do you have a copy of the original so he can do a search for Duke Burgundy's version?"

"Yes," Winterfall said, handing her a data chip.

"Let me see what he can do." She crossed to the side door leading into the Prime Minister's office, knocked once, and opened the door. "My Lord?" she called, stepping through the opening and closing the door behind her.

Leaving Winterfall alone with his thoughts and fears.

And, maybe, some hope.

Everything else he'd tried had led to a dead-end. Over the past six weeks he'd investigated the members of the Palace's household staff, as many as he could get to without attracting the attention and ire of the Queen's Own. He'd looked at the Cabinet support staff. He'd checked out the technicians who kept the Lords' computer systems running. He'd even delved into the life and history of Burgundy's still-forlorn personal secretary, Louisa Geary. None of them had shown any signs of being Breakwater's private information source.

Winterfall had nearly given up when he'd suddenly thought about Tarleton.

She had worked beside Burgundy for over fifteen T-years. He'd had far too much work to do; she'd had far too little. Just as Breakwater had shifted some of his background work load to Winterfall, it seemed possible, even likely, that Burgundy might have done the same with Tarleton.

And if he had, Breakwater would certainly have sniffed out that connection and done his best to exploit it.

Not that any such exploitation was obvious. Tarleton's finances didn't show any mysterious influxes during the years she'd worked beside Burgundy. Nor were there extra bonuses, free vacations, or any of the payoffs that traditionally accompanied such espionage.

Still, the lack of a smoke trail didn't mean anything. Surely Tarleton was smart enough to avoid leaving such evidence behind her. And if she wasn't that smart, Breakwater certainly was.

Winterfall was gazing at the wall behind Tarleton's desk, idly mapping out the locations on Manticore and Sphinx represented by the various trip mementos lined up on the display shelf there, wondering if any of them was too costly for her salary, when the door opened and Tarleton returned.

"Any luck?" he asked.

"Yes and no," Tarleton said, walking over to him and holding out his data chip. "Baron Harwich was able to find His Grace's copy of your document. But there were no notes or comments attached."

"Really?" Winterfall asked, frowning as he took the chip. "That's very strange. His Grace made it clear at the time—I remember him mentioning it in two separate conversations—that he would be delivering a number of far-ranging thoughts to Breakwater."

"Baron Harwich's search was very thorough," Tarleton said. "Perhaps His Grace did that work at home."

"Maybe," Winterfall said heavily. "In that case, we'll just have to go with what we have tomorrow. Thank you for your time, Ms. Tarleton, and please thank the Prime Minister for me."

"I will," Tarleton said. "Have a good day, My Lord."

"And you."

It had been very nicely done, Winterfall decided as he headed down the hallway toward his own office. Nice, neat, and really pretty defensible. Harwich was notorious for not sticking to any particular work or lunch schedule, so a normal visitor would have no way of knowing whether the Prime Minister was in or not. A little judicious fuzzing of the computer's timestamp for the search, and no one would be able to prove without a doubt that it had been Tarleton, not Harwich, who had just cracked into the Prime Minister's computer and dug out the old document Winterfall had chosen for his test.

It was just Tarleton's bad luck that Winterfall had

spent the previous hour and a half staking out the Lords' dining hall, waiting specifically for Harwich to appear before hurrying to the Foreign Secretary's office for his test.

Winterfall had laid his trap carefully. And Tarleton had fallen into it.

He scowled to himself. He had Tarleton dead to rights, with enough evidence that she had Burgundy's access codes to at least open up an official investigation. But that didn't mean he could prove a connection between her and Breakwater, or even that an investigation would find such proof. He certainly couldn't prove that Tarleton was the one who'd passed Breakwater the late Prime Minister's list of possible Royal Consorts.

No, Winterfall's work wasn't yet done. Not by a long shot.

And he was running out of time.

The rumors and gossip continued to circle, but there had been silence from the Palace and an even deeper silence—some commentators called it *ominous*—from the Lords. Breakwater had said he would deliver his outrageous ultimatum to the Queen in four or five weeks. It had already been six.

And once that message was delivered, the clock would start an inexorable countdown.

Winterfall hoped the scheme would backfire, that the Lords and Commons would rally behind their Queen and against the Chancellor. But he didn't dare risk it. However such a confrontation ended, it carried the potential to sully reputations, ruin careers, bloody all the participants, and create a blot on the Star Kingdom's history that future generations would read about with incredulity and contempt.

The Star Kingdom didn't deserve that. The Queen didn't deserve that. And Winterfall was determined that it wouldn't happen.

He just didn't have the faintest idea how he was going to stop it.

But he would find one. Somewhere, he would find one.

And quickly.

☆   ☆   ☆

"I trust you realize," Chomps commented into the silence, "that this whole thing is *your* fault."

Travis turned his head, being careful not to bump his chin on the collar ring of his vac suit. "Excuse me?"

"The logic's impeccable," Chomps said. "You're the one who trotted out Special Order Seven and pissed her off. You're the one who made all those promises to the Andermani and pissed her off. You're the one who burgled the Volsung offices and stole their files."

"How did *that* one piss her off?"

"I don't know," Chomps admitted. "But it got us out here in the middle of nowhere, so I'm going to count it."

"Fair enough." Travis waved toward all the empty space pressing against the shuttle cockpit's viewports. "Interesting, isn't it, how this can simultaneously be the most boring spot in the universe *and* the least boring spot?"

"Ooh—existentials," Chomps said. "Great. Just the thing to break up the monotony."

"Let's just hope the monotony continues for—how much longer?"

"To closest approach?" Chomps leaned forward from the pilot's couch. "At our current massive velocity, I make it . . . four hours and two minutes."

Travis nodded. *Current massive velocity*. Chomps's pointedly casual way of suggesting Travis should have fought this particular battle a little harder.

Ironically, perhaps, of all of Travis's recent battles with Captain Clegg, this was the one he'd been the most content to lose.

He peered out the side viewport. Walther was an unusual system, with two asteroid belts inside the orbit of Walther Prime, its single habitable planet. Their shuttle was currently en route to pass between the outer of those two asteroid belts and Prime, running a hyperbolic path that would take them to within thirty-two light-seconds of the planet.

The planet that, according to their best information, was the base of the Volsung Mercenaries.

Clegg had insisted on getting a closer look at the place before they did anything else. But that was easier said than done.

They could hardly bring *Casey* in for a visit. All indications were that Walther was officially owned by Telmach's governor, unofficially occupied by the Volsungs, and almost certainly closed to any traffic that didn't have business with the mercenaries. That didn't preclude Clegg from coming in openly at full acceleration, blasting straight across the system, and punching back out before the Volsungs could scramble anything to hit her. But that approach would require them to stay reasonably far from Prime, which would glean them little or no useful information. Even worse, it would alert the mercenaries that there was trouble on the horizon and give them time to bolster their defenses or even abandon the base and relocate elsewhere.

Alternatively, *Casey* could try the stealthy approach, slipping as close to Prime as she could on a ballistic path with her wedge down. But again, there was only so close that a ship the size of a light cruiser could get before the Volsungs' sensors picked her up.

A smaller vessel could get in closer. A smaller vessel with its power completely shut off could get closer still. A smaller, unpowered vessel crammed to the gills with sensor equipment and a couple of sets of eyes and hands to ride herd on it and make any last-second adjustments to the shuttle's attitude to line up those sensors, and they might be in business.

It had taken a day and a half to create, jury-rig, and install the sensor equipment strapped to the shuttle's belly. Five hours and twenty-one minutes ago, not quite a hundred twelve million kilometers behind Travis's flight couch, *Casey* had translated out of hyper, accelerated to five thousand KPS, and then, just short of the hyper-limit, detached the modified shuttle on a ballistic heading which would carry it to within those thirty-two light-seconds of Prime. Even as the shuttle sailed silently away, *Casey* had ducked back into the alpha bands, micro hopped across the star system, and settled back into n-space on its opposite side to await their arrival at the farther hyper-limit.

Whatever personal problems Travis had with Clegg, he had to admit she was smart and knew her job. She'd had her newly-created remote reconnaissance platform repainted a sooty black which, combined with its already minimal radar signature, should make it as hard as possible to detect. She'd carefully crafted its flight path to carry it to sunward of Prime, where Walther's torrential radiation would further conceal it, but not directly across the star's disk, where an alert sensor operator might spot its occultation.

And over Travis's original objections, she'd limited its initial speed to five thousand KPS instead of the ten thousand he'd originally asked for, turning a ten-hour trip into one that was twice that long.

But again, she'd had solid reasons for the decision. The charged-particle scatter in the shuttle's shockwave would be noticeably lower at the slower speed, again decreasing the chance that any of the Volsungs would notice them. More importantly, given that he and Chomps would have only the single pass at the planet, the longer they stayed in sensor range the more data they could pull.

Travis appreciated the captain's logic. He just hoped the sensor package would hold up its end of the bargain. Shoehorning passive and optical sensors with the necessary range and sensitivity into a small enough package—and with only the components available aboard *Casey* to work with—had been a nontrivial exercise. Commander Norris's Engineering division had worked round the clock to put the whole thing together, with some unsung genius actually fabricating the electronically-steered tracking system for the optical heads on the fly.

Travis had no doubt about the sensor package's theoretical capabilities. But he really hated trusting a single system, without backup, that had never been fully tested.

But this was what they had, and this was where they were, and they would have to make do.

With the survival of the Star Kingdom very likely resting in their hands.

His stomach growled. "Lunchtime," he announced, pushing the dark thoughts and concerns away. Reaching behind his couch to the cabinet holding their water bottles and MREs, he pulled out three of the latter and passed two of them to Chomps. "By the way?" he added.

"Yes?"

"It's 'you're the one who trotted out Special Order Seven and pissed her off, *Sir*.'"

Chomps grinned. "Right, Sir. I'll remember that, Sir. Toss me a bottle of water, please, Sir? This time see if you can bank it off the com panel cover. Ten bucks says you can't."

"You're covered, Chief." Snagging a bottle, Travis held it in front of his right eye and took careful aim.

☆   ☆   ☆

"There," Chomps said, pointing at the monitor on Clegg's desk as he dropped a cursor into the display. He tapped in a command, and the computer-scrubbed, light-amplified image expanded to fill the screen.

"So," Clegg said, her voice almost casual as she peered over Chomps's shoulder. "A station."

"Yes, Ma'am," Travis confirmed from his position at the other end of her desk. He was trying hard to read Clegg's face and body language, and as usual he was failing miserably. "Decent size, large spin section. Perfect place for a mercenary force to set up shop."

"What makes you think it's Gensonne's?" Clegg asked. "You said Governor Bilshing owned the system. Why couldn't it be his?"

"Because of those docks," Chomps said. "There, there, and two more around there."

Clegg motioned, and Chomps vacated her chair. She sat down, frowning as she leaned closer to the display.

"You're sure those are docks?" she asked, tapping the images. "They look more like loading berths to me."

"They're Silesian MiniBs, Ma'am," Travis said. "It's a minimalist type of space dock. Quick and easy to set up, and relatively cheap. We heard a fair amount about them during our investigation."

"We also got a quick look at the specs," Chomps nodded. "Pretty ingenious design, though most of the money saving comes from skipping safety redundancies. The point is that when you add that many docks to that big an orbiting station, the setup is too large even for the most pretentious governor's entourage. More significantly, two of those docks are way too big for anything a governor will likely be flying around in."

"You're saying they're designed for battlecruisers."

"Yes, Ma'am," Chomps said. "The problem is that there don't seem to be any ships that size anywhere in the system. At least not within our sensor range, and we did a complete three-sixty sweep as we went past the planet. Given how close to the station most of their units were parked, I'm pretty sure we'd have seen any battlecruisers that were present. Problem is, we also know he has at least one battlecruiser left, and it has to be *somewhere*. It might be that he's sent his big ship—or ships—on a mission." He looked at Travis, his face tightening. "We're hoping that mission wasn't a second try at Manticore."

For a moment Clegg remained silent, her expression tight, her eyes on the display and the sidebar listing of the ships Travis and Chomps had spotted around the station during their flyby.

"If the big ships are gone," the captain said at last, "there's no way to prove this is Gensonne's base."

"I think there is, Ma'am," Chomps said, tapping the sidebar. "None of the ships had their radars or tracking systems up, but these two are obviously destroyers, and they look a *lot* like some of our telemetry from the battle."

Clegg rubbed her cheek. "Fine, let's say you're right. What next?"

"Even MiniBs aren't easy to break down, pack, and transport once they've been set up, Ma'am," Chomps said. "So we're pretty sure he's planning on coming back."

"With one or more battlecruisers," she added pointedly.

"Presumably," Travis said. "But they're not here now, which means we have a window of opportunity."

"An opportunity for...?"

"As the Chief says, this place represents a lot of money. If we swoop in and wreck everything, that should seriously cramp his warmaking ability."

"Oh, just *wreck* it? Just like that?" Clegg jabbed a finger at the sidebar. "With three cruisers and eight destroyers ready to take exception?"

"Actually, we think now that it's just two cruisers and five or six destroyers, in addition to the freighters," Travis said. "And three of them might be Silesian *Ordra*-class frigates. But you're right, of course. No matter what the exact details, there's still no way we could take all of them on."

"Succinct analysis, TO," Clegg said acidly. "So what *are* you recommending? That we head back to Manticore and ask Admiral Locatelli to loan us a couple of battlecruisers?"

Travis winced. If Manticore was even still there.

"We could do that, Ma'am," he said. "But with a five-month round-trip, plus whatever time it takes to prep an expeditionary force, there's a good chance Gensonne would be back, possibly with his entire fleet, by the time we were ready."

"And I don't think that's a battle the Royal Manticoran Navy's ready for," Chomps said soberly.

"Agreed," Clegg said. "So you're dropping this one in *my* lap?"

"Not entirely, Ma'am," Travis said, suppressing his reflexive annoyance at her tone. One way or another, of course, it was already in her lap. She was the captain, and no matter what happened the final decision would be hers. "We have another suggestion."

"Well?"

Travis braced himself. She wasn't going to like this. "We know *Hamman*'s search schedule, and we know Kane's been tasked with finding Gensonne. If we can find him and—"

"You can stop right there, Commander," Clegg cut him off. "Are you seriously suggesting we bring a freighter—a *foreign* freighter—into our mission? And even if Kane was willing, you think even a Q-ship will magically change *those* odds?" She pointed again at the sidebar.

"I don't think Kane is alone, Ma'am," Travis said. He'd been right; she hadn't liked it. "His last message mentioned other Andermani in Silesia. I'm guessing there are more Q-ships, possibly even a warship or two tucked away somewhere."

"He never mentioned warships."

"No, but they have to be here," Travis said. "You heard how Kane talked about Gensonne. They want him, badly, and they surely wouldn't risk running an intel mission that might spook him unless they were ready to follow up with an immediate attack."

"And you assume they think that way why? Oh—right," she added before he could answer. "Because that's the way *you* would do it."

With an effort, Travis pushed back his anger. Clegg was smart, efficient, and experienced. Why couldn't she see the logic here?

Or wasn't it the logic she couldn't see past? Was it her animosity toward Travis himself, along with Special Order Seven, that was getting in her way?

Probably. And that meant he was endangering the mission. Just by being who he was, he was endangering the mission. He looked helplessly at Chomps—

"I was just thinking, Ma'am," the Chief spoke up thoughtfully. "That comment Kane made at the end, the one about cooperation including reasonable joint military support?"

"What about it?" Clegg demanded, her eyes still on Travis. "It was pretty clear he was talking about some kind of official Andermani/Manticoran operation at some vague future time."

"That's what I assumed, too, Ma'am," Chomps agreed. "But he's a reservist, not an official member of the Andermani government. He shouldn't even be making suggestions like that, let along something that sounds like a promise."

Almost unwillingly, Travis thought, Clegg turned away from him and looked at Chomps. "So you're saying that Kane *is* thinking like Long?"

"As Commander Long said, the Andermani want Gensonne very badly," Chomps reminded her.

"So what you're advising is that we go look for *Hamman*—hat in hand, figuratively speaking—and ask Kane to help us out?"

"More or less, Ma'am," Chomps said. "If he can't help us himself, he should at least be able to give us an introduction to whoever can."

"Mm." For a moment Clegg gazed at the image of the Volsung base. "You make it sound easy," she said. "Only it's not. The Andermani want Gensonne and the Volsungs dead."

"Good, because that's what we want, too," Chomps said.

"Is it?" Clegg countered. She transferred her glare back to Travis. "Is it, Long?"

"No, Ma'am," Travis said. "Our primary objective is information on why Gensonne attacked us. The Andermani may not care about that."

"Very good," Clegg said, inclining her head microscopically. "So how would you go about *making* it their objective?"

"I don't know, Ma'am," Travis admitted.

"Even though they think just like you do?"

Travis felt his lip twitch. "I don't have diplomatic skills, Ma'am." He hesitated. "As I'm sure the Captain has noticed."

Something that might have been a small smile twitched across Clegg's lips. "Indeed, the Captain has," she agreed. "Chief? How about you?"

"I'm no better than Commander Long, Ma'am," Chomps said, shaking his head.

"You just know better when to keep your mouth shut?"

"Yes, Ma'am." There was no doubting that it was

a smile that now crossed Chomps's face. "I'm sure he'll learn, Ma'am."

"If he lives long enough." Clegg gave a snort. "I have to say, gentlemen, that if this is the best Calvingdell can do, SIS is already in pretty bad shape." She cocked an eyebrow at Chomps. "Or will *she* learn, too?"

"I would never say such a thing about a Peer, Ma'am," Chomps protested mildly.

"I'm sure you wouldn't," Clegg growled. "I'll take your suggestions under advisement. Dismissed, both of you."

☆   ☆   ☆

For a long moment after they left, Clegg stared at the office door. Then, huffing out a sigh, she turned her attention back to the display.

There were many officers in the Navy who were gifted in managing people. She wasn't one of them.

Granted, most of that was because many of the people she was supposed to manage were self-seeking careerists, or lazy, or just plain stupid. She'd been forced to deal with officers who were marking time while seniority pushed them steadily upward to positions they were unfit for. She'd had to lead enlisted personnel who were neither led nor driven to true competence in their own duties, watching them lapse into mediocrity.

So what was it about Commander Travis Uriah Long that set her teeth on edge?

Because he wasn't any of the things she'd grown to loathe. He wasn't incompetent, or lazy, or unmotivated. He was smart, he was dedicated, and sometimes he could be borderline brilliant.

And in many cases, in many of their disagreements, he'd turned out to be right.

Was *that* what bugged her about him? She hoped not, because that attitude would be the very depths of pettiness.

Maybe it was his earnestness, or his stubbornness, or the way he shot off his mouth without thinking things through that drove her crazy. The problem was that, more often than not, her knee-jerk reaction was to do exactly the same thing.

Going to Kane and the Andermani made sense. In fact, given the size of the Volsung force, it was really the only option she had.

Mentally, she shook her head. What was that she'd said to Long about officers who didn't think through the logical implications?

Long was a lieutenant commander who lacked people skills. Clegg was a captain. She really ought to be better at this than he was.

Muttering a curse at herself, she keyed her intercom.

"Bridge, Woodburn," the XO's voice replied.

"Clegg," she identified herself. "Pull up *Hamman*'s itinerary and figure out where we can make rendez-vous with her. Compute the two best options, plus a couple of alternatives in case she makes better time than Kane expected."

There was just the briefest silence.

"Yes, Captain," Woodburn said, his voice studiously neutral. "I'll send you the courses as soon as they're ready."

"Thank you." She keyed off the intercom.

And sighed again. Long would undoubtedly feel

relieved, and he and Townsend would both feel vindicated. Worse, they'd both know she'd changed her mind and succumbed to their logic, or at least to their arguments.

Put one way, they'd know she'd recognized the validity of their suggestions and overcome her own resistance to accept them. Put another way, they'd know they'd manipulated her into doing things *their* way.

But it didn't matter. The survival of the Star Kingdom was at stake. With that threat hanging over them, she could afford to let Long and Townsend think whatever they liked.

She turned back to her computer, her mind filling with thoughts of strategy and tactics.

And diplomacy.

CHAPTER TWENTY-EIGHT

ELIZABETH HAD KNOWN THIS DAY WOULD come. But even with foreknowledge and mental preparation, some events could still deliver a shock.

Today's was one of them.

"I had hoped this would not be necessary, Your Majesty," Breakwater said, his voice as grave and earnest as if he actually meant it. "But my duty, and indeed the duty of all your Ministers, is to the Constitution of the Star Kingdom. It is thus with a heavy heart that I must make the following statement."

He cleared his throat, and Elizabeth braced herself. Here it came.

"Unless Your Majesty takes a commoner husband within the next thirty days, so that the Kingdom may be given an heir as prescribed by the Constitution, I will be forced to submit a resolution to the House of Lords that will bring the whole thing into the open and force you to publicly address the issue."

It was as if a terrible weight had been lifted from Elizabeth's shoulders. Thirty days. Breakwater had vacillated for six months on this issue; and now he was giving her *another* thirty days?

It was like a gift from God. With thirty more days, assuming Joshua Miller was still willing—

"I understand, My Lord," she said gravely. "I disagree entirely with your premise, but you must of course do what you think is right. As do we all."

"Of course, Your Majesty," Breakwater said. "And again, I regret that this has become necessary."

I'll just bet you do. "Again, I understand," Elizabeth said. "Thank you for your honesty."

She waited ten minutes after he'd left the Palace, just to be on the safe side. Then, with only a little trepidation, she screened Joshua.

"He's a real prince, isn't he?" Joshua commented after Elizabeth brought him up to speed. "Okay. So what do we do?"

"The same thing we have been doing," Elizabeth said. "At least now we've got a definite timetable and deadline."

"I suppose," Joshua said, a bit doubtfully. "Though you know what stress can do to this sort of thing."

"Try not to think about it," Elizabeth said. "We'll just have to do what we can, and hope for the best."

"Yeah. Hope," Joshua rumbled. "I've never liked that word. I especially don't like having to hang my hat on it."

"I don't, either," Elizabeth confessed. "But right now, it's all we've got."

"I suppose," Joshua said. "Do you want me to come over tonight?"

"You think it'll do any good?"

"I think so, yes," Joshua said. "Besides, if we make

it work, we'll need to have some answers and statements ready. If we can't think of anything else, we can always work on that."

Elizabeth sighed. He always made it sound so... *clinical*.

"That's a good idea," she said. "I'll send Adler. The usual time?"

"That will be fine," he said. "I'll see you later. Your Majesty," he belatedly added the obligatory honorific.

Elizabeth smiled sadly. So very, very clinical.

But that was her life now. That was the life of the Queen. "I'll see you at eight, then," she said. "Good-bye, Joshua."

"Good-bye, Your Majesty."

☆　☆　☆

The realities of space travel, particularly the fact that courier ships were no faster than warships, meant that a ship that came calling on a neighbor seldom if ever had the chance to announce her arrival in advance. If the warship was particularly large and threatening, or the neighbor was particularly nervous, that could create complications and diplomatic panic.

A destroyer like *Damocles* wasn't particularly large or threatening, particularly to a system as well-armed and well-defended as Haven. Haven itself was certainly not the nervous-neighbor type.

Which made Haven Control's coolly formal communications both puzzling and, in Lisa's view, more than a little ominous. Surely the government and Republic Navy hadn't forgotten their successful joint venture at Secour ten T-years ago, and should accord a visiting Manticoran ship a welcome that was warm or at least cordial.

The situation bugged her all the way in, and she was pretty sure Captain Marcello was feeling just as puzzled. Fortunately, they were nearly to Haven orbit when the reason was made clear.

"Because I wished to greet you in person, of course," Commodore Gustave Charnay said, his wide and expansive face beaming from the com display. "Please forgive my theatrics, but it is seldom that one has a chance to renew acquaintances with long-lost comrades in arms." He cocked his head to the side. "Though perhaps you don't remember me, Commander Donnelly? I was merely the XO of *Saintonge* under Commodore Jason Flanders, and sadly did not acquit myself as well as I might have."

"I don't think any of us started out looking very good, Captain," Lisa said diplomatically. She remembered Charnay quite well, in fact. But the years hadn't been kind to the man. "But once we caught on, we ended up all right."

"You're very kind to say so," Charnay said, inclining his head. "I trust that later you'll indulge my curiosity as to the lives and further careers of Captain Eigen and Commander Metzger."

"I'll be delighted," Lisa assured him, noting out of the corner of her eye the satisfied look on Captain Marcello's face. Some commanders, she knew, would find it insulting to be effectively ignored while a more junior officer attracted this much attention. But Marcello had his eye firmly on the mission, and the more friendly and cooperative Haven's top people were with his officers—*any* of his officers—the better. "I'd also like to hear how Commodore Flanders has fared."

"We shall make sure to have a time of reminiscences,"

Charnay promised. "And perhaps a third will join us. Brigadier? Are you there?"

"I'm here, Commodore," a familiar voice came. The com display split; and on the other half—

"Colonel *Massingill*?" Lisa asked. The question was pure reflex; aside from considerably more white in her hair, Massingill looked exactly as she had ten T-years ago. Leaving Manticore to come work for the Havenites had clearly been healthy for the woman. "I'm sorry: I see it's *Brigadier* Massingill."

"It's good to see you, too, Commander," Massingill said with a smile. "And in the spirit of full disclosure, I should acknowledge that I'm the one who asked Commodore Charnay to delay a formal welcome until I could arrive aboard *Saintonge*. As soon as I saw your name on the officer list Captain Marcello sent, I knew that I had to be here."

"I'm glad you're here, Brigadier," Lisa said, mentally crossing her fingers. Here was where all the warm fuzzies could suddenly disappear. "This isn't just a social call, or even a show-the-flag voyage."

"Of course not," Charnay said calmly. "It was obvious from the start that you'd come to discuss the attack on Manticore. That was the main reason Brigadier Massingill and I waited until now to speak with you."

"There are some in the Nouveau Paris political sphere who would frown on assisting Manticore, especially if that aid took resources away from Haven," Massingill added. "Fortunately, there's another side to that sphere." She gave Lisa a half smile. "Most of whom remember Secour very well."

"Still, it's not something we wish to banter around freely," Charnay said. "As far as the public is concerned, you're here to deliver your new Sovereign's greetings and best wishes to the Republic." He smiled. "And while Captain Marcello is wined and dined and endures speech after speech, perhaps Commander Donnelly, Brigadier Massingill, and I will have discussions of our own. Will that arrangement work for you, Captain?"

"Absolutely," Marcello said. "In fact, that was largely what I was going to suggest." He inclined his head to Massingill. "The fact that Manticore would once again be privileged to enjoy Brigadier Massingill's services is an unexpected but welcome bonus."

"More of a privilege than you know," Charnay said. "The Brigadier has become Haven's leading expert on the discovery, assessment, and elimination of pirate and black-merc groups."

He raised his eyebrows. "So tell me, Captain Marcello. What exactly do you want from us?"

"We've brought you a small sampling of debris from the battle," Marcello said. "Some of it appears to be Havenite in origin."

"I presume you don't suspect us of direct involvement."

"Not at all," Marcello assured him. "Our thought is that either someone in the Republic is working with our mysterious Admiral Tamerlane or, more likely, Tamerlane purchased Havenite equipment somewhere along the line. Either way, we're hoping our attackers left a trail you can follow."

"I presume it will be best for everyone if such inquiries are off-the-books," Lisa added.

"Absolutely," Charnay agreed. "If for no other reason than an official investigation might alert the wrong people." He smiled, his eyes glittering with anticipation. "Let me screen the head of Naval Intelligence and find out what we can do."

☆ ☆ ☆

The file was so obscure, so vague, and so old that Winterfall's search nearly missed it. But he *did* spot it, and a few evenings' worth of work took him all the way back to its source and a long-buried truth. A few more evenings' worth of talking to archivists and spinning stories, and he had a copy of the original document.

It was explosive. Fusion-bomb-level explosive. It might make the difference in Breakwater's quiet campaign to undermine the Queen.

The problem was, Winterfall had no idea what to do with it.

He couldn't just turn it over to the Lords. Not the entire body, nor any subset of it. He couldn't really take it to the Queen. He certainly couldn't go public with it. If the whole thing blew up, Winterfall's reputation and future would be well within the resulting blast zone.

But he couldn't just sit on it, either. Breakwater's confrontation with the Queen was coming to a head, and everyone in government was figuring out where they wanted to be lined up when the fireworks started. Winterfall had to find a way to get this to the right people, and he had to do it fast.

There was only one person he could think of to turn to. His brother Travis had the kind of overdeveloped sense of duty that would surely put him on his Sovereign's side in any political struggle. And he would probably know military people who could get the document in the right hands without leaving Winterfall's fingerprints on it.

There was just one small hitch.

"No, he left here about five months ago," Travis's landlord said. "Happens all the time with Navy people."

Winterfall clenched his teeth. And the one time he not only wanted but needed to make contact with his brother, naturally, was the time his brother would be nowhere to be found.

"Do you know when he'll be back?"

"Nope," the man said. "He paid rent for a year, which is a lot longer than they're usually gone. But even with shorter deployments they're not always right about the timing. That's why the Navy has a rent payment guarantee, y'see, that keeps us from just booting them out if—"

"Yes, yes," Winterfall interrupted him. "What about his friend, Lisa Donnelly?"

"No idea," he said. "She doesn't live in any of my buildings. But I think she shipped out about the same time Long did."

"And she'll be gone a year, too?"

"No idea," he said. "They don't exactly check in and out with me. You need to talk to someone in the Admiralty if you want that kind of information."

"I may do that," Winterfall said. "Thanks."

Still, he reflected as he walked back toward his aircar, it might not be a problem. Breakwater had said he would be giving the Queen an ultimatum soon, but he seemed to have changed his mind. Certainly he hadn't said anything about the confrontation happening any time soon.

He hated to sit on this any longer than he had to, but maybe it wouldn't be so bad. Travis would probably be back in seven months, and Breakwater had already dithered that long on this. If the Chancellor dithered another few months, Winterfall could still pull this off.

And if, somewhere down the line, Breakwater informed him that the ultimatum's delivery was imminent... well, he would worry about that when it happened.

"Hello, Gavin."

Winterfall jumped, nearly wrenching his back as he spun around. Invisibly, inaudibly, Baroness Castle Rock had managed to come within three meters of him. "My Lady," he managed. "You startled me."

"Really? My apologies," she said, her lined face showing bemusement. "I didn't realize I was walking so softly. What brings you to this neighborhood?"

Winterfall felt his face stiffen. Did she somehow know about his private research? What could he say?

An instant later, he realized that he didn't have to come up with anything at all. He had the perfect reason to be here.

"I was hoping to drop in on my brother," he said. "But the landlord told me he'd been deployed somewhere."

"Yes, out to Silesia," Castle Rock said, her eyes steady on his face. "I thought you knew that."

"I'm afraid I'm not as good at keeping track of Travis as I should be," Winterfall admitted. "What about you? You have family or friends around here?"

"I enjoy long walks sometimes," she said. "You could have saved yourself a trip if you'd just screened him."

"Yes, I suppose I could have," Winterfall agreed. "Probably should have, too. But sometimes I just have to get out of the Lords. That place can drive even the sanest person crazy."

Castle Rock smiled. But it was a perfunctory smile, without any warmth Winterfall could detect.

And really, why *should* she offer him a genuine smile? She'd startled him, thrown a couple of perfectly innocent-sounding questions in his path, and watched him stumble over them.

She knew something was up. Hopefully she hadn't guessed any of the details. But she'd certainly come to the obvious conclusion that it was probably something neither she nor Breakwater would like.

Or maybe she *had* guessed the details. Maybe she, or Breakwater, was fully aware of his nighttime researches or his evening visits to archivists.

And suddenly, Winterfall was freshly aware of the damning data chip in his pocket.

"It's not always a pleasant place," Castle Rock agreed. "But it's where the business of the Star Kingdom gets done. Speaking of which, I'm sure you have some meetings or debates you should be attending."

"Yes, I have one later today," Winterfall said, resisting the urge to slowly back away from her. He already looked guilty—there was no point in adding the appearance of panicked paranoia to the mix.

"Good," she said. "I'll see you back there, then."

"Yes, My Lady," Winterfall said.

She gave him another perfunctory smile and turned away. Winterfall watched her for a few steps, to make sure she was actually leaving, then turned and continued on toward his aircar.

At least she hadn't called the police and had him searched. He had no idea whether she could make that work legally, but he was pretty sure she had tricks up her sleeve that he'd never heard of.

Thankfully, he was off the hook. For now.

But his time was running out. He had to find someone to pass this information to, and fast.

In the meantime, he was still a Member of Parliament, and he had a job to do. He would head back, and he would do that job.

After all, the House of Lords was a big place. Surely he could avoid running into Breakwater or one of his cronies for the rest of the day.

And later tonight he would figure out what he was going to do.

CHAPTER TWENTY-NINE

MOST BUSINESS BETWEEN THE LORDS AND the Commons went via digital transfer. But occasionally there was a document that was deemed too sensitive or too cumbersome, and a courier was engaged to hand-carry the data chip between the two buildings.

It took Winterfall a week to contrive such a document, and to find a reason to deliver it himself.

He hadn't been to the Commons for nearly three years. But as he walked the corridors, he could see that the place hadn't changed. Whereas the Lords always seemed to resonate with activity and purpose, the Commons seemed almost placid, even lethargic.

On one level, it made no sense. When Queen Elizabeth I had taken over from her father, she'd worked hard to upset the neat little members-only governing club that the Constitution's framers had made of the House of Lords. The Queen had taken that carefully constructed centralization of power and spread it out to both the Commons and the Crown. The Lords had squawked furiously, but with the Commons' help the Queen had forced it through.

But on another level, it made perfect sense. Governing was hard work that required time, attention to detail, and sheer perseverance. Most of the Peerage had been raised to think of themselves as leaders and governors, even those who had to split their time between Parliament and their day jobs, but most commoners hadn't. And so, despite the legacy of shared power that Elizabeth I had tried to leave them, over the years the Commons had gradually ceded much of their power back to the Lords.

Most of the Lords undoubtedly thought of that as a good thing, if indeed they thought about it at all. Winterfall himself was of two minds. Concentration of power was certainly more efficient, but it could also be more easily abused.

Fortunately, political philosophy wasn't on today's agenda. All he had to do was deliver his data chip and a short message and get out. Preferably without anyone important seeing him.

His target office was in an otherwise unremarkable hallway. There was a name on the wall beside the door, but no secretary or other gatekeeper sat watch outside. Very unlike the circle of high-level Lords he usually ran in. The door itself was half open; taking that as a tacit invitation to potential interlopers, Winterfall tapped gently on the door and pushed it open.

The office was smaller than Winterfall had expected, and only sparsely decorated. The man sitting behind the desk was equally unadorned, his jacket off, his neckwrap undone and hanging loose, his sleeves rolled partially up his forearms. But as he looked up, Winterfall had the sense that the man felt completely at home here.

"Can I help you?"

"Excuse me," Winterfall apologized. "The door was open. You don't know me, Mr. Miller, but—"

"Oh, I know you, My Lord," Joshua Miller interrupted calmly. "I daresay everyone in Landing knows you. At least, those who follow politics. What can I do for you?"

"I need to ask you a favor," Winterfall said, reaching behind him and closing the door. Miller's eyes narrowed slightly as he did so, but he made no comment. "I have a document I need delivered to the Queen. I was hoping you'd do that for me."

Miller's eyebrows went up a fraction of a millimeter.

"The Palace really isn't that hard to find," he said. "Just ask someone on the street. They'll point you the right direction."

"I can't take it to her myself," Winterfall said. "It's . . . let's just say it's of a sensitive nature. I can't afford for there to be any public notice taken of the delivery."

"So what makes you think there'll be less notice if *I* take it?"

"Because I'm guessing the guards at the door are more familiar with you," Winterfall said. "They may let you in with less fuss."

"I think you've got the wrong person," Miller said. "I've been to the Palace exactly twice, and the last time was six months ago. You want an unobvious courier, you'd do better to send it in with your patron, Breakwater. He's always walking the halls there."

"Yes," Winterfall murmured, feeling his throat tighten. Yes, *that* would be a clever idea. "But you're also a prominent MP. No one will worry if you—"

"Let me see it."

Winterfall frowned. Miller's expression hadn't changed, but he was now holding out his hand.

"Excuse me?"

"Let me see the document."

"Will you take it to the Queen?"

"I can try," Miller said. "I know a couple of people in the Palace. But I'm not going to bother them until I know it's worth wasting their time over."

"It can't go through anyone else," Winterfall warned. "It has to go to the Queen directly."

"Yes, I got that," Miller said. He wiggled the fingers of his outstretched hand. "The document."

Winterfall hesitated, a sudden surge of doubt freezing his resolve. Miller's speeches and bill submissions clearly showed that he was one of those who wanted the Commons to regain some of its eroded power. That was the main reason Winterfall had decided to approach him. On top of that, he was on Burgundy's list, so he must at least be a decent man.

But even decent men could be ambitious for power, and the document in Winterfall's pocket cut in more than one direction. If Miller's true goal was *personal* power, with the restoration of the Commons' authority merely a means to that end, taking Winterfall's data chip elsewhere would guarantee him all the power he could ever want.

And it would spell Winterfall's instant and permanent ruin.

It was a risk. But then, all of life was a risk.

And eventually, every man had to trust *someone*.

Steeling himself, he pulled the chip from his pocket. "For the Queen," he said, placing it in Miller's outstretched hand.

"Interesting choice of phrase," Miller said, peering briefly at the chip and then slipping it into his own pocket. "Did you mean that in the sense of *Deliver it to the Queen*, or more along the lines of a formal battle cry."

"Actually, a little of both."

And to his mild surprise, Miller smiled.

"I'll do what I can, My Lord," he said. "No; better. I'll do everything I can."

"Thank you, Mr. Miller," Winterfall said. "Good day to you, sir. And good luck."

☆   ☆   ☆

"I'm bored," Hester Fife declared, folding her arms across her chest.

"Really?" Llyn asked, eyeing her across the table.

"Really." Hester unfolded her arms and started pointing to the four chess boards set up between them. "I've won this one, this one, and this one."

"Really," Llyn said again, dropping his gaze to the boards. They were barely ten moves into each of the games. And she was declaring victory already?

Apparently so. The worst part was that she was probably right. "What about this one?" he asked, pointing to the fourth board.

"You could still win," she conceded. "But you probably won't. You have a bad habit of only thinking five or six moves ahead, so you'll probably blow it. You usually do."

"Well, let's at least give me a fighting chance," Llyn said, frowning down at the board. A minute ago, he'd been confident about his strategy. Now, he probably ought to give his plan another quick review.

"Whatever," Hester said. "Can I reset these?"

"Sure," Llyn said, still mentally running through the moves. "Go ahead."

Normally, of course, he hated to lose. Hated it with a passion. But with Hester he was willing to put his Alpha-male instincts aside. Partly it was because fighting against her in chess was futile anyway, but mostly it was because she was too valuable to be left to spin her wheels in frustration and boredom. Anything that kept her sharp, even if it was rolling boulders over him, was worth whatever pain it cost.

And speaking of spinning wheels . . .

"How are you doing on that other little problem I gave you?" he asked as he eased his remaining knight to a cautious attack.

"Oh, I'm finished," she said as she pushed all the pieces to the side of the first board with the back of her hand and began returning them to their starting positions. "I figured it out just before you traded me the bishop for the knight in the second game."

Llyn frowned. "So you *haven't* finished it?"

"Yes, I finished it," she said with strained patience. "I just said that."

"But you haven't broken the encryption yet?"

"*Yes*, I broke the encryption," she repeated, her patience even more strained. "I just haven't written it down yet, that's all."

"Ah," Llyn said. "Had you a time in mind for doing that?"

"Oh, I don't know," she said, starting on the second board. "After a couple more wins, probably."

"I guess that'll work," Llyn agreed, making a mental note not to try *too* hard to beat her on this new round of games.

"I don't know what you want Gensonne's com encryption broken for, anyway," she added, pausing in her board resetting to counter Llyn's knight move with her rook. "They're not *really* going to say anything important when you're close enough to tap in, are they?"

"You never know," Llyn told her, glaring at the rook. That was *not* the move he'd expected her to make. "Gensonne's arrogant enough to think he can get away with it."

"And stupid enough to try?"

"Basically."

"Idiots." Shaking her head, she returned to her resetting.

"Don't disparage idiots, Hester my dear," Llyn said. "They're quite useful. Find a stupid person who thinks he's clever, and you can get him to do almost anything you want."

"You mean like getting him to play chess all afternoon even when he hates to lose?"

"Or like getting her to solve an encryption problem even though she gets bored with the datawork part of it."

She gave him a startled look. Her shoulders rounded, and she lowered her gaze to the table. "That wasn't very nice," she said in a low voice.

"I'm sorry," Llyn said, silently berating himself. The woman was a mathematical genius, but her sense of self-esteem was a piece of pie crust, and he of all people should know that. "It was a joke." He reached over, put a finger under her chin, and eased her head up to face him again. "Just like yours," he added, giving her a reassuring smile.

She frowned, and then her face cleared. "Oh. Right. Jokes. Because neither of us is *actually* stupid."

"That's right," Llyn agreed, starting to breathe easier. "We're not stupid, we're not expendable—"

"—and we're not going," she finished the old comedy routine line, grinning brightly now, the momentary hurt forgotten. The grin vanished into another frown. "We're *not* going, are we?"

"Not at all," he assured her. "At least, not all the way."

"Good," she said. "Because it doesn't sound like fun."

"It'll be fun for us," Llyn said. "Just another game. Like this one."

"Right." She gestured to the reset boards. "Ready?"

"Ready," he said, moving his king's pawn on the first board. "And you'll program in the decryption coding right after the games. Right?"

"Yes," she said, jumping her knight over her home-row pawns. "Right after the games."

☆　　☆　　☆

Making rendezvous turned out not to be quite as easy as Kane had implied when he laid out his projected movements.

It was no one's fault, really. Coordinating interstellar movements was hard enough even when both ships had firmly fixed schedules. Coordinating them when neither side knew exactly when the other would reach a given point made it far more difficult.

Clegg had known from the moment they left Walther that her window for catching Kane at Lau Hiler would be a bit tight. But there should be enough time. Moreover, it was only four T-days in hyper to Lau Hiler but nine T-days to Sachsen, the next target system on Woodburn's list. If she caught Kane at Lau Hiler, she could save eight full days. If she missed him there, though, it would cost ten more T-days to make the trip to Sachsen on his heels.

As it happened, she didn't catch him at Lau Hiler.

Clegg sat in her command chair, glowering at the display. Travis sat at the TO's station, trying not to make himself noticed. It was hardly his fault that Kane wasn't on his planned schedule, but he suspected Clegg would try to make it his fault just the same.

Unfortunately, Pasha was Lau Hiler's only inhabited planet. If *Hamman* wasn't there, or on her way in or out, she wasn't likely to be anywhere else in the system.

"Kill our acceleration, XO," the captain said after a moment. "Com, is Pasha's station in laser range?"

"Yes, Ma'am," Lieutenant Sulini Hira said.

"Lay a laser on the station and transmit a request for any stored messages."

"Aye, aye, Ma'am. Transmitting now."

Travis checked the status board. *Casey* had been in-system for an hour and forty minutes, putting her roughly five minutes and four point eight million kilometers inside the hyper-limit, sixty-two million kilometers short of Pasha's orbit. At that range, a round-trip transmission delay was almost seven minutes.

Stifling a sigh, Travis, along with Clegg and everyone else on the bridge, settled in to wait.

The seven minutes passed, plus four more, before a soft chime sounded.

"Transmission from Pasha Station, Ma'am," Hira reported.

"Very good, Com," Clegg said. "Decrypt and switch to my display."

"Aye, aye, Ma'am."

For a few seconds Clegg gazed at her display. Surreptitiously, Travis looked at her, saw her eyes tracking back and forth as she read. Then, her lips compressed briefly.

"Missed him by less than fifteen hours, XO," she said, looking across at Woodburn.

Travis winced. Fifteen hours, after a journey of nine light-years. Clegg was *not* going to be happy.

To his surprise, the expected explosion didn't happen. "I guess we follow them to Sachsen," she added.

"Assuming he's actually there," Woodburn said, a bit sourly.

"He will be," Clegg said calmly. "Captain Kane indicates his route hasn't changed; he just managed to clear Lau Hiler almost seventy-two hours earlier than he'd anticipated. So we *ought* to catch up with him in Sachsen."

She glanced at Travis, with no particular emotion he could detect, then turned to the astrogator.

"Take us back across the limit, Ms. Lukanov," she ordered. "Then put us on course for Sachsen."

☆　　☆　　☆

Eleven days later, *Casey* crossed the Sachsen hyper limit and headed inward.

"We'd better find some good news, Sir," the ATO, Lieutenant Kojong Ip, commented from the TO spot. "I think the captain's going to start chewing hull plates if we don't."

"Watch what you say about senior officers, Mr. Ip," Travis warned. Under some circumstances he would have let Ip's comment pass, but as Officer of the Watch he had to maintain higher standards.

Not that he disagreed with the ATO. Over the last few days he'd watched Clegg's quiet tension slowly ramping up as they approached Sachsen.

Once, he would have assumed she was mad at him, or at Chomps, or at *somebody* aboard, and reacted with his usual approach of walking on eggshells and waiting for the explosion to happen. But after a long talk with Chomps three days ago, and some of the insight that the Chief had that Travis sorely lacked, he finally understood.

It wasn't just Clegg's natural irascibility, though there was certainly some of that in her personality. Mostly, it was her deep awareness that her actions here in Silesia would set the pattern for the entire RMN.

Andermani captains like Kane served in a navy that routinely deployed its ships across multiple star systems, and had done so for years. Cruising the interstellar lanes, far from any immediate contact with superiors, was something to which they'd had ample opportunity to become accustomed. For that matter, back when Gustav Anderman had been perhaps the Solarian League's most successful mercenary commander, the ships under his command had never known where they might travel in any given month, or the month after that.

The pattern for the Royal Manticoran Navy had been almost the exact opposite. Ever since the days of the Brotherhood's reign of terror its ships had rarely left the home system. On the few occasions when they had they'd usually gone in squadron or at least divisional strength.

Clegg was breaking new ground here. She and *Casey* were on their own, farther away from home space than any RMN ship had ever before operated. Clegg wasn't simply Manticore's senior naval representative, but also its senior diplomatic representative. Her words, her decisions, her actions—all of them could have far-reaching repercussions for the Star Kingdom.

If she committed herself too closely to a relationship with someone like Kane, perhaps creating expectations which Queen Elizabeth's government chose to repudiate, the consequences for future relations with the Andermani might be dire. By the same token, if she *offended* the Andermani by declining to cooperate with them, that could have equally serious repercussions. And those same diplomatic considerations applied to every other star system in the area that *Casey* visited.

But stacked right alongside those were the military considerations. *Casey* had no support, no backup. If anything happened to her that couldn't be repaired with local resources, or if there was an ordinary operational accident, she'd be marooned in one of the local star systems until a relief could be sent from Manticore.

If she was lucky. If she wasn't, *Casey* might simply disappear, never to be heard from again.

And every bit of that responsibility devolved upon Captain Trina Clegg. She wasn't just a subject of the Star Kingdom of Manticore. She *was* the Star Kingdom of Manticore.

"Whoa—there we go, Sir," Ip said, and there was no mistaking the relief in his voice. "Happy days, Commander."

"Happy days, indeed, Lieutenant," Travis said, gazing at SMS *Hamman's* transponder beacon burning brightly on the plot. Sachsen was a busier system than Lau Hiler, with a more sprawling infrastructure, and Kane's message had explained that he would require more time here for his search. Currently, the Andermani freighter was orbiting Dresden, the system's single inhabited planet, and Travis wondered briefly how much of Kane's investigation he'd completed.

He also wondered how Kane was going to react to what he and Chomps had discovered at Walther.

He pressed the intercom button.

"Clegg," the captain's voice responded.

"Long, Captain," he said. "We've just crossed the hyper-limit. We're picking up *Hamman's* transponder at niner-point-five light-minutes, in Dresden orbit."

"Very good, Mr. Long," she half-grunted. "Transmit our initial message. I'll be there in five."

"Aye, aye, Ma'am."

☆   ☆   ☆

Captain Kane, to Travis's relief, was delighted to hear from them. He listened carefully to Clegg's report about Walther, asked a few questions and seemed eminently satisfied with her answers.

And then, instead of inviting them inward to Dresden, he suggested they all head out to the hyper limit and follow him somewhere.

Clegg had asked a few questions of her own. The only answers Kane would give boiled down to promising the journey would be well worth the Manticorans' time.

For the past sixteen hours, *Casey* had followed *Hamman* through the alpha bands. Finally, four and a half light-days from Sachsen, Kane signaled that they'd arrived.

Hamman apparently had a very good astrogator. After a moment's orientation, Kane announced they'd arrived five light-minutes from their goal, and again invited *Casey* to follow.

Two hours of acceleration, followed by two more hours of deceleration. Travis gazed at the displays, listening to the silence of *Casey's* bridge, wondering what Kane was up to.

And then, ten minutes from their final destination, they began to see the lights.

"XO?" Clegg invited. She was leaning forward in her seat, as if putting herself that much closer to the display would give her a better view.

"There appear to be several ships out there, Ma'am," Woodburn said. "Lying to—no wedges. They seem to be waiting."

"For Kane?" Clegg asked. "Or for us?"

"Hopefully, both," Woodburn said, his voice coming through the speaker from CIC. "Assuming those are running lights, that one closest to us is probably a cruiser. That one further back and to portside may be a battlecruiser. The two to starboard look to be a destroyer and another cruiser—"

And then, behind the frigate and battlecruiser, another set of running lights abruptly came on.

Travis caught his breath. What the hell was *that*?

"XO?" Clegg called. Her voice was mostly calm, but there was a definite edge to it. "Tell me what we're seeing."

"It's not a battlecruiser, Ma'am," Woodburn said, his voice about as stunned as Travis had ever heard it. "It's too big, and we're reading too many launchers. Unless the Andermani have dreamed up some kind of customized hull—" He paused, and Travis could visualizing him shaking his head "—Captain, I believe that is a genuine, honest-to-God battleship."

Someone on the bridge whistled softly. The sound

broke Travis's own awed paralysis, and he keyed for the files.

"That's . . . impressive," Clegg said into the silence. "I was under the impression that only the League had warships that big. TO?"

"That's what *Jayne's* says, Ma'am," Travis confirmed. "According to them, the SLN's the only navy with battleships."

"Apparently, their bean-counters missed one," Clegg said.

"Yes, Ma'am," Travis agreed.

And apparently he, Clegg, and everyone else aboard had *seriously* underestimated how badly Gustav wanted Gensonne put out of business.

"Com, let's open a hail," Clegg continued. "See who we're dealing with here."

"Already have one coming in, Captain," Lieutenant Hira announced. "It's from an Admiral Gotthold Riefenstahl, Graf von Basaltberg."

"Thank you," Clegg said. "Put him through."

The com display lit up to show an elderly man with a lined face and a close-trimmed skullcap of pure white hair. His haircut, as well as his overall demeanor, reminded Travis of Gensonne.

But whereas Gensonne's uniform had been hidden by a vac suit, with only the collar peeking out, Basaltberg's elaborate white uniform, edged in red piping and encrusted with gold braid, was on full and grand display.

"Captain Clegg," the man's booming voice came from the speaker. "This is Admiral Gotthold Riefenstahl, Graf von Basaltberg, commanding His Majesty's Ship *Vergeltung*. I apologize for the inconvenience of our rendezvous point, but I'm sure you can appreciate that our presence in the Confederacy must be kept very quiet so as to avoid alerting our quarry."

"I understand completely, Admiral," Clegg assured him. "I was starting to wonder if Captain Kane had decided that tracking you down would be a good test of our patience."

"He is certainly not above such tests," Basaltberg agreed with a smile. "But in this case, he recognizes, as do I, that time is of the essence. He tells me you have discovered the location of the traitor Gensonne's base?"

Traitor. Travis noted the word with interest. Clearly, there was more going on than Kane had told them.

"We do," Clegg confirmed. "Has he also described the quid pro quo we're asking in exchange for that information?"

"He has," Basaltberg said. "He also suggests you have doubts that an admiral and noble of the Andermani Empire would listen to a lowly freighter captain."

"I'll admit to having some reservations, yes," Clegg said. "Though to be fair, I also had certain reservations about just how lowly a freighter captain he truly was."

"Clearly, you have the gift of insight, Captain," Basaltberg said, his smile fading into seriousness. "I have personally known many freighter captains who would say and do whatever would maximize their profits. But I think you will find—" his eyes flicked to his side "—that in this case, your reservations were unnecessary."

The com screen split in half, and Captain Kane appeared beside the admiral.

But he was no longer wearing the utilitarian coveralls

he'd worn during their meeting aboard *Hamman*. Now, he was dressed in a version of the same uniform Basaltberg wore.

"Permit me to introduce Major Chien-lu Zhou," Basaltberg said. "Director of Silesian Operations for Abteilung III, our Department of Intelligence." He smiled wryly. "He is also my son-in-law. He believes that a joint operation between our two forces would be a good and proper idea."

"As do we, Admiral," Clegg said calmly, to Travis's somewhat grudging admiration. The surprises were coming fast here, and she was taking each of them in stride. "And as you said, time is of the essence."

"Time and information both," Basaltberg agreed. "Now. Major Zhou tells me that your request in return for Gensonne's location is our aid in capturing his base's computer intact." He learned forward a few centimeters. "I believe we can work with that."

CHAPTER THIRTY

"SO MUCH WORK," COMMODORE CHARNAY SAID, shaking his head. "So few results."

"Yes," Lisa murmured as she ran her eye down the list of serial numbers, manufacturers, buyers, and destinations. The analysts had been sifting through the possibilities for two and a half weeks, and about all they'd been able to say with certainty was that much of equipment the RMN had blown into pieces during the Battle of Manticore had been made by Haven manufacturers and sold to buyers in Silesia.

Which everyone had mostly already known.

"Still, it hasn't been a complete waste," Marcello offered. "A couple of the Silesian buyers are almost certainly general importers who then resell to their clients. If we can dig into their records, we may be able to track the nodes to their ultimate destination."

"Unless the final transfer was done off the books," Charnay pointed out. "It probably wouldn't have been in the case of a reasonably honest mercenary, like Gustav Anderman used to be, but that doesn't exactly describe your friend Tamerlane. There are dishonest arms brokers in every star nation, and that's the sort *he'd* be dealing with. You can certainly try to find his suppliers, but I'm guessing you'll hit a dead end every time."

"You may be right," Marcello said. "But that decision will be someone else's headache, not mine. Regardless, we greatly appreciate your help."

"Glad to do it," Charnay said. "I've been assured that we'll continue to dig into things at this end after you leave. Tamerlane probably isn't another Brotherhood cult leader; but then again, he might be the beginning of one. It's in Haven's best interests to get a handle on him and whatever his long-term plans are." He glanced at his uni-link. "Excuse me, please—I have a screen coming in."

He raised the uni-link to his lips. "Charnay."

"He's right about the wheel-spinning," Marcello said quietly to Lisa. "And I doubt the Admiralty's going to be overjoyed at the cost-per-datum ratio we've racked up this trip."

"Everyone knew it was a long shot, Sir," Lisa reminded him. "And we *did* confirm they're somewhere in Silesia."

"We confirmed they *were* somewhere in Silesia," Marcello countered. "That doesn't mean they're there now. The Brotherhood was famous for moving their whole infrastructure around with them. Tamerlane wouldn't have to be a cultist leader to take a page or two from their book."

"True," Lisa conceded. "So do we head home, or wait and let the analysts take another run at the data?"

Marcello pursed his lips—

"Excuse me, Captain; Commander," Charnay broke in, his voice suddenly grim. "Something's come up. They need us in Command One right away."

☆   ☆   ☆

Command One was four floors up in the enormous Octagon Building which housed the central nervous node of the Republic of Haven's military. It was also down what seemed like the better part of no more than ten or twelve kilometers of corridors from the conference room in which they'd been working, and the lengthy trek put the difference between the Octagon and the Manticoran Admiralty's far more modest housing into stark contrast. Commodore Charnay led them through the bustling command center and into a smaller, secure briefing room on the other side.

"I tell you, I don't *know* who they are," the older of the two men seated in the witness chairs growled, his eyes flashing at the semicircle of Havenite officers gathered around a large conference table as Lisa, Marcello, and Charnay slipped into the room. "All I know is that Master Baird has been a prisoner of these criminals for six months, and someone has to *do* something about it."

A Havenite officer wearing admiral's insignia on his collar and the name Dorvelle on his nameplate spotted the newcomers.

"Ah—Commodore," he spoke up, his voice grim as he beckoned to Charnay. "Welcome to hell's little hectare. This is Captain Lionel Katura, fresh in from the Walther System over in Silesia. He tells us that his employer, a Solarian merchant named Max Baird, has been captured by a gang of pirates."

"Not captured; *kidnapped*," Katura corrected tersely. "*Captured* makes it sound like Master Baird was attacking them or provoking them. He wasn't. We were reaching out to the Silesians, as per Master Rowbtham's instructions, when we were attacked. *Attacked*."

"Who's Master Rowbtham?" Charnay asked.

"Master Rafe Rowbtham," the man in the second chair said. Unlike Katura, he spoke with a Havenite accent and had the look and posture of a civilian. "Solarian merchant, quite well-off. He opened a local office on Danak Alpha twelve T-years ago. I met him myself on one of my regular business trips to Danak. According to our records, he's only been there a couple of times himself, but it's used by his sales and marketing agents whenever they're in the area."

"This is Daval Weissman," Dorvelle put in as Charnay raised an eyebrow. "He's our representative on the Jerriais Consortium board. Major development group," he added to Lisa and Marcello. "They're doing a lot of work in the Danak system."

"I see," Charnay said. "And we know for a fact that Captain Katura is one of Master Rowbtham's people?"

"Of course," Weissman said, bristling a little. "The system authorities always check ship credentials, as do the Consortium's security personnel. Besides, they have the entry passcodes."

"No offense, Mister Weissman," Charnay soothed. "This whole kidnapping thing sounds so incredible I wanted to make sure we had some actual facts nailed down."

"If you think that's incredible, wait till you hear what the pirates want," Dorvelle said grimly.

"A moment more, if I may, Admiral," Charnay said. "Mr. Weissman, you say you've met Master Rowbtham. Have you also met Master Baird?"

"Not personally, but several of my colleagues have," Weissman said. "He was last through the system about three T-years ago, and I believe he's on record then as saying he was on his way to the Silesian Confederacy." He gestured to Katura. "At any rate, when Captain Katura came to us with the horrible news, I knew we had to talk to the Navy right away."

"You see, they're coming," Katura said. "The pirate gang—all of them. And they're bringing two battle-cruisers and probably six heavy cruisers with them."

Lisa felt her eyes go wide. A pirate gang had a pair of *battlecruisers?*

"To Danak, he means, not Haven," Weissman hastened to add. "Master Baird apparently told them that there were some top-of-the-line League missiles coming into our shipyards, and—"

"Wait a minute, wait a minute," Charnay interrupted, flashing a startled look at Dorvelle. "*League* missiles are being sent to *Danak?*"

"No, of course not," Weissman said before the admiral could respond. "What would Jerriais be doing with *missiles?*"

"But Master Baird had to tell them *something,*" Katura put in, his voice edging toward pleading. "They had his whole family—his wife and both daughters. The pirates' leader—he calls himself Admiral Swenson—somehow got it into his head that Master Rowbtham has connections with some of the League's major arms manufacturers. The pirates think he's been selling weapons to the Andermani and getting rich off of

Emperor Gustav's building program, and the ransom demand was that some advanced missile systems be installed on *their* ships, too. So Master Baird spun them the story about missiles already being on their way."

"*Does* Rowbtham have such connections?" Charnay asked.

"Not that we're aware of," Weissman said. "If he did, though, I suppose it might be logical for him to use local contacts in Danak to actually warehouse or even install them." He shrugged. "The Consortium's been expanding its shipyards, but we're ahead of projections and don't really need all the capacity we've got right now. Consignment work is a way to use that overcapacity rather than letting it stand idle, and we've been doing a fair bit of local shipbuilding and overhaul work. If Rowbtham really was going to install missile systems for someone, Danak would be a good place to do it."

"It doesn't matter whether Master Rowbtham really has munitions contacts or not," Katura bit out. "The point is that Master Baird had no choice but to promise whatever Swenson wanted or watch his family be tortured to death."

Lisa felt a shiver run up her back. Fleetingly, she wished that Breakwater and all those other anti-Navy people who thought the galaxy was an inherently safe place could hear this.

"So as I said, he told them that there were some missiles and upgraded launchers en route to Danak," Katura continued, "and that for a reasonable fee, the Danak government would look the other way while they were misdirected to Swenson's ships. But he also said the shipyard people would refuse unless they had authorization from the Jerriais office here in Nouveau Paris."

"Why would they believe that?" Charnay asked.

"According to Master Baird's recorded message, Swenson believes Rowbtham brought the missiles in openly through the Republic's inspectors," Weissman explained. "That's not as ridiculous as it sounds, given the Danak government's stakeholder position in the Consortium. We've got a twelve percent interest, and nobody on the Jerriais side would want us to think they were involved in black market arms sales. So it makes sense for them to insist that Rowbtham bring them in only with our knowledge."

"Yes, exactly," Katura said. "That was the only way Master Baird could convince Swenson to let me come ahead. He said that the office here had to sign off on the missiles' release. I'm supposed to deliver Master Baird's authorization here, then race back to Danak."

"But Master Baird was smart enough to tell them none of this would work unless he came along personally to confirm the orders in Danak," Weissman said. "And he insisted his family accompany him, as well."

"Aboard one of these pirate battlecruisers, no doubt," Charnay growled.

"No, I don't think so," Katura said. "Master Baird and his family were traveling aboard *Pacemaker*, but we were in company with *Banshee*, one of Master Rowbtham's freighters. When Swenson sent me with *Pacemaker*, Master Baird insisted on moving to *Banshee* instead of one of Swenson's ships."

He took a shuddering breath.

"These pirates are brutal, Commodore. We've heard about cases in which their captives have been beaten, raped, tortured—even killed. Master Baird wasn't going to have that happen to his family, and he threatened to blow up *Pacemaker* and *Banshee* and kill everyone aboard rather than put his wife and daughters in their hands."

"Gutsy move," Charnay said. "What if they'd called his bluff?"

Katura's throat worked. "He wasn't bluffing," he said softly. "Fortunately, the pirates realized he wasn't bluffing, so they let him transfer to *Banshee* with his wife and the girls. It's slower than anything Swenson has, so it can't run away, and Swenson insists it stay within a quarter million kilometers of his flagship where it's under his guns. I know Captain Rhamas, *Banshee's* skipper, and he won't try anything stupid."

"Let's certainly hope not," Dorvelle said.

"So officially, I'm here to arrange the missile release and authorization for the Jerriais yards to install them," Katura concluded. "But my *real* message was the one I delivered first to Mr. Weissman and now to you."

"I'm sure the Consortium was thrilled," Charnay said sourly. "And I'm willing to bet Danak will be even more thrilled when they find out a pair of pirate battlecruisers are on the way. How much time do we have, Admiral?"

"Therein lies the problem," Dorvelle said heavily. "Baird's original plan was to stall the pirates' departure from Walther long enough to give Captain Katura plenty of time to reach Haven and for us to gather up a proper welcoming committee to send to Danak with *Pacemaker*. Unfortunately, Swenson isn't the patient type, and refused to give Katura any more time than absolutely necessary."

"They didn't want to give him *any* extra time, but Master Baird convinced them it would take at least twenty-four hours to process the release here in Nouveau Paris," Katura put in. "And they don't know how fast *Pacemaker* really is."

"Luckily, he was able to shave almost forty-eight hours off his projected transit by bulling his way through the Gamma bands," Dorvelle said. "Bottom line: the pirates are due to arrive in eleven T-days, and it's seven from here to Danak."

"Leaving you four days to put together a response," Lisa murmured, wincing.

"That is, unfortunately, the relative math," the admiral said. "But it's worse than that. *Saintonge* and her escorts are really the only battlecruiser group we know we can get to Danak in time."

Lisa sent a startled look at Marcello. "I thought..." She broke off.

"You thought we had the biggest navy in the sector," Charnay said. His voice was odd, his eyes gazing out at nothing. "But we also have a lot of associated systems who look to us for collective security. Aside from the Capital Squadron—"

"Which we can't touch," Dorvelle put in.

"—which I wouldn't touch even if I could," Charnay agreed, "especially with a major pirate force in the neighborhood, the majority of our strength is in battlecruiser groups covering all those other star systems. Admiral, are *Artois* and *Provence* still in the yards?"

"Yes," Dorvelle said. "And *Poitou* is down with a bad alpha node. We can hope the pirates aren't as skilled or well-armed as we are, but that's just an assumption. The numbers themselves certainly aren't promising."

"I've brought along Captain Rhamas's best estimates on their ship types and acceleration profiles," Katura offered.

Everyone turned to look at him. "Excuse me?" Dorvelle asked.

"Rhamas served in the Solarian Navy for twenty-three T-years before Master Rowbtham hired him," Katura explained. "He knows his warships, and he had plenty of time to work his passive sensors. He couldn't guarantee his acceleration numbers, but he's confident about his class identifications and armaments."

"Well, that will definitely help," Charnay observed. "Not as much as another battlecruiser or two, but right now we'll take everything we can get."

Beside Lisa, Marcello stirred.

"Commodore Charnay; Admiral Dorvelle? A private word, if I may?"

Some of the other Havenite officers frowned. But Dorvelle took it in stride.

"Certainly," he said. "This way."

The admiral led the way into a small office just off the briefing room. Marcello started to step inside, then paused at the doorway.

"By the way, Captain Katura. Would you happen to have any recordings of Swenson or any of the other pirates?"

"No," Katura said, his lips compressing briefly with memory. "The first thing they did after they captured us was to go into both ships' computers and erase all the com logs and everything else pertaining to them."

"Of course they did," Marcello said. "Thank you."

He continued into the office with the others, closing the door behind him.

"I know what you're going to say, Captain," Dorvelle said before Marcello could speak. "And while I appreciate the offer, I'm afraid I can't allow *Damocles* to assist."

"That's indeed a question I'll be addressing in a moment, Sir," Marcello said. "But I first wanted to raise the possibility that this might be some kind of elaborate ruse."

"To what end?" Dorvelle asked.

"Possibly to pull your ships out of position," Marcello replied. "As you said, you're stretched thin. They may be hoping you'll uncover Nouveau Paris itself in order to respond to Danak. You said you wouldn't touch your Capital Squadron, but Swenson may not know that. For that matter, they may expect you to bend the rules with an innocent family's life on the line."

"I don't like thinking about that," Dorvelle said grimly. "But that decision's not negotiable."

"Of course not," Marcello said. "Again, Swenson might not realize that."

"Or the target could be *Saintonge*, herself," Lisa added. "If they know you won't touch the Capital Squadron, and also know about the rest of your deployments, they may figure that a single battle-cruiser group is all you'll be able to spare."

"And we only have Katura's word regarding the enemy's numbers," Marcello said, nodding. "I'm not necessarily saying he's lying, but he could have been deliberately misled. If you go in expecting eight ships and find yourself facing twelve or sixteen, even the Republic's edge in weapons and training might not be enough."

"Or worse," Lisa added. "What kind of gang has the resources to buy and operate a pair of battlecruisers? Or *needs* ships that heavy, for that matter? Frankly, everything Katura has said sounds to me more like mercenaries than pirates."

"Possibly connected to your friend Tamerlane?" Dorvelle suggested.

"I'm sure that thought has occurred to all of us," Marcello said. "That's why I hoped some of *Pacemaker*'s recordings were intact. My point is that if Swenson *is* Tamerlane, and if the group is bigger than we know, this could be one of several coordinated attacks on specific Havenite targets."

"I suppose that's possible," Dorvelle said, his forehead furrowed with thought. "But highly unlikely. A group that big would need a huge local logistics support structure, and I can't see that hiding anywhere nearby. Not with Brigadier Massingill poking sticks into all the likely termite hills."

"And there are ways a pirate gang could have picked up a pair of battlecruisers," Charnay said. "That's exactly what the group at Secour was trying to do, remember."

"Point," Marcello agreed. "And actually, I doubt anyone would actually try a scheme like I described. But I wanted to make sure the possibility had been raised."

"But you still think Swenson is connected to Tamerlane?" Dorvelle asked.

"I think it possible," Marcello said. "And if that's the case, I respectfully submit that, under our existing treaty, *Damocles* has not only a right but also a duty to be involved."

Dorvelle gave out a low whistle. "And with that, the can of worms is officially open," he said. "You realize, I presume, that not only would the CNO have to sign off on that, but Legal Affairs would also have to get involved, not to mention the State Department. I'm not at all sure that four days is enough time to sort through all of that."

"I realize that, Sir," Marcello replied. "Nevertheless, I stand by my request."

Dorvelle looked at Charnay.

"The Navy's got a long tradition of giving the commander on the scene wide latitude in carrying out his orders, Commodore," he said. "Right now, it looks like you're going to be that commander. Thoughts?"

"I agree CNO would have to be aboard, Sir," Charnay said. "If nothing else, so that he could lean on Legal and State. I guarantee they're not going to be happy at the image of a Manticoran warship getting shot up under Havenite command."

He looked at Marcello and Lisa.

"On the other hand, Captain Marcello makes a valid point about the moral imperatives here. We've also worked well with Manticore in the past, not just at Secour but also in our joint pirate-hunt program. Their people and capabilities are well known to both our line personnel and Command." He smiled tightly. "As a purely practical matter, I'll remind the Admiral that *Damocles* was a major contributor to one of the RMN's three enemy kills at the Battle of Manticore. I think I could find a use for an extra destroyer."

"Very well," Dorvelle said. "I'll run it up the flagpole and see if anyone wants to take potshots at it. I just wish you didn't have quite as good a point about how useful you could find them. If I could scare up a few more hulls of our own for you, I would."

"I know that, Sir." Charnay looked at Marcello and Lisa. "So our roster is *Saintonge*, three heavy cruisers, four destroyers, a frigate, and RMN *Damocles*. Not the most cheerful of line-ups against two battlecruisers and six heavy cruisers, but I've seen worse. And we'll have seven days en route to plan." He looked back at Dorvelle and stiffened to attention. "Do I have my orders, Admiral Dorvelle?"

"You do, Commodore Charnay," Dorvelle said, also coming to attention. He didn't look very happy, Lisa thought, but happiness seemed in generally short supply at the moment. "Start your spin-up immediately. Requisition whatever you need; I want you ready to sortie within thirty-six hours."

"We will be, Sir."

"Good," Dorvelle said. "Good luck."

"Thank you, Sir," Charnay said. "And if I may make a suggestion, I recommend that you not mention our discussion about feints and ruses in front of Katura or Weissman."

"In case this *is* a ruse?"

"Yes, Sir." Charnay said. "Exactly."

☆　　☆　　☆

Saintonge and her escorts were indeed ready to depart within Dorvelle's window. So was *Damocles*.

"I doubt the Admiralty would be thrilled if they knew what we were up to," Lisa warned Marcello as they headed for the hyper-limit.

"Lucky for us they're not here," Marcello replied. "Or was that a roundabout way of saying you had your own qualms?"

"Not *qualms*, exactly, Sir," Lisa hedged. Marcello wasn't as rigid on quiet criticism as some officers she'd worked with, but that didn't mean she should abuse the privilege. "I'm just a little concerned about the logistics. Not to mention this new software."

"We can hardly work with Charnay if our computers and sensors can't talk to his," Marcello pointed out. "And don't forget that even though the Havenite ships are built locally, all of us are basically Solarian-designed. In a way, we were *built* to interface."

"Yes, sir," Lisa said. And really, their hardware was mostly compatible, though of course the Havenite versions were newer upgrades. "I'm mostly worried about how far they'll be able to get into our systems."

"Mostly it'll just be our communications interface," Marcello said. "I wish we could do more—a fully distributed fire-control network, for instance, would be extremely useful. But our missiles are too old and don't interface with their systems well enough for that."

"There's still all the sensor data and com traffic," Lisa said. "I'm not worried so much about whether the access filters will work as I am about the access we had to give them. Even with Papadakis's people looking over their shoulders, who's to say they didn't slip in a worm or gatherer program?"

"Hard to see what we could possibly have that they might want," Marcello said with a hint of dryness. "Anyway, we theoretically ice-walled all of our encryptions and private data and protocols before we let them into the system. If they've got a worm that can tunnel through all that—and there's some reason for them to try it—then yes, we could be in trouble. Still, encryptions and protocols can be changed, and

I imagine the Admiralty will do exactly that as soon as we return."

"Yes, Sir," Lisa agreed, her throat unpleasantly dry. When they returned.

If they returned.

In many ways, this was worse than even the invasion of Manticore. There, they'd had barely hours to realize what was happening, and all of that time had been filled with frantic work as every ship in the Navy scrambled to get combat ready.

Here, they were going to have days to handle all that prep work. Days which would give everyone aboard plenty of time to lie in their racks thinking about what lay ahead.

Their training was supposed to have prepared them for this kind of situation. But as Lisa looked back now, she realized it hadn't prepared them nearly well enough.

But then, probably no training really could.

"So let's forget about potential problems with our allies and focus our attention on the definite problems with our opponents," Marcello continued. "We have seven days to make sure everything and everybody is ready for whatever's coming at us. I trust you've made that point to Ravel?"

"Yes, Sir, I have," Lisa assured him. "Not that she needed the reminder. She's been elbow-deep in analysis, simulations, and layered plans since we got the news."

And she was a competent enough TO, Lisa knew. Still, she didn't seem to have that spark of outside-the-box thinking Travis did.

She wished Travis was here. Not just because his way of thinking could prove crucial in the battle ahead, but because she missed him.

"And we've received Commodore Charnay's proposed drill schedule?"

"Yes, Sir, his operations officer sent it over," Lisa said again. "Not that I've shared that schedule with anyone yet."

"Are you planning to?"

"Actually, Sir—with your permission, of course—no."

"Good," Marcello said. "Though I trust you realize that if our people flub our very first joint exercise with the rest of the squadron, it's not going to look good."

"I discussed that with Commander Laforge," Lisa said. "I told her what I had in mind, and she grabbed it and ran."

"She's not going to tell their people the schedule, either?"

"Exactly," Lisa said. "So if there's any flubbing, it'll probably be pretty broadly shared."

"Good enough," Marcello said. "Just be aware that if Ravel and her people turn in a subpar performance, they'll pay for it in more work and less sleep."

"Understood, Sir," Lisa said. "The last thing we want is to hit Danak without everyone running at peak performance."

Marcello gave a little snort. "Remember the old days, Commander? The days when we ran drills and exercises with plenty of advance warning?"

"You mean the old days a year ago?"

"Those are the ones."

Lisa nodded. Those had indeed been slower, lazier, more comfortable times.

Part of that had been from necessity, as recalcitrant or downright broken ship systems needed to be babied into something approaching readiness. But another part of it had been the "old pals" network in action, making sure the officers involved had as much time as possible to bring their departments up to snuff. Career-essential efficiency reports had ridden on how well they performed, after all, and it would never have done to have someone blot his or her copybook simply because they hadn't had a couple of weeks to get ready.

But those days were gone forever. The Star Kingdom had been attacked, and the RMN would never again be simply a comfortable place to tread water and drift along until an equally comfortable retirement.

When the old days faded, the old habits and systems had to fade with them.

"Still, *sic transit gloria mundi,* as the saying goes," Marcello continued. He raised his eyebrows. "You *were* planning to share the schedule with *me,* weren't you?"

"Of course, Sir," Lisa said in her most respectfully innocent voice. "How could you possibly think otherwise?"

☆   ☆   ☆

"You realize, of course," Joshua Miller warned, "that on its basic, fundamental level this document is largely worthless as a lever."

"True," Elizabeth conceded. "And if he chooses to play it on that level, it will make a messy situation that much worse."

"Breakwater won't fight," Michael said from across the table. "He understands reality, but he also understands the intangibles of appearance. He'll do what you want, Elizabeth, if only to preserve his reputation for future options."

Elizabeth felt her throat tighten. *He'll do what* you

want. Not what the former king wanted, or what a prominent member of the Commons wanted, or even what all three of them wanted together. *What* you *want*.

It had been over a year since Elizabeth had been crowned Queen. In all that time, there'd been maybe half a dozen brief periods when she'd actually *felt* like a true sovereign.

Now, with that single word, the full impact of her title, position, power, and responsibility suddenly hit her.

"I hope you're right, Your Highness," Miller said, inclining his head toward Michael. "I suppose only time will tell." He paused. "But whatever happens, Your Majesty," he added to Elizabeth, his voice going almost shy, "I want to thank you for allowing me to be part of it."

"You're quite welcome, Mr. Miller," Elizabeth assured him. "For my part, I'll forever be in your debt for the service you've provided to the Crown, to the Star Kingdom, and to me personally."

"It was a duty I was more than happy to perform." Miller's shoulder shifted, as if he wanted to reach over and touch her hand. Not in a forward or inappropriate manner, Elizabeth sensed, but merely a friendly, companion-like touch.

But at the last second, he seemed to sense it would be inappropriate or unwelcome. The shoulder shifted back, and his hand remained where it was.

And so, since Elizabeth was likewise feeling a sudden yearning for human contact, she took the initiative, reaching over to touch his hand.

Miller seemed to stiffen, just slightly. Across the table, Elizabeth sensed her father stir, as if about to speak, then go still again.

She withdrew her hand. "You'd best go, now," she said. "We still have a lot of work to do."

"Indeed, Your Majesty," Miller said, standing up and bowing to her. "Just let me know when you need me. I'll be ready." He swiveled around, bowed to Michael. "Your Highness."

"Mr. Miller," Michael said gravely.

Miller turned and headed across the study toward the door, where Sergeant Adler waited to escort him home.

Elizabeth watched his back as he walked. In another time, in another place...

She shook the thought away. Or rather, the thought faded of its own accord. As long as Carmichael's memory danced through her mind and heart and soul, there could never be another man allowed to take the empty place at her side.

It was almost funny, in a crudely ironic sort of way, how everyone had thought Burgundy's final data file had been a list of potential suiters. She'd thought that, the Prime Minister's own secretary had apparently thought it, and whoever had leaked the names to Breakwater had clearly thought it.

Maybe that list would have come next, had the Prime Minister lived a few more weeks. What everyone had clearly forgotten was that Burgundy was a servant of the Crown as well as a close friend to the Wintons. He'd seen the coming fight over succession as clearly as Breakwater had.

And so had left his Queen his final legacy.

Across the office, Miller and Adler slipped out into the empty corridor, Adler closing the door behind them. "He's a good man," Michael murmured. His tone, Elizabeth noted, gave no hint as to which of the two possible implications her father might be going for with the words.

"Yes, he is," Elizabeth agreed. For a moment she was tempted to tease the double meaning back at him, just for the fun of it. But she was Queen, and fun was no longer something she could engage in spontaneously. It was, instead, a precious commodity to be carefully saved for specific times and places. "He'll make a good ally in the Commons."

Again, she sensed her father's shift in posture, though whether in relief or disappointment she couldn't tell. "And the others?"

"Jacques Corlain will certainly stand alongside Mr. Miller," Elizabeth said. "Placido Amadeo—"

"You really *can* call him *Joshua*, you know," Michael pointed out gently. "At least when we're alone. It's quite obvious you like the man."

"Placido Amadeo and his company have a great deal of influence on several of the other MPs," Elizabeth continued doggedly. "I'm confident that he'll also answer Mr. Miller's request to use that pressure when needed. All in all, I think we've got a good chance."

Her father gave a barely-audible sigh.

"I agree," he said. "Though if Breakwater doesn't— but of course he will," he corrected himself hastily. "And now, I believe it's time to put these old bones to bed. Unless you need me some more tonight?"

"I'll always need you, Dad," Elizabeth said, reaching across the table and squeezing his hand. "But for now, pleasant dreams."

"You won't always need me, Elizabeth," Michael said. He squeezed her hand in turn, then let go and stood up. "In fact, I'm not sure you need me right now. And I'm glad of that. Very glad." He smiled. "But if you don't *need* me, I hope you'll always *want* me."

"Always, Dad," Elizabeth said quietly. "Sleep well, and be sure to kiss Mom for me."

"She's probably already asleep."

"Then just kiss her very, very gently."

CHAPTER THIRTY-ONE

BETWEEN THE TIME REQUIRED TO CHASE *Hamman* from Lau Hiler to Sachsen and the flight time from there back to Walther, thirty-nine T-days would elapse by the time *Casey* returned to the Volsungs' home system. With no idea of the mercenaries' operational patterns, it was impossible to predict whether or not some—or all—of the rest of their vessels would have returned in the cruiser's absence.

That thought continued to nag at the back of Travis's mind. Still, Clegg, Basaltberg, and Kane—Riefenstahl, rather—didn't seem particularly concerned about it. They continued to plan, and to hold frequent conferences, as the Allied force headed back to Walther.

Or at least, they weren't showing any particular concern. Which was not, of course, the same thing.

Still, Travis could sense a certain oddness about the Andermani and their attitude towards Gensonne. It was an attitude Chomps had also picked up on, and the two of them discussed it on several occasions over a beer in Travis's quarters.

They never found a conclusion to safely land on, but both agreed that Basaltberg was being driven by more than just a desire to deal with a potential threat to their empire's security.

Still, if the Andermani were reticent about exactly what Gensonne might have done to awaken such ire, they'd been far more forthcoming about their navy and its capabilities than Travis had anticipated. It was eye-opening, and more than a little astonishing.

Unexpectedly, at least to Travis, it was also a little humiliating.

The Andermani were sharing information and advice so enthusiastically because the Royal Manticoran Navy wasn't remotely in their league. Even *Casey*, the most modern ship in the RMN, was simply outclassed.

In a purely technological sense, *Casey* was in at least shouting distance of her new consorts. But she was the RMN's outlier, the only ship they had which could make that claim. Basaltberg's ships all mounted equally—uniformly—modern weapon systems and electronics.

Yet, in many ways, the Star Kingdom's Navy's technological inferiority might very well be its *least* glaring weakness. The far more serious detriment was that the RMN lacked the Andermani's institutional knowledge, their infrastructure, their technology, and—most damning of all—their experience.

The Andermani hadn't drawn attention to it, of course. They'd accepted Travis and Clegg's proposal for dealing with the mercenary base's missile platforms, and had been highly complementary about *Casey*'s role in the Battle of Manticore. Yet below the surface Travis could sense that they also thought the RMN had won that battle as much by sheer luck as by actual military skill. None of them seemed to question the Manticorans' courage and determination, but he'd had the distinct impression that they'd found it hard not to roll their eyes during discussions of both participants' tactics during the battle.

As *Casey*'s tactical officer, Travis had been deeply involved in the planning sessions carried out en route back to Walther. Many of those had been com conferences, but at Basaltberg's insistence he and Clegg had dined several times on *Vergeltung* as the admiral's honored guests. Technically, those dinners had been social occasions, but there'd been quite a bit of professional conversation as well. Somewhere along the way, Travis had realized that Basaltberg, Riefenstahl, and Captain Luitpold Huschens, *Vergeltung*'s captain and Admiral Basaltberg's flag captain, were quietly conducting a seminar for the benefit of the Manticorans.

Travis had no problem with that. On the contrary, he had determined to soak up any insight they offered like an eager sponge. It was harder to tell about Clegg, though he noted that when she offered a response or a comment it was always succinct, to the point, and thoughtful. Clearly, she was as aware as he was of just how much the RMN still had to learn.

But she'd also been a King's—and now a Queen's—officer a lot longer than Travis had. She'd been one of the people who'd fought for decades to simply keep the Navy alive. Having to now face the evidence of what the RMN *could* have been, and had never been allowed to be, had to be harder on her than it was even on Travis.

Vergeltung was a perfect case in point.

The battleship was far newer than the RMN's battlecruisers. No one, even in the Solarian League, had been building ships this big when Manticore purchased the *Lexington*-class battlecruisers nearly a T-century ago.

But Travis knew a refitted ship when he saw one. In fact, he suspected that *Vergeltung* hadn't been refitted so much as rebuilt. There were clear signs of heavy damage, including both external and internal stiffening plates, the kind used to relieve stress on hull frames and decking after significant breakage.

After that kind of damage a hull seldom survived. The repair costs had probably been close to the purchase price of a newer ship of the same class. Gustav Anderman must have wanted her badly to invest that much in putting her back together again.

But however old the basic hull was, and however severely it might have been mauled in the past, Travis had no doubt of its soundness and integrity. And there was nothing at all old, obsolete, or worn out about *Vergeltung*.

Her electronics were cutting edge. He hadn't personally examined her missiles, but they were listed as Starstorms, the same round the SLN had used as recently as twelve T-years ago. The fusion boosters that kicked those missiles out of their tubes were at least twice as powerful as those aboard Manticoran ships, allowing the weapons to get safely clear of the wedge and on their way correspondingly faster. Her single spinal laser was a massive weapon, again at least twice as powerful as anything the RMN mounted. She was lavishly equipped with active antimissile defenses, including heavy autocannon, advanced defensive electronic warfare suites, and a towed decoy system that would make any tactical officer's mouth water. The improvised Allied squadron exercised together a half-dozen times during the voyage from Sachsen back to Walther, and even in the exercises it had been painfully obvious that *Vergeltung*'s ECM were far more advanced than *Casey*'s, even after her refit, far less the rest of the RMN's units.

Basaltberg's other ships presented much the same picture. Though not all of them were new, they'd all been carefully maintained and upgraded on a regular basis by a navy which understood the advantages of operational homogeneity and believed in keeping its ships ahead of anything they were likely to encounter.

Travis could only wish some of the people responsible for Manticoran naval priorities could see what he was seeing, and from Clegg's dark moods after their visits to *Vergeltung* he guessed she had the same thoughts. She'd been watching the Navy—*her* Navy—slowly fall apart, disintegrate into a hollowed out shell, for a lot longer than he had.

And now, she was about to take the least hollow ship of that shell into battle.

☆　　☆　　☆

All the way back from Sachsen Travis had had the nagging fear that the Andermani might have been putting too much trust in the data he and Chomps had picked up during their flyby of the Volsungs' base.

Now, sitting in n-space ten light-minutes outside the Walther hyper limit, on the farthest side of the system from Walther Prime, he found out why Basaltberg hadn't been worried.

"I have *got* to get me one of those," Chomps muttered as he, Travis, and a dozen other Manticorans gazed at the viewscreen and the vac-suited Andermani techs working on *Vergeltung*'s hull. Travis hadn't gotten a good look at this bit of SMS tech during the trip, and he rather doubted they were going to get one now.

"I wonder how they crammed everything in," Chomps continued, rubbing his chin thoughtfully. "It can't be more than half again the size of a standard shuttle."

Travis nodded. Only a shuttle and a half; and yet somehow the Andermani had crammed in a sensor suite far better than the one *Casey*'s techs had rigged up.

And had even had room for a set of impellers.

It had to be Solarian tech. Somehow, even way out in the Andermani Empire, Gustav must still have a pipeline back there that enabled him to get hold of this kind of cutting-edge equipment.

Did that mean that the Solarians also had these recon drones? Probably.

All that mattered at the moment, though, was that *Vergeltung* had one of them.

Such marvels came with a cost, of course. The drone was big enough that the battleship had been required to give up a missile launcher site in order to provide a hull mooring point for it. In the missing tube's place was a housing which—intentionally, no doubt—closely mimicked the weapon mount which had been removed. The housing was more than just camouflage, though, almost certainly providing an atmosphere seal and allowing a shirtsleeve environment for the drone's maintenance.

The drone was too big for the housing to hold it in fully assembled form. Putting the bits and pieces together and testing them had occupied a sizable number of *Vergeltung*'s technicians for the last seven and a half hours. But the suited figures were drifting back towards the battleship, now.

And then, without fanfare, the drone was away.

It was hard to make out, even with the viewscreen set to maximum zoom. Like the modified shuttle Travis and Chomps had ridden, it was painted a black so deep that the light from the Andermani techs' helmet lamps had seemed to simply melt into it. At the moment, its running lights were glowing, but when those winked out, the drone would just disappear. Unless it occluded a star, no optical sensor had a hope of spotting it.

According to Commander Anholt, Admiral Basaltberg's operations officer, the drone was capable of a max acceleration of fifteen hundred gravities, not quite half that of a missile in long-range cruise mode. But unlike a missile, the drone's impellers could be turned off and then on again. That was vital, given the limits of their power supply—even the Andermani couldn't squeeze a reactor into something that small. The impellers would only be used for relatively brief accelerations and decelerations, with lengthy ballistic phases in between. That made for a prodigious operational range, as well as contributing enormously to its stealthiness along the way.

The deeper implications of such a system were enormous. Not just for tactical drones or missiles, but also for small craft. Travis's mind flashed back to all the slow shuttle rides he'd taken over his years in the RMN. If those shuttles had been equipped with impellers, he could have saved many dreary hours of his life.

In the distance, the drone's lights vanished. Probably because they'd been switched off, but equally possibly because when something pulled away at fifteen hundred gravities it got itself out of sight in a hurry.

"And, they're off," Chomps murmured. "Wonder what it'll find."

"Whatever's there," Travis said. "*I* wonder if it'll really be able to find its way back home."

"I don't think even a drone would risk pissing off Admiral Riefenstahl by getting lost," Chomps assured him. He shook his head. "But yeah. I really, really want one."

☆   ☆   ☆

"My congratulations yet again, Captain Marcello," Commodore Charnay said from the com display, a tight but satisfied smile on his face. "*Damocles* did you proud. Again." The smile morphed into a grimace. "I wish all of *my* ships performed that well and that consistently. *Intrépide*'s crew, in particular, needs to work on scrubbing away the rust."

"Thank you, Commodore," Marcello said, fully appreciating the depth of the other's compliment.

Intrépide was one of Charnay's modern, powerful destroyers, but her skipper had been taken by surprise by the first of Commander Laforge's drills. Once she'd recovered from the surprise, she'd performed adequately.

Just not as well as *Damocles*. Despite the destroyer's age and the Royal Manticoran Navy's relative inexperience, only three of the Havenite ships had reached full combat readiness before Marcello's crew even in the first exercise. And his people had performed equally well in all of the subsequent drills the commodore had laid on, consistently placing in the top five scorers in each exercise.

The results had been well worth the time and effort. A T-week of Charnay's and Commander Laforge's drills had turned an already professional group of officers and crews into a group that now operated with a clean, snappy precision Marcello wished the RMN possessed.

Not surprising, really. Under normal circumstances, training was just training. But here, every man and woman aboard the Havenite ships was fully aware that the drills would be followed by actual, vicious combat . . . and that they would be on the short end of the firepower ratio.

"Have you decided on the initial deployment yet, Sir?" he asked Charnay. The last three or four drills had tested alternative deployment plans, and Marcello knew which one he preferred. But *Damocles* was the visiting member of the team, and that decision would be the commodore's alone.

"I have," Charnay said. "Assuming we manage to beat the pirates to Danak, we'll go with Embuscade. If they get there before us, we'll go to Mascarade and hope we can convince them to leave the system intact."

"Which would mean abandoning Baird and his family," Marcello pointed out.

"I know," Charnay said heavily. "Letting them get away is clearly less than optimal, for other reasons as well. But we don't have the firepower to take them head-on. Besides, much as I hate what'll almost certainly happen to the Bairds, I can't possibly justify a fleet battle in the heart of the Danak System if there's any way to avoid it. The collateral damage there could be enormous, even if the mercenaries didn't threaten to deliberately destroy its deep-space infrastructure for tactical leverage."

"Understood," Marcello said.

Like Charnay, he hoped they wouldn't have to go with Mascarade, even if *Damocles*'s antics during the Barcan incursion into Manticore had served as its inspiration.

That had been an interesting set of conversations. Their Havenite hosts had been politely skeptical when he and Lisa described Commander Long's boosted impeller deception—mainly, Marcello suspected, because they'd been astonished anyone had fallen for such an ancient chestnut.

But slowly that attitude had changed. It *was* an ancient trick, but that also meant it was so old a lot of navies had completely forgotten about it. In addition, as Charnay had reminded them, the reason the tactic had once been so common was that until an attacker reached detailed sensor range, he *had* to assume he truly was looking at the larger and more powerful ships. The consequences if he decided it was a ruse and was wrong would have been disastrous.

And so Charnay had dusted the concept off and incorporated it into the Mascarade deployment. If the mercenaries were already inside the inner system when the Allied squadron arrived, his two modern heavy cruisers—*Jocelyne Pellian* and *Jean-Claude Courtois*— would run up their impellers to simulate battlecruisers, while *Courageux* and *Intrépide* ran theirs up to simulate heavy cruisers. That much apparent firepower should give the pirates pause and add weight to Charnay's demand that they depart Danak space upon pain of attack.

It might even work.

Hopefully, that situation wouldn't arise. If the pirates kept to their timetable—which they had every reason to do, given Baird's insistence that they had to be a scheduled arrival—Charnay's squadron would arrive over a day and a half before they did. In that case, Embuscade offered a much higher chance of success. There was only one part Marcello considered truly chancy, although he understood why Charnay had included it.

"Is Brigadier Massingill confident her people will be able to get aboard both ships, Sir?" he asked.

"Brigadier Massingill," Charnay replied with a somewhat lopsided smile, "is confident her people can do *anything*. And, to date, she's always managed to back that up. In this case, I'll admit I'm a bit more concerned than usual. But given the data Captain Rhamas was able to provide on the pirates' ships, I'm willing to risk her teams if it means a chance to take one of their damned battlecruisers out of play early."

"*If* Admiral Swenson isn't too skittish about splitting his force."

"And if I were him I'd be leery about doing that," Charnay agreed. "We just have to convince him that he's expected and there aren't any unfriendly welcoming committees around. I figure there's maybe a thirty percent chance he'll bite. If he does, I'm guessing he'll send *Loki*."

"Because that's not his flagship?" Marcello suggested.

"That, and because the *Bayezid*-class ships have older compensators. She's slow, so it would make more sense to detach her. Assuming he bites, of course."

Marcello nodded. It would be better for the Havenites if Swenson sent *Odin*, which was far and away the most powerful of the pirates' ships. But Charnay was right. If Swenson detached any of his ships it would probably be the one most likely to hold down his fleet acceleration rate.

"And one bite is all it'll take," Charnay continued. "If the Brigadier's people get aboard, any battle-cruiser is toast. Even if Swenson has the equivalent of a Marine detachment—which they might if they're mercenaries and not pirates—they aren't going to be armored and ready when the commandos come storming in. Personally, if *I* found myself trapped inside a ship with the Three-Oh-Third, I'd surrender so fast I'd sprain something."

"Hopefully, they'll feel the same way," Marcello murmured. Privately, both he and Commander Donnelly had some serious reservations about this part of the plan. Still, if it worked it would certainly be a masterstroke.

And even if Swenson declined to take the bait, it shouldn't leave them worse off than they were already.

He felt far more confident about the rest of Embuscade. It was about as straightforward as a battle plan got, and it should offer them the best tactical situation anyone could hope for.

And if Swenson *did* allow Massingill's commandos to take half his battlecruiser strength off the board, the numerical odds would be the next best thing to even.

Having drilled with Charnay's ships for the last six days, Marcello liked their chances in that kind of a fight.

☆   ☆   ☆

Ten hours after the drone's departure, *Casey* once again floated off *Vergeltung*'s flank, this time ten light-minutes outside the hyper limit on Walther Prime's side of the system. In the distance, the dim firefly of the decelerating drone approached the hidden fleet.

Despite the small size of those impellers, it had

required barely 40 minutes and only 41,731,000 kilometers—little more than 2.3 LM—to attain a velocity of 35,000 KPS. It had done that long before it crossed the Walther hyper-limit in-bound, then coasted ballistically across the entire hyper-sphere in less than six hours before exiting on the far side. It had then reengaged its impellers and begun braking for recovery by its mothership.

Now Travis watched the faint signal of that stealthy impeller wedge come to rest less than five hundred kilometers clear of *Vergeltung*, wondering what its sensors had found.

The answer, it turned out, was quite a lot.

"I have to say, Admiral," Captain Clegg said to Basaltberg's image on the bridge com screen in front of her, "that your probe has definitely added new meaning to the old adage that bad news travels fast."

"It's a concern, certainly," Admiral Basaltberg conceded. "We're fortunate it passed close enough for the drone to get a decent look at it."

"Have you identified it?" Clegg asked. "Nothing from our ship archives comes closer than eighty-two percent probable."

"It appears to be one of the old Beowulfan *Stilio*-class ships," Basaltberg said. "Beowulf retired them decades ago, but obviously there are still some in service elsewhere."

Travis had already keyed his display. The entry came up, and he ran his eyes quickly down the entry. *Stilio*-class ships ran to about two hundred thousand tons, and were somewhat more modern than the RMN's *Lexington*-class battlecruisers. The original weapons systems were listed, but since the Volsungs had probably upgraded it over the years that information was only marginally relevant.

He also noted in passing that that particular class had come in at only seventy-nine percent probable in their own archive search. Yet another area in which the Andermani were ahead of them.

"A significant weapons platform," Basaltberg continued, "but not anything *Vergeltung* can't handle."

"No doubt," Clegg replied. "Though I'd just as soon not have had this added to the mix at the last minute."

"You should learn to look upon the positive, Captain," Major Zhou offered. "The more ships which are present, the more ships we can dispose of."

"Exactly," Basaltberg agreed. He tapped the plot in front of him. "And not just present, but so conveniently gathered together for us."

Travis nodded silent agreement as he shifted his eyes again to the plot on the tac display. The Andermani drone had passed close enough to get a detailed look at the group of ships in orbit around Walther Prime in company with the Volsungs' space station. There were twenty-six of them in all, three more than Travis and Chomps had observed in their own flight through the system.

Two of the newcomers were freighters, which were unlikely to matter as far as the upcoming combat was concerned, bringing the total freighter count to nine. One of those was obviously a tanker, while another, judging from the hab sections, was probably a personnel transport. The rest appeared to be standard freighters, most in the two million-ton range. Most showed no sign of armament, although it was possible they were more conventional Q-ships than *Hamman* and simply chose to keep their teeth hidden. But that seemed unlikely, and Travis suspected the majority were prizes the mercenaries had acquired.

That left seventeen warships: two light cruisers, ten destroyers of one sort or another, and five *Ordra*-class Silesian frigates.

Plus, of course, the newly-arrived *Stilio*-class battle-cruiser.

Under the circumstances, Travis thought, one might wonder just how conveniently what had been gathered, and for whom.

"Certainly an impressive collection of hulls," the Andermani admiral continued. "Commander Anholt's best estimate is that they out-mass us by a bit more than two-to-one, not counting the base missile platforms, now that the *Stilio*'s been added to the equation."

Again, Travis nodded silently to himself. That fit his estimate, as well.

"Of course, if all goes according to plan, the missile platforms will cease to be an issue shortly before battle is fully joined," Basaltberg said. "We also estimate that at least five of the destroyer-range vessels and three of the frigates are down for maintenance. Several appear to be undergoing long-term refits, and need not enter into our calculations. The others seem to be undergoing more limited repair, but given the probable efficiency of technicians working for Gensonne, I doubt that any of them can be made combat-ready in the available window."

Travis and Clegg exchanged looks. Both of them, Travis had no doubt, were remembering another star system and another group of warships trying frantically to clear their maintenance docks.

"That leaves only nine combat-capable mobile units as opposed to our seven," Basaltberg said, "and I venture to say that our ships are better armed and equipped then theirs on any ton-for-ton comparison."

His expression hardened. "But there is more to war than tonnage or hardware. There is a vast difference between mercenaries who prey upon the weak and the helpless and a navy which stands between them and their victims. It is a difference we Andermani understand better than most, perhaps. Firepower and numbers matter, but so does the willingness to stand and fight."

"I can't argue with any of that, Sir," Clegg said. "However, as you say, firepower and numbers *are* significant factors, and we can only hope there aren't more battlecruisers wandering around the outer system the way this one was."

Basaltberg shook his head. "I doubt there will be any more of them."

"May I ask why?"

"Because I don't believe this one *was* wandering the outer system, as you suggest," Basaltberg said. "It seems obvious that we caught her arriving from out-system. Any additional ships would almost certainly have been in company with her and therefore also have been spotted by the drone."

"I agree it's likely she was inbound and not just returning from some kind of exercise," Clegg said, frowning. "May I ask why you believe it *obvious* and not simply *likely*?"

Basaltberg gestured to Major Zhou, standing silently at his side. "Major?" he invited.

"Gensonne has certain habits, Captain," Zhou

explained. "Habits to which he insists all of his captains conform. A final loop around a fixed or orbiting base whenever one of his ships arrives on station is one of those habits. That's what this ship was doing."

"Really?" Clegg peered hard at the plot. "What does he hope to accomplish with that kind of maneuver?"

"A dog circling its bed," Travis murmured to himself.

"You have something to add, TO?" Clegg asked.

"Sorry, Ma'am," Travis apologized, feeling his face warming. "My mother breeds dogs, and I was remembering that some breeds like to circle their beds before lying down. Goes back to when they slept in the wild and wanted to drive out any snakes or large insects that might be hiding in the grass."

"Exactly correct, Commander Long," Basaltberg said, inclining his head in Travis's direction. An especially impressive feat, given that Travis wasn't within the field of view of Clegg's com. "Gensonne knows how vulnerable orbiting stations are to sneak attacks, so he likes to take occasional looks, hopefully unexpected, behind any blocking planet or moon. An incoming ship which is already on the move is ideal for that purpose. That's why, as Major Zhou points out, he has always had standing orders to that effect."

"I suppose that makes sense," Clegg said, a bit doubtfully.

"It represents a hard learned lesson of the Imperial Navy, Captain," Basaltberg said. "Though had he taken the *entire* lesson to heart, he would order periodic, erratically scheduled sweeps with the ships already in-system."

"Or post a unit in a position to watch their backs," Clegg said.

"Exactly," Basaltberg said. "Though in face of our proposed tactics, any decision on their part to sweep the far side of Prime would have been of no utility. Regardless, I believe the vessel's flight profile positively confirms that she is a recent arrival, not something that your people missed on *your* probe of the system."

"I understand, and concur," Clegg said, inclining her head.

Basaltberg nodded back. "I also point out in passing, Captain, that our drone's information matches almost perfectly with your own sensor records. An impressive feat indeed for an improvised installation."

"And if it *is* a recent arrival," Zhou said, his voice going darker, "it's possible that Gensonne himself may be aboard her. He prefers to be shipboard rather than spend time on a station or on the ground. Especially as a ship offers the option of running away if he so chooses."

"Exactly," Basaltberg said. "I believe we have gleaned all that we can from the drone's data. Instruct all units that we will initiate Operation *Verräterweg* in one hour."

☆   ☆   ☆

"To tomorrow," Gensonne said, lifting his glass toward the com screen.

"To tomorrow," Llyn echoed, his image lifting his in turn.

It was an odd dinner, Gensonne thought as he set his glass back on his table. Bizarre, even, if one thought too hard about it. He'd originally invited Llyn to *Odin* for a last meal together before they reached Danak and Llyn's promised missile upgrade could begin. Part of the invitation had been to see what additional information he might be able to worm out of Llyn on various subjects; part of it had been to have the option of politely insisting Llyn stay in his sight during the early stages of the operation, just in case.

Maybe Llyn had sensed that second part lurking under Gensonne's courtesy. Maybe he had preparations of his own to make before Danak and simply didn't want to be away from his ship even for a couple of hours this close to the end of their voyage.

Or maybe he felt that it was time for him to host one of their infrequent dinners. He'd counteroffered to treat Gensonne this time around, an invitation that the Volsung admiral had likewise found an excuse to decline.

And so here the two of them sat, eating in their individual ships, conversing via com like people in a long-distance relationship.

Still, if the second part of Gensonne's plan was out, the first was still viable. He'd been watching Llyn's alcohol intake closely, paying particular attention to the minute but clear evidence of impaired motor skills. Now, as the meal drew to a close, was his best chance at persuading the little man to get talkative.

"So tell me, Mr. Llyn," Gensonne said as he forked one last bite of steak. "How smoothly do you really think this is going to go?"

"That's always hard to predict out here on the frontier," Llyn said with a shrug. He took another sip from his glass and returned it to his table. "I don't expect any problems, though. The schedule's a bit tight, but I'm fairly confident Katura will have managed to make it to Nouveau Paris and then back to Danak in time."

"If he didn't?"

"Then you'll have to hang around outside the hyper-limit until he gets back, I'm afraid," Llyn said. "But aside from the boredom factor, that shouldn't be anything to worry about. I doubt they'll be worried if we behave ourselves and the authorization comes through within a day or two. There's always a little slippage in interstellar arrangements."

Gensonne nodded. The Axelrod operative had said all the right things about the Volsungs' future utility to his employers, and what he'd said made sense.

On the other hand, what he'd said before the attack on Manticore had *also* seemed to make sense.

But Llyn was damned straight that the squadron was staying safely outside the limit if the expected invitation hadn't gotten back from Haven. Gensonne wasn't making any commitment until he was positive Llyn hadn't arranged something nasty under the table.

If he had, then the last thing Gensonne would do before escaping back into hyper would be to send the slippery little bastard straight to hell.

"We'll just have to hope any slippage is minimal," he told Llyn. "I'd feel better if I knew exactly which local politician's palm we had to grease. We *will* have to grease some politician's palm, right?"

"I assume so," Llyn said. "Rather, *I'll* have to apply the grease—you won't need to be involved with that part. Unfortunately, those names and faces often change out here. But the message Katura brings back from the Jerriais office in Nouveau Paris will take care of that."

"You think we'll only have to pay off one person?"

"Probably only one politician," Llyn said. "There might also be a yard foremen or two with their hands out. But that should only be loose change by comparison."

"And after that how long before I get my missiles?"

"*Releasing* the missiles shouldn't take long," Llyn assured him. "Not more than a day or so for the paperwork. As for the systems installation and then the actual loading, you'd have a better idea about that than I would. How long does a weapons upgrade like this usually take?"

"Depends on how urgently it's pressed, and who's doing the work," Gensonne replied. "In a proper yard accustomed to military work, maybe a couple of weeks. In a civilian yard, it could take a month or longer. I'd feel happier if I knew where Jerriais falls on that scale."

"No idea, I'm afraid," Llyn said. "The people who handle Axelrod's hardware could probably give you a decent estimate, but that's not my department."

"Right—your department is hiring mercenaries," Gensonne said, watching the little man closely. "So what exactly does Axelrod want with Manticore, anyway? Is it something on one of the planets? Some extra-rich ores in one of the asteroid belts? It's not the treecats, is it?"

Llyn pursed his lips, gazing hard at Gensonne. Gensonne studied his face, searching for signs of intoxication, wishing mightily that he could smell the other's breath. "Well, I don't suppose it will be a secret much longer," Llyn said at last with a small shrug. "Besides, it will be obvious as soon as you get your next assignment. We want to turn Manticore into a staging area for an attack on the Andermani Empire."

Gensonne sat up a bit straighter in his chair. They were going to take down *Gustav*?

"Seriously? Why?"

"Oh, now *that's* still a secret," Llyn said with a slightly hazy but distinctly smug smile. "Why, does it bother you?"

"No, no, exactly the opposite," Gensonne assured him. "I have a bit of history with Gustav Anderman. I hope you'll allow me to be present at his downfall."

"Absolutely," Llyn promised. "Why do you think we chose you for this job in the first place? So I take it you're fully aboard?"

"Absolutely," Gensonne said, feeling better than he had in days. In years. Revenge for the embarrassing freak defeat at Manticore *and* the chance to burn Gustav Anderman down to bedrock? Damned right he was aboard. "What's our timetable?"

"Patience, Admiral," Llyn reproved him mildly. "First the missiles, then Manticore, *then* Anderman."

"Yes; the missiles," Gensonne said, forcing his mind away from visions of vengeance against Uncle Gustav. "How exactly do you expect that to work?"

"I thought we'd already covered that," Llyn said, frowning. "We go to the designated platforms—probably Bergen One since that was their most capable yard as of my last information. Once we arrive—"

"No, no, I mean the sequencing," Gensonne interrupted. "Surely they won't be able to refit all eight ships at the same time."

"Probably not," Llyn agreed. "It'll also depend on how busy they are when we get there. Hopefully, they can do, say, four at once. Maybe more, but four's a safe guess."

"During which time the rest of the ships will just be sitting there?"

"Or taking a tour of the mining facilities, or going

in for a closer look at the gas giant or the Twins, or buying reactor mass and fresh entertainment chips." Llyn frowned again. "Why, are you worried that you'll be bored?"

"I'm concerned about awkward questions from people we *haven't* bribed," Gensonne countered. "What's going to keep those people and their questions off our backs?"

"That's why we sent Katura ahead, remember?" Llyn said. "All your people have to do is to remember they're part of the Imperial Andermani Navy." He wrinkled his nose as he took another sip from his glass. "Though I'll admit your ship types are a bit of an odd mix. Still, everybody knows—or assumes—Gustav keeps some nonstandard ships tucked away. Plausible deniability, you know, if that becomes necessary."

"I imagine Axelrod's also found that approach useful a time or two?" Gensonne suggested.

"Definitely," Llyn said, his eyes briefly taking on a far-away look. "The point is, nobody's going to question your ID as long as the paperwork from the home office says that's who you are. And no one wants to get on Gustav's wrong side without a damned good reason."

"I suppose you're right," Gensonne said reluctantly.

"Of course I'm right," Llyn assured him. "Oh, and I think I may have forgotten to tell you that they know me here as Max Baird, an agent for a rich Solarian merchant named Rowbtham. So don't be surprised if you get a call for me by that name."

"Understood," Gensonne said. So the slippery little bastard was slippery here as well? Somehow, that didn't surprise him.

"And now, I should go," Llyn said, glancing at his

chrono. "Big day tomorrow, with important screens to make and field. I need to be at my best."

"As do we all," Gensonne agreed. "It'll be interesting to see how much dock space they have available."

"If Captain Katura performed as well as he always has in the past, that information should be waiting for us when we check in with Danak Traffic Control."

"All right," Gensonne said. "We'll talk again after we translate back to n-space."

"Right." Llyn reached toward the com control, then paused. "By the way, I trust you haven't told anyone else about my connection with Axelrod?"

Gensonne felt his muscles tense. Which answer was Llyn expecting? More importantly, which one should he give him?

"Don't be silly," he said. "Knowledge is power. Shared knowledge is useless."

He watched Llyn's face closely. But there was nothing there but a contented nod.

"Good. My employers would be very annoyed with me if they knew our connection had gotten out. Good night, Admiral. Sleep well."

"I will," Gensonne said softly. So he'd given the right answer. Distantly, he wondered what would have happened if he'd given the wrong one. "You, too."

CHAPTER THIRTY-TWO

TRAVIS LONG FELT VERY, VERY LONELY as he sat at his station on *Casey*'s bridge.

They were thirty-one light-minutes from the Walther System's fiery central furnace. Nine hours ago, the entire Andermani squadron had accelerated away, their impeller signatures disappearing from *Casey*'s sensors an hour after their departure.

Leaving *Casey* all alone.

He thought back to where this had started, back when he'd suggested that Clegg try to link up with the man they knew then as Captain Kane. Never would he have guessed that this was where it would all end.

What surprised him most was how much he'd grown to like and respect these people.

True, the Andermani could be a little stuffy, and there was that subtle but ever-present sense that they thought the Manticorans still had a lot to learn. But they'd been more than generous about teaching some of those lessons, and in many ways they'd treated *Casey*'s officers like the equals they definitely weren't.

And they hadn't had to agree to Captain Clegg's request to leave the base and its computer files intact if possible.

Of course, it remained to be seen whether or not they'd agreed in good faith. And if *Casey's* proposed tactic for dealing with the missile platforms didn't work, the whole question would probably be moot anyway.

Those platforms weren't especially well protected, but they mounted a lot of launchers. If they had the ability to manage that many missiles simultaneously, they were going to be dangerous as hell in a missile engagement. In fact, at that sort of range, the two of them were probably worth at least another battle-cruiser, maybe even two.

Clegg's approval of Travis's idea for dealing with them had been another surprise. The fact that she'd given him credit even while officially putting her own neck on the line was also more than he had expected.

For his part, Basaltberg had been quick to come on board with the tactic, as well as with Clegg's own suggested psychological warfare flourish to encourage the mercenaries' mobile units to stand and fight.

"Lieutenant Lukanov?" Clegg said abruptly into the tense silence.

"Yes, Ma'am?" the astrogator replied.

"It's time," the captain said, her voice glacially calm. "Take us into hyper."

☆   ☆   ☆

HMS *Casey* blasted into normal-space just outside the Walther System hyper limit in a bleeding cascade of transit energy. They had arrived just under two-hundred-seventy-two million kilometers from Walther Prime, Travis noted from his board, and within seven thousand kilometers of Clegg's designated locus.

And all on a ten-light-minute micro jump.

"Impressive job, Ms. Lukanov," Clegg said. "Tell me how we line up."

"Yes, Ma'am," Lukanov said, tapping rapidly on her keyboard. "If we accelerate at two hundred gravities for three-six-seven seconds, we can drop back and be right on profile."

"Very good," Clegg said. "Commander Woodburn, take us in."

Unlike *Casey*'s first visit to Walther, this time she would make no effort to conceal her presence. She aimed at the point in space where Walther Prime would be in six hours and forty-two minutes and ran Lukanov's specified numbers. Then, with the ship now exactly on her carefully planned profile, she reduced her acceleration to 190 gees and bored straight in.

Travis sat back in front of his own panel, feeling the long hours that now stretched ahead of him. Against all doubts—his own as well as, he suspected, Lady Calvingdell's—he and Chomps had actually pulled it off. With the backing of Delphi, Delphi's training and equipment, a lot of hard work, and probably more than a little luck, they'd tracked Manticore's attacker to his lair.

And yet, despite the satisfaction of that accomplishment—and despite Chomps's assertion that Travis was a born spy—he was slowly coming to realize that the tactical officer's chair was where he felt most comfortable. Sitting here, preparing to put himself, the men and women under his command, and his ship between his Star Kingdom and her enemies, was where he needed to be.

Even more, it was where he *wanted* to be.

That wasn't where he thought he would end up when he first enlisted. The Navy had been an escape, both from the desolate wasteland of his life and from the more immediate threat of jail if he'd been incriminated in the robbery he hadn't known was about to occur. It had offered him a haven, a refuge, and he'd grabbed it with both hands. In time, he'd discovered he was good at it, but in so many ways, it had still been just a job.

Yet even before the Battle of Manticore that had begun to change. Slowly, so slowly that he hadn't even noticed it until now, the concept of a *job* or even a *career* had turned into a *calling*. Somewhere in those years he'd realized, only subconsciously at first, that there were people and principles he would die to protect.

He had no idea when that had happened. But it was where he stood now, though he would probably be too embarrassed and self-conscious to ever admit it out loud to anyone, except possibly Lisa.

He'd thought he was searching for rules and structure. Instead, what he'd really been searching for were clarity and purpose.

Ahead in the distance were eighteen warships belonging to a mercenary fleet which had already attacked his home once.

Whatever else happened, he thought darkly, these particular ships would never do that again.

☆   ☆   ☆

There was really no way, Gensonne knew, that eight warships and a freighter translating into the Danak system in tight sequence could be seen as anything but someone's military.

Fortunately, that was precisely the role the Volsungs were trying to play in the first place.

Not that he'd mind if the Danak authorities were just a *little* nervous. Llyn had said the Volsungs would be on the hook for the launchers' installation, and long experience had shown Gensonne that nervous people were less likely to price-gouge their customers.

Of course, in this case there was an additional reason not to worry about Danakan anxiety. He was supposed to be an admiral of the Andermani Navy, and Emperor Gustav's people didn't spend their time worrying about other people's tender sensibilities.

He scowled at the displays. The formation had come in tight, but their translation locus was almost twenty-one light-seconds off, putting them better than ten light-minutes short of their most probable destination on a least-time course.

A genuine Andermani captain would probably ream someone out for that. Once they were underway, he would see about doing precisely that.

"Spin up our transponders," he ordered Captain Imbar. "Andermani warships *always* respect the niceties of interstellar law. Just make sure we're showing the right ones."

☆   ☆   ☆

Ten minutes later, the reply came.

"Andermani ship *Winterfeldt*, this is Danak Traffic Control," a voice said from the bridge speaker.

"Welcome to Danak. We've been expecting you. Jerriais Operations Manager Dostoyevsky sends her greetings, and Secretary of Industry Charnay has been asked to relay President Nelson's welcome, as well."

Gensonne leaned back in his chair, gripping the armrest tightly with satisfaction and released tension. So Llyn's man Katura had made it to Haven and back with the necessary paperwork. Perfect.

He allowed himself a few seconds to gloat, then pressed the com stud.

"Thank you, Traffic Control," he replied, giving free rein to the Andermani accent he'd spent years getting rid of. "This is Admiral Koenig of the Imperial Andermani Navy. I assume from your greeting that you know why we're here?"

He leaned back, busying himself with status reports and fine-tuning the Volsung formation as he waited out the twenty-minute round-trip communications lag.

"We do, indeed, Admiral," DTC's voice came right on schedule. "We've been instructed to inform you that Master Rowbtham's authorization for the work on your ships has been approved by the Jerriais office in Nouveau Paris. We only learned about the work order a day ago, but we've done some shuffling and I think we'll be able to fit you in as expeditiously as Master Rowbtham's requested."

☆   ☆   ☆

"Andermani ship *Winterfeldt*, this is Danak Traffic Control. Welcome to Danak. We've been expecting you."

"Here we go," Captain Marcello murmured.

Lisa nodded, gazing at the navigation display as she listened to the cheerful greeting. On the display, more or less exactly where Commodore Charnay had predicted, a cluster of icons labeled *Swenson One* had just appeared.

She checked the boards, doing a quick calculation. DTC's message had been transmitted simultaneously just over thirteen minutes ago, both to the newly arrived pirate fleet and to the Allied squadron. That meant Swenson One had received it 213 seconds earlier and undoubtedly replied by now. Presumably, Swenson's response had already been relayed to *Saintonge* by DTC, but she and *Damocles* wouldn't know about that for at least another nine minutes.

"I suppose it's a good thing we got here with two days to spare," Marcello added.

"Beg your pardon, Sir?" Lisa asked.

"Sorry—talking to myself," Marcello apologized. "I was just thinking that it's lucky we got here with two days to spare. If we hadn't, the Danakans would still be dragging their feet."

Lisa nodded wearily. "Yes, Sir. That they would."

Nobody had told the Danakan government that its star system was about to be turned into a battlefield, and System President Nelson's response to Commodore Charnay's news had been far less than happy.

And *extremely* less than cooperative.

Danak's population was still extremely small, most of it centered on Danak Alpha, the larger of the system's twin planets. At any given moment, though, at least a third of that population was distributed out in Bergen's Ring, an asteroid belt notable for its density and rich resources, its relatively short transit distance to Alpha, and the fact that it lay well inside the system's hyper limit. That meant the limit was a less-than-optimally long haul from the shipyard and mineral extraction platforms the Jerriais Consortium was busily building, but at the same time it also offered a certain degree of military security, since any potential attacker had at least a four-hour transit time even at two hundred gravities' acceleration. For a zero-zero solution, that went up to over five hours, which—in theory, at least—should give a defender time to respond.

It also gave time for the civilians in an invader's path to refugee out. Quite a few of them, Lisa noted, had done exactly that over the past eighteen hours.

The Jerriais shipyards and orbital mining facilities were the real reason for the system's development. Major concentrations of manufacturing, shipbuilding, and repair platforms would eventually be established in twelve equidistant nodal positions around the Ring, but at the moment only two were fully operational. A third was in the process of spinning up, however, and the initial hab module for a fourth had just been brought online. Danak was on its way to being one of the galaxy's success stories, which probably explained President Nelson's lack of enthusiasm at the prospect of entertaining such energetic visitors.

In fact, for almost twenty-four hours, she'd flatly refused to go along.

Her initial response had been to instruct Danak Traffic Control that Swenson was to be informed that he was not welcome, that Danak contained no missiles or upgraded launchers for his ships, and that a Havenite squadron was prepared to open fire upon him if he violated the system hyper-limit. The thought of what might happen to the Baird family had clearly weighed upon her, but her overriding responsibility

was to the citizens of her own star system, not to the
family of a Solarian merchant.

For some reason, no one in the Republic of Haven—
or aboard HMS *Damocles*—had considered the possibility of such a thoroughly rational attitude on the
Danakan government's part. Obviously, they should
have, and changing Nelson's mind had required all the
persuasiveness Commodore Charnay, Captain Katura,
and Jerriais representative Weissman could bring to bear.

It must have been an interesting discussion, Lisa
thought. From all accounts, President Nelson was a
stubborn woman, and she'd had a lot of good reasons
on her side.

The decisive point had probably been Charnay's
argument that it was in everyone's interests to take
a pirate force this powerful out of play. His appeal
to the collective security treaty between the Republic
and Danak had played its part, as well, although Lisa
suspected Weissman's position as the home office
representative of what was Danak's major employer
and an official member of the Republic's government
had played a rather larger role than any sense of
interstellar obligation on Nelson's part.

As for Katura, after recounting Max Baird's desperate
situation to the president, he'd left it to Weissman and
Charnay to convince her to go along while he took
Pacemaker to the gas refinery complex and refueling
station orbiting Helier, Danak's innermost gas giant.

It wasn't an unreasonable request—after all the
high-speed running around he'd done, his ship had
needed reactor mass badly. Still, Lisa wondered if
his prime motivation had been to get away from the
discussion. He'd made his personal anguish over the

Baird family's situation clear enough, and sitting on the sidelines while it was all hashed out yet again couldn't have been easy on him.

In the end, however, President Nelson had agreed that Traffic Control would cooperate in Operation Embuscade.

If Embuscade worked as designed, no one would be firing off missiles anywhere near important system infrastructure. That had been another factor in Nelson's decision to cooperate. But she'd flatly refused to commit any of the Danak System Navy's handful of lightly-armed corvettes to the battle. Instead, she'd ordered her naval commander to hold them in a covering position for Danak Alpha.

If anyone was getting killed in the Danak System, she clearly intended for the casualties to be incurred by the people who'd brought this trouble to her citizens in the first place.

Lisa Donnelly understood Nelson's attitude. But that hadn't made her any happier about it.

"I guess the important thing is that Nelson came onboard in the end," she said.

"Agreed," Marcello said. "I wish Massingill and her people had had a little longer to get settled in at Three, though. Still, she seems confident that everything's in place."

Lisa hissed softly between her teeth. "I hope she's right, Sir."

"Yes. So do I."

☆   ☆   ☆

"... Master Rowbtham had hoped Jerriais could accommodate you at Bergen One," Danak Traffic Control said, "but I'm afraid they're swamped right now. They can't clear any of their slips for at least a T-week, possibly two. It's our understanding your navy needs this upgrade expedited, correct?"

Gensonne ground his teeth. Of *course* he wanted it expedited.

But what was this about not being able to clear any slips for at least a week? Some last-minute play of Llyn's?

He forced back the reflexive flicker of suspicion. He was in control here, and Llyn knew it.

"Correct," he confirmed. "So what exactly are you saying? That Jerriais can't accommodate us?"

"Oh, no, Admiral, Jerriais can certainly accommodate you," Traffic Control said after another twenty-minutes lag. "They just can't take your ships at Bergen One. Most of the heavy work is going to have to be done at Bergen Two instead. Unfortunately, Two is still in its expansion phase and its capacity is considerably lower than One's. But all that means is that they'll only be able to handle four of your ships at a time. Or only three, if the first round includes both of your battlecruisers.

"However, Jerriais understands you need to expedite, and so they've arranged to undertake some of the preliminary work at Bergen Three. They can't install the full suite of systems you require there, but they *can* strip out the old systems and offload your old ordnance, which would get that part of the installation out of the way. Secretary Charnay and Ms. Dostoyevsky have run the numbers and concluded that if you send one battlecruiser and one heavy cruiser to Three it would ultimately cut the time for your second set of refits at least in half."

Gensonne frowned as he studied his navigation plot, where Astrogation had brought up the icons of the new destinations. It wasn't as bad as it could have been, but it was bad enough. Bergen 2 and Bergen 3 were on almost opposite sides of the primary, Bergen 3 laying roughly 16.2 LM to port of *Odin*'s current vector, Bergen 2 laying 23.27 LM off the Volsungs' starboard bow as the Volsungs continued heading for Bergen 1.

He didn't like putting that much separation between his units, especially since he hadn't planned on splitting them up at all. On top of that, he knew how local governments and shipyards functioned out here, especially with someone they expected to be a one-time visitor. One of their favorite ploys was to surreptitiously damage or incapacitate critical systems and then charge through the ceiling to fix the damage their techs had fortuitously discovered.

It would take a lot of nerve to try to gouge an Andermani fleet that way. But the Empire was a long way from Danak, and the locals might just think they could take even Uncle Gustav's money and run.

He swiveled toward the com screen he had tied to *Banshee*'s bridge. "You heard?"

"Of course," Llyn said. "Doesn't sound all that unreasonable to me."

"Yeah, well, *you're* not the one being told to split up his fleet," Gensonne growled. "Who's this Secretary of Industry Charnay, anyway? One of the people you're going to have to bribe?"

"I told you, there was no way to be sure who it would be," Llyn said with clearly strained patience. "The last time I was here, the Secretary of Industry was a woman named Bradshaw. But that was a long time ago. According to my records, though, there *was* a Charnay—I don't have a first name—as an under-secretary in that department." He dropped his gaze to something off screen. "He's apparently a trained engineer with a strong background in shipbuilding." He looked up again. "Does sound like he's our guy."

"I'm not real fond of *sounds like*," Gensonne said warningly.

"Don't worry about it," Llyn advised. "Remember what he said about relaying the President's welcome? That's the kind of thing someone says when they want a face-to-face. A *quiet* face-to-face."

"So that they can collect their credit chip?"

"Exactly."

Gensonne frowned. Still, the analysis sounded reasonable. Of course, it didn't say anything one way or the other about the locals' possible avarice.

On the other hand, if he played his cards right he might have a way to find out before they got their hands too deeply into his pockets.

"I would prefer to continue to keep both my battle-cruisers together and under my supervision while the work is being carried out," he said into the com microphone. "However, Ms. Dostoyevsky's suggestion for expediting the prep work sounds reasonable. Therefore, I propose..."

☆　　☆　　☆

Llyn's computer pinged. Listening with half an ear to Gensonne's response to DTC, he checked the display.

His slightly-out-of-date records indicated that Adelaide Bradshaw was still Secretary of Industry in the Danak System Government. There was no mention of an undersecretary named Charnay.

But the records *did* list a Captain Gustav Charnay of the Republic of Haven Navy.

He huffed out a silent sigh of relief. He'd known that Katura had come through the minute Traffic Control greeted *"Winterfeldt"* as an expected arrival. Now, if the Charnay DTC had named was the same one as in his database, it would appear Haven had bought the kidnapping story and decided to respond with force.

Whether they'd responded with sufficient force remained to be seen. But they probably wouldn't have come if they didn't think they had it under control.

Though this ploy to split up Gensonne's force didn't sound promising. If they needed to divide the Volsungs into more bite-sized pieces—

"Sir?" Rhamas's voice murmured from the intercom. "We have a burst transmission from *Pacemaker*."

Llyn peered at the plot and the caret marking the transmission's sender. The ship showed no ID code, but it was well to port of the Volsungs' current vector, about two minutes inside the hyper-limit on a heading for Danak Alpha from the vicinity of Helier.

Or, rather, it *had* been heading for Danak Alpha. Now, suddenly, the ship had stopped accelerating and was actively decelerating, obviously hoping to stay clear of any possible confrontation.

It also meant that, assuming the diversion to Bergen 2 worked and *Pacemaker* held her current heading, Katura was going to land in almost exactly the right spot to complete his part of the operation.

Things could still go south in a major way, of course. But between Katura's smooth competence and Gensonne's obsessive punctuality, all the pieces on the board seemed to be where Llyn wanted them.

Hopefully, Haven had sent along enough firepower to take care of the Volsungs once and for all. If not,

Llyn himself would be able to make sure that whatever Gensonne knew about Axelrod and its interest in Manticore, that information would go no further.

"Decrypt?" he asked Rhamas.

"Coming through now, Sir," *Banshee*'s captain said, and fresh text appeared on Llyn's display.

Even transmitting over a relatively short distance and from well to one side of the Volsung formation, there was always the chance that a burst transmission over a tightly focused com laser might find unintended ears. But Katura knew that, and had chosen an encryption similar to the ones the Jerriais Consortium used for their own internal communications. Anyone who noticed it would probably assume it was routine traffic.

Havenite force under Commodore Gustav Charnay. One BC, three CAs, five DDs, one FG. Also attached one Manticoran DD.

So Charnay had been promoted to commodore since Llyn's last file update. Not really surprising.

What *was* surprising was that the Havenite force had a Manticoran destroyer in the mix.

Llyn scowled. And if there was one RMN ship, were there others? Maybe even a whole fleet that Katura didn't know about?

Probably not. Still, it was a possibility Llyn couldn't reject out of hand. Gensonne's after-action report had indicated that the RMN he'd left behind had been considerably more mauled than the RMN that Llyn had encountered a couple of weeks later. He'd downplayed that discrepancy in his conversations with the Volsung admiral, but it was a puzzle he hadn't yet sorted out.

Llyn had detected five battlecruisers; Gensonne had insisted he'd left behind only three. That meant two of them must have been visitors, almost certainly Havenite, no matter what their transponders had said.

So far that was the best sense he'd been able to make of the puzzle. Still, it fit with the Republic's efforts to establish a collective security arrangement in what was coming to be known as the Haven Quadrant. Granted, their presence at that particular time had been annoyingly fortuitous, and there was still the matter of the Manticoran transponder codes.

Still, what mattered was that Manticore surely wouldn't have risked sending any of its own heavy ships away from the home system when they had no way of telling when their attackers might return. Detaching one or two lighter units for joint operations with Haven, on the other hand, made a great deal of sense.

In a way, that was too bad. Llyn would have preferred Haven to have a crushing force advantage, and a horde of Manticoran ships supporting them would have been a welcome addition.

On the other hand, the presence of an unexpected Manticoran ship could prove problematic. Gensonne had disguised himself a bit—at Llyn's insistence—but it was a quick and rudimentary disguise, not nearly up to Llyn's own standards. A sharp-eyed Manticoran might be able to see past the Prussian-style mustache and prominent cheek scar, and a sharp-eared one might recognize the voice of the man who'd invaded their space and called for their King's surrender. If that happened, the Manticorans might be able to persuade the Havenites to offer Gensonne his life in exchange for information.

Fortunately, thanks to Hester, Llyn still held the hole card.

"Sir, Imbar is signaling the rest of the Volsung force," Rhamas reported. "He's warning them to keep a close eye on us and be ready in case we make a run for it. Apparently, Gensonne doesn't trust us."

"I'm so very disappointed. Any replies?"

"*Copperhead* and *Fomalhaut* report they each have their laser manned and a missile prepped for launch," Rhamas replied. "Imbar's warning them not to paint us with active targeting, lest Danak wonder why they're targeting their own freighter. *Fomalhaut* is offended that Imbar feels the need to point out the obvious . . . *Copperhead* seconds that opinion, but with more profanity."

Llyn smiled. And Hester probably *still* thought all of the little jobs he'd given her over the past few months, such as hacking Gensonne's com encryptions, had been just busy work.

"I think we can trust them to hold their fire, at least for now," he told Rhamas. He looked at the master plot, watching as vectors and projected arrival times began to shift. "It looks like about three and a half hours until Exodus."

"Yes, Sir," Rhamas said. "I'll be sorry to see her go."

"You'll get over it," Llyn assured him. "And don't worry. I'll get you an even shinier toy when this is done."

☆   ☆   ☆

"However, Ms. Dostoyevsky's suggestion for expediting the prep work sounds reasonable," the pirate admiral's voice came from *Damocles*'s bridge speaker. "Therefore, I propose a compromise. My main body is altering course for Bergen Two now, but I'll be detaching three of my cruisers—*Mollwitz*, *Burkersdorf*, and *Rossbach*—to Bergen Three. Three heavy cruisers should be about the same workload as one battlecruiser and one heavy cruiser, and that would allow me to personally supervise *Winterfeldt* and *Boyen*'s refits."

"Damn," Marcello murmured, looking across at Lisa.

Lisa nodded. She'd already pulled up the ship list Captain Katura had provided, but she didn't really need it. Like her captain, she'd committed it to memory, and *Mollwitz, Burkersdorf,* and *Rossbach* were more properly known as *Adder, Copperhead,* and *Mamba,* Swenson's three *Thu'ban*-class ships.

"Well, *that* was unexpected," Marcello continued.

Lisa nodded again, wondering how Brigadier Massingill and her commandos were going to handle this one.

Bergen 3 consisted of two active platforms and two more still in the process of construction. Massingill's operations plan had divided her troops evenly between the operational platforms, under the assumption that she would face only two ships. *Three* of them would not only spread her available combat power thinner on at least one platform, but it also offered a greater opportunity for the timing to go awry.

Still, as Commodore Charnay had pointed out, if anyone could handle that situation it would be Massingill and the 303rd. Heavy cruisers were also less likely than battlecruisers to have sizable ground combat components aboard, which should offset some of the brigadier's dispersal problems.

"I assume you heard that, Captain Marcello?" Charnay said from the captain's com display.

"Yes, Sir," Marcello replied. "Has DTC responded yet?"

"Unfortunately, there wasn't time for them to run it past us before they did," Charnay said out. "They couldn't very well tell him *no* without a good reason. After all, on the face of it, it's a completely logical suggestion."

"Wonderful," Marcello murmured.

"Agreed," Charnay said. "This is going to make things a lot trickier for the Brigadier. And unfortunately, she's not the only one whose timing it's likely to impact."

☆   ☆   ☆

"There they go," Captain Imbar growled as the designated cruisers headed for Bergen 3. "Von Belling and Michelson behaving like hot dogs as usual. Should I com them to slow it down?"

"No, let them have their fun," Gensonne said, eyeing the plot. "Besides, everyone knows the Andermani do things better than anyone else in the galaxy. Let them show the Danakans how good they really are."

He didn't bother to add that the main reason he'd chosen them for detachment was that nobody else could keep up with them anyway.

The *Thu'bans* were the fastest ships in the Volsungs' inventory, with a six-gravity maximum acceleration advantage over even *Odin*, and compensators that were equally robust. As a result, their captains routinely operated them at eighty-five percent power, rather than the more normal eighty percent, whenever they could cut loose from the rest of the fleet's apron strings. Given their primary role of defending the battlecruisers from missiles, that didn't happen very often, and they relished any opportunities that came their way.

And so as *Odin* continued towards Bergen 2 at the formation's stately 185 gravities, *Adder*, *Copperhead*, and *Mamba* accelerated steadily away from them at 223 gravities.

"Just make sure von Belling and Schneider know they're not supposed to let any of Danak's techs on board until Michelson's had a chance to see how competent they are," Gensonne added. "I don't want the locals getting near anything critical until we're positive this isn't an attempt to hit us up for extra fees before they dock."

"I doubt that's really necessary, Admiral," Llyn spoke up from the link to *Banshee*. "You may be a one-time customer, but Master Rowbtham is local and does a fair amount of business in Danak. You're also rather forgetting that you're units of the Andermani Navy, and no one wants to get blacklisted by Gustav Anderman. His personal disapproval aside, his word still carries a lot of weight with the Solarians."

"Maybe," Gensonne said curtly. "But I'm not taking any chances. I'll be keeping my eye on things at Bergen Two. Von Belling and the others had damn well better do likewise."

☆   ☆   ☆

"*That* much faster, Sir?" Marcello asked.

"That much faster," Charnay confirmed grimly.

Lisa winced as she punched numbers into her console. When they'd come up with the plan to divert some of Swenson's units they'd assumed that one of the battlecruisers would have been included. Ideally, Swenson would have taken his flagship into the trap, enabling Massingill to capture him and decapitate his entire force. The more likely scenario, though, had been that he would detach *Boyen*, otherwise known as *Loki*, whose maximum safe acceleration was only 185 gees.

At the moment the three cruisers—now designated *Swenson Two*—had separated from the main formation, Swenson One had been 9.84 LM from her original destination at Bergen 1. That had put it 23.27 LM from Bergen 2 and 16.2 LM from Bergen 3. From that starting point, *Loki* would have been seven hours and two minutes from a zero-zero with Bergen 3.

But at the *Thu'bans'* higher acceleration, they were only six hours and twenty-three minutes away. That meant Swenson Two would arrive thirty-nine minutes earlier than *Loki* could.

Which meant Massingill's attack might well have to begin over a half hour earlier than the plan had assumed.

Even worse, the rest of the pirate fleet would be thirty-nine minutes—and a solid 4.9 million kilometers—farther away, and traveling 4,254 KPS faster than Commodore Charnay's battle plan had allowed for.

Lisa punched more numbers, studying them closely. Swenson One would still be too deep into the inner-system to kill its velocity and accelerate back out of engagement range. But if the balloon went up early at Bergen 3 and the rest of the bad guys were smart enough to cut and run the instant it did, it would probably make intercepting them more difficult. Depending on how *much* too soon it went up, it could make things very difficult indeed.

On the other hand, the timing here had always been problematic. Even *Loki* would have reached Bergen 3 eighty-four minutes before the rest of the fleet reached Bergen 2. The transmission lag between Bergen 3 and Bergen 2 was 15.8 minutes, which would have bought some of that time back, but that had still left an interval of well over an hour in which *Loki* might have warned her consorts they were headed into a trap.

No one had been willing to assume that Massingill's people could take out two ships before at least one of them got a message off. Accordingly, they'd designed a carefully choreographed set of procedures intended to burn at least forty to fifty minutes between *Loki's* arrival and her actual docking. That would have kicked off the boarding attempt only about ten minutes before the rest of the pirates were at Commodore Charnay's desired range from Bergen 2, at which point any warning messages from either section of their forces would have crossed one another in transmission.

That thirty-nine-minute difference was going to make the timing a lot trickier. But that was the reality, Lisa knew as she watched CIC project the pirates' newly diverging vectors onto *Damocles's* main plot. They would all just have to deal with it,

☆   ☆   ☆

And of course, right in the middle of Gensonne's work on rethinking and reworking his schedule, Llyn's face popped up on his com display. "What do you want?" Gensonne growled. "I'm busy. Thanks to your helpful friends."

"I understand," Llyn said in one of those soothing tones he used when he wanted something or didn't think Gensonne would understand some complicated plan he was going to pitch. "And I don't want to add any extra complications to your life. I just wanted you to know that I've received a coded burst transmission."

Gensonne sat up straighter. "What kind of transmission?"

"It's not a problem," Llyn assured him hastily. "Quite the contrary. It's merely confirmation that Secretary Charnay is, indeed, the one waiting for our credit chip."

"Good." That particular concern had been pushed into the back of Gensonne's mind by everything else, but it had never entirely left. "So we're good to go?"

"Mostly," Llyn said. "It appears we'll also have to deal with a couple of yard foremen. Again, not a problem, but I'll need to figure out how much extra this is going to cost."

"And why are you bothering *me* with this?"

"Because you need to be aware that there could be a brief delay when we reach the yard platforms while the arrangements are being made."

"Really," Gensonne said, turning up the voltage in his stare. "Have I ever mentioned how much I dislike delays?"

"I'm not particularly fond of them either," Llyn said with a scowl. "Especially when my original instructions were crystal-clear. Unfortunately, there doesn't seem to have been anything Katura could have done about it. We're going to need to discuss the foremen's demands, then authorize their payments, *then* find a way to slip the money into their accounts without Jerriais bookkeepers noticing."

"You're not making me any happier," Gensonne warned.

"Don't worry, it's nothing I haven't done dozens of time before," Llyn assured him. "But it's likely to keep me busy for the next few hours, and I wanted you to know why I'll be on the com a lot and therefore why I might not be instantly available if you need my help with something."

Gensonne snorted. Like he would *need* the little man's help at this point.

"Fine," he said. "You're the one signing the slips. Go see how many credits you have to fork over this time."

"How many credits my *employer* has to fork over, you mean," Llyn replied, and Gensonne suppressed a smile at the irritation in the other's tone. Apparently, Llyn didn't like being gouged any more than he did, even when it wasn't his own personal money.

"Whatever," he said. "Just make sure the details are settled before we're ready to dock. I want to get this show on the road."

"Of course, Admiral," Llyn assured him. "As do I."

☆   ☆   ☆

"Damn," Brigadier Jean Massingill muttered under her breath as she punched numbers and flung names back and forth across her tablet. "Damn, damn, damn, and damn again."

The schedule had called for her to delay the pirates' incoming battlecruiser forty to fifty minutes before getting her commandos aboard and launching their attack. Now they needed to drag that out another thirty to forty minutes. The plan had called for two teams, one each for a battlecruiser and heavy cruiser. Now, it was going to be three teams for three *Thu'ban* heavy cruisers.

So not only did she need to find a way to tapdance for a full hour and a half, she also needed to split two teams into three. And those three teams needed to take a crash course in *Thu'bans* architecture.

"Brigadier?"

Massingill looked up to see Major Elsie Dorrman striding up to her, another tablet in her hand. "Yes?"

"I've pulled up specs for the *Thu'bans*," Dorrman said. "Everyone's looking them over, and Bastonge and Danzer are mapping out the routes and procedures."

"Good," Massingill said. Major Bastonge and Captain Danzer had been the leaders of the two thirty-man teams who would have taken on the pirates.

Only now each of their teams would be reduced to twenty. That was not a hell of a lot against a shipful of pirates.

"At least they won't have to cut their way out of cargo containers this time," Dorrman reminded her.

"True," Massingill said, feeling a ghost of a smile at the memory of the Solway operation. That one had gone off without a hitch.

But that one had had extensive planning ahead of time, and no last-minute surprises.

"What about the teams?" she asked. "Have you and the others figured out how to split them up?"

"We've come up with two options," Dorrman said, handing over her tablet. "The first would leave Bastonge's and Danzer's core groups intact. The downside is that would make the third team mostly made up of less experienced fighters."

Massingill scowled. With the bulk of the 303rd off on training exercises elsewhere in the Republic, these sixty men and women were all she'd been able to scrape together on the short notice she'd been given. They'd had a few days in transit to train together, but they were far from being fully coherent units.

"The second would strip five commandos from each

of the core groups to form the core of the third," Dorrman continued. "That would lower the experience level of Groups One and Two, but give Three a more solid center."

"Understood," Massingill said, studying the options. "Do you have a recommendation on Three's commander?"

Dorrman shrugged slightly. "The only logical choice is me."

Massingill suppressed a sigh. Yes, she'd pretty well seen that one coming.

Only she didn't want it. Dorrman was experienced, but she was older than the average 303rd and therefore somewhat lower on the strength and stamina scales. Ironically, perhaps, that same age detriment—along with her gender—tended to make opponents underestimate her. That gave her a huge advantage in the ambush and subterfuge categories, which was why Massingill had set her up as one of the lower-level techs with Danzer's team. Getting close to the people in charge of critical systems was one of Dorrman's specialties, and Massingill had hoped to take advantage of those skills.

But she was right. Experience and leadership, not to mention her rank, argued for Dorrman commanding Group Three.

"And your recommendation on the split?"

"Leave the other two groups their cores and give me the newbies," Dorrman said without hesitation. "As long as I have Rushkoff, I can make it work."

Massingill nodded. Rushkoff was one of their best-trained ship techs, and would probably be the first to get the *Thu'ban* details under his belt. On top of that, he had a gift of gab that enabled him to convince the most hardened skeptic that he knew exactly what he was talking about.

"All right," she said, handing the tablet back. "Get on it. I'll go corral the yard dogs and figure out how we're going to vamp for an extra half hour."

"If all else fails, Ma'am," Dorrman offered, "you could always start reminiscing about the good old days."

"I'll keep that in mind, Major," Massingill said. "Go prep your team."

CHAPTER THIRTY-THREE

"COMMANDER?" LIEUTENANT WOLFGANG MOELLER, ATO OF the Volsung battlecruiser *Tarantel*, called back across the bridge. "Something odd, sir."

Lieutenant Commander Marco Feyman, *Tarantel's* tactical officer, looked up from his novel, a trickle of hopeful interest rising in him. Duty at Walther Prime's *Schmiede* space station was about as cripplingly boring as anything the Volsung Mercenaries had to offer, and anything that could lighten that uniformly gray lifescape would be welcome.

Though probably it was nothing more than a twitchy reading on one of *Tarantel's* systems. Still, anything was better than nothing.

"What is it, Moeller?" he asked.

"We've just picked up an incoming impeller wedge, Sir," Moeller replied, turning his head to look over his shoulder at Feyman. "I checked the schedule update from *Schmiede*, and we're not expecting anyone for at least two months."

"I see."

Feyman bookmarked his page, unstrapped, and swam leisurely across the bridge to Tactical. He grabbed one of the handholds on the back of Moeller's chair and frowned past the younger man's shoulder at the icon gleaming on the tactical plot.

There was a wedge there, all right. And it was heading inward.

Straight toward the Volsung station.

Moeller had already pulled up Captain Hauser's last two schedule updates on a different display. Feyman ran an eye over them, confirmed that there were no visitors expected, and looked back at the icon.

Odd, certainly. Still, hardly a cause for panic. The mercenary business didn't run on a public transport system's schedule, after all. There could be any number of reasons a single ship—from the impeller signature, he tentatively identified it as either a destroyer or a cruiser—could be incoming to Walther.

At the moment, though, he couldn't think of any reason that made sense. If everything had gone according to schedule, Admiral Gensonne had only just now arrived at Danak. He couldn't possibly have gotten there, learned anything important enough to justify sending a courier back to Walther, and gotten the courier here by now. And it was highly unlikely that anyone else would be sending them couriers.

So the odds were that whoever this was, it wasn't a Volsung.

Which raised all sorts of interesting questions of its own.

"Com?" he called over his shoulder. "Raise *Schmiede*. Inform Captain Hauser that we've detected an incoming impeller wedge, inbound at just over four thousand

KPS, and accelerating at one-niner-zero gravities. She's about—what do you make the range, Wolfgang?"

"Call it fourteen-point-niner light-minutes, Sir," Moeller replied. "She's just over four million kilometers inside the limit."

"Append that information to your message, Com."

"Yes, Sir."

Feyman shifted his eyes to the status board. At the moment, *Leuchtfeuer* was down for long overdue maintenance on her alpha nodes, but her sisters *Heliograph* and *Semaphore*, the designated ready-duty ships, were properly on station. Whoever this intruder was, they could at least give it a proper Volsung welcome.

"Think they've seen us yet, Sir?" Moeller asked quietly, looking up at Feyman.

"You tell me," Feyman countered. Moeller had promise, but he was also young and inexperienced. This would be a good exercise for him.

"Yes, Sir." Moeller considered. "Probably not."

"Why?"

"Only four ships have hot nodes at the moment: *Heliograph*, *Semaphore*, and two of the freighters," Moeller said. "It would be very difficult for them to pick up anything other than an impeller wedge at that range."

"Anything else?" Feyman asked.

"Well . . . it's not exactly scientific," Moeller hedged, "but if that's not one of our ships, they'd be crazy to head in-system if they had any clue what was waiting for them here."

"Good," Feyman complimented him. The kid definitely had promise. "All right. If they're headed for a zero-zero with the planet—which looks likely from their projected vector—they'll hit turnover in another hundred and sixty minutes. By that time, they may be able to see more. If they don't turn around *before* then, they're pretty much committed to coming all the way into our parlor."

"So if they break off before turnover, that'll mean they've definitely seen us?" Moeller suggested.

"Or they suddenly remembered they forgot to turn off the stove back home," Feyman said. "And if they leave things too close to turnover, they'll still wind up in our range even if they then wise up and run for it."

Moeller nodded. "So no matter how it goes, they're in for an unpleasant surprise."

"That they are." Feyman made a face. And speaking of unpleasantries . . . "Com, you'd better ask Captain Stoffel to join us on the bridge."

He leaned a little closer to Moeller. "We're going to need him to sit on Hauser," he added softly.

The ATO nodded. "Yes, Sir."

There was a reason Soren Hauser commanded *Schmiede*, an orbiting station well away from the pointy end of things. The base commander was an excellent logistician, a meticulous record-keeper, and set a decent table for his fellow officers.

But he wasn't the calmest and most methodical combat officer in the history of the galaxy.

Still, Feyman thought as he looked back at the icon, just how calm and methodical did someone have to be to deal with a waddling duck?

☆   ☆   ☆

"Why aren't you bringing up your impellers?" Captain Soren Hauser demanded, his face starting to turn a familiar shade of red as it glared out from the com screen on *Tarantel*'s command deck.

Schmiede's CO sounded distinctly nervous, Captain Ditmar Stoffel noted without any particular surprise. Feyman had been right about Hauser's probable reaction, although it was a bit hard for Stoffel to understand exactly how even he could panic over a single incoming cruiser. Especially one so stupid—or so pig-ignorant— that it clearly had no idea what it was accelerating into.

Fortunately, Stoffel was senior to him, which meant Hauser was going to be denied the opportunity to screw this one up.

"Because, Captain," he said, trying to sound as if he didn't consider Hauser a complete idiot, "our visitor is still an hour from his turnover point for a zero-zero with Prime. I'd prefer for him to get past that point before he figures out what he's poking his nose into. The closer he is to turnover, the less likely he'll be able to evade us when we move out in pursuit."

"And if he gets close enough to fire off a couple of missiles?" Hauser demanded. "You may not realize how damned near naked *Schmiede* is."

Stoffel pursed his lips. There, at least, the other had a point.

The base itself was completely unarmed. Its only defense was the pair of missile platforms floating in space over a thousand kilometers away from it. And while those platforms were great at offensive fire, each mounted only a single counter missile launcher and a single autocannon to defend both themselves and the base.

And with no impeller wedges or sidewalls on either base or platforms, it was for damn sure none of them would be taking evasive action.

So if the intruder decided to fire missiles at them,

the chance that something would get through was a definite, even high, probability. Assuming *Tarantel* and the other ships didn't prevent that from happening.

"I understand," Stoffel soothed. "Don't worry. Even if he comes all the way in, we'll be able to nail him long before he starts shooting. More likely, at some point he'll realize he's bitten off more than he can chew, and then his full attention will be on getting his skin out in one piece."

"I don't like it," Hauser rumbled. "Why should somebody decide to come buzzing around out here? And *especially* when the Admiral's away?"

"Assuming any of his personnel survive—and I'm feeling generous; I'll at least give him the option of surrendering—we'll ask them," Stoffel replied. "Whatever their thinking, though, they obviously don't have a clue what they're facing. Even without *Tarantel*, we have more than enough mobile units to deal with a single cruiser."

☆   ☆   ☆

"Turnover in three minutes, Ma'am," Lieutenant Lukanov announced into the quiet of *Casey*'s bridge.

"Very good," Clegg replied.

It was odd, Travis thought, how utterly calm the captain sounded.

To some extent, she was like this during training exercises. But even there, he'd always been able to hear the tension bubbling below the surface, the hawkeyed attention to detail that would get some hapless officer or tech a hot-to-icy reprimand in the after-action analysis.

But there was none of that now. Not today. Not facing an exercise, but actual combat.

Just as Travis himself had realized a TO's chair was where he was supposed to be, perhaps the command chair was Captain Trina Clegg's designated place. She'd spent three decades of her life preparing to defend her Star Kingdom.

Now, in this moment, all that training and experience was going to come together.

Maybe this was a turning point in her own character. Or maybe she'd go back to being prickly once the shooting stopped.

Unless they managed to get killed during it.

Travis shook his head to himself. Now *there* was a cheerful thought.

"Turnover in thirty seconds, Ma'am," Woodburn reported.

"Execute on profile," Clegg said with that same calm.

"Aye, aye, Ma'am. Executing...Now."

HMS *Casey* flipped end for end and began burning off her speed toward Walther Prime at the same hundred and ninety gravities.

☆   ☆   ☆

"And *that*, Captain Hauser," Captain Stoffel said quietly under his breath, "is why I didn't bring up any wedges."

Feyman smiled tightly in agreement. He was actually a bit surprised the intruder hadn't already spotted *Tarantel*, despite the battlecruiser's inactive impeller nodes, with the range down to only seven and a half light-minutes. But that was still over 135.9 million kilometers, he reminded himself. Quite a few things could get lost in the background noise at that range. Especially with all of the emissions coming from *Schmiede*.

And if their sensor resolution was so bad they'd missed *Tarantel*, it was highly probable that they'd put the orbital station's missile platforms down to additional bases or simply orbital warehouses, as well.

Feyman smiled again. That should make Hauser happy.

☆   ☆   ☆

"About *now*, I think, Captain Rhamas," Llyn said thoughtfully.

Three hours and forty minutes had passed since Gensonne's force had split up. During that time, *Banshee*'s velocity had risen to 23,999 KPS, and she'd traveled just over 158,397,400 kilometers towards Bergen 2. In thirty-three minutes Gensonne was due to begin decelerating in his approach to the Danak shipbuilding platforms.

It was time for Exodus.

"Yes, Sir," Rhamas said. "The programming's locked in on both the primary and the backup systems, and I've double-checked everything. The only thing I'm really worried about is the com side. What if Gensonne insists on talking to you? Those recordings aren't perfect, you know."

"The computers will be up to the task," Llyn said. "Worst-case, he gets suspicious and pushes the button early, at which point *Banshee* does its magic trick and everybody on both sides wonders what the hell just happened. Not as neat and tidy as I'd like, but it would do the job."

"Yes, Sir," Rhamas said. He was still a little doubtful, Llyn knew.

But there was no need for either doubt or worry. Axelrod believed in providing its operatives the best computer support available, and Llyn had taken full advantage of those capabilities during the voyage to Danak. He and Rhamas had spent hours refining the list of keywords the software would look for in any incoming transmission. They'd spent even more hours providing the computer with prerecorded responses, both audio and video.

Unfortunately, those responses had to be fairly nonspecific, which was where the fancy software came in, choosing which message to use in any given set of circumstances. In a pinch, the software could also manufacture its own CGI talking heads if the prerecorded messages weren't adequate for the task.

Llyn wasn't crazy about using the latter, mindful of its weaknesses. But in this case he doubted anyone would have time to do the kind of scrub that would unmask it.

Actually, Llyn was rather looking forward to having Gensonne carry on a conversation with his computer doppleganger. After all, he'd been setting up for that the entire trip from Walther, making a habit of letting his attention apparently drift away during conversations, acting preoccupied and then suddenly jumping back in.

Gensonne had probably assumed he was doing that simply to annoy him. But what the Volsung believed didn't matter. The pattern had been established, and that was all Llyn cared about.

A shame, really, that it had to end this way. It wasn't often that Llyn came across someone so easy to manipulate.

Taking one last look around, Llyn picked up his minicomp and the single briefcase racked beside his console.

"Time to go, Captain." He gestured toward the hatch. "After you."

☆   ☆   ☆

Massingill's delaying tactics—with all the supposed miscommunication, lost orders, missing supervisor signatures, mislaid tether connectors, inexperienced platform crews, tug malfunctions, and enough official and long-winded apologies to fill a light cruiser—was over and had been successfully played. The three pirate heavy cruisers were docked at their respective platforms at Bergen 3 and the boarding tunnels extended. No one aboard, as far as Massingill had been able to ascertain, suspected a thing.

And then, completely unexpectedly, the whole plan started to unravel.

"That's ridiculous," Massingill said, staring at the displays. "That's what they're *here* for."

"I know," Major Bastonge murmured over the com. "I don't understand it either. All they said was that no one was getting aboard *Mollwitz* and *Burkersdorf* until *Rossbach*'s commander had satisfied himself that the techs knew what they were doing and weren't going to screw anything up."

Massingill ground her teeth. "Probably worried they'll get charged for extra breakage."

Which made no sense at all. Just because one team didn't screw up or start stealing everything that wasn't nailed down didn't mean the next team wouldn't, no matter how long they made that team wait.

"Can you see the hatch?"

"Oh, yeah, it's right there straight down the tunnel ahead of us," Bastonge confirmed. "Sealed tight."

Massingill shifted her eyes to one of the other

monitors. Theoretically, that meant Bastonge could pull back until such time as the pirates graciously allowed them access. If he could get to Dorrman's dock fast enough...

But he couldn't. On Platform Three's monitor she could see that *Rossbach*—or as Massingill knew her, *Mamba*—had already opened her hatch. Dorrman and her three-man team were prepping their equipment cart and getting ready to head across the boarding tunnel. Even if Bastonge or Danzer could magically teleport across Bergen 3, the fact that Dorrman's techs were suddenly being replaced by someone else was bound to raise eyebrows, questions, and suspicions.

Bottom line was that Massingill's very best teams were going to have to sit on their hands while Dorrman and her group walked into enemy territory alone.

And if they screwed up, and the alarm was given to all three ships, the 303rd might lose two of its intended targets. Maybe even all three.

Massingill took a deep breath. Plan A had been sidetracked. On to Plan B.

"Sergeant Frijtom, you copying all this?" she asked.

"Yes, Brigadier," Frijtom confirmed, his voice muffled and oddly echoey inside his heavy assault armor. "You want us to do a full breach?"

"Not yet, but be ready," Massingill said. "We'll give Dorrman a chance first to beguile their way aboard *Mamba* and lock the hatch open for her assault team. But if that blips and the alarm goes up, I want you ready to charge in and try to open them up the hard way. You got that, Bastonge?"

"Yes, Ma'am," the Team One commander said. "You want me to call it, or will you?"

"I'll call it," Massingill said. She was the only one with clear contact with Dorrman and Team Three, which meant she would be the first to know if the balloon had gone up. "Same instructions for you, Broussard," she added.

"Understood, Ma'am," the leader of Danzer's heavy-weapons attack leader confirmed. "We'll be ready whenever you need us."

"Copy as well," Danzer said. "Also, I'm seeing just one camera by *Copperhead*'s hatch that's inside the tunnel. If we can blind that one, it'll give the breach team a few extra seconds before anyone inside knows what's happening."

"Same here," Bastonge said. "Give us a few seconds' head's-up, and we can take care of it."

"Understood," Massingill said.

She would try to give them those seconds. She really would.

Because the entire plan was suddenly on the tightrope here. Plan A had counted on the disguised tech squads getting aboard at the same time and then being able to simultaneously lock the hatches open and let the armored full-assault teams swarm inside. Now, only Dorrman's team would be able to follow that procedure.

The catch was that once the alarm went up, *Adder* and *Copperhead* would still have a solid hullmetal hatch between themselves and the commandos. In theory, they could probably breach the hatches within ninety seconds ... but ninety seconds was enough time for a competent commander to figure out a good counter response.

It was more than enough time for an incompetent one to panic.

And for an armed ship with hot nodes tethered to

a floating space dock, there were a *lot* of nasty forms a panic reaction could take.

Dorrman and her people were on the move now, rolling their cart down the tunnel. "Good luck," Massingill murmured. "All of you."

☆   ☆   ☆

"Elsie Dorrman," the head of *Mamba*'s six-man reception committee growled out Dorrman's name as he stared at her ID tag.

"That's right," Dorrman confirmed, looking casually around the airlock area. There had been two cameras outside the hatch, one of them partially obscured by the boarding tunnel, but there was only one in here.

And it was right below one of the floodlights the pirates had rigged up to point at the hatch.

Mentally, she shook her head. No doubt they thought having a light they could shine in an attacker's eyes as he charged through the hatchway would be to their advantage. No doubt they also thought that putting their camera beneath it would help hide it from view.

But with the light currently running at maybe half power, putting out just enough to illuminate the visitors, neither half of the ploy actually worked. In fact, in this instance, they'd have done better to shut the light down completely.

She looked over at Corporal Rushkoff, currently standing stolidly for his own hard-eyed visual exam. She caught his eye, nodded microscopically toward the light and camera, got his confirming microscopic nod in return, and settled down to wait for the reception committee to finish with the other two jumpsuited members of their team.

"Fine," the *Mamba*'s spokesman growled at last.

Maybe he wasn't trying to be intimidating; maybe that was just his normal voice. "Two things. One: you keep your hands to yourselves. You don't mess with anything that doesn't have to do with missile launch systems. Two: we'll be with you every minute you're aboard to make sure you keep your hands to yourselves. Got that? What?"

"Sorry," Rushkoff said, sounding a little confused as he lowered the hand he'd raised. "But I think that was actually *three* points."

For a moment the pirate seemed at a loss for words. He looked back at his silent companions, then back at Rushkoff, then finally at Dorrman. "Point Four: smart mouths get spaced. Got that?"

"Certainly," Dorrman said with just the right degree of nervousness. "We don't want trouble with representatives of the Andermani Empire."

A flicker crossed the pirate's face, as if he'd momentarily forgotten the role he was playing. "Right," he growled. "Let's go—"

"You got that, Rushkoff?" Dorrman interrupted, turning a two-barreled glare at the corporal. "Because I'm fed up with your games, too, and I swear that if *they* don't space you *I* will."

"Yeah, yeah," Rushkoff said, rolling his eyes. "Heard it before. So has my uncle."

"If you *dare*—" Dorrman broke off, and for a long moment she and Rushkoff stared at each other, Dorrman glaring, Rushkoff responding with smug innocence. Out of the corner of her eye, she saw the other two techs quietly moving the equipment cart off to the side of the hatchway, their attitude clearly that of innocent bystanders who wanted to keep it that way.

Finally, with a muttered curse, Dorrman turned back to the pirates. "Sorry," she muttered. "Personnel problem."

"So *now* are you ready?" the spokesman asked. Dorrman had been wrong; his growly voice could also contain sarcasm. "Good. Let's get on with it."

He gestured, and one of his men reached past the equipment cart to the hatch control. He watched while the hatch slid closed, then spun around and led the way out of the airlock, beckoning one of his men to his side. Dorrman and Rushkoff followed, the other two techs behind them, the last four pirates picking up the rear.

As Dorrman stepped into the corridor, she threw a casual glance over her shoulder. The equipment cart was in position, its hidden electronics package ready to inductively feed the open-hatch command into the control line whenever Dorrman or Sergeant DuMonde and his heavy-weapons squad called for it.

And as an extra bonus, her little drama with Rushkoff had bought enough time and drawn enough pirate attention that the techs had been able to adjust one of the cart's shiny surfaces to reflect the floodlight back into the camera beneath it.

Which meant that when DuMonde was ready to move, she should be able to get her team well down the corridor toward the spin section and the reactor beyond it before the alarm went off.

Of course, before that DuMonde would have to deal with the hatchway's outside camera. But she was a resourceful woman. She'd figure out something.

☆   ☆   ☆

The calm before the storm.

Lisa had heard that phrase a thousand times during

her life. But never before had she appreciated it as much as she did right now.

The Havenite forces were ready. Commodore Charnay's mobile force was waiting silently at the spot he'd dubbed Point Fusillade, 130,000 kilometers short of Bergen 2 on Swenson One's approach vector. His ships' impeller nodes were hot, but their wedges, transponders, and every active sensor were down. With the enemy now only ten light-seconds away, they were effectively invisible.

Of course, they couldn't eliminate the waste heat from their reactors. But it was highly unlikely the pirates would notice them against the background thermals of Bergen 2's platforms and busily moving work boats.

Damocles was also ready. Lisa ran her eyes down the status displays; and as she did so it occurred to her that for the first time in her professional life—in exercises, as well as actual combat conditions—her ship was about to go into battle without a single down-checked system. It made her realize all the more pointedly just how hand-to-mouth the RMN's existence had been.

And not just in equipment, but also in leadership and experience.

It was impossible for her to imagine Charnay dividing his forces, exposing them to defeat in detail, the way the Star Kingdom had deployed her own ships to three separate worlds after the Battle of Manticore. Charnay had experience, and the institutional experience and memory of the RHN behind him in his tactical planning.

In fact, and in contrast, he'd persuaded the pirates

to make that very same mistake themselves by sending three of their ships to Bergen 3.

Lisa scowled. Though that one had the potential to come back and bite both sides on this one. Charnay had picked Point Fusillade on the assumption that Admiral Swenson would either hold his force together or would send *Loki* to Bergen 3. It hadn't occurred to any of the planners that the *Thu'ban*-class cruisers might be sent as a group in *Loki's* place, nor that they would run with such a high acceleration rate.

And that one small change now threatened the entire operation's timing. Had *Loki* been sent, she would have arrived only forty minutes ago, allowing Brigadier Massingill's people enough time to launch their boarding attempt without giving their targets time to warn Swenson One across the intervening 15.8 LM before the main pirate force reached Point Fusillade. Now, with the faster *Thu'bans* in play, Massingill had to add an extra half hour's worth of stalling to get back on Charnay's schedule.

The good news was that, according to her last transmission, she'd managed to stall for almost an hour so far. The bad news was that Swenson Two had apparently decided that they were only going to open one ship at a time to the tech teams.

Danak Traffic Control had been good about feeding them a steady stream of reports, all of it relayed through communications satellites well to one side of the intruders' approach vector to keep the com lasers clear of enemy ears. But that roundabout approach necessarily added an extra time delay—not critical in regards to Swenson One's steady approach, but potentially disastrous with the volatile situation about to erupt at Bergen 3. Once Massingill sent up the balloon there, things at Fusillade were likely to get very hot indeed.

In fact, allowing for the time-delay, it was entirely possible that Massingill had already launched her attack. That even as she sat here on *Damocles*'s bridge the com signal announcing that Massingill's commandos were locked in mortal combat with the pirates was crawling its way toward her.

But whatever was happening at Bergen 3, Swenson One was already too deep in-system to escape. Even if its ships went to a zero safety margin on their compensators, *Loki* would require twenty-three minutes simply to decelerate to zero relative to Bergen 2. At that point, she would be half a million kilometers from the platforms, and 140,000 kilometers inside Charnay's squadron's missile envelope.

Obviously, the closer and slower they could get the enemy before they fired, the better. Still, barring some sort of cataclysmic disaster—

The ping announcing an incoming transmission sounded shockingly loud in the quiet. Lisa turned towards the com section.

Just in time to see Chief Ulvestad's eyes go wide.

"Chief?" she asked.

"You'd better view this, Ma'am," Ulvestad said grimly. "You'd better view it right now.

"Someone over at Bergen Three has just raised a wedge."

☆   ☆   ☆

Orders, Captain von Belling thought sourly, *were orders*.

Unfortunately, even stupid orders were still orders.

He looked around *Copperhead*'s bridge, noting every face gazing at nothing and every pair of hands doing nothing. And it was going to stay that way for the foreseeable future.

All because Admiral Cutler Gensonne was paranoid about being ripped off.

Von Belling took a sip from his coffee bulb. Stupid, stupid, stupid. They'd come all this way to be given the most advanced missiles anyone out here had ever seen; and instead of enthusiastically expediting the hell out of the procedure, Gensonne was worried about getting nick-and-dimmed over the cost of the launcher upgrades?

It made no sense. Especially since the whole issue could have easily been avoided. All Gensonne had had to do—what he *should* have done—was insist that part of the Volsungs' next payment, maybe a third of it, be the launcher instillation. That way, if the Danak techs tried to pad the bill Llyn would be the one on the hook, and he would be the one who had to argue or suck it up.

If Gensonne had done it that way, von Belling and *Adder* could be getting their old launchers pulled apart right now instead of sitting out here on half-kilometer tethers waiting for Captain Lucian to decide it was okay to let the techs aboard.

Von Belling would have made it work if *he* was in charge.

Maybe someday he would be.

"Captain, I'm getting some odd readings from *Mamba*," the man at the sensor station spoke up. "Did Captain Lucian say anything about shutting down his reactor?"

"No," von Belling said, peering at the sensor image that now appeared on his display. Clearly, not everyone on *Copperhead*'s bridge was sitting idle.

The heat reading definitely showed a decrease. "You sure the heat signature's not just being occluded by one of the tugs and transports running around?"

"That's what I thought at first," the man said. "But the heat output's been going down steadily for the past six minutes."

Von Belling frowned and checked his chrono. The last communication from Lucian hadn't mentioned any problems. "Maybe the techs needed to get at something," he said. Even to himself the words sounded stupid. "Com, get Lucian on the line."

"Yes, Sir." There was a pause. "Sorry, Sir, but the tether line isn't working. I'm getting a recording that says the system's having problems."

"Is it, now," von Belling said, frowning a little harder. Work platforms like Bergen 3 typically ran all communications, including ship-to-ship, through tether lines and a cell system so as to save radio bandwidth and com laser pathways for tugs and shuttles and others that couldn't be hardline linked.

Well, to hell with *that*. A real Andermani captain wouldn't put up with that kind of sloppiness on Bergen 3's part, and von Belling was damned if he would, either. "Com laser on *Mamba*," he ordered.

"Sir, the laser's been locked down."

"Then *unlock* it," Von Belling bit out. Ship com lasers were routinely disabled in shipyards to prevent them from going off accidentally and punching holes in equipment, platforms, or random personnel. But this was a special case, and he was an Andermani captain, and to hell with the usual niceties. "While it's coming up, get on the radio," he added. "Tell whoever answers to ask Captain Lucian to kindly tell the rest of us what the hell he's doing."

"Yes, Sir."

He turned back to his keyboard, punching himself into the circuit so he'd be ready to chew someone out the moment he answered—

And jerked back in his seat as a flood of static exploded from the bridge speaker.

He jabbed the button hard enough to hurt his finger, shutting off the noise. "What the *hell*?" he snarled.

"I don't know, Sir," Com said, his words stumbling over each other. "It's—they say—"

"Looks like a malfunctioning spark-weld on one of the repair tugs," the sensor officer put in. "It's about half a kilometer aft working on that barge—"

"Half a kilometer *aft*?" von Belling snarled. "They just *happened* to have a noisy spark-welder sitting right where it would kill our radio?"

And in that frozen, horrible second suspicion became certainty. He knew what was about to happen.

Or rather, what was happening *right now*.

He jabbed for all-ship intercom. "Red alert!" he shouted. "All crew, all departments—red alert. Secure all hatches, and prepare to be boarded."

The alert klaxon cut off the flurry of curses that erupted from the rest of the bridge crew. Von Belling fumbled for the internal security controls, trying to remember how to pull up the hatch camera. He got it and keyed for the image.

There they were: sixteen heavily armored commandos, armed with heavy infantry submachine guns, computer-controlled soft-slug room-sweepers, and shoulder-mounted short-range missile doorbusters. They were gathered around the hatch, busily attaching what were undoubtedly shaped charges around the edges.

There was no time to wonder where they hell they'd come from, or how this had happened. Once those charges were blown and the hatch was open, *Copperhead* would be trapped. All the commandos needed to do was pop the boarding tunnel, open the ship to space, and then cut through the maze of decompression doors at their leisure until they reached the bridge, reactor, and impeller rooms.

Mamba had apparently already been taken. Von Belling would be damned if *Copperhead* fell the same way.

"Helm, get us free," he ordered. "Full thrusters and whatever else you have to do, but I want those tethers off my ship."

"I don't think—"

"Don't *think*," von Belling bellowed. "Just *do it*."

"We can't, Sir," the helm moaned. "They're too strong. We can't just pull away."

Von Belling clenched his teeth. This whole thing going to hell in a coffee bulb, and now his own bridge crew was starting to come apart? "Then don't pull," he said. "Rotate. Spin us around, damn you, and *get those tethers off*."

"Aye, aye," the man said, his voice marginally less panicked. The thruster warning chimed, and on the plot *Copperhead*'s attitude began to change as the cruiser started a slow rotation.

Painfully slow. Von Belling swore under his breath, shifting his attention back and forth between the attitude readings and the view of the commandos trying to break into his ship. Briefly, he wondered what was happening with *Adder* and whether it, too, was already aswarm with commandos. But Captain Schneider was also out of laser line-of-sight, and von Belling had no doubt there was another radio jammer sitting between the two of them.

But maybe there *wasn't* one between him and Gensonne.

"Signal to *Odin*," he ordered Com. "Dump our data into a burst transmission and warn him that we've walked into a trap."

"Yes, Sir."

Only it would very likely be too late, von Belling knew. Here at Bergen 3, he was nearly sixteen light-minutes from Gensonne at Bergen 2. Sixteen minutes until the slow lightspeed crawl of his warning made its way across the Danak system.

Unless...

"Helm, how long until we can bring up the wedge?" he called.

"Three minutes, Captain," the reply came.

Three minutes... and the gravity wave from a wedge traveled instantaneously. Gensonne would know something was wrong, even if he had no idea what.

A small shudder ran through the bridge. Von Belling looked back at the attitude plot to see that *Copperhead* had stopped its rotation. "Helm?"

"Sorry, Sir, but the tethers are still holding."

Von Belling smiled humorously. "Then rotate us the other way," he ordered. "Get us moving as fast as you can, build up some momentum. Snap them, or tear them out by their roots, I don't care which."

"Yes, Sir."

In the boarding tunnel, all but one of the commandos had pulled back a couple of meters. The charges must be nearly ready. "Push it, helm, damn it," he bit out. "Everyone who's not doing something else, grab a gun and get the hell to the main hatch."

"Captain, I'm picking up twenty tugs," Sensors called tensely. "Coming around from the other side of the platform—looks like they're converging on us."

"Of *course* they're converging on us," von Belling said between clenched teeth. Thanks to Gensonne's money paranoia, the stealth strategy that had cost the Volsungs *Mamba* was a no-go for *Copperhead*, and thanks to von Belling's alertness the slightly less stealthy commando assault was about to fail, too. Whoever was running this circus had apparently gone to Plan C.

Only Plan C would be catastrophic. With all the Danakans' finesse stripped away, Plan C would be the hit-it-with-a-hammer option. Possibly an all-out armored assault on every hatch, vent, and opening on the ship; more likely a matter of nuclear warheads attached to all the critical parts.

He couldn't let that happen. Whatever he had to do, he couldn't let that happen.

"Sir—the boarding tunnel!"

Von Belling looked at the display.

Just in time to see it break at the far end, rippling briefly as the air rushed out of it, then going still and stiff as the *Copperhead*'s rotation stretched it outward.

And to von Belling's immense satisfaction, the commandos lost their grip and footing and tumbled out, disappearing into the vacuum beyond.

He bared his teeth in the first genuine smile he'd

had in hours. Now if they could just get those damned tugs and their double damned nukes to wave off.

Only that wasn't going to happen as long as *Copperhead* was tied to the platform. "Reverse rotation," he ordered again. If they could just keep stressing the tethers...

"Sir, wedge is forming," Helm announced.

Von Belling snarled his second smile of the day. Finally. If he couldn't stress the tethers into mechanical failure, then maybe he could just fly away, even if he had to drag the whole damn platform along with him.

And then, too late, a horrible realization bubbled through him.

Like all visitors to Bergen 3, the Volsung cruisers had been carefully tethered to the platform in such a way that an accidental impeller activation would lay out the stress bands safely far above and below the station.

Only *Copperhead* was no longer in that attitude.

Copperhead had rotated.

And in the far distance, as the wedge ceiling coalesced across the platform and the inhabited parts of the station beyond it, Bergen 3 began to disintegrate.

Bergen 3... and *Mamba* and *Adder*.

CHAPTER THIRTY-FOUR

"WELL, XO," CLEGG COMMENTED, A SLIGHTLY lighter edge peeking through the glacial calm of her voice. "I suppose it's time we noticed them."

Travis looked again at the numbers. *Casey* was twenty-five minutes past turnover, her inward velocity towards Walther Prime down to under twenty KPS, her range a hundred three million kilometers. At her current acceleration, she would reach zero-range relative to the planet in the next hundred and seventy-six minutes.

"Yes, Ma'am, I suppose it is," Commander Woodburn agreed from CIC.

"Com," Clegg said, "let's introduce ourselves."

"Aye, aye, Ma'am."

☆   ☆   ☆

"Well," Captain Stoffel commented from *Tarantel*'s bridge. "It would appear they've finally noticed us."

"Or if not us, then one of the other ships," Feyman said. Because, really, the intruder's response to a battlecruiser should have been considerably different.

But at least its identity was no longer a mystery.

The cruiser had brought up its transponder beacon, broadcasting its identity in the clear.

It was the sort of gesture that mercenaries, and even most respectable navies, no longer bothered with. But like an old wet-navy raising the battle flag, it was undeniably dramatic. It announced a ship's determination, and its readiness to fight.

And so there it was: HMS *Casey* of the Royal Manticoran Navy was charging in on them.

"*Casey*," Stoffel said in a rather different voice, and Feyman felt his stomach tighten as he, too, recognized the name.

Tarantel had missed the Battle of Manticore, but all of Gensonne's senior captains had reviewed the records of the battle. Few lower-ranking officers had seen the full details, but as always the rumor mill had taken up the slack.

Which meant everyone aboard *Tarantel* knew they were facing the ship that had killed the battlecruiser *Tyr* at Manticore.

The numbers on Feyman's displays shifted. "Deceleration's increased by forty Gs, Sir," he reported. "New decel at two-point-two-five KPS, about a twenty-one percent increase. If it was running at safe margin, it's just redlined its compensator."

"Profile change?"

"They'll reach zero-zero relative to Prime thirty-one minutes sooner. Call it a hundred and forty-five minutes. Range at that point will be seventeen-point-three-million kilometers."

"Interesting." Stoffel leaned back in his chair, rubbing his chin. "Any side component to her vector?"

"No, Sir. Still coming straight down the pike."

For a moment Stoffel drummed his fingers on his armrest. "Well, they've got chutzpah, I'll give them that. I wonder if they really think they can get away with it twice."

"Sir?"

"Their trick at Manticore was to slide right past *Tyr* and *Odin* at Manticore on reciprocal headings," Stoffel said. "I'm just wondering if they really think they can pull that off again."

Fey frowned. "But if they want to dodge past us, then why are they decelerating so hard?"

"Maybe they're hoping to draw us into heading out to meet them," Stoffel said. "If they can make us commit to an intercept vector they'll have a lot better look at any holes in the fence they might squirm through. If we *don't* accelerate out to meet them and they manage to reduce their relative velocity to zero, we don't have anything that could catch them if they stick with their current acceleration."

"If they're just planning to run, why the transponder beacon?"

"Either they turned it on before they fully realized what's waiting for them—assuming they've realized that even now—or else they're waving it to convince us that they really, really still want to fight." He shrugged. "It's not much, but what *else* do they have?"

He straightened up in his chair. "So, a hundred and forty-five minutes to relative zero," he continued "We'll give them another two hours, then raise wedge and head out to meet them. Might as well let them reduce their closing rate and give us a better target."

"And it'll make Hauser happy by keeping them out of range of his precious base?" Feyman suggested.

"Farthest thing from my mind, TO," Stoffel assured him. "But since you mention it, why not?"

☆   ☆   ☆

The minutes stretched into hours. Feyman filled the time by double-checking every system under his command, and making sure everyone else checked theirs.

The ship that had killed so many of their friends and colleagues was going down.

Finally, it was almost time.

And then, on Feyman's displays...

"Com, I want updates from all units," Captain Stoffel ordered. He touched a stud on his chair arm. "Engineering, this is the captain. What's our impeller state?"

"Holding at Readiness, Sir," Commander Eric Becker replied. "Three minutes, and we're hot."

"Good. Stand by to raise wedge in twenty-three minutes. Com? Where are those updates?"

Feyman lifted a finger. "Captain? You need to take a look at this."

"This better be important, TO," Stoffel warned as Feyman keyed the image to his station. "What exactly am I looking at?"

"I don't know yet, Sir," Feyman said. "But there seems to be something else out there."

"What do you mean *something else*?" Stoffel demanded. "Something else *what*?"

"Something out there just occluded a star, Sir," Feyman said, rapidly keying his board. "I've just trained the heat sensors around to take a better look."

A momentary silence fell on the bridge as the sensors did their work.

"Well?" Stoffel prompted.

"Heat signatures, Captain," Feyman said, hearing the fresh grimness in his voice. "At least two of them. Consistent with reactors at minimum power."

Stoffel sucked in a short breath. "Where?"

"Same bearing as *Casey*, Sir, and just under five hundred thousand kilometers ahead of them. If *Casey* maintains its current deceleration, their vectors will merge—merge *exactly*—in just under eleven minutes at seven-zero-six-zero KPS and eighteen million kilometers short of Prime."

"Damn it all," Stoffel said, his tone the bitter iciness of deep space. "They *wanted* us to see him! To see *him*, and not whoever the hell these other bastards are."

"Yes, sir," Feyman said, rushing to crunch these new numbers. "They would have had to sneak across the hyper limit hours before *Casey* crossed, coming in low and slow."

"And then they showed us *Casey*, coming in hot," Stoffel bit out, his tone as disgusted as his expression. "Showing its impellers to the entire frigging galaxy. And it damned well worked. Like trained fish we kept looking exactly where they wanted us to look."

Another dozen seconds passed. Feyman kept quiet. So did the rest of the bridge crew.

Stoffel huffed out a sigh. "Well," he growled, his eyes blazing. "For a pissant little navy from a nowhere little star system, they're just full of clever tricks, aren't they? Well, they're in for a surprise. They must have better intel on Walther than I thought. We'll have to ask the survivors how they got it."

"They must have gotten it after the Admiral pulled out for Danak, too," Feyman added. "Even with a couple of their ancient battlecruisers there's no way in hell they would tangle with us here unless they knew most of our big ships were gone."

"So they found out he was gone and decided to take a run at our base," Stoffel said, nodding.

It was crazy, of course. Feyman knew that. Crazy and gutsy both. Matching a pair of old battlecruisers with outdated equipment against the base missile platforms and the combat-capable destroyers and frigates at Walther would be iffy at the best of times, even with surprise on their side. Which, sadly for them, they no longer had.

On the other hand...

"If you're right, Sir," he said. "it's very likely they don't know *we're* here."

"Exactly," Stoffel agreed. "They also probably figure we still think *Casey* is alone."

Feyman shook his head. This was getting complicated. "So what do we do, Sir?"

"What we *don't* do is go charging out to meet them any sooner than we have to," Stoffel grated. "We'll keep *Tarantel's* wedge down and leave them in blissful ignorance as long as we can."

"And *Schmiede*?"

Stoffel pondered a moment. "All right—here's the plan. For now, nobody stirs. I'll bring up our wedge five minutes before they enter missile range—that'll keep them ninety thousand kilometers out of Hauser's range when they fire. It'll only take a minute for them to cross the zone, but they'll have to honor *our* threat and concentrate their initial fire on us."

"Sounds wonderful," Feyman murmured.

"Don't get smart," Stoffel warned. "We may get

hammered harder than I'd like, but they'll get hurt, too. Probably pretty badly. And that'll turn *Schmiede* into our reserve. When they *do* enter its range and it opens fire, it should be a hell of a lot harder for them to intercept its birds."

Feyman wrinkled his nose. He didn't much like the plan, but it offered the best way to maximize their own firepower.

And chance of survival.

"So we all play like quiet little mice," Stoffel said. "Right up to the point when we stop being mice and turn into tigers."

☆ ☆ ☆

HMS *Casey*'s base vector merged with the Andermani squadron's.

The cruiser dropped neatly into her assigned slot in *Vergeltung*'s screen and stopped accelerating.

"Communications request from Admiral Basaltberg," Ulvestad said.

"Put him through," Clegg ordered.

The main display lit up with the Andermani admiral's face. "*Very* well done, Captain Clegg," he said warmly. "I'm sure they've realized by now what we're up to, but I very much doubt they've figured out what they're up against."

"I would have put it that they don't have a hope in hell, Sir," Clegg suggested.

"Indeed," Basaltberg said, smiling. "Well. Since they seem to be shy about coming out to meet us, I think we should leave them in blissful ignorance for another—" he consulted his chrono "—eleven minutes and forty-one seconds."

☆ ☆ ☆

The Manticoran force inched closer.

Feyman scowled as he shifted his eyes back and forth between his displays, looking for something—*anything*—that would give him more of a clue as to what exactly was bearing down on them.

Casey had joined the incoming formation of unknowns. That much was obvious. But the cruiser's wedge was still the only one showing, and it was generating a substantial blind spot.

Active sensors were useless at this range, and thermal sensors couldn't see through an interposed impeller wedge. There were still a couple of thermal signatures showing, one each above and below *Casey*'s wedge, but he knew damned well there was also something on the other side of the cruiser. The blind spot it was creating was the only reason for the ship to take station directly in the center of the vertically stacked intruders.

But what the hell was she hiding?

There was only one possibility. Manticore had talked Haven into sending along some firepower.

Feyman snorted under his breath. Only one possibility, and it didn't make any sense at all. Haven and Manticore might have cooperated—once—years ago, and he could see Haven not being pleased with unprovoked mercenary attacks on independent star nations anywhere in its vicinity.

But there was no way in the universe that the Republic Navy would have been willing—or able—to cut loose the modern firepower to support Manticore this far from home. For starters, *Casey* and its friends couldn't have come all the way from Manticore just to attack this star system. They *had* to have discovered its location only after they got to Silesia, so there was no way they could have convinced Haven to send along—

"Status change!" Lieutenant Moeller snapped suddenly. "I have one, two, four…six…A minimum of *six* additional impeller wedges!"

"What the *hell*?" Captain Stoffel demanded. "*Six* wedges?"

"And there might be a seventh directly behind *Casey*," Feyman said, his pulse thudding suddenly in his throat as he peered at the icons on his own plot.

Stoffel swore viciously. "Fine. What can you tell me about the ones we *can* see?"

"Range is still twelve-point-seven million kilometers, Sir," Feyman said. "Not much resolution at that range. But they've begun decelerating at two hundred gravities, which puts them right on top of us at zero velocity in exactly sixty minutes."

"Tentative class IDs on two of them, Sir," Moeller spoke up. "Both at least heavy cruisers. CIC makes it a sixty-five-percent chance one of them is a battlecruiser."

"Probably couldn't hide both of them behind a single frigging light cruiser, even at that range," Stoffel growled. "So Manticore wants to gamble its entire navy on a throw of the dice? Fine. Let's show them what it costs to play with the big boys."

☆　☆　☆

"All right, Commander Long," Clegg said. "This is your show. Do us proud."

"Yes, Ma'am," Travis replied. This was it. Taking a deep breath, he pressed the button.

A pair of green telltales turned red.

☆　☆　☆

Feyman's eyes darted back and forth between his displays, his fingers tapping his board as he tried to squeeze every last bit of data he could out of *Tarantel*'s sensors. The incoming Manticorans had been decelerating for just over thirty-five minutes since bringing up their wedges, and would enter missile range in another eleven minutes. *Tarantel*'s own wedge and sidewalls would be coming up in approximately six. Feyman's initial salvo was ready and waiting to launch, and he'd set up firing solutions on the wedge CIC had determined was definitely a battlecruiser. There was still time to alter the targeting setups, however, and he needed to be ready in case the Manticorans had another trick or two up their sleeves.

And then, without warning, *Casey* shifted to port, staying in its same plane, deftly clearing a line of sight for whoever was hiding behind it, while at the same time not blocking any of the other ships' fields of fire.

"*Casey* is shifting position, Sir," he called the warning. "Opening sight lines to something behind it—"

"Transponder beacons!" Communications shouted suddenly. "I have transponders, and—oh my *God*."

Feyman barely heard the last three words as he stared at his own display. The transponder beacons of seven ships flashed onto his plot: SMS *Hamman*, SMS *München*, SMS *Ao Qin*, SMS *Loreley*, SMS *Zhong Kui*, and . . .

"They're not Manticorans." Through the pounding of his heart he could hear his voice coming from between numbed lips. "They're Andermani.

"And that's *Vergeltung* out there."

☆   ☆   ☆

"I imagine there are some very unhappy people over there," Captain Clegg murmured as, all around *Casey*, Andermani impeller wedges and sidewalls began to come up.

Travis nodded, his full focus on cataloguing targets. It looked like the recon drone's data on who could and couldn't get underway was pretty much on the money.

Still, just because a ship couldn't move and couldn't raise sidewalls didn't mean it couldn't throw missiles before it died.

☆　　☆　　☆

"I guess that settles whether or not we go out to meet them," Stoffel snarled with an anger and viciousness Feyman had never heard from him before. "Hauser's just going to have to suck it up, because we're *definitely* going to need *Schmiede*'s missile platforms against that kind of firepower. I don't like engaging from such a low base velocity, but we've got to bring them into *Schmiede*'s missile envelope."

"Yes, Sir."

☆　　☆　　☆

"CIC makes it one active battlecruiser, two light cruisers, plus three destroyers and three frigates, Ma'am," Travis announced. "That matches just about perfectly with the Andermani drone's data."

"Glad to hear it," Clegg replied. "Let's hope our brilliant idea works. Because if it doesn't those two missile platforms will more than compensate for a bunch of ships that can't move."

Travis clenched his teeth. "Yes, Ma'am."

"Relax, TO," the captain calmly. "I signed off on your brilliant idea because it *was* brilliant."

"Oh," Travis said. "Ah...thank you, Ma'am."

"Mind you, you've had a few others I didn't think quite so highly of," she added. "But this one—well, I think this one will actually work."

Travis took a deep breath. "I hope so, Ma'am."

☆   ☆   ☆

"*Zhong Kui*'s our target," Captain Stoffel said. The anger was gone from his voice, leaving a harsh bitterness in its place. "The destroyers and frigates will have to deal with *their* cruisers and destroyers. And *Schmiede...*"

He trailed off, his eyes on the main plot. Eyes full of ice and hatred.

And fear. Feyman could feel the captain's fear.

The same fear everyone else on the bridge was feeling.

Including Feyman himself.

Vergeltung changed everything. Feyman tried not to reflect on the bitter irony which had brought that ship, of every ship in the Andermani Navy, to Walther. Distantly, he wondered what the odds against that must have been.

But those odds were meaningless today. The only thing that mattered was the cold, hard fact that *Vergeltung* all by herself could almost certainly have defeated every Volsung combat-capable ship in the system.

Including *Tarantel*.

Zhong Kui was a locally built variant of the *Seydlitz*-class battlecruisers Gustav Anderman had brought with him to the Potsdam System. It was larger, faster, and more powerful than *Tarantel*, but not impossibly so. With a little luck, and a superior crew, *Tarantel* could take it on with a good chance of coming out on top.

Then there was *Ao Qin*. It was based on the *Drachen*-class frigate, and the Andermani navy still classified them as such, though most navies would consider them light cruisers. *München* was a *Bremen*-class. Feyman knew its type well; he'd served aboard a *Bremen* as a midshipman. They were missile-heavy, with no beam weapons at all, uncompromisingly designed for the long-range missile engagement. He had no profile on *Hamman*, but from her gravitic and electronic signature—and the fact that she was here—she had to be well armed, despite her apparent freighter hull. Probably one of the *Musketier*-class ships.

But all of them—the entire force, for that matter—paled in comparison to *Vergeltung*. Not only did it have twice *Zhong Kui's* missile armament, but also two thirds again the battlecruiser's *anti*missile capability.

Stoffel hadn't completed his last sentence. He hadn't had to. Everyone aboard *Tarantel* knew that *Vergeltung* was *Schmiede's* only possible target. It was unlikely that even the missile platforms could throw enough armament to saturate the battleship's defenses, especially backed up by *Vergeltung's* sophisticated ECM. But if *Schmiede* couldn't do it, then no one could.

At least there wouldn't be any more surprises. Now, it had become a face-to-face shootout, with everything depending on who shot first.

Though as a practical matter, with a head-on approach like this there wouldn't be much difference between who fired first and who fired second.

Feyman's stomach seemed to have turned into a permanent cramp, and he could feel the sweat gathering at his temples and in his armpits. He'd seen combat before, but never against an equally capable opponent, far less a *more* capable one.

For the first time in his career, he finally understood how all the Volsungs' victims must have felt.

☆   ☆   ☆

"Missile range in sixty seconds," Lieutenant Ip called from the ATO station.

"Tracking links enabled," Travis added. "Targeting update confirmed." He looked up at the timer ticking down in a corner of his display. "Fifteen seconds, Ma'am."

"Very good, TO," Clegg said. "Let's roll those dice."

"Ten seconds. Five . . . four . . . three . . . two—"

☆   ☆   ☆

"*Sir!*" ATO Moeller gasped. "Sir—*Schmiede*—"

"*God,*" Feyman breathed, though whether it was a curse or a prayer even he didn't know.

Two pairs of missiles had suddenly materialized less than eight thousand kilometers from *Schmiede*. They couldn't be there. They just *couldn't*.

But they were, springing into existence at the very edge of *Schmiede*'s active radar envelope, coming in ballistic with a base velocity of 3,640 KPS. To be there, moving at that speed and factoring in the enemy's deceleration rate, they must have been deployed eighteen minutes earlier. It was the only possible geometry.

But there had been no booster flares from any of the incoming ships. So how—?

Casey.

In that single, blindingly clear instant, he knew how it had been done. He'd seen Gensonne's reports, and heard all the rumors, but only now did he recall that, unlike any of her Andermani consorts, the Manticoran carried railgun launchers forward. Her missiles needed no boosters, gave no betraying thermal flares when they launched. *Casey* had simply launched four of them, drives down, and allowed them to run silently ahead of the approaching fleet. They'd coasted onward from their base velocity at launch, with no betraying impeller wedge, while *Casey* itself continued to decelerate, falling farther and farther behind them.

And now, forty seconds before *Schmiede* could possibly fire, those four missiles' impellers sprang to life and hurled them at their targets at an acceleration of ten thousand gravities.

It took them just under two seconds to cover the 7.8 thousand kilometers between them and those targets. Two seconds in which the defenders could see them coming but couldn't possibly stop them. There simply wasn't enough tracking time, enough response time. They were *inside* every defensive system, and Feyman watched in impotent horror as both of *Schmiede*'s missile platforms disappeared in blossoms of nuclear flame.

"Captain, I have an incoming transmission," the com officer half-whispered into the stunned silence.

Stoffel, his expression as stunned as Feyman felt, waved at the main com display.

"Put it up," he grated.

A white-haired officer in the uniform of the Andermani Navy appeared.

"You know who I am," he said. His voice could have been frozen helium. His eyes somehow managed to be even colder. "You also know you will

be in my engagement range in thirty seconds. If
you want to live longer than the next five minutes,
strike your wedges.

"You have twenty-five seconds to comply."

☆   ☆   ☆

The silence of *Odin's* bridge roared around Gensonne as he stared at Captain von Belling's face on
the com display. He couldn't look away. For a handful
of seconds, he literally *couldn't* while his brain tried
to process the burst transmission's information. Tried
to understand that *Adder* and *Mamba* were simply
gone, blown treacherously out of space in a sudden,
unprovoked attack.

No, not in an *attack*, he realized.

In an *ambush*.

One which had to have been carefully planned far
in advance of its execution. He didn't know—yet—
how von Belling had managed to avoid the fate of
Copperhead's consorts. But that didn't matter right
now. What mattered was that the ambush must have
been prepared well ahead of time, and that meant—

"Com, get me *Banshee*," he snapped. "And I don't
want any more damn excuses from Rhamas about how
busy Llyn is talking to these people."

He switched his glare to *Odin's* captain. Imbar
was pale, his expression as shaken as Gensonne felt.

"Bring us to a reciprocal heading immediately," he
grated. "And take us to two hundred gravities decel."

"Yes, Sir," Imbar said, and started barking orders.

Gensonne took a deep breath, trying to force his
mind into some sort of logical action. All right. *Adder*
and *Mamba* were gone. *Copperhead* was running
from Bergen 3 as fast as his wedge would take him,

though if their attackers had been smart there would undoubtedly be another layer or two waiting between him and the hyper limit.

That left *Odin* and the rest of the Volsung ships currently heading into their own ambush. Imbar would have ordered the others to conform to *Odin's* movements, which should at least start buying them a little time.

The problem was that until he knew more about the Bergen 3 ambush he couldn't anticipate what might be waiting for them at Bergen 2. Until he had some kind of clue, all he could really do was to slow his approach.

But until then, there was one other matter that he would be more than happy to attend to.

On the com display, Captain Rhamas's dour face appeared. "Admiral Gensonne," he said with a small nod. "How can I help you? I'm afraid Mr. Llyn is still—"

"I know *exactly* what Llyn is doing," Gensonne cut in savagely. "And if he doesn't want to get blown out of space in the next three seconds, he'd better get on the damn com."

Rhamas looked at him a bit oddly, without any concern, let alone panic, in the face of Gensonne's threat. A small part of Gensonne's mind took note of that and wondered.

But there was too much else going on for him to care. He opened his mouth to underline the threat—

"Of course, Admiral," Rhamas said. "Give me a moment."

"*One* moment." Gensonne's voice was icy.

☆　　☆　　☆

Banshee's main computer had spent the last four and a half hours monitoring the Volsungs' communications. It hadn't had a great deal else to do during those hours.

Its software had been called upon to tweak the Captain Rhamas image a half dozen times during various exchanges with Admiral Gensonne, but its artificial Rhamas personality had managed to deflect any actual conversation between the artificial Llyn and the Volsung commander.

That would no longer be possible. The computer's filters had recognized no less than eleven flagged keywords in *Copperhead's* transmission to *Odin* even before Gensonne demanded to speak to Llyn. That had triggered an entire cascade of commands.

And deep inside *Banshee*, half a dozen systems none of the Volsungs had ever suspected were already spinning up.

☆   ☆   ☆

"Course change on Swenson One," Lieutenant Commander Ravel announced crisply from *Damocles's* TO station. "They've reversed acceleration and increased to two-point-one-two KPS squared. That's eighty-six percent of theoretical max for a *Bayezid*-class battle-cruiser, Captain."

"Obviously they've heard the news, too," Marcello said quietly to Lisa, his voice grim. Like the rest of *Casey's* bridge crew, he was clearly trying to grapple with the report from Bergen 3.

"You think he's seen us, Sir?" Lisa asked.

"I can't see how he could," Marcello replied. "But he doesn't have to see us to realize we're out here. And if he does—"

"All units, this is the Flag," Commodore Charnay's voice came over the squadron frequency. "Stand by to bring up wedges in ninety seconds from...mark."

"Set it up, Maneuvering," Marcello ordered. "Confirm receipt, Com."

"Wedge in ninety seconds from mark, aye," Lieutenant Vespasiano Guiccardini said.

"Order receipt confirmed, Sir," Chief Ulvestad added. "And the Flag is transmitting to the pirates now."

☆   ☆   ☆

"Admiral Gensonne," Llyn said from the com display. His tone was so much like Rhamas's last greeting, Gensonne thought, that it had to be clearly and infuriatingly deliberate. "What can I do for you?"

"You can die like the lying bastard you are," Gensonne told him harshly. "And if you even *blink* wrong from now on, you're going to do it. I know you've been screwing with us, and I also know you'll be dead before anything *else* happens."

Deep in *Banshee*'s computer, the programmed systems quietly jettisoned two small sections of hull plating, then shifted the com program to a slightly different communications file.

Llyn smiled.

Gensonne stared, feeling his blood pressure soaring. He *smiled*?

"I see," the face on his display said. "Should I assume something unfortunate has happened?"

For a second Gensonne couldn't find his voice in the face of such utter chutzpah. Unfortunate? *Smiling*? "Is *that* what you call this?" Gensonne demanded. "*Unfortunate*? Because you're about to find out what unfortunate *really* looks like. Whatever you did to my cruisers at Bergen Three isn't going to work here. We're on to you, you smug little bastard. We're not going to Bergen Two, and if Danak's pathetic little system force tries to get in our way, we have more than enough firepower to turn the whole damn thing into superheated atoms. They cough up reparations for *Mamba* and *Adder* fast enough, I might not do the same thing to the rest of the system."

He ran out of words and turned up his glare another couple of notches. If Llyn wasn't shaking in his fancy boots, he damn well ought to be.

Only he wasn't. The damned little snake was still just looking at him, eyebrows raised politely.

Gensonne ground his teeth. His thumb twitched toward the red button on his armrest; with a supreme effort he forced it to stop.

"And I wouldn't count on any last-minute surprises," he continued. "See, Danak hasn't got a beef with us. There's no way they would have attacked us unless *you* goaded them into it. So if they balk at reparations, I'm going to offer to sweeten the pot.

"I'm going to give them *you*."

He paused again. But Llyn just continued to gaze placidly out of the display.

"You're the one who kicked off this mess," Gensonne went on. *Something* in here had to get a rise out of the man. "You're the genius who just got a whole bunch of their citizens killed. I'm pretty sure that once they know what happened, they'll be *real* eager to get their hands on you. I'll trade you for a promise that I won't come back and grind their pathetic little star system into dust."

Still nothing.

"And after *that*," Gensonne concluded, "I'll make sure Manticore knows who hired us to trash *their* miserable star system."

"I see you're upset," Llyn said soothingly. "Surely we can work this out somehow, Admiral."

Gensonne stared at him. Had the little man even been *listening*?

"Incoming burst transmission, Sir," the com officer broke into Gensonne's confused disbelief. Gensonne turned a glare on him—

The man's mouth was hanging open, his face rigid. "Sir, it's from a Commodore Charnay."

Gensonne's first reflexive thought was that Com had stupidly gotten it wrong. Charnay was Secretary of Industry, not a—

The thought broke off. Of course. Charnay was just another part of Llyn's scam, and a pretty pathetic part on top of it.

"Commodore Charnay?" he bit out. "*Commodore?*" He spat contemptuously. "Danak has one hell of a delusional government if they think they rate a commodore. Or was a promotion *your* idea?" he added to Llyn's image.

"He's not Danakan, Sir," the com officer managed, his voice coming out half strangled. "He's Havenite."

Gensonne felt an icy hand grip the back of his neck. *Havenite?*

And with that, his improvised plans, his quick-thinking adjustment to Llyn's treachery—it flashed away like vapor in vacuum.

And if the man really was a commodore...

"Put it up," he ordered, his lips feeling numb.

On the secondary com display a man appeared:

middle-aged, grim-faced, wearing the uniform of the Republic of Haven Navy.

"I am Commodore Gustav Charnay, Republic of Haven Navy," he identified himself. "Be advised that my squadron is in position and prepared to intercept and engage your forces. You will stand down and strike your wedges to await my boarding parties upon pain of your destruction."

His eyes narrowed another millimeter. "You are also informed that should any harm befall the Baird family, you individually and all of your personnel collectively, will be held personally responsible and tried accordingly. Charnay, clear."

Gensonne blinked. *Baird*—wasn't that the alias Llyn said he used in the Republic? When the hell had he picked up a family?

He brushed the thought aside, trying to think. All right. If Charnay had the firepower to back up his warning, then it was over.

Still, despite a questionable activity or two in the Volsungs' past, there was no reason Haven should be mad at them. Certainly there was no paper trail connecting them to anything Nouveau Paris might take exception to. As far as Haven knew, he and his people were as respectable as any other mercenary group, and as far as Gensonne himself knew the Republic had no extradition treaties with the Andermani Empire. Surrender might be professionally disastrous, but surrender and survival beat the hell out of glorious defiance and fiery death.

Besides, as he'd just told Llyn, he had plenty of information to trade. Haven would probably pay even more for it even than Danak would.

"Admiral, *Banshee* is changing attitude," Tracking announced suddenly. "Rolling to starboard and changing heading to zero-three-seven degrees."

Gensonne's eyes darted to the tactical plot. Where did the sneaky little bastard think he was going?

Because if the RHN was really waiting out there somewhere, the last thing Gensonne wanted was for his best bargaining chip to go running off somewhere.

"Whatever you're thinking, Llyn, forget it," he snapped at the com. "I swear to God, I'll blow you right out of space if you don't."

"I don't understand why you seem so irritated," Llyn said.

"Still changing heading, Sir."

"Llyn, stop," Gensonne bit out. "I said *stop. Now!*"

"What was that you said, Admiral?" Llyn asked, his expression still placid. "I'm afraid I didn't hear you clearly."

"Sir, *Banshee*'s increased its acceleration," Tracking said, the urgency in his voice mixed with disbelief and rising panic. "It's pulling away to starboard."

"It's been a pleasure doing business with you Admiral," Llyn continued from his display. "Regretfully, I must inform you that I'm terminating our relationship. One final parting gift: a warning to you that Captain Katura has informed the Republic of the sizable reward that's been posted for you by the Andermani Empire. I'm sure you recall the relevant incident. Under the current circumstances, I imagine the only question Nouveau Paris will have for Emperor Gustav is whether he would prefer you alive or dead."

Raw, red fury boiled suddenly in Cutler Gensonne's brain.

Fury, and deep, gut-wrenching fear. Screwed. He was absolutely and utterly screwed.

All he had left was to screw Axelrod in return. And if Llyn himself was going to be useless as a bargaining chip...

He looked at the visual display centered on *Banshee*, his lips curling back in a savage smile. Reaching to the red button, he slammed his fist onto it.

Nothing happened.

He stared at the image in disbelief, and hit the button again.

Again, nothing.

"Something wrong, Admiral?" Llyn inquired calmly. He frowned as if thinking, and then his expression cleared. "Of course. You just triggered the bomb, didn't you?"

Gensonne's jaw dropped.

"I must say, I was deeply saddened when I learned you'd planted it on *Banshee*'s hull," Llyn continued, his tone gently chiding. "I'd thought we were building a mutually trusting relationship. And then for you to go and demonstrate how wrong I was..." He shook his head sadly. "I couldn't decide whether I was more disappointed by your treachery or by your assumption that I was stupid enough to fall for it." He shrugged. "But then, there really isn't any point in being disappointed with you. Not anymore."

And in that moment, Gensonne knew that death had arrived for him.

"Llyn," he breathed, the word a curse, a last spitting of defiance.

The computer image on Gensonne's display froze as the masquerade came to an end. "Goodbye, Admiral," the recorded message said through the now motion-less lips.

"Tactical!" Gensonne roared, shaking himself out of his paralysis. "Target *Ban*—"

The pair of torpedo launchers in *Banshee*'s port broadside fired.

Energy torpedoes were light-speed weapons, devastating in their ability to slice through hull and plastic and ceramic.

But battlecruisers were big, tough ships. They didn't die as instantaneously as smaller ships might have under the same punishment. Gensonne had one final, fleeting fragment of a second, his mind finally understanding the full extent of Llyn's treachery, before *Odin* vanished in a twisting, roiling eruption of fury.

Three seconds later, the bomb Gensonne had planted on *Banshee*'s hull detonated and a second small, furious star blazed briefly in the Volsung formation.

☆   ☆   ☆

Charnay's mouth tightened as a pair of impeller signatures abruptly disappeared from his tactical plot. Ten seconds later, his passive sensors caught the light-speed emissions of the explosions.

And as the associated beacons cut off, his worst fear was confirmed.

One of the destroyed ships had been *Banshee*.

That was the thing he'd feared most from the outset. Not that his plans for dealing with the pirates might fail, but that the innocent merchant family might be killed right before his eyes.

"Sir, CIC is reporting something . . . a little strange," Commander Laforge said.

Charnay shook away the hollow feeling in the pit of his stomach. What was done was done, and there was no longer anything he could do about it.

"How do you mean *strange*, Isadora?" he asked.

"Sir, the bigger of those explosions was one of the battlecruisers—presumably *Odin*, given its proximity to the freighter, but it could conceivably have been *Loki*," Laforge said. "The strange part is it looks like she blew up just before the freighter did."

"*Before?*"

"Yes, Sir," Laforge said. "The range is over ten light-seconds, and we're still refining the data. But the timing seems pretty clear."

Her eyes met Charnay's, and the confusion in them matched his own.

"Well, keep at it," he told her. "We'll get to the bottom of it eventually."

In the meantime, the cost in lives for *Banshee's* death could now be added to the deaths that Brigadier Massingill's people and the civilians aboard Bergen Three had suffered in these bastards' hands.

It was time to balance that debt.

"Com," the commodore called. "Alpha One. Transmit execution."

☆   ☆   ☆

"Execute Alpha One, Sir," Ulvestad called from *Damocles's* com station.

"Acknowledge receipt, Com," Marcello ordered.

"Acknowledging, aye, Sir."

Finally.

"Helm, execute Alpha One."

"Aye, aye, Sir. Executing Alpha One."

☆   ☆   ☆

Captain Harcon Jaeger stared in disbelieving horror at the visual display. The news from *Copperhead* had been devastating enough, but he'd had no idea just how spectacularly wrong things had gone until Commodore Charnay's surrender demand.

The blood-freezing implications of that had still been sinking in when *Banshee's* vector began to change.

And then, without a whisper of warning, *Odin* had blown up. Jaeger's brain was still reeling over that when Llyn's freighter had also disintegrated.

Jaeger didn't have one single clue what the hell had just happened.

"Sir, we're picking up impeller signatures, range two-point-five million kilometers," *Loki's* tactical officer spoke up, her voice holding disbelief and sudden dread. "Directly between us and Bergen Two."

"Numbers?"

"We make it ten, Sir." The TO said, her dread edging toward panic. "At least one battlecruiser, probably three or four cruisers. The rest are showing as destroyers; CIC thinks one may be a frigate."

Jaeger inhaled deeply, trying to think. With *Odin* and two *Thu'bans* gone—and *Copperhead* too far away to be of any use, even if it managed to escape—all he had left were *Loki*, *Aldebaran*, *Fomalhaut*, and *Shirokawa*. *Loki* was slow, but it had a disproportionately heavy throw weight in a missile engagement.

But if that truly was a Havenite battlecruiser out there, it was probably a *Saintonge*-class. *Loki's* chances against that kind of modern heavyweight weren't good. Adding that to his two-to-one numerical disadvantage . . .

Fine. *He who fights and runs away . . .* "All units,

Execute Himmel Rakete," he said sharply. "Signal *Shirokawa* to remain in company with us."

There was a moment's silence, and then—

"Executing Himmel Rakete," his maneuvering officer said.

☆   ☆   ☆

"Sir, the enemy is dispersing," Lieutenant Ravel said.

"Scatter maneuver," Marcello said softly, watching the plot.

Lisa nodded to herself as she gazed at the tac display. Whoever was in command over there had run the odds, come to the logical conclusion, and was wasting no time in getting the hell out. The brutally truncated Swenson One had blossomed, spreading out from a common center like the bursting of a celebration skyrocket. They were splitting up to flee on four—no, only three—headings, spaced 120° apart.

"Their accelerations are increasing," Ravel continued. "Not uniformly. It looks like two of the cruisers— probably *Aldebaran* and *Fomalhaut*—are proceeding independently. Flag is redesignating them Swenson Two and Swenson Three. The third seems to be staying in company with the remaining battlecruiser. Flag is redesignating them Swenson Four and Swenson One. We're still not positive whether Swenson One is *Odin* or *Loki* at this point, but *Saintonge*'s CIC thinks it's *Loki*."

"If it's *Loki*, Swenson Four's probably *Shirokawa*," Lisa murmured to Marcello. "She's the slowest of their cruisers."

She checked the numbers, ran a quick plot. It would be close.

"Enemy acceleration is settling down," Ravel said

after a moment. "Swenson Two and Three are at two-point-two-niner KPS squared. Swenson One and Four are at two-point-one-six."

Lisa winced. Or not.

"I guess that's that," Marcello murmured, echoing Lisa's own conclusion. "If Two and Three are the *Antares*-class ships, that's a ninety-five-percent acceleration setting."

"And if One is *Loki*, that's about the same setting for her," Lisa agreed. "If it's *Odin*, it's only about eighty-six percent." She scowled. "Probably settles the question of which one she is. Not that it matters a lot to *us*."

"I'm afraid not," Marcello agreed.

Swenson One's current acceleration was eight gravities higher than *Damocles*'s maximum acceleration with no safety margin at all. For that matter, it was higher than either of the older Havenite destroyers could manage at zero-margin compensator settings, and no commander in his right mind could justify going to a zero margin to pursue a clearly defeated and fleeing enemy.

Lisa looked back at the slow-motion skyrocket. Yet another galling example of the RMN's obsolescence. When the enemy's slower battlecruiser could pull a higher acceleration than a destroyer massing less than a quarter of its tonnage, it was time to start upgrading compensators.

"Signal from Flag, Sir," Ulvestad said.

"Put it through."

Charnay's face appeared on the com display.

"I'm sure you've seen the acceleration numbers," the commodore said.

"Yes, Sir," Marcello said. "Afraid we're not quite fleet-footed enough."

"Not your fault. For that matter, *Hache de Guerre* and *Poignard* are no fleeter of foot than you are."

Marcello nodded—agreement, apology, or commiseration, Lisa couldn't tell which. "Orders, Sir?"

"I don't like to do it," Charnay said, "but I see no alternative to breaking the squadron into divisions. *Topaze, Courageux, Aigrett,* and *Saintonge* will go after Swenson One and Swenson Four. I'm sending *Jocelyne Pellian, Jean-Claude Courtois,* and *Intrépide* after Swenson Two. Unfortunately, that means Swenson Three is very likely going to get away clean."

"Yes, Sir," Marcello said, and Lisa could see her own frustration hidden behind the calmness of his expression.

Bringing a fleeing enemy to action short of the hyper-limit was seldom easy if the enemy in question didn't want to fight. In this case, despite the pirates' ability to generate velocity perpendicular to their initial vector, they couldn't avoid interception, because their original vector would force them to overrun Charnay's pursuing vessels whether they wanted to or not. What they *could* do—or at least attempt—was create enough separation to guarantee extended engagement ranges and limited engagement time. If they could stay at the three to four-hundred-thousand-kilometer long-missile range and maneuver to keep her impeller wedge interposed, it would be impossible for a single pursuer to generate a firing angle. In order to force Swenson One to turn and fight, it would be necessary to get someone into position to fire directly up her kilt, and that required multiple platforms. In fact,

Charnay was spreading himself dangerously thin to go after even two of the pirates.

Still, the pursuit was beginning deep inside the hyper-sphere. That, combined with *Saintonge*'s higher base acceleration rate, meant Charnay could probably overhaul *Loki* short of the limit in a stern chase even if the other battlecruiser crossed his initial missile range undamaged.

"I'm leaving *Hache de Guerre* and *Poignard* behind with you," Charnay continued. "You'll be the senior captain, so command will devolve on you. I want you to begin decelerating and prepare to conduct search and rescue operations along the pirates' original vector."

Out of the corner of her eye, Lisa saw Marcello's eyebrows twitch. "Of course, Sir."

Charnay evidently saw the eyebrow thing, too. "I understand your skepticism, Captain," Charnay said. "Frankly, I have no idea what the hell happened out there. But I'd really like to find out. And it *is* at least remotely possible Baird managed to get himself or at least his wife and daughters off in a life pod between the time the pirates started decelerating and when all the shooting started. It's not likely, but if there are civilians out there who managed to not get killed, it's our job to keep them that way."

"Understood, Sir."

"Then we'll see you later, Captain," Charnay said more formally. "Charnay, clear."

The com display blanked, and Marcello sighed.

"You heard the Commodore, Chief Ulvestad," he said. "Contact the other skippers and let's set up some coordination."

"Yes, Sir," Ulvestad replied.

Lisa sat back in her own command couch, listening with half an ear as Ulvestad started her dual conversation, watching the icons of the hunters and the hunted accelerate steadily away from *Damocles*.

She checked the chrono, mentally shaking her head. After the hours and hours spent waiting, anticipating, planning, and watching Charnay's plan proceed perfectly, it had all come apart in less than ten minutes. Indeed, only seven minutes had elapsed since the pirate battlecruiser and *Banshee* had blown up.

And now more hours would stretch out as the survivors fled across the star system.

Travis had had it right, she decided, trying to remember the exact words of his quote. *War: ninety percent boredom and ten percent screaming panic.* Something like that, anyway.

She exhaled a quiet sigh. Some things, apparently, never changed.

☆   ☆   ☆

"Well, that's that," Llyn said, sitting in the copilot seat of the special ops shuttle.

And with the drama over, it was time to turn his mind to other things.

Such as doing something extra nice for Hester.

The obvious answer was a raise or bonus. That was his plan for Rhamas and Katura and the rest of their crews.

But Hester? What would she even do with extra money?

There was no question that he had to do *something*. Hester was the reason, after all, that everyone else was still alive.

She'd started by cracking the Volsungs' com encryption, which was the task Llyn had first set for her. But that hadn't been the end of it. She'd next tackled the software of the bomb Gensonne had surreptitiously placed on *Banshee*'s hull, the Volsung's rather ham-handed insurance policy.

He'd never decided whether Gensonne had expected the bomb to go undetected, or whether he'd expected Llyn to spot it and thus recognize the sword hanging over his head. The deadman protocol Gensonne had built into it rather argued for the latter idea, since Llyn would know that messing with the bomb or running out of range of the reset signal would mean his death.

Sadly for Gensonne, he hadn't known about Hester. Nor would it ever have entered his petty little mind that Llyn's eccentric genius would give him access to the bomb's programming long before they reached Danak. The system had continued to respond properly to each of Gensonne's reset signals, but unbeknownst to the admiral he'd been locked out of the actual detonation command and sequence.

Llyn could have removed it anytime he wished after that, but it had been a handy way to get rid of *Banshee*. He had no doubt that Captain Jaeger and *Loki* would react by blowing the freighter out of space seconds after her concealed energy torpedoes took down *Odin* and sent Gensonne's inconvenient secrets into eternity. But the bomb had guaranteed the freighter's *complete* destruction.

And that was almost as important as ensuring Gensonne's silence. He couldn't very well let anyone discover *Banshee*'s unique capabilities, or to query her computers about who'd built her and where she'd been over the last few years.

Now, given the timing, Haven and Danak would

have little choice but to conclude that the shadowy mastermind behind the Volsungs' most recent operations had been killed by the vengeful Gensonne when he realized he'd been betrayed.

Meanwhile, he, Rhamas, and Rhamas's crew had an appointment to keep.

Llyn, like most Axelrod operatives, liked to keep a few aces up his sleeve. *Banshee*'s second shuttle, tucked away out of sight and out of paperwork in the Number Two cargo hold, was one such ace. Even someone who'd examined its normal radar signature might not have realized just how stealthy the design actually was, since it incorporated strategically placed radar reflectors to strengthen its return when Llyn wanted to appear more or less normal.

In full stealth mode, however, those reflectors disappeared under sliding panels of radar-absorbent synthetic. On top of that, the shuttle used a special version of cold thrust—far more expensive than conventional thrusters, and with a significantly lower maximum acceleration, but with a thermal signature that was so low as to be virtually undetectable.

The only downside was that the extra equipment meant the living space was somewhat restricted. Still, it was large enough to accommodate all of *Banshee*'s small crew, certainly for the short length of time they would be penned up inside.

For the first five minutes after separation from *Banshee*, they'd simply drifted while Gensonne and his ships continued accelerating away from them toward Bergen 2. Then, with the Volsungs a safe seven million kilometers away, Rhamas had fired up the cold-thrust engine, expending virtually all of the shuttle's reaction mass on a fifty-minute, eight-gravity burn. The end result had been a paltry 235 KPS of velocity, but a more than satisfactory 350,000 kilometers of distance from its original vector.

Gensonne's turnover and deceleration towards his zero-zero with Bergen 2 had reversed the original process, with the ballistic shuttle now starting to catch up with the slowing Volsung fleet. But the additional side vector, along with the shuttle's inherently stealthy design, had meant little danger it would stray into Gensonne's detection range. By the time the velocities equalized once again, sixty-six minutes after separation and thirty-three minutes after the beginning of Gensonne's deceleration, Llyn was over half a million kilometers off the Volsungs' course.

Easy range for passive sensors against a starship. Against the shuttle, those same passive sensors were well-nigh useless, and they were well beyond the range at which any active sensors might have found such a stealthy target.

By the time *Banshee* executed her final instructions, it would be just thirty-six minutes until the shuttle once again crossed the hyper-limit.

Where *Pacemaker* would find it, rendezvous with it, take its passengers on board, and shake the dust of Danak from its sandals forever.

Llyn smiled out at the stars. No, not money. Not for Hester. Maybe a nice new chess program, something she couldn't take nine falls out of ten.

Yes. *That* would make the dear, crazy, frustrating, indispensable genius happy.

CHAPTER THIRTY-FIVE

"COM REQUEST FROM BERGEN TWO, SIR," Chief Ulvestad said.

"Put it up," Marcello ordered.

The image of Floyd Koski, the Jerriais Consortium's manager for Bergen 2, appeared upon the main com display.

The Danakan looked less than delighted. Lisa could hardly blame him.

The stream of follow-up reports from the debacle at Bergen 3 were getting worse and worse. The casualty totals were horrendous and continued to climb, and at least two of Bergen 3's platforms were total losses.

And Brigadier Massingill was among the seriously wounded. That was the one that dug most deeply into Lisa's gut.

It could have been worse. Bergen 3 had been chosen as the ambush site because any damage to it would risk far fewer lives and be a far lighter blow to the Jerriais development plan than either of the other two platforms. But that was little more than the coldest of comforts.

"Captain Marcello," Koski said as Marcello's face appeared on his own display. His voice was taut, and it was clear he was struggling to remain civil.

"Good afternoon, Mr. Koski," Marcello greeted him in turn. "What can I do for you?"

"I've been asked to relay a report to you," Koski said after the half second time lag. "DTC appears to be having some difficulty maintaining communications with *Pacemaker*."

"Excuse me?"

"Traffic Control is unable to get a response from *Pacemaker*," Koski said with strained patience. "They wondered if you or Commodore Charnay might have some idea what she's up to."

"As far as I know, she's not up to *anything*," Marcello replied. "May I ask why DTC is worried?"

"Because she's accelerating across the inner system at just over two KPS squared," Koski said. "She didn't alert DTC to any change in flight plan, and she's not responding to their hails. They're wondering if Captain Katura is proceeding under orders from Commodore Charnay."

"To the best of my knowledge, Captain Katura's sole concern was to recover Master Baird and his family," Marcello said. "My understanding was that *Pacemaker* would return to Danak Alpha orbit and wait out the engagement."

"That was our understanding, as well," Koski said, his civility starting to sound even more strained. "Are you saying Commodore Charnay *hasn't* given Katura new instructions?"

"Not as far as I'm aware," Marcello said. "Do we know where she's headed?"

Koski looked somewhere off screen.

"You should have it now."

"XO?" Marcello prompted.

"I've got it, Sir," Lisa said, keying the incoming vector data onto *Damocles*'s navigation plot.

She frowned. *Pacemaker*'s projected vector cut a chord across the Danak system that would take her at least fourteen light-minutes clear of *Damocles* or any of the surviving Volsungs and their Havenite pursuers.

What *was* Katura up to?

"So?" Koski prompted.

"I'm sorry, but I don't have any idea what he's doing," Marcello said. "It looks like he's running."

"It does, doesn't it?" Koski said darkly. "I find that highly suspicious. Under the circumstances, my government would very much like another conversation with him."

"I don't doubt it," Marcello said. "I'm sorry I don't have any further information for you."

"I rather doubted you would," Koski said with a touch of acid. "Let us know if the SAR effort bears any fruit. Koski, clear."

His image disappeared.

"I don't think President Nelson's going to get that chat, Sir," Lisa said. "Did you note where *Pacemaker*'s vector crosses the hyper-limit?"

Marcello frowned at the plot. "Well," he said, his face clearing just a little. "Damn."

Lisa nodded, feeling her lips compress. On *Pacemaker*'s currently projected heading, she would cross the hyper-limit less than four light-seconds from the point at which *Banshee* would have crossed had she survived and maintained her own heading.

"You think Katura's on his way to pick up a survivor from Swenson One?" Marcello asked.

"I don't see any other reason why he'd pick that particular spot," Lisa said. "It's certainly not the closest route to the hyper limit from his original position."

For a moment Marcello was silent.

"I suppose we could be generous and assume he's simply playing backstop for any life pods from *Banshee* that we missed," he said. "But I doubt you believe that any more than I do."

"No, Sir." Lisa shook her head. "This whole thing stinks to high heaven. Katura spun a good story, and for a while everything seemed to be going exactly as anticipated. But after what happened to *Odin* and *Banshee* . . ."

"And now *Pacemaker*," Marcello agreed. "It appears, TO, that the whole thing was a con, right from the beginning. Somebody wanted Swenson and his fleet eliminated, and he thoughtfully invited us and the Havenites to do all the heavy lifting for him. The big question is *why*."

"And *who*," Lisa added.

"Right," Marcello said. "And it doesn't look like we'll get those answers. At least, not today."

Lisa sighed and nodded as she ran the numbers. Nothing in Danak could possibly intercept *Pacemaker* on her current heading until several hours after she crossed the hyper-limit outbound. Her eyes drifted to the icons of the fleeing mercenary ships and the Havenite vessels steadily and vengefully closing the range.

"Not today," she echoed. "But unless Swenson's people are complete idiots, maybe we'll have some of those answers tomorrow."

☆　☆　☆

Only fifty of the pirates had survived the battle. Of those, only a handful were in good enough shape to be interrogated immediately. Commodore Charnay himself, joining with a handful of other officers, was in overall charge of the questioning.

But while it was Charnay who asked the questions, and it was Charnay who got the answers, it was Massingill who most of the prisoners watched while they supplied those answers.

Small wonder. The Commodore and the other officers had the appearance of stern victors who wanted information and were prepared to go to whatever lengths necessary to get it.

Massingill had the appearance of death incarnate.

She was in pain, despite the drugs coursing through her system. She didn't care. Much of her face was swathed in bandages. It didn't matter. All that mattered was that her eyes were clear and open...and that the pirates could see the look in those eyes.

Her teams had been killed. Bastonge, Cochran, Frijtom, Rushkoff—Elsie Dorrman—all of them and more wiped out in the flailing wedge that had shredded *Adder* and *Mamba* and half of Bergen 3. Sixty of the 303rd's finest, killed where they stood.

Murdered where they stood.

Massingill didn't care what vague guesses the prisoners had as to what had happened, or why *Copperhead* had acted the way she had. All Massingill knew was that someone aboard that cruiser had coldly and deliberately made the decision to commit mass murder.

With the rest of Charnay's forces occupied with Swenson One, *Copperhead* had managed to escape the Danak system. She was beyond Massingill's reach.

But someone had given the cruiser's captain his orders. Someone had connived and conned and manipulated the situation to the point where that decision had been made, and Massingill's commandos had been murdered.

That person might be beyond her reach for now. But he wouldn't stay that way. Somehow, someday, she would find him.

In the meantime, she would sit in on Charnay's interrogations, and stare at the prisoners, and learn everything she could about what was left of their organization.

Because if she stared hard enough, maybe something genuinely useful would shake loose.

☆　　☆　　☆

"Well?" Llyn asked.

Captain Katura shrugged.

"They're not happy," he said. "But they've accepted the situation with the grace of men who don't really have a choice."

"Yes," Llyn murmured, looking over the displays and the reports that were still coming in as he sipped his tea.

It was good. All of it. Gensonne was dead, his main ships had been destroyed—he'd always suspected that Jaeger had a streak of go-down-with-his-ship dramatics that would guarantee that *Loki* fought itself to death rather than surrender—and most of the mercenaries dead or captured. The survivors were mostly ordinary spacers who'd never even seen Llyn, let alone knew anything about him. A couple of midlevel officers were reputed to be among the prisoners, but that wouldn't be a problem, either.

Of course, *Copperhead* had managed to get away from Bergen 3. But that shouldn't be a problem. Gensonne would hardly have shared his damning Axelrod information with anyone aboard a lowly cruiser.

That was really the only potential chink in the trap Llyn had so carefully engineered. If Gensonne had lied about being the only one who knew Llyn's connection to Axelrod, this could still come apart.

But that was vanishingly unlikely. As Gensonne himself had said, knowledge was power, and Gensonne was too smart to hand that power to any of his officers.

He would have left a backup data package, of course, if only to prevent Llyn from murdering him as soon as his usefulness was ended. But the backup was almost certainly deeply buried in one of the computers at the Walther base. If *Shrike* and the Axelrod Black Ops task force Captain Vaagen had been ordered to collect were on schedule, the station and remaining Volsung ships and men would be an expanding ball of superheated gas long before any news of the Danak debacle could reach them.

Really, the only downside to this whole thing was that he'd now burned his Max Baird identity and could never return openly to this part of space. But that was all right. There were other representatives of the mysterious Master Rowbtham who could make an appearance if and when Axelrod needed someone to poke around Havenite space.

And they well might need to do that. Because while the Volsung Mercenaries had been dealt with, the problem of Manticore was still there. The Star Kingdom remained blithely unaware of the awesome economic power they were sitting on, and it was still Llyn's job to figure out how to put that asset firmly onto Axelrod's balance sheet.

It would take some thought. Some very deep, very cunning thought.

But Llyn had the time. He certainly had the cunning.

"Destination, sir?" Katura asked.

"Solway," Llyn said. "There should be a ship at the facility there that Rhamas and his crew can be certified for. They can then head to Jasper or back to Beowulf for new orders. I'll probably have Rhamas take Hester with him—the places I'll be going will bore her to death, and I'm tired of losing all those chess games."

"Yes, sir." Katura gave his employer half a smile. "I *am* sorry *Banshee* had to go, though. It was a good ship, and I know Rhamas really liked it."

"Yes, it was," Llyn agreed. "But don't worry. I'll make sure his next one is even better."

☆   ☆   ☆

The station was quiet, on minimal power, and except for a few Andermani still poking around the corners it seemed deserted.

"It wasn't difficult," Basaltberg commented as he led the way around the inner edge of the spin section. "Once their ships were lost, the station forces had little incentive to fight."

Which didn't exactly address the question of whether they'd surrendered or gone down fighting, Travis noted. But he had no intention of bringing up that particular subject. Not to the man who commanded a ship that had taken out an enemy battlecruiser in a single, massive, three-wave missile salvo.

At least there were no bodies lying around that Travis had to look at. He was grateful for that.

"I appreciate your willingness to join me aboard the station, Captain Clegg," Basaltberg continued. "I wanted to show you personally that we have indeed taken the main computer system intact, and wished you present during the final download process."

"Thank you, Admiral," Clegg said. "We're very grateful for your courtesy. Especially given that you carried most of the load of the battle."

"Hardly a fair assessment," Basaltberg said with mild reproof, "since it was your plan that laid the groundwork for the battle. You should be justly proud of your contribution, as I'm certain your Navy is justly proud of you." He shifted his eyes to Travis. "And you, Commander Long. I will be recommending to His Excellency that the Navy look into installing such launchers, with an eye toward using your tactic in future engagements."

"Thank you, Sir," Travis said.

"A question, Captain," Basaltberg said, turning his eyes back to Clegg. "I find it interesting that you initially proffered this idea as your own, and that only after I accepted it did you identify it as Commander Long's tactic. May I ask why?"

"Certainly, Sir," Clegg said. "I wished to make it clear that anything that came from *Casey's* officers or crew came with my authority and approval. Should the plan have been rejected, nothing more would need to have been said. But once it was accepted—" she shot Travis an unreadable glance "—it was my responsibility to give full credit where due."

"I see," Basaltberg said. "Interesting. Is this common Manticoran military procedure and standards?"

Clegg seemed to hesitate—

And in Travis's mind's eye, a kaleidoscope of names and faces and voices appeared, the long line of men and women he'd served with throughout his career. Some of those people had been honorable and brave. Others had been cheaters, loafers, or back-stabbers.

The Navy had books full of regulations and procedures. Travis had read them through, absorbing the information until it became a part of his core. Sadly, not everyone lived up to the standards laid out there. Maybe not even half of them.

That wasn't something the Navy was proud of. But it also wasn't something they needed to share with a foreign officer.

"It's the procedure and standard held by the very best," he said before Clegg could come up with her own answer. "Unfortunately, not everyone in the Navy can be the very best."

"Perhaps not," Basaltberg said, his face stern. "Though I will say that those who are not the best do not survive long in the Andermani Navy." His expression softened a little—"But we have tasted a great deal of war. The Star Kingdom has not."

"We have now," Clegg murmured.

"Indeed you have," Basaltberg agreed. "Let us pray that you will learn quickly the lessons necessary to survive."

"Yes," Clegg said. "Speaking of survival, Sir, have you

ascertained whether the prisoners and their planetside dependents will all fit aboard the Volsung freighters?"

"They will," Basaltberg said. "They won't be comfortable, but they'll survive. I've detailed *Ao Qin* and *Loreley* to escort them to Sachsen, where they'll be turned over to the authorities. I wish them luck dealing with them."

He gestured to a hatchway ahead, flanked by two armored Andermani. "And now, let us see if the spoils of victory are ready for us to share."

Chomps and Hauptman were in the computer room, along with two Andermani techs and another four soldiers. Chomps was seated at one of the consoles, while Hauptman was hunched over a rolling cart covered with small electronic components.

"Ah—Captain," Chomps greeted Clegg. "You're just in time. We're downloading the last data files now."

"You've got everything?" Clegg asked, frowning at Hauptman's cart. "Hidden files, segmenteds, ghosts?"

"Everything," Chomps assured her. "It'll take a while to sort through it, possibly months or years for some of the more stubborn ones. But that's what techs are for." He nodded toward Hauptman. "Right now, Mr. Hauptman's the one with the interesting haul."

"Possibly," Hauptman cautioned. "Townsend didn't need my help with the computer, so I decided to poke around the supply rooms to see where Gensonne had been shopping. A lot of the stuff is Silesian, of course, with some Havenite thrown in."

"No big surprise on either," Chomps added.

"Right." Hauptman gestured to his cart. "*This* stuff, though, I think may be Andermani."

"Do you, now," Basaltberg said, a frown creasing

his head as he stepped toward the cart for a closer look. "Your evidence?"

"Mostly negative," Hauptman admitted. "I know that the serial code patterns don't look Havenite, Silesian, or Solarian, and they're definitely not Manticoran." He gestured again. "I pulled some of the more portable pieces together, in case you wanted to take it with you before we destroy the station."

"I would indeed," Basaltberg said. "Thank you, Herr Hauptman."

"My pleasure." Hauptman looked at Clegg. "We *are* still going to destroy the station, right?"

"Admiral Basaltberg will handle that part," Clegg said. "Our orders didn't specify the station's destruction. His did. Ergo, he gets to spend the missiles."

"Done," Chomps announced, uncoupling a pair of data modules from the computer and standing up. "Here it is, Captain. Admiral, I understand your people have already made their own copies?"

"They have," Basaltberg said. "And with that, Captain Clegg, I believe it's time for both of us to return to our respective homes." He offered her his hand. "Thank you for your assistance, and the assistance of the Star Kingdom of Manticore."

"I was glad we could make this work, Sir," Clegg said, taking the proffered hand and shaking it. "I hope this will mark the beginning of a closer relationship between our nations."

"To be candid, I doubt that very much," Basaltberg said. "Manticore is quite distant, and the Emperor's thoughts are much closer to home." His face hardened a bit. "Remember, too, Captain, that our joint effort here was in no way sanctioned by either of our governments. What will come of it, or whether my superiors will chose to make Manticoran involvement in *Vergeltung*'s mission part of the official record, I cannot say."

"Understood," Clegg said. "To be honest, the whole thing will probably be even more sensitive from our end. Given Manticore's current political atmosphere, this could fan flames that would be better left alone. I'll make sure my officers and official records treat this with all the sensitivity required."

"Then let us say our farewells—" Basaltberg smiled faintly "—and let us hope our next meeting will be under more pleasant circumstances."

☆   ☆   ☆

Casey was thirty minutes from the hyper limit when gravitics spotted the fresh hyper footprint seventy degrees around the edge of the system.

"Report," Clegg said as she pulled herself onto the bridge.

"Looks like six ships," Woodburn reported from CIC. "Their wedges read like warships. Small ones—cruiser or destroyer class. Their transponder codes won't get to us for another twenty-one minutes, which means we won't know who they are until we're just about ready to translate."

"Assuming they're even running transponders," Clegg said as she floated to a halt at Travis's station. "Options, TO?"

"We could cease acceleration, Ma'am," Travis said cautiously. Clegg wasn't really thinking about going back to meet an unknown force alone, was she? "That would give us more time to collect data before we hit the hyper limit. But at this distance, we're not going to get much no matter what we do. We could try shutting down our impellers and hiding, but there's a good chance they've already spotted our wedge."

"Any chance of finding Basaltberg? He might like to know Walther has new arrivals."

"No, Ma'am," Travis said, checking the log. "*Vergeltung* translated to Alpha nearly an hour ago, and on an entirely different vector from ours. She's long gone."

"Yes, I thought that would be the case." Clegg lowered her voice. "I assume you don't have a plan up your sleeve for taking on six cruisers all by ourselves?"

Travis clenched his teeth. Was she mocking him? Probably.

"No, Ma'am."

"Pity," she said in the same low voice. "You seem to have a knack for such things. I suppose Delphi's gain is the Navy's loss."

Travis frowned. A compliment? From Clegg? "I—uh—thank you, Ma'am."

"You're welcome, Commander," Clegg said. "We may not mesh very well personality-wise, but you're good at combat. And I can appreciate that."

"Thank you, Ma'am."

"Everyone as you were," Clegg said, raising her voice to normal volume again. "Continue course. Keep the transponder off—if they're who we think they are, we don't want them to know who just wrecked their base. CIC, call Chief Townsend, and tell him he's got one hour to pull everything he can on the visitors." She tapped Travis's shoulder. "And while everyone else is looking backwards, TO, you keep a sharp watch everywhere else. Just in case they're not alone."

☆   ☆   ☆

"Bogey One just translated to Alpha, Sir," the XO reported from *Shrike's* CIC. "They never activated their beacon, and we weren't able to get anything but their wedge strength."

Captain Vaagen scowled. So one of the Volsung ships had escaped. Unwittingly, probably unknowingly, given that she had already been well on her way before he and the Black Ops force even hit the hyper limit.

Still, when the vagrant returned to a ruined base her captain would hardly have trouble putting two and two together.

Mr. Llyn wouldn't be pleased. He hated loose ends. But there was nothing Vaagen could do about it. He, and Llyn, would just have to live with it.

In the meantime, he had a job to do.

"Continue on course," he ordered. "And keep trying to raise the Volsung base. There must be *somebody* awake there we can talk to."

☆   ☆   ☆

"Good day, My Lord," Elizabeth said as she seated herself at the Palace conference room table. "Thank you for coming by on such short notice."

"As always, Your Majesty, I serve at my Monarch's convenience," Breakwater said, bowing courteously.

But the smoothness of his words belied the wariness in his face. Even as he seated himself, he threw a surreptitious look at Elizabeth's father, seated at the far end of the table.

The Monarch, the former Monarch, and the Chancellor of the Exchequer, alone at a meeting. In Breakwater's place, Elizabeth reflected, she would probably feel a little nervous, too.

"I'll get right to the point, My Lord," she said. "Four points, actually. First point: I'm pregnant."

Breakwater's eyes widened. "You're—? Ah ... my congratulations, Your Majesty. May I ask ... ?"

"Who the father is?" Elizabeth shook her head. "No, you may not. Second point: this child is the rightful heir to the Star Kingdom, and will succeed me to the Throne. Third point—"

"Excuse me, Your Majesty," Breakwater interrupted. The initial shock had passed, and he was back on track again. "Once again, I must remind you that the Constitution requires the Monarch to marry a commoner, which carries the strong implication that the heir must come from such a union. If the child you carry is your late husband's, you're in violation of that provision."

"The Constitution may imply, but it doesn't explicitly state," Elizabeth said. "Which brings me to Point Three: with the backing of the House of Commons, I intend to propose an amendment to the Constitution that will remove that ambiguity, and bring my child fully within the law."

Breakwater's face stiffened. "With the *Commons*, Your Majesty?"

"Yes, My Lord," Elizabeth said. "You see, my final gift from Prime Minister Burgundy wasn't a list of potential suiters, as we all first thought. It was, instead, a list of potential allies in the Constitutional crises he knew would be coming."

"I see." Breakwater drew himself up. "There is, of course, another way to avoid such a crisis."

"There are several," Elizabeth agreed. "But since I don't feel like bartering my future for your support, this is the one I'll be using." She keyed the file on her tablet over to Breakwater's. "Especially given Point Four."

Breakwater glanced down at his tablet. Took a second look. Carefully picked up the tablet and held it a bit closer.

And as he read, Elizabeth watched the color slowly drain from his face.

It seemed a long time before he finally looked up. "This wasn't me," he said, his voice almost a whisper.

"I know that," Elizabeth said. "But the guilty parties were your supporters. *And* you knew what they'd done."

"*After* the fact," Breakwater insisted. "Only *after* the fact."

"Irrelevant," Michael spoke up. "The point is that you knew, and you said nothing. No one should have profited from the *Phobos* disaster the way Castle Rock and Chillon did. Even worse, the very nature of their under-the-table deals strongly suggests they knew in advance about the sloop's flaws, yet they said nothing. And a hundred thirty men and women died."

"They've been your close political allies for over fifteen T-years," Elizabeth said. "A brush that tars them will also tar you."

Breakwater's lip twisted. "So you blackmail me," he bit out. "And for something I didn't even do."

"Would you feel better if we blackmailed you for something you *did* do?" Michael offered. "I'm sure your long career includes deals and quiet profits you'd rather the Star Kingdom not hear about. But this is what we've got. So this is what we use."

Breakwater looked back down at his tablet. "I told them it was wrong," he said quietly. "That's the irony.

I warned them to make restitution, and to immediately distance themselves from the people they'd made their deals with. But they wouldn't listen."

"And then you let it lie," Elizabeth said. "*That's* the true irony, My Lord. You had the chance to hold the moral high ground, but you gave it away to further your own political agenda and power. And now you lose it all."

"*All?*" Breakwater challenged, looking back up at her.

"All," she said firmly. "But not all at once. I need you to remain in your current position, and to hold your peace when Joshua Miller brings up my resolution in the Commons. You don't have to openly support it. You just have to *not* oppose it."

Breakwater shook his head. "You underestimate the Lords, Your Majesty," he said. "Or else you overestimate the Commons."

"I don't think so," Elizabeth said. "On the contrary, I think *you* underestimate the people. Would you like to hear the speech I'll be delivering after Mr. Miller announces the resolution?"

Breakwater's eyes had gone hooded. "A speech to Parliament?"

"A speech to the entire Star Kingdom," Elizabeth said. The image of a tiger in a corner, crouched and trapped, flicked to mind. "The core will go something like this.

"This is the child of my late husband, the child we always intended to have. I've lost the man I loved; I will not give up his child, as well. I believe any fair minded person can understand the need to clear up the Constitutional ambiguity the recently introduced amendment will address. Whatever the outcome of that process, and whatever future political battles may have to be waged before simple sanity is allowed to rule, I *will* have this child, and its existence will in no way affect all the other legal arguments—for *or* against—my proposed solution to the Constitution's ambiguity where the marriage of the ruling monarch is concerned."

She finished, and for a moment no one spoke.

"You understand the language will probably be more elaborate," Elizabeth said. "Certainly more formal. But I think the message speaks for itself."

For another moment no one spoke. Elizabeth wanted to look at her father, to try to get his read on Breakwater. But this was between her and the Chancellor, and she needed to face him down alone.

Breakwater stirred.

"And if I bow to your demands?"

"Six T-months from now you'll hand in your resignation from the Cabinet," Elizabeth said, watching him closely. He had a whole repertoire of gambits to throw, everything from guilt to pity, and he was surely spinning up at least one of them. "You'll be permitted to remain in the Lords, and wield whatever influence you still have." She gestured toward his tablet. "But it won't be as much as you're expecting, because at approximately that same time this document will be revealed, and there's a good chance Castle Rock and Chillon will be brought up on charges."

"But I'll be left out of it?"

"Provided you continue to cooperate, yes," Elizabeth said. "As you said, this wasn't you. But that's the future. For now, just know that in two days Mr. Miller will bring the Constitutional issue before the Commons. You have until then to decide whether to maintain your reputation and dignity, or to allow the political landscape to devolve into war."

"Of course, if that happens this document will be released much sooner," Michael added.

"I'm sure it will," Breakwater murmured. He blanked his tablet and for another moment he gazed down at it. Then, slowly, he raised his eyes again.

"If there's nothing more, Your Majesty?"

The tiger in the corner had sheathed its claws.

For now.

"There's nothing more, My Lord," Elizabeth confirmed.

"Then I take my leave," Breakwater said, standing up and bowing. "Your Majesty." He half turned and bowed to Michael. "Your Highness."

"Well," Elizabeth said after the door had closed behind him. "That went more smoothly than I'd expected."

"Don't believe it," Michael said sourly. "He may be bowing on the outside, but he's standing up straight and defiant on the inside. He's going to be working this, just as hard and as fast as he can. You can bet on it."

"Oh, I am," Elizabeth assured him. "But I'm also betting that part of his scheme will involve Susan Tarleton and his private back door into Prime Minister Harwich's office and computer. Once Joshua has pushed through the bill, and Breakwater starts planning his comeback, I'll be taking that back door away from him."

"That should crimp his style a bit," Michael agreed. "Have you thought about who to suggest as Foreign Secretary?"

"I have the perfect candidate," Elizabeth said, smiling. This had actually been Joshua's idea, but she'd enthusiastically agreed with it. "Baron Winterfall."

"*Winterfall*?" Michael's eyes widened. "You're joking."

"Can you think of a better way to mollify Breakwater's supporters?" Elizabeth asked. "I doubt any of them knows of Winterfall's defection, so it'll look like I'm bowing to some unseen pressure."

"At least until the bottom drops out with his resignation," Michael said thoughtfully. "And by then it'll be too late to object to any of it. Not a very big bone to throw them, though."

"Oh, I don't know," Elizabeth said. "With our increasing contacts with Haven and the ongoing regional pirate hunt, Foreign Affairs may someday become more than just a sinecure position."

"Maybe," Michael said. "That would certainly be a change."

"Change can be good, Daddy," Elizabeth said quietly.

"Yes, it can." Michael shrugged. "Sometimes."

CHAPTER THIRTY-SIX

TRAVIS HAD COME HOME FROM LONG voyages before. But never one this long.

And never one that held so much hope, anticipation, and pure terror for the two solid months that he waited nervously for Lisa to come home, too.

But finally—finally—she was there. Safe and sound.

And with an impressive story of her own.

"I'm just hoping Massingill comes out of it okay," she commented as Travis ferried dishes from her cupboard to the dining room table. "You remember Jean Massingill, right?"

"Yes," Travis said, carefully lining up the spoons with the knives. "Was there any improvement in her condition before you left?"

"It's going to be a long haul," Lisa said. "But the look in her eyes—you should have seen it. If she ever figures out who was behind her teams' slaughter, and if you happen to be standing in her way, get to one side quick."

"Trust me," Travis assured her, wincing a little as

he smoothed out a wrinkle in her napkin. Jean Massingill on a blood-hunt was definitely an awesome and terrifying image.

"She was talking about taking a leave of absence if she couldn't get someone in Nouveau Paris to kick off a full and proper investigation—her words—and take it on herself and you're being *really* quiet tonight."

"I know," Travis said. "But you're a little talkative, so it evens out."

"I'm talkative because you're nervous," Lisa said, eyeing him closely. "You being nervous makes *me* nervous. You're not picking up incoming bogies, are you?"

"No, no, nothing like that." Travis took a deep breath. Frankly, he'd rather face an enemy task force. "Lisa...we've been friends for a long time. I really like your company, and you put up with me, so I guess you like mine, too."

"Yes, I do," Lisa said solemnly. "Very much." And then stopped.

Travis took another deep breath. Did she already know where this was going? Probably. She was a much better judge of people and emotions and facial expressions than he was. She probably knew exactly where this was going.

But she was going to make him go through the whole thing anyway.

Typical senior officer.

"The thing is, I had a lot of time to think while we were on the Silesia mission," he continued. "And you were at Haven; and if I'd had even a hint that the rest of Gensonne's mercenaries were heading your way, I'd have been worried sick. *Was* worried sick once we found the computer files about Danak."

"Likewise," Lisa said, her voice still not giving anything away. "If I'd known they'd left a force where you were...but I wouldn't have been so worried."

Travis felt his heart plummet into his gut. "You wouldn't?"

"No," Lisa said, a small smile finally touching her lips. "Because I've seen you in action. I know what you can do. I'd have known that, whatever you came up against, you would find a brilliant plan that would win the day."

"Well...sometimes," Travis said. Wishing like hell that he had a brilliant plan for this one.

And then, finally, she took pity. "You're right, Travis, we know each other pretty well," she said, reaching over and taking his hand. "If you have something to say, you don't have to be clever. Just say it."

Travis took one final deep breath. "Lisa Donnelly," he said, impulsively dropping to one knee. That *was* the correct form, wasn't it? "Will you marry me?"

☆　　☆　　☆

Deep inside Elizabeth's abdomen, the baby kicked again.

"Goodness," Elizabeth said, leaning back from her desk, wincing as she clutched at her silken robe. She winced again at the sight and feel of her newly spherical figure. *You can dress up a balloon*, she thought dryly, *but it's still just a balloon*. "Patience, please. You've still got three months to cook."

The baby—David—took no notice. He kicked once more and then went silent again. Elizabeth waited a moment, then readjusted herself in her chair. It was getting increasingly difficult to find comfortable positions, and she suspected it was only going to get worse.

Her intercom pinged, and she tapped the key. "Yes, Martine?"

"Your Majesty, Prime Minister Harwich and Defense Minister Dapplelake are here to see you. Lord Harwich says it's urgent."

Elizabeth felt a stirring in her gut that had nothing to do with her fidgety baby. Had they dug up something fresh about Gensonne? Or worse, was there new evidence that the battles at Walther and Danak hadn't fully eliminated him as a threat?

"Send them in," she said.

Across the office, the door swung open and the two ministers stepped inside. "Please come in, My Lords," Elizabeth said, waving them forward. "What can I do for you?"

"Our apologies, Your Majesty," Harwich said as they crossed to her desk. His expression was grim, the same way he'd looked just before the threatened Constitutional crisis passed with more of a whimper than a bang.

Was Breakwater making fresh trouble?

"We're sorry to intrude on short notice," the Prime Minister continued. "But we've just received some information from SIS that we thought needed your immediate attention."

Elizabeth inclined her head. "Of course. Please continue."

"Lady Calvingdell's team has been going through the records her agents obtained from the Volsung base at Walther," Dapplelake said. "There are a number of layers, plus an unknown number of hidden files that could take months or even years to dig out and decrypt. But we *have* ascertained three very important points.

"First: the force that came briefly into Manticore space three weeks after Gensonne's attack was indeed units from the Free Duchy of Barca."

"Are you sure?" Elizabeth asked, frowning at Dapplelake. "I thought we'd concluded they were more of Gensonne's ships running false IDs."

"We'd *assumed* that, Your Highness," Dapplelake corrected. "But we never had any data either way. But the Volsung records confirm without a doubt that the Barcans were involved."

"But why?"

"Apparently, the same reason the Volsungs were involved," Harwich said grimly. "Money. Lots and lots of money."

A chill ran up Elizabeth's back. "Money from whom?"

"That, we still don't know," Dapplelake said. "But that leads to point two: even with just the money trail we've been able to track it's clear that a huge amount of money has already been spent on the goal of destroying the Star Kingdom of Manticore. That implies deep pockets, and people with deep pockets aren't likely to give up just because the Volsungs are out of the picture."

"And point three," Harwich said. "The money trail Dapplelake mentions unfortunately fades out too soon for us to track it back to its source. But we're fairly confident that it extends all the way back to the Solarian League."

The chill grew even colder. "The *League* wants us destroyed?"

"Or someone inside the League," Harwich said. "Some star nation, perhaps, or possibly a transstellar corporation." He shrugged. "Theoretically, it could even be a group of wealthy individuals who for some reason don't want Manticore to succeed."

"I see," Elizabeth said, forcing calmness. "So what we know is that someone's out to destroy us, but we don't know who or why. We can also assume that, whatever the answers are to those questions, the attacks will continue."

Harwich and Dapplelake exchanged looks. "Yes, Your Majesty," Harwich said. "That's the situation as we read it."

Elizabeth nodded, freshly aware of the baby growing inside her. Her job as the Queen was to protect the Star Kingdom's people. Her job as a mother was to do everything she could to make sure this particular problem was resolved here and now, and not get handed over to her son.

"In that case, we had best get to it," she said. "Have Lady Calvingdell redouble her efforts to dig into the Volsungs' records. You're to see she has all the resources she needs."

"Understood, Your Majesty," Dapplelake said. "Calvingdell is already doing all that she can, and we're working together to get her whatever resources and personnel she can use."

"Good." Elizabeth took a deep breath. "We're standing on a precipice, My Lords. We need to know exactly how close we are to the edge, before our unknown enemy pushes us off."

EPILOGUE

"... WHICH IS ONE OF THE MANY reasons I find it difficult to evaluate this officer's efficiency without permitting personal opinion to color my judgment.

"Having said that, and making all due allowance for the clashes between our personalities, I continue to believe this officer is far too conscious of the exact letter of the regulations. This makes him, in many ways, a less than ideal leader during routine shipboard operations. He is clearly not comfortable dealing with subordinates outside the strictest interpretation of regulations and standard operating procedures, and one cannot avoid the impression that he takes refuge behind them rather than seeking opportunities to generate a sense of rapport. In addition, he is often awkward in social situations with civilians when serving as a formal representative of Her Majesty's Navy. It has also been my observation, from personal experience, that he is not always articulate or possessed of an appropriate sense of timing in presenting contrarian points of view to his superiors.

"These are significant faults in any Queen's officer, and, as his commanding officer on the deployment just concluded, my relations with him were frequently strained. I also found him perversely impetuous, for one so enamored of regulations, and on many occasions he clearly formed opinions and judgments on the flimsiest of evidence and with minimal time to consider all implications of the matter in hand.

"In short, he was not an easy officer for me to command.

"He is also, however, fundamentally incapable of giving less than his best to any task to which he may be assigned. He does not appear to know even the definition of the term 'dereliction,' and despite his obvious preference for clearly defined hierarchies and the social insulation of regulations and SOP, he excels at identifying and correcting weaknesses in the training of his own subordinates. Nor does that preference for defined rules prevent him from thinking quickly, clearly, and concisely or from conceiving inventive, original, unconventional, and highly successful tactical solutions, even under severe pressure. And while I would be far more comfortable with his judgment if he could bring himself to spend an additional few minutes before reaching his conclusions *outside* immediate tactical problems, he almost invariably reaches the *proper* conclusion, however haphazard his reasoning must appear to any outside observer.

"Perhaps most importantly, this officer possesses the intellectual integrity and moral courage not only to shoulder responsibilities which should never have been assigned to someone of his relatively junior rank, but also to accept the potentially disastrous personal consequences of exercising his judgment in meeting those responsibilities.

"In short, it is the undersigned officer's opinion that Lieutenant Commander Long is one of the most competent—if frequently infuriating—and valuable officers with whom she has been privileged to serve. He is unreservedly recommended for independent command at the earliest possible moment.

"Trina Miranda Clegg, Captain, Royal Manticoran Navy.

"Commanding officer, Her Majesty's Ship *Casey*, CL-01.

"19 Tenth, 75 AL."

Admiral Carlton Locatelli finished reading aloud, laid the memo board on his desk, and leaned back in his chair.

"And there you have it, Clara," he said. "Since you were never a serving officer and thus never had the opportunity to make Captain Clegg's acquaintance, you'll just have to take my word for it that getting an efficiency report like that out of her..." He shook his head wryly. "Let's just say she's not noted for the effusiveness of her praise."

"That's exactly my point." Countess Calvingdell leaned forward in her own chair and tapped her index finger emphatically on his desktop. "*Exactly* my point."

Locatelli shook his head. "Out of the question," he said. "It's going to take a while for Her Majesty and Dapplelake—and Harwich, of course—to get it rammed through Parliament, but after what Gensonne did to us, the Navy's *got* to be updated. And not just our hardware. Hell, not even *primarily* our hardware."

He raised his hands shoulder high, then lowered them, his expression hardening. "We've got some good people—some *very* good people—but you know from your time as Defense Minister that we've also got a lot of deadwood that needs clearing away. And I hate to say this, but not even our best people really know their jobs the way they ought to."

"Yourself excepted, I assume?"

"Myself *not* excepted," Locatelli conceded. "It's not their fault, really. The point is that before we can start teaching ourselves to do our jobs properly we've first got to figure out what it is we don't know. That's going to take a lot of time and a lot of sweat."

He raised his eyebrows.

"*And* a lot of people like Lieutenant Commander Long."

"If you need him so badly, why is he still just a lieutenant commander?" Calvingdell countered.

Locatelli snorted out a half-laugh.

"You know the answer to that, My Lady. Politics, of course. You know even better than I do how that gets in the way every damn time we turn around. Long's brother's association with Breakwater has always left him in a sort of limbo."

"As far as I can tell, Long is about as apolitical as it's possible for anyone to be," Calvingdell pointed out.

"I agree," Locatelli said. "But who's going to believe that? No one in the Navy, let alone Parliament, can ever forget who his brother is. So every single time he's nominated for a decoration or a promotion board thinks about him, the political implications of decorating or promoting *Winterfall's brother* loom up in everyone's mind."

He scowled. "Including mine. That's the only damned reason he hasn't already gotten the recognition he deserves, and if I could figure out a way around that, I'd already have taken it. So far I haven't, but that doesn't mean I can justify letting an officer—especially a *tactical* officer—of his proven capability be frittered away as a spook when we've got such a deep hole to dig ourselves out of."

"I might point out that Commander Long and Chief Townsend are the only reason we know as much as we do about the Volsungs," Calvingdell reminded him tartly. "Let me also point out that this recent mission clearly indicates the two of them as a team are greater than the sum of their parts."

"As long as they have Special Order Seven to trot out?"

Calvingdell made a face.

"Fine—I deserved that. Much as I hate to admit it, in retrospect I agree completely with Clegg's original objections to that order. By the same token, her own report makes it clear that it was only Long's willingness to overrule her that led to the Andermani cooperation against Walther and the capture of Gensonne's backup data base. You may need tactical officers to figure out how to *fight* the enemy, Carlton, but *I* need superior intelligence assets to figure out who the hell the enemy *is*."

"I'm not giving him up," Locatelli said flatly. He smiled crookedly. "On the other hand, I'll concede your point about the team of Long and Townsend. Actually, I'm more than half inclined to insist that Townsend come back to regular service, too."

"Dream on, Carlton," Calvingdell said, returning

his smile. "You're not getting Townsend back, so don't even go there. You'll need a better lever than *that* to pry Long out of Delphi's grip."

"Except that he's not officially *in* Delphi's grip," Locatelli pointed out. "Technically, he's just *on loan* to Delphi, which means I can take him back anytime I want."

For a handful of seconds they just looked at each other. Then, Calvingdell shrugged.

"Fine. If that's your final word, I suppose I'll just have to go over your head."

Locatelli snorted. "*Dapplelake*? Seriously, Clara. When you were Defense Minister, how did *you* react when a couple of your senior subordinates behaved like kids fighting over a sandbox toy?"

"Not well," the countess conceded.

"Exactly," Locatelli said. "I doubt the Earl will react any better than you did. Besides, the First Lord's already made his opinion clear."

"*Cazenestro*'s made the call?" Calvingdell's eyebrows arched. "Why didn't you just say so?"

"I said he's made his opinion clear," Locatelli said. "I didn't say he's decided who gets Long."

"And what exactly would that opinion have been?"

"That he doesn't want an argument over ONI's and Special Intelligence's spheres of authority," Locatelli said. "His exact words were 'Earl Dapplelake doesn't want to hear about it, *I* don't want to hear about it, and—trust me—neither of you want *Her Majesty* to hear about it.' So unless you're planning to appeal to God, it looks like you've run out of options for appeal."

"I suppose that makes sense," Calvingdell said reluctantly. "Cazenestro isn't exactly in a position to give us direct orders, but I can see his point. The last thing any of us want is to turn intelligence-gathering into a political food fight in the Lords."

"With everybody and his brother sticking a spoon into the soup," Locatelli said sourly,

"Exactly," Calvingdell said. "So if we don't want that, we need to work out the relationship between ONI and Delphi ourselves. Seems to me the simplest solution is for me to just take Long off your hands."

Locatelli snorted. "My Lady, I am a senior officer in the Royal Manticoran Navy," he said sternly. "Senior officers of the Navy do not simply strike their wedges and surrender."

"Then just how do *you* suggest we work this out, Admiral?"

"After much thought and mature consideration," Locatelli said, unfolding his arms and sliding a hand into his tunic pocket, "I've come up with what I believe is the only possible solution."

"Which is?"

"This," he said gravely, drawing his hand from his pocket. He held it out towards her across the deck and opened it to show the small, gleaming disk on his palm.

"Since you're the peer of the realm, My Lady," he told her, "the choice is yours. Heads or tails?"

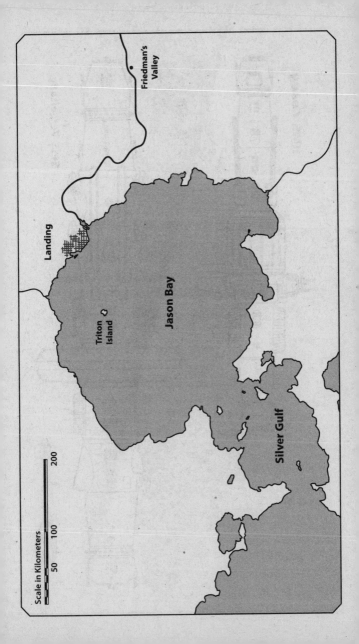

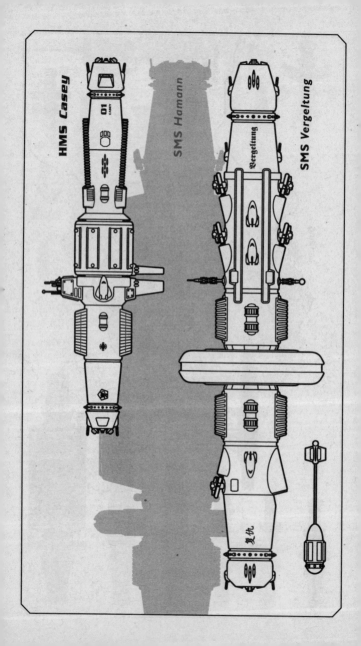

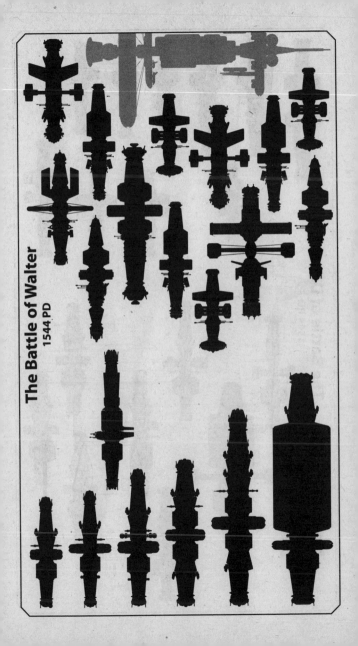

The Battle of Walter
1544 PD

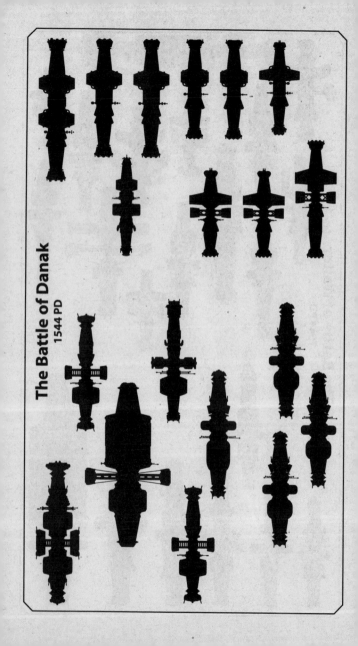

The Battle of Danak
1544 PD

"SPACE OPERA IS ALIVE AND WELL"*

And *New York Times* Best Seller
DAVID WEBER
is the New Reigning King of the Spaceways!

HONOR HARRINGTON NOVELS:

On Basilisk Station   pb • 0-7434-3571-0 • $7.99
"... an outstanding blend of military/technical writing balanced by supderb character development and an excellent degree of human drama ... very highly recommended."—*Wilson Library Bulletin*

The Honor of the Queen   pb • 0-7434-3572-9 • $7.99
"Honor fights her way with fists, brains, and tactical genius through a tangle of politics, battles and cultural differences. Although battered she ends this book with her honor, and the Queen's, intact."—*Kliatt*

The Short Victorious War   pb • 0-7434-3573-7 • $7.99
"This remarkable story will appeal to readers interested in warfare, science, and technology of the future or just in interpersonal relationships, and important part of the story. Gratifying, especially to female readers, is the total equality of the sexes!"—*Kliatt*

Field of Dishonor   pb • 0-7434-3574-5 • $7.99
"Great stuff...compelling combat combined with engaging characters for a great space opera adventure."—*Locus*

* *Starlog*

Flag in Exile pb • 0-7434-3575-3 • $7.99
"Packs enough punch to smash a starship to smithereens."—*Publishers Weekly*

Honor Among Enemies pb • 0-671-87783-6 • $7.99
"Star Wars as it might have been written by C.S. Forester
. . . fast-paced entertainment." —*Booklist*

In Enemy Hands pb • 0-671-57770-0 • $7.99
After being ambushed, Honor finds herself aboard an
enemy cruiser, bound for her scheduled execution. But
one lesson Honor has never learned is how to give up!

Echoes of Honor hc • 0-671-87892-1 • $24.00
pb • 0-671-57833-2 • $7.99
"Brilliant! Brilliant! Brilliant!"—Anne McCaffrey

Ashes of Victory pb • 0-671-31977-9 • $7.99
Honor has escaped from the prison planet called Hell and
returned to the Manticoran Alliance, to the heart of a furnace of new weapons, new strategies, new tactics, spies,
diplomacy, and assassination.

War of Honor hc • 0-7434-3545-1 • $26.00
pb • 0-7434-7167-9 • $7.99
No one wanted another war. Neither the Republic of
Haven, nor Manticore—and certainly not Honor Harrington.
Unfortunately, what they wanted didn't matter.

At All Costs pb • 1-4165-4414-3 • $7.99
The war with the Republic of Haven has resumed. . . disas-
trously for the Star Kingdom of Manticore. The alternative
to victory is total defeat, yet this time the cost of victory
will be agonizingly high.

Mission of Honor hc • 978-1-4391-3361-3 • $27.00
pb • 978-1-4391-3451-1 • $7.99

The unstoppable juggernaut of the mighty Solarian League is on a collision course with Manticore. But if everything Honor Harrington loves is going down to destruction, it won't be going alone.

A Rising Thunder trade pb • 978-1-4516-3871-4 • $15.00
pb • 978-1-4767-3612-9 • $7.99

Shadow of Freedom hc • 978-1-4516-3869-1 • $25.00
trade pb • 978-1-4767-3628-0 • $15.00
pb • 978-1-4767-8048-1 • $7.99

The survival of Manticore is at stake as Honor must battle not only the powerful Solarian League, but also the secret puppetmasters who plan to pick up all the pieces after galactic civilization is shattered.

Shadow of Victory pb 978-1-4814-8288-2 $8.99

"This latest Honor Harrington novel brings the saga to another crucial turning point. . . . Readers may feel confident that they will be Honored many more times and enjoy it every time." —*Booklist*

Uncompromising Honor hc 978-1-4814-8350-6 $28.00

When the Manticoran Star Kingdom goes to war against the Solarian Empire, Honor Harrington leads the way. She'll take the fight to the enemy and end its menace forever.

HONORVERSE VOLUMES:

Crown of Slaves (with Eric Flint) pb • 0-7434-9899-2 • $7.99
Torch of Freedom (with Eric Flint) pb • 978-1-4391-3408-5 • $8.99
Cauldron of Ghosts (with Eric Flint)
hc • 978-1-4767-3633-4 • $25.00
pb • 978-1-4767-8100-6 • $8.99

Sent on a mission to keep Erewhon from breaking with Manticore, the Star Kingdom's most able agent and the Queen's niece may not even be able to escape with their lives. . .

House of Steel (with Bu9)
hc • 978-1-4516-3875-2 • $25.00
trade pb • 978-1-4516-3893-6 • $15.00
pb • 978-1-4767-3643-3 • $7.99

The Shadow of Saganami
hc • 0-7434-8852-0 • $26.00
pb • 1-4165-0929-1 • $7.99

Storm from the Shadows
hc • 1-4165-9147-8 • $27.00
pb • 1-4391-3354-9 • $8.99

A new generation of officers, trained by Honor Harrington, are ready to hit the front lines as war erupts again.

A Beautiful Friendship
hc • 978-1-4516-3747-2 • $18.99
YA tpb • 978-1-4516-3826-4 • $9.00

Fire Season (with Jane Lindskold)
hc • 978-1-4516-3840-0 • $18.99
tpb • 978-1-4516-3921-6 • $9.99

Treecat Wars (with Jane Lindskold)
hc • 978-1-4516-3933-9 • $18.99
tpb • 978-1-4767-3663-1 • $9.99

"A stellar introduction to a new YA science-fiction series."
—*Booklist* starred review

A Call to Duty (with Timothy Zahn)
hc • 978-1-4767-3684-6 • $25.00
pb • 978-1-4767-8168-6 • $7.99

A Call to Arms (with Timothy Zahn & Thomas Pope)
hc • 978-1-4767-8085-6 • $26.00
pb • 978-1-4767-8156-3 • $7.99

A Call to Vengeance (with Timothy Zahn & Thomas Pope)
hc • 978-1-4767-8210-2 • $26.00

Journey to the early days of the Star Empire. The Royal Manticoran Navy rises, as a new hero of the Honorverse answers the call!

ANTHOLOGIES EDITED BY WEBER:

More Than Honor
pb • 0-671-87857-3 • $7.99

Worlds of Honor
pb • 0-671-57855-3 • $7.99

Changer of Worlds	pb • 0-7434-3520-6 • $7.99
The Service of the Sword	pb • 0-7434-8836-9 • $7.99
In Fire Forged	pb • 978-1-4516-3803-5 • $7.99
Beginnings	pb • 978-1-4767-3659-4 • $7.99

THE DAHAK SERIES:

Mutineers' Moon	pb • 0-671-72085-6 • $7.99
The Armageddon Inheritance	pb • 0-671-72197-6 • $7.99
Heirs of Empire	pb • 0-671-87707-0 • $7.99
Empire from the Ashes	tpb • 1-4165-0993-X • $16.00

Contains *Mutineers' Moon, The Armageddon Inheritance*
and *Heirs of Empire* in one volume.

THE BAHZELL SAGA:

Oath of Swords	trade pb • 1-4165-2086-4 • $15.00
	pb • 0-671-87642-2 • $7.99
The War God's Own	hc • 0-671-87873-5 • $22.00
	pb • 0-671-57792-1 • $7.99
Wind Rider's Oath	hc • 0-7434-8821-0 • $26.00
	pb • 1-4165-0895-3 • $7.99
War Maid's Choice	pb • 978-1-4516-3901-8 • $7.99
The Sword of the South	hc • 978-1-4767-8085-6 • $26.00
	trade pb • 978-1-4767-8127-3 • $18.00
	pb • 978-1-4814-8236-3 • $8.99

Bahzell Bahnakson of the hradani is no knight in shining armor
and doesn't want to deal with anybody else's problems, let
alone the War God's. The War God thinks otherwise.

OTHER NOVELS:

The Excalibur Alternative	hc • 0-671-31860-8 • $21.00
	pb • 0-7434-3584-2 • $7.99

An English knight and an alien dragon join forces to over-
throw the alien slavers who captured them. Set in the
world of David Drake's *Ranks of Bronze*.

In Fury Born pb • 1-4165-2131-3 • $7.99
A greatly expanded new version of *Path of the Fury*, with almost twice the original wordage.

1633 (with Eric Flint) pb • 0-7434-7155-5 • $7.99
1634: The Baltic War (with Eric Flint) pb • 1-4165-5588-9 • $7.99
American freedom and justice versus the tyrannies of the 17th century. Set in Flint's *1632* universe.

THE STARFIRE SERIES WITH STEVE WHITE:

The Stars at War I hc • 0-7434-8841-5 • $25.00
Rewritten *Insurrection* and *In Death Ground* in one massive volume.
The Stars at War II hc • 0-7434-9912-3 • $27.00
The Shiva Option and *Crusade* in one massive volume.

PRINCE ROGER NOVELS WITH JOHN RINGO:
"This is as good as military sf gets." —*Booklist*

March Upcountry pb • 0-7434-3538-9 • $7.99

March to the Sea pb • 0-7434-3580-X • $7.99

March to the Stars pb • 0-7434-8818-0 • $7.99

We Few pb • 1-4165-2084-8 • $7.99

Empire of Men omni tpb • 978-1-4767-3624-2 • $14.00
March Upcountry and *March to the Sea* in one massive volume.

Throne of Stars omni tpb • 978-1-4767-3666-2 • $14.00
March to the Stars and *We Few* in one massive volume.

Available in bookstores everywhere.
Or order ebooks online at www.baen.com.

"[Timothy] Zahn keeps the story moving at a breakneck pace, maintaining excitement. . . ." —*Publishers Weekly*

Multiple *New York Times* Best Seller

TIMOTHY ZAHN

The Moreau Clan—Galactic warriors, walking weapons, heirs of a fallen legacy. After thirty years of peace, the Troft invaders have returned. The long exile is over: the Cobras shall rise once more!

The Cobra Trilogy
978-1-4391-3318-7
$12.00 US/ $15.99 Can.

Cobra War

Cobra Guardian
HC 978-1-4391-3406-5
$24.00/$26.99 Can.

Cobra Gamble
PB 978-1-4516-3860-8
$7.99/$9.99 Can.

Cobra Rebellion

Cobra Slave
TPB 978-1-4516-3899-8
$15.00/$17.00 Can.

PB 978-1-4767-3653-2
$7.99/$9.99 Can.

Cobra Outlaw
TPB 978-1-4767-8034-4
$15.00/$17.00 Can.

Cobra Traitor
TPB 978-1-4814-8280-6
$16.00/$22.00 Can.

"[F]inely wrought space adventure . . . [with] social, political and emotional complications, all of which Zahn treats with his usual skill." — *Booklist*

Available in bookstores everywhere.
Or order ebooks online at www.baenebooks.com.

Robert A. Heinlein

"Robert A. Heinlein wears imagination as though it were his private suit of clothes. What makes his work so rich is that he combines his lively, creative sense with an approach that is at once literate, informed, and exciting."
—*New York Times*

ASIGNMENT IN ETERNITY	978-1-4516-3785-4 TPB $13.00
BETWEEN PLANETS	978-1-4391-3321-7 $7.99
BEYOND THIS HORIZON	978-0-7434-3561-1 $6.99
EXPANDED UNIVERSE	978-0-7434-9915-6 $7.99
FARNHAM'S FREEHOLD	978-0-671-72206-7 $7.99
THE GREEN HILLS OF EARTH & THE MENACE FROM EARTH	978-1-4391-3436-8 $7.99
THE MAN WHO SOLD THE MOON & ORPHANS OF THE SKY	978-1-4516-3922-3 TPB $13.00
THE PUPPET MASTERS	978-1-4391-3376-7 $7.99
REVOLT IN 2100 & METHUSELAH'S CHILDREN	978-0-671-57780-3 $7.99
THE ROLLING STONES	978-1-4391-3356-9 $7.99
SIXTH COLUMN	978-1-4516-3872-1 $7.99
THE STAR BEAST	978-1-4516-3891-2 $7.99
STARMAN JONES	978-1-4516-3844-8 $7.99
WALDO & MAGIC, INC.	978-1-4767-3635-8 TPB $14.00

Available in bookstores everywhere.
Or order ebooks online at www.baen.com.

DID YOU KNOW YOU CAN DO ALL THESE THINGS AT THE
BAEN BOOKS WEBSITE?

* Read free sample chapters of books

* See what new books are upcoming

* Read entire Baen Books for free

* Check out your favorite author's titles

* Catch up on the latest Baen news & author events

* Buy any Baen book

* Read interviews with authors and artists

* Buy almost any Baen book as an e-book individually or an entire month at a time

* Find a list of titles suitable for young adults

* Communicate with some of the coolest fans in science fiction & some of the best minds on the planet

* Listen to our original weekly podcast, The Baen Free Radio Hour

Visit us at www.baen.com